OPERATION FIREBRAND

JEFFERSON SCOTT

PROMISE PRESS
An Imprint of Barbour Publishing

OPERATION FIREBRAND

ISBN 1-58660-586-0

Acquisitions & Editorial Director: Mike Nappa
Editorial Consultant: Liz Duckworth
Art Director: Robyn Martins
Cover: Lookout Design

Published by Promise Press Fiction, an imprint of Barbour Publishing, Inc., P.O. Box 719, Uhrichsville, OH 44683, www.promisepress.com

Printed in the United States of America.

For my son,
Nathan Patrick Scott

ACKNOWLEDGMENTS

IT WOULD not be overstating the case to say that this book would not have been possible without my friend and brother, Steve Watkins. Steve is a pastor in Kentucky now, but once upon a time he was a Navy SEAL. In a sense, he *is* Jason Kromer, the hero of this book. Steve's advice on all things military—from a Christian point of view, no less—was instrumental in enabling me to write this novel at all and to give it its feel of authenticity.

Just as crucial was the medical advice I received from Clark D. Gerhart, MD, FACS. On top of the technical information he provided, this writer, surgeon, and Christian brother suggested or enhanced some of the more memorable scenes in this book. Thanks for all the help, Clark.

Thanks also to Mike Nappa and Rod Morris, friends and editors; and to Julee Schwarzburg, friend, editor, and copyeditor. Thanks to my endorsers, James Scott Bell and Alton Gansky. Thanks to Lance Woodward for the Russian help. Thanks to Pastor Flanvius Joey Johnson for his help with the city of Akron and for the use of his sermon. Thanks to Terri McFadden for the use of her metaphor of a vision-on-a-rope. Thanks to Megan Burke for her information about orphanages in Kazakhstan. Thanks to Liz Duckworth for her editorial insight. Thanks to Lookout Design Group for their awesome cover.

Thanks to my read-along gang: Kirk DouPonce, Stu Ehr, Mark and Laurie Francis, Tim Kizziar, John and Anne Gerke, Chris Gilbert, Jim Lund, and Sarah Purswell.

Special thanks to Gordon Golden, who has hopefully saved me from offending thousands of potential readers because in my rough draft I had inadvertently implied that no Christian should serve in the military. I certainly do not mean to say this. Thanks, Gordon.

Thanks to those who gave me information about Kazakhstan in general and Baikonur City in particular: Valentine Romanov, Carl Rising, Loi Pietro, James Neihouse, Victoria Kim, and Oksana with British Airways.

As always, a tremendous thanks goes to my wife, Robin, without whose support, encouragement, and brainstorming none of my novels would happen. Thanks to my children for being wonderful. And thanks to my Lord for letting me live the dream.

GLOSSARY OF MILITARY TERMS

Term	Definition
BUD/S	Basic Underwater Demolition/SEAL. The navy's training program for SEAL candidates.
e-and-e	Escape and Evasion. Also written as E&E.
GPS	Global Positioning System. A network of satellites that allows people with ground receivers to pinpoint their geographic location.
ghillie suit	Camouflaged clothing that incorporates grass and other organic materials to help a sniper blend into the terrain.
In-country	Deployed to a nation in which a war is being waged.
LZ	Landing Zone.
SAM	Surface-to-Air Missile.
SEAL	SEa, Air and Land. This term indicates that the navy's special warfare commandos can infiltrate through the use of diverse insertion platforms such as aircraft, ships, submarines, and land vehicles.
The Teams	The Navy SEAL Teams.

Part I

Death of a Navy Seal

CHAPTER 1

Target of Opportunity

Today I am going to kill a man in cold blood.

The thought felt wrong in Jason Kromer's mind, like a rock in the heel of his boot.

He watched the thick Indonesian jungle glide by the side of the Mark V Special Operations Craft as it purred upstream toward the insertion zone. Gasoline and engine exhaust mixed with the stink of the river mud churned up beneath them. The soldier's fingers slid down the smooth barrel of the sniper rifle in his lap. It had a camouflage polymer stock. Perfect for killing from a distance in hiding.

Jason could see Lieutenant Stemper forward, in the boat's cabin, talking on the satellite radio. He paused from penciling coordinates and glanced back at Jason, his sun-bleached eyebrows bunched. Then he turned away and signed off. Stemper called Doug "Chimp" Bigelow and Tom Sikes over to him. Chimp was Jason's spotter in the sniper team; Sikes was First Squad's radioman. The three of them walked aft to Jason.

Jason felt like standing and saluting, despite all his years of SEAL conditioning against the trappings of traditional military protocol. He managed to restrain himself.

"Well, it's confirmed, you lucky dogs," Stemper said. "Looks like we're going to get ourselves some real action today after all."

Oh, great.

Bigelow's wide face and prominent ears turned to Jason and Sikes and then back to Stemper. "Hoo-yah, baby." He shook Jason's shoulder until they were both grinning like idiots. "Gonna party today!"

The other four members of First Squad, Foxtrot Platoon, SEAL Team Three, scooted into earshot. The boat's crewmen were close, too, but managed to at least appear not to be eavesdropping.

"What's the op, sir?" Jason asked.

"Target of opportunity," Stemper said. "Intel boys have been flying one of them remote model airplane drones right around here, and they think they got themselves a real bad boy. Back in—" He noticed the others crowding around and gestured to Jason, Bigelow, and Sikes. "You boys mind if they listen in?"

"No problem, sir," Sikes said.

"All right, then, gather 'round, children, and I'll tell you a bedtime story."

The SEALs came forward, along with members of the boat's crew. A few grinned enviously at Jason and Bigelow and Sikes.

"As you boys remember," Stemper said, "back in the early nineties there was some really bad action over in East Timor, just a few hundred miles that way." He pointed southeast. "Massacres, soldiers firing on peaceful demonstrators, rapes. All that. Things have pretty much died down, thanks to us being here, among other things. But there's still bad blood. Lots of the military thugs behind those crimes were never caught.

"Well, the intel boys think they've located one of the worst. Muslim extremist militiaman named Amien Dewantoro. One of the leading triggermen behind the Dili massacre. As I was telling our lucky fire team here, one of those radio control recon drones has pinpointed Dewantoro right here in our backyard. Local informants tipped intel off that he was coming out of hiding to see the family. The locals don't think the target will stay put for more than a few hours, so it's up to us four to go in and take him out."

Jason, Bigelow, and Sikes accepted the hand slaps and mock punches from the team.

"Now you see why I always make you two lug that Remington and spotter scope wherever we go, don't you, boys?" Stemper said to Jason and Bigelow.

"Yes, sir."

"You never know when you're going to get asked to the dance." Stemper turned to the group. "Kromer and Chimp Bigelow will be the sniper pair; Sikes will be handler for the guide; and I'll go to be sure everybody keeps their heads down."

He handed a color printout to Jason. It was a blurry photo of a brown-skinned militiaman holding a Russian-made assault rifle over his head in victory. "Here's our guy. You boys take a good look at that face because we'll have to ID him in the field. Kromer, I want you to hang onto that for the op. All right, the rest of you apes clear outta here. Everything else is just for my sweethearts."

The group dispersed.

Jason stared at the photo of the man he was going to kill. How many times he'd longed for an op like this. But now. . . ?

Stemper brought his team of three close. "Here's the deal, boys: This ain't just your usual assassination."

Jason leaned forward with the others. Stemper was barely whispering.

"See, we're not supposed to be conducting any combat activities," said Stemper. "Just little recon patrols like we did today. But. . ." He looked over his shoulder, as if one of the river crocodiles might've slithered onto the deck. "But, you see, the East Timor honchos want this guy bad. And it seems that Washington wants to do them a favor." He looked intently at each one of them. "So, no mistakes."

Jason tried to read Stemper's expression. "Are you telling us what I think you're telling us?"

"Absolutely."

Bigelow looked at Jason. "You ever been on a black op before, Jace?"

"No, I haven't, Chimp. Have you, Sikes?"

"Not unless you're referring to my date last month with Miss Ophelia Johnson."

They traded high-fives. Jason and Bigelow did the hand jive handshake they'd worked out in BUD/S training.

"Yeah, yeah," Stemper said, "you think it's a good thing. But I'm here to tell you it ain't all that great. We'll never be able to tell anyone about it. We'll never win a medal for it. And. . .*and*. . .if we get into trouble out there, we're pretty much on our own. The navy's not going to scramble an F-18 to save our necks, and I guarantee the army's not going to flush an Apache to give close cover, not for a mission that isn't supposed to be happening. You understand me?"

"Yes, sir."

"Boy, sir," Bigelow said, "when you talk like that I get all excited."

"Well, stow it, mister. I want you sharper than my ex-wife's tongue when we get off this boat." Stemper waved a mosquito from his ear and took a notepad out of his chest pocket. "Here's our GPS coordinates. Get out your maps. We're putting in where the local guide is. That's about fifteen minutes away, so listen up."

Five minutes later the briefing was over, and Stemper moved forward in the boat.

Sikes followed him. "I'm not too sure about your sniper team, Lieutenant," he said in a faux whisper that was loud enough for the long-legged waterbird wading near the shoreline to hear.

"What are you talking about, Sikes?"

"Well, just look at them. Neither one's in his ghillie suit. They don't have a really long-range rifle between them. And Bigelow's got those big ol' flappy ears. I'm just afraid they're not up to the job."

"Well, what would you suggest, Sikes?" Stemper said.

"I don't know, sir. I was thinking we'd have a better chance of operational success if we gave the sniper rifle to those orangutans we saw this morning."

That brought a chorus of simian sound effects from the peanut gallery.

"Plus," Sikes said, all humor gone from his voice, "I just don't think Kromer has the chutzpa to pull the trigger. Not with his WWJD bracelet on and all."

Instantly, the appraising look returned to Stemper's eyes as he looked at Jason.

Jason felt his face flushing.

Finally Stemper slapped Sikes on the back of the head. "You just worry about getting yourself ready, Sikes."

"All right, partner," Bigelow said to Jason. "I'm gonna go prep. See you in ten."

Jason nodded and turned his attention to the .308 Remington Model 700 rifle. His murder weapon. He could feel someone watching him. He looked up and caught the lieutenant's gaze. Stemper motioned Jason over to him.

They leaned over the railing to look at the brown water moving by. "What about it, Kromer?"

"What about what, sir?"

"About what Sikes said. I'd be lying if I said that same thought hadn't come to me. You're a fantastic operator, Jason, one of my best. But when you got religion. . .I don't know. I don't have a problem with religion; don't get me wrong. But if religion gets in—no, if *anything* gets in the way of a SEAL doing his job, I have to be concerned." There was something like pleading in his eyes when he looked at Jason. "Do you know what I'm saying?"

Jason sighed then smiled. He watched as they passed some locals in a long, narrow canoe. “I do, sir. I’ve asked myself the same question a million times. When I was. . .you know—*before*—I never had a problem with any part of this job. I mean, ‘I’m sorry, pal, but you chose to work for the wrong government.’ But now. . .I don’t know.

“It’s not just that I’m a Christian, though. That’s not it. I know tons of Christian guys who serve in combat roles and have no problem with that as a part of their faith. Captain Miller, who leads the military fellowship back in San Diego, for one. I don’t mean to say that all Christians ought to get out of the military. No way. King David was a warrior and a godly man, for crying out loud. But I’m just wondering if it’s okay for me.”

Stemper rubbed the blond stubble on his chin. “I should send Lemke in your place. I’ll make Bigelow sniper.”

“No, sir, please don’t do that. I’m still a SEAL and I’m still the best you’ve got.”

“Kromer, you’ve just told me you’ve basically become a conscientious objector. How can I make you the sniper?”

“Please, sir, I want to be in on this,” Jason said. “I wouldn’t be in the Teams if I didn’t want to be where the action is.”

Stemper shook his head and smiled. “I know what you can do, Kromer, or I wouldn’t have picked you for my platoon. I want you on this mission, and if you want to go, then that settles it. But let me be clear that I’ve got you under evaluation. If I have the slightest doubt that this Jesus thing is interfering with the performance of your duties or endangering my men, you will be out of here so fast your luggage won’t catch up with you for a week. Understand?”

“Perfectly, sir.”

“All right, then,” he said, thumping Jason on the back. “Now get with your partner and come up with our e-and-e.”

“Aw, no, no, no,” Bigelow said, approaching. “Us four ain’t going to need no escape and evasion plan. We’re going to sneak in there like little rats, tap the bad guy, and be back here in time for tea. Aren’t we, shooter?”

"You got that right, spotter," Jason said.

"No way," Stemper said. "I want an e-and-e and I want it now. Sikes, get over here for this. You, too, Lemke. You're going to be in charge while I'm away."

The boat's skipper called back to Stemper. "We're there in two, Lieutenant."

"Affirmative, skipper, thank you." He turned back to his sniper team. "Well?"

Jason pulled out his map. "Extraction point is here. If this point is compromised, we'll head downstream and come to the beach in hundred-yard increments at half-hour intervals, on the hour and half hour. If it's daylight, we'll signal with our flashlights or mirrors. If it's night, we'll use red lenses."

"Good," Stemper said. "And the signal will be. . . ?"

"Morse for 'tea time,' of course," Bigelow said.

"Right. Got that, Lemke?"

"Aye, aye, sir."

The boat decelerated. "We've spotted the local," the skipper said. "Moving in now, sir."

"Very good, skipper. okay, little rats, checklist." Stemper lifted his G3AR rifle. "Primary weapon?"

Jason showed his Remington. "Check."

Bigelow showed his MP-5 submachine gun. "Check."

Sikes showed his M16. "Check."

"Secondary weapon?"

They all displayed their 9mm SIG Sauer P226s. "Check."

"Spotter scope?"

Bigelow held up the big lens. "Check."

"Intersquad radio?"

"Check."

"Map?"

"Check."

"Watch?"

"Check."

"Mirror, light, and lens?"

"Check, check, check."

"GPS locator?"

"Check."

"Horse sense, SEAL pride, and dumb luck?"

"Check!"

"Very well," Stemper said, "we are good to go. Now let's get out there and make the navy proud."

"Yes, sir!"

"Lemke, hang around here for when we get hungry for tea and crumpets."

"You got it," Lemke said.

The young man waiting for them on shore wore black sneakers, rolled up gray pants, and a brown Guns N' Roses T-shirt. He watched from beneath a brown corduroy hat, turned up in the front, as the boat approached. He looked nervous, and his tongue appeared and disappeared between his lips like a pink cuckoo clock. He wore a purple fanny pack across his chest as if it were a belt of ammunition. His dark brown eyes peered into Jason's with intensity. When the boat's prow edged into the tall grass, he broke into a bright smile.

"Welcome, American navy! Come, come, quick." He extended his hands to the SEALs.

All four men ignored his offer and vaulted onto the spongy turf.

Lemke tapped his radio headset. "Same protocol, Lieutenant? Wrestling?"

"That's right," Stemper said. "You're Body and we're Undertaker."

"Aw, sir," Bigelow said. "I wanted us to be Stone Cold Steve Austin this time."

Stemper shook his head. "Very well. Lemke, you are Body and we are Stone Cold."

"Got it."

The SEALs pushed the special operations craft back into the

current and watched their only support float away.

"Come, come," the guide said, smiling and nodding.

Bigelow followed him along the trail. Stemper and Sikes fell in behind. Jason brought up the rear, his sniper rifle in his hands.

Oh, Lord Jesus. Today I am going to kill a man in cold blood. . . .

CHAPTER 2

ASSASSIN

JASON followed their guide, Ibnu, as the young man led them away from the river along a barely perceptible trail that plunged deep into the tropical forest.

Sunlight and shadow skittered over the brown path and gnarled tetrastigma vines. Bloated flies buzzed beneath the canopy, floating from one "corpse flower" to another. The jungle always carried an earthy musk of life and death, but whenever they passed a patch of corpse flowers—meter-wide parasitic flowers that smelled like rotting meat—the scent of death won out.

Jason couldn't help thinking it might be a premonition of what was to come. Of what he was going to cause.

As he walked, a song he'd learned in church played in his mind. People said it was an old hymn, but for him, all the songs were new.

Jesus, lover of my soul, let me to Thy bosom fly,

While the nearer waters roll, while the tempest still is high.
Hide me, O my Savior, hide, till the storm of life is past;
Safe into the haven guide; O receive my soul at last.

It was a good walking song, the downbeats matching his footsteps. It also happened to be a pretty accurate expression of what was going on inside him at the moment.

Other refuge have I none, hangs my helpless soul on Thee;
Leave, ah! Leave me not alone, still support and comfort me.
All my trust on Thee is stayed, all my help from Thee I bring;
Cover my defenseless head with the shadow of Thy wing.

Twenty minutes into their hike, Ibnu led them down into a ravine. The water at the bottom was clear and emerald green and frothed white at the edges. As they descended, the air turned cool. The boulders littering the creek bottom were slick. They rattled as the five men passed. Ibnu led them upstream.

Soon the creek widened as it crossed a mud flat. Mangrove trees towered over them, their brown trunks a mass of tubes and sinews like the legs of skinless giants. Their breathing snorkels peeked out of the mud, an armada of submarine periscopes. As Jason stepped onto the shore, mudskippers bounded away over the flat to hide in the mangrove roots.

The raucous, braying call of a black palm cockatoo rose over the chorus of birdsong, and Ibnu stopped. He took off his corduroy hat and pointed up the creek bank with it.

"Here, you go up here."

Stemper took a step in the direction indicated. "Dewantoro, he's that way?"

"Yes, yes. Very bad man. That way."

Jason took out his map and studied it a moment. "Are you sure? If I've been calculating right, we're in here somewhere," he said, pointing at the map. "Lieutenant, we've still got another five miles to go."

"Well, let's get to it," Bigelow said.

"No, no," Ibnu said, his tongue darting in and out. "You get lost in jungle." His smile was broad.

Stemper took out his GPS locator and compared it to Jason's map. "He's right, Ibnu. We need to head northwest from here."

"Let's get after it then," Sikes said. "The sun's heading down."

"Your map place old," Ibnu said. "Bad man move. Ibnu see him. Ibnu's friends follow. He here now."

"But I thought he was going to his family's home," Stemper said.

"Yes, but big family, more than one wife." His laugh sounded like he thought Dewantoro had a pretty good thing going.

Jason put his map away. "I don't like it. Something stinks here besides the plants."

"Ibnu, how far away is Dewantoro?" Stemper asked.

"Not far. Just over this way. Not far."

Bigelow looked at Stemper. "Sir, why don't we at least go check it out? If Ibnu IDs him, we're set. If he's wrong, we head to the other site."

"Sounds good," Stemper said.

Jason blew air through his lips. "I still don't like it."

"Come on," Bigelow said to Jason, unshouldering his MP-5. "We'll get in and out quick. It'll be just like the time we snuck into the Alpha Delta Pi house at San Diego State U. Oh," he said, his grin turning into a smirk, "I forgot you don't do that kind of thing anymore."

Sikes snickered. Stemper tried to hide a grin.

Jason blinked at him. "So you're saying that when a man becomes a Christian, he stops liking beautiful women?"

"Am I wrong?"

"You're wrong."

"Then what are we waiting for? Let's go. Lead on, Ibnu of the Jungle."

Ibnu found a gap in the overhanging brush and scampered up the far side of the ravine. At the top, he led them through dense foliage bordering a wide clearing. Jason could see glimpses of white-walled houses on the far side of the clearing.

After a hundred yards, Ibnu crouched and put his finger to his lips. "Dewantoro in house on other side of next field. There, past banana trees."

"All right," Stemper said. "We'll take it from here."

"Wait a minute, sir," Jason said. "Ibnu, you're sure Dewantoro is there?"

"Yes, yes."

"Can you point him out to me?"

"Jason. . ." Bigelow said.

"No, Doug, forget it. Unless he can give me a positive ID, I'm not shooting. This photo could be almost anybody. We may already be at the wrong place; I don't want to shoot the wrong guy, too."

Ibnu's brown eyes narrowed. He looked about to say something but settled for licking his lips. Above them, a flying squirrel—looking like a square Frisbee with a head and a tail—sailed from one tree to another.

"Here," Bigelow said to Ibnu, "take this scope and show me Dewantoro, okay?"

Ibnu looked at it uncertainly but shrugged and took it. He crept into the wall of ferns and low banana trees and went prone. The SEALs lay down beside Ibnu as he brought the scope to his eye. Jason could see cows and chickens in the clearing, along with some children and women.

"There!" Ibnu hissed. "Dewantoro. Very bad man, there, there."

Jason brought up his rifle and peered through the Leupold scope. Bigelow took the spotter glass and looked through.

"That's him?" Bigelow asked. "The guy with the rifle?"

"Yes, yes."

Jason spotted the man in his scope. The range was less than a hundred yards, so he could see him with much more clarity than the photo in his pocket.

The man whose sternum lay beneath Jason's crosshairs was old enough to be Dewantoro. He was wiry and small after the manner of Indonesian men. He wore tan pants cut off below the knees, a black shirt with a blue zip collar, and black deck shoes with a ring around his left ankle. He carried a short-barreled hunting rifle. Like Ibnu, he wore a pouch diagonally over his chest.

Jason studied the man's face. He had the broad nose and dark features of his people. His thick black hair swept back over a high forehead, wrinkled by age or care. He crossed the grass slowly, angling toward one of seven white houses bordering the clearing. Something about the way the man carried himself made Jason's stomach churn. "This isn't right."

"What are you talking about?" Bigelow said. "This is perfect. Ibnu ID'd the guy, just like you wanted, and you've got a clean shot. You take him out and we'll exit the way we came in. We'll be back in time for tea *and* biscuits."

Jason looked again. The man was inspecting something on the underside of a cow in the field. He had laid his rifle down. Some children shrieked and ran toward him.

"Look at this picture, Lieutenant," Jason said, pulling it out.

Stemper took the picture, then took Jason's rifle and peered through the scope. He checked the photo again. "Yeah, it's him. Look at the jawline and the way he kind of hunches over. That's the guy."

"Come on, Jace," Bigelow said. "It's just like intel said. He's come home to see the family from wherever the scumbag hides out. Pop him quick before he goes in to see his wife, or we'll have to wait until he's done his business."

Jason's mind raced. Everything about this seemed wrong. But he couldn't be sure of himself. Did it feel wrong because something was up with the mission or because he was a Christian now and didn't want to just shoot a man who was not his enemy?

He took his rifle back and looked through the scope. The man had picked up one of the little brown-faced cherubs and was laughing with the others. Was this the face of a triggerman?

"I. . .I mean, there's a little wind," Jason said. "I need to recalculate my range."

"Jace, what's up with you, man?" Bigelow said. "I've never seen you hesitate like this."

"I'm not hesitating."

"It sure feels like it to me, Kromer," Stemper said. "Bigelow, you take the shot."

"No, sir. Please," Jason said. "I'll do it. Just. . .just let me get a better position."

"A better. . . ?" Stemper swatted at another mosquito buzzing his face. "Whatever. You're the sniper. Just do it already."

"I don't like this, sir," Bigelow said. "I'm starting to get that feeling in my gut."

"Stow it, Bigelow."

Jason crawled ten yards to his left. When he was in position, he looked back at the fire team. Bigelow was looking through the spotter scope. Stemper and Sikes had moved off with Ibnu a few paces. A trio of bright yellow and green tropical birds flitted by at head level.

Jason sighed and drew a bead on his target. The man was holding a little girl close to his face. Jason almost couldn't tolerate the thought of shooting a man who was not attacking him. But to do it while he was holding his baby girl?

He raised the crosshairs to center on the man's ear.

The target gave the little girl a kiss on the cheek.

Jason flipped the safety off.

The target put the girl on his shoulders.

Jason began his slow squeeze on the trigger.

As if in slow motion, the target rotated slightly, giving Jason the clearest shot he could want. He would probably injure the girl, too, not to mention scar her psychologically for life. But this was his job.

He looked at Bigelow, who gave him a "What are you waiting for?" gesture.

Oh, Lord, please forgive me.

Jason reacquired his target.

The man was laughing.

He squeezed on the trigger.

Then the grenades went off.

The first explosion detonated twenty yards away in the field behind them. The shockwave struck Jason physically. He rolled over, just as a deafening *pow!* went off on his right, shattering the trees beside him. Bark and rocks pelted his leg. His right ear rang and went deaf.

Halfway across the field—and closing—came thirty men with assault rifles. They were not in any uniform, but they were well-equipped and coming hard.

Jason scrambled to Bigelow. "Let's get out of here!"

"You didn't take the shot!"

Stemper crouched behind a bush and looked at Jason. "You didn't shoot?"

"I was about to when—"

"Get back up there and take the shot! No, wait. Bigelow, you take the shot."

"But, sir!" Jason said. He scrubbed at his ear, which was beginning to clear.

"Do it, Bigelow," Stemper said. "That's an order."

"Yes, sir." When Bigelow reached for the rifle, he glanced at Jason for only a moment. "You should've taken the shot, Jace."

As Bigelow crawled into position, another grenade exploded thirty feet in front of them, showering them with grass and earth.

Stemper and Sikes opened fire. The grenade thrower went down, and the rest of the attackers ducked into the tall grass.

Jason grabbed Bigelow's MP-5 and chambered a round. He fired a quick burst toward the attackers.

Behind him he heard the Remington's deep report, followed by the sound of Bigelow working the bolt action rifle. Bigelow fired again.

"He's down!" Bigelow shouted, crawling toward the others.

"Check," Stemper said. "Kromer, give that gun to Bigelow. You and Sikes take the local to the ravine and we'll cover."

Jason and Bigelow exchanged a look.

"Do it!" Stemper said. To punctuate his order, he let out a sustained burst with his G3AR. In the clearing, men cried out in pain.

Jason gave up the submachine gun and received his sniper rifle back. He patted Bigelow on the back and moved behind him toward Sikes and Ibnu, just as bullets sprayed their position. Both men went down.

Stemper and Bigelow fired to suppress the shooter, and Jason went to check on the fallen.

Sikes was all right. He'd taken a bullet in his left calf. Ibnu was very clearly dead.

"Lieutenant," Jason shouted, trying not to throw up, "the local is dead. Sikes took one in the leg. I'll get him to the ravine."

Stemper nodded and continued to fire.

Jason plunged into the thicket with Sikes in tow. Behind him he heard Bigelow's MP-5 submachine gun firing on full auto, its distinctive report answering the *crack* of the assault rifles' supersonic bullets flying by overhead, followed by the delayed *whump* of the barrel report. Stemper fired his G3AR in three-shot bursts. Another grenade went off near where Jason had been taking aim with his sniper rifle.

Jason drew his P226, the 9mm pistol feeling like a toy against AK-47s. "Come on, Tom. Let's get you to where you can call for help."

Sikes had his own pistol out. "No air support, remember?"

Bigelow burst through the brush and tumbled onto the turf next to Jason. "They're right on us! Lieutenant's falling back."

They ran toward the ravine. The brush clung to them. Vines and roots snarled their feet and brought them down. Fibrous branches resisted their progress. The pursuers closed the distance.

"We've got to cut back toward the field!" Jason said.

"No way!"

"We can't get out with these vines!"

Jason angled Sikes toward the clearing and the undergrowth eased up. He saw four attackers through the fronds. They were shouting and shooting into the brush. Jason fired his handgun at them—aiming for the legs—and some of the enemy gunfire was replaced by cries of pain. But other men were beating the hedges behind them. They ran.

At the top of the ravine, Jason saw that they were at a spot farther down along the mud flat. They skidded and tumbled down the slope. At the bottom, Jason helped Sikes apply a tourniquet and Sikes cranked up his radio.

"Body, this is Stone Cold. We are on the ropes. How copy? Over."

Jason scanned the sun-dappled mud flat for enemies. All he saw was jungle and mud—and a bird of paradise swooping beneath the canopy, its overlong white tail feathers trailing behind it like a smoke trail. Jason could hear the firefight in the near distance.

The radio squawked. "Stone Cold, this is Body." It was Lemke's voice, but it was punctuated with what sounded like machine-gun fire. "Acknowledge on the ropes. We are on the ropes, too. How copy, over?"

Sikes and Jason exchanged an anxious look. "Body, Stone Cold. Affirmative. Can you provide tag team? Over."

"Stone Cold, Body. Negative. Be advised that extraction point is compromised. Exchanging heavy fire. Will call when bell rings. Over."

"Body, Stone Cold. Understood. Over and out."

Someone was coming to the edge of the ravine. Jason and Sikes raised their handguns.

It was Bigelow. Even from the distance up the slope, Jason could see his friend was sweating and breathing hard. "Lieutenant's coming," Bigelow said. "Get moving!"

Jason helped Sikes to his feet, and they moved downstream at a good pace, scattering a horde of large black dragonflies.

The sound of gunfire neared. Bullets struck mango trees on the far side of the ravine. Jason turned to look just as Stemper burst over the ridge and rolled down the hillside. Bigelow crouched, fired a long burst in the direction of pursuit, then turned to come down the slope.

He never saw the grenade.

It exploded behind him almost at his feet. He catapulted through the air all the way down the hillside into the mud at the bottom of the ravine. He landed like a rag doll, facedown. His pants were scorched and shredded. The mud around him quickly turned dark red.

"Doug!"

Jason dropped Sikes and ran to his friend. Stemper gained his feet and interposed himself between them and the trail at the top of the ravine.

As Jason reached Bigelow, the wounded man let out a moan and moved his head. Jason rolled his face out of the muck and was about to flip him over when he noticed the deep gash halfway down his spine.

"Doug, it's your back. I can't move you."

A whisper from the top of the ravine startled Jason more than any shout. The attackers were massing behind the thick fronds at the edge of the ridge. Stemper fired at the sound.

"Get him, Kromer!" he shouted. "We've got to move."

Bigelow let out an awful scream. "Ah! It hurts! My legs! Jace, I can't feel my legs!"

Two men slid down the ravine upstream, trying to flank them. Jason dropped his sniper rifle and went for Bigelow's MP-5 from the mud. But before he could fire, Stemper shot at the attackers. Both men fell into the stream.

For the moment, all gunfire ceased.

"Get him out of here, Kromer!" Stemper said.

Jason threw the MP-5's strap over his arm and hoisted a mud-drenched Bigelow off the ground. *Better paralyzed than dead.* His friend screamed bloody murder, but Jason put him over his back in a fireman's carry. He saw that Sikes had already limped downstream a ways. The best he could, his feet sticking in the mud and his ankles twisting on the slippery boulders, Jason hustled Bigelow up the creek.

He left his sniper rifle behind.

Jason and Sikes finally reached the place where Ibnu had brought them into the ravine. A huge tree trunk towered overhead. A small orangutan looked down at them from its perch on a thick vine.

Jason made a run at the hillside, but Bigelow's extra weight caused his boots to slip and they fell.

"Aaaaaaagh!"

Far upstream, he heard shouts. Stemper, covering their retreat, fired single shots now. Jason could hear his footsteps splashing nearer.

"Come on, Chimp, help me out," Jason said. "I've got to get you up the hill. Can you use your arms?"

Bigelow's eyes were cloudy. "My legs, Jace. What's wrong with my legs?"

"You're going to be all right, buddy. We're going to get you out of this."

Sikes cranked up the radio. "Body, this is Stone Cold. How copy? Over."

Bigelow moaned. "It hurts, Jace."

"I know."

"You did this to me, Jace. You and your Jesus. You waited. Why didn't you just take the shot? We'd have been long gone."

Jason shut his eyes. "Doug, I. . ."

"Stone Cold, Body. How copy? Over."

"Body, Stone Cold, copy fine. We are still on the ropes. Over."

"Stone Cold, Body. Copy you are on the ropes. Our round is over and can tag team now. Over."

Stemper reached them. His left hand was bleeding. "They're coming, but slow, and not as many." He nodded at Bigelow. "How is he, Kromer?"

"He's bad, sir," Jason said. *Because of me.*

"Do what you can for him quick. And then let's move."

"Yes, sir."

From the looks of it, Bigelow had gone into shock. His pulse was weak but regular, and he was breathing. Jason rolled him over and did what he could to staunch the blood loss.

"Stone Cold, Body," Lemke said over the radio. "Be advised that your extraction point is compromised. Proceed to e-and-e point, over."

Stemper shot an intense look at Sikes. *"What?"*

"They came under fire."

Stemper sat down heavily on the slope.

Sikes spoke into the radio. "Body, Stone Cold. Understood. Proceeding to e-and-e point. Body, be advised that we have wounded. Over."

There was a pause before Lemke spoke again. "Stone Cold, Body. Copy your wounded. Medical help standing by. Over."

Jason heard a splash not far downstream. He eased forward, the MP-5 ready.

The radio crackled. "Stone Cold, Body." The volume was far too high now. Sikes brought it close and turned it down. Lemke's voice continued. "Be advised we are arranging a welcoming committee for you at secondary extract. Reach for your tag team, Stone Cold. Over."

"Body, Stone Cold," Sikes said quietly. "Copy. Over and out."

Jason eased back into the stream, behind a long fronded plant. The men were looking for them up on the ridgeline. They didn't see Jason.

This is different, Lord, isn't it? This is self-defense.

But it wasn't different.

One of the men looked right at Jason—and fired. Jason returned fire.

Bullets flew both ways, but the attackers were no match for a Navy SEAL in combat. Their shots flew wide. Jason's didn't. All five fell into the water.

And yet they weren't dead. Jason had placed every bullet where he'd aimed it. Assuming these guys could get medical help, they would live. For the moment, though, they were incapacitated.

Stemper sloshed forward to stand beside him. The look he gave Jason was complex. His jaw moved left and right as he examined him. "Okay, Kromer," he said. "Let's move."

He grabbed Bigelow's legs and Jason grabbed his arms. Sikes held onto Jason's belt and they made it up the side of the ravine. Then Jason took Bigelow over his back again and began to run.

Jason lost track of time. He was running and running. That's all he knew. Step, step, step, step. . .The sun was still up, but at that moment he didn't know if it was even the same day they'd started the mission on. His friend was on his back and might die, might already be dead. Every SEAL in the fire team was wounded—except him. And all because he didn't take that shot when he had the chance.

Step, step, step, step. . .

Finally, he broke out of the undergrowth at a spot where he could see the river through a line of trees across a clearing. Two plumes of black smoke rose at the water's edge. A crocodile was mauling something on the grass. Jason estimated a spot a hundred yards downstream from the smoke and lumbered toward it. Stemper helped Sikes limp along. There was no sound of pursuit.

As they veered away from the original extraction spot, an AK-47 opened fire toward them. They were visually shielded by ferns but had nothing hard between them and their attacker. Jason heard shouting behind him and another gun opened fire. The guns were getting closer.

Blood seeped over his forehead into his right eye. He had no idea whether he'd been shot or if the blood was from Bigelow. He just kept plodding forward in the longest hundred-yard dash of his life.

The pursuers were firing wildly now. There were more than two of them. Bullets whizzed over Jason's head and *thunked* into the ground beside him. Every now and then he heard footsteps behind him. His teammates, he hoped.

Step, step, step. . .

Then from in front of him Jason heard a sound he knew—a tubular *toink* followed instantly by a *whissht.* An M203 40mm grenade launcher. A SEAL weapon. Then he heard it again. Behind him the grenades exploded with a muted *boom,* followed by the sound of dirt falling back to earth. The pursuing rifles fell silent.

From the wall of brush in front of him, four SEALs advanced to envelop the fire team. They fired at anything that moved—and a few things that didn't—and walked backward with Jason and the others, collapsing the ring.

When they got into the cover of the brush near the riverbank, Lemke and Jensen helped Jason lower Bigelow to the ground and began tending to his wounds. The Mark V Special Operations Craft waited prow first in the grassy bank. Hernandez saw to Sikes's leg. Jason saw that Stemper's sleeve was soaked in his own blood. Turner approached him, but Stemper pushed him away.

"Not now, Turner. Cover our exfil."

"Yes, sir."

"Everybody, we're pulling out," Stemper said. "Lemke, you and Jensen get Bigelow onto the boat. Hernandez, you and Kromer get Sikes aboard. When you're there, Sikes, get on the horn and have a search-and-rescue helicopter from the *Stennis* meet us en route for medevac. Turner, you and I will cover our exfil and get on the boat. Now move!"

CHAPTER 3

FALLOUT

JASON pushed two sailors aside and vaulted through the oval doorway in the bulkhead. The men wore bright red shirts with a black stripe, marking them as "B-B stackers," men who loaded the missiles and bombs onto the aircraft topside on the flight deck. Jason was still in full battle gear, dried blood and all.

He hurtled the next knee-knocker, the raised part of the bulkhead opening, and clattered down the *USS John C. Stennis*'s passageway. He was running down what looked like a hall of mirrors with no reflection. Identical but ever smaller oval openings receded into the distance as the passage stretched away. Was he gaining any ground? It felt like a bad dream. Some part of his mind registered the aroma of spaghetti wending its way to him from the galley.

Suddenly the passageway widened into a medical supply room. Like the rest of the carrier below decks, the walls of the sick bay were pale green. The fluorescent lights bounced off the white linoleum floor, making the whole place feel devoid of warmth and hope. He felt as if he were in a sci-fi virtual reality world like *The Matrix.*

A black man sat at a desk in the cluttered office on Jason's left. He wore a white long sleeve turtleneck with his stripes stenciled on his sleeve. He looked startled to see a commando in his doorway. "Can I help you?"

"You a doctor?"

"No, man," he said, pointing a thumb over his shoulder. "This is my supply room. You need anything?"

"You got a wounded man here? A SEAL. Doug Bigelow. Is he okay?"

"Hold on, hold on. Yeah, we got a SEAL in about an hour ago."

Jason winced. "I got here as soon as I could."

The man stood up. "Come on, I'll take you back."

He led Jason down the hall and to the left. Jason saw offices and closets but no beds. They passed the dentistry room, consultation rooms, and a medical records office. Down this second hallway, Jason saw two medical staffers in white turtlenecks examining an X-ray on a light board. The supply clerk went up to the closest one.

"Sir, this here's a friend of the back injury. He wants to know how he is."

The doctor looked over his half glasses at Jason. "All right, Seaman, thank you." To the other doctor he said, "File these films. I'll be with you in a minute." Then he touched Jason's elbow and pointed with his chin at a small consultation room. Jason went in and sat on a metal folding chair. The doctor pulled the curtain shut and sat.

"You're a friend of Mr. . . ."

"Bigelow," Jason finished.

"I'm Commander Neal, senior medical officer. And you are?"

"Jason Kromer. Sir, can you tell me how he's doing?"

Dr. Neal was a hawkish man with black hair graying above the ears. His light blue eyes seemed to penetrate like X-rays. "Jason, your friend's been hurt pretty bad. I understand it was a grenade?"

"That's right. Went off right behind him. Blew him thirty feet through the air, down a hill."

Neal nodded. "He's got shrapnel pressing into his spinal cord. That will have to come out, but I'm not going to do it. We've stabilized him for transport. He'll be headed off to San Diego in just a few minutes."

"Is he. . ." Jason swallowed. "Is he going to be. . .you know. . . ?"

"Paralyzed?" Neal shook his head. "No way to tell yet. Spinal cord injuries are tricky. If there's just pressure on it, they could remove the shrapnel and he could return to full function. If it's severed, he may have paraplegia. There are degrees of that, but it is usually permanent. If the cord's injured but not severed, his impairment could fall anywhere between full function and no function. We'll have to wait to know."

Jason's weariness suddenly caught up with him. It stopped, backed up, and dumped on him like fifty tons of wet sand.

"Jason," Neal said, "does your friend have any family back in San Diego?"

Jason shook his head. "He always said we were his family."

"All right. Now listen, son. I don't know what happened out there, but I can tell it was bad." Neal's eyes seemed to scan Jason's soul. "I'm sure you did what you could for him."

Jason dropped his gaze. He found his head was shaking like a palsied old man.

"Whatever happens," Neal said, "he's going to need friends like you to come through this. Tell you what: Why don't you come see me in a day or two, and we'll just talk. What do you say?"

Jason was staring at a smudge on the linoleum. "We'll see, Doc."

Neal stood up. "Well, do you want to see him?"

"Can I?"

"Sure. But be quick. They're coming any minute to get him on the helicopter."

Neal led Jason into a wide ward with twelve beds along the walls.

One man sat up against the wall writing a letter, bandages on his nose and chin. Another lay asleep, his arm in a heavy cast atop the covers. On the far side of the ward Neal pulled aside a curtain separating off the intensive care bed.

There was Bigelow, staring straight up at the ceiling, a stiff cervical collar on his neck. His wrists were tied loosely with gauze to the bed rail to protect the IVs hanging from his arms. Wires ran from his bare chest to the beeping heart monitor standing beside the bed. A tube came snaking out of in his nose. Stitches lined the skin above his right eye. His cheekbone was red and beginning to bruise and his hair was still caked with mud. A corpsman was giving him a sponge bath with a brown cloth that had once been white.

"Kyle, you finished?" Neal asked.

The corpsman dropped his rag into a basin. "Yes, sir."

"Why is he lying on his back?" Jason said. "Isn't that like the last thing he should be doing?"

"It's to keep him immobilized," Neal said. "You're going to have to be directly over him if you want him to see you."

"Doc!"

"What is it, Mr. Bigelow?"

"Get him out. I don't want to talk to him."

Jason winced. Neal patted him on the arm and backed out, closing the curtain behind him.

Jason leaned into Bigelow's field of view. "Hey, Chimp."

"Get out."

He smiled. "Make me."

Bigelow's arms lifted toward Jason but were quickly halted by the gauze. He settled for moving the only part of his body with complete freedom: He turned his eyes away from Jason and stared at the beeping heart monitor.

"Hey," Jason said, "how was the chopper ride? Those S&R guys get it done, don't they?"

No response, just beeping.

"We had to come the old-fashioned way. I got here as soon as I could."

Beep, beep, beep, beep.

"Oh, you'll be happy to know that Sikes is going to be fine. He's milking it like crazy, though. Says he'll never bowl again."

Beep, beep, beep, beep. Out in the ward, someone went into a coughing fit.

"Hey, it looks like you're going to get back to California before the rest of us, you dog. Doc says they're packing you off to San Diego in just a few minutes. Leave everybody's girlfriends alone, all right?"

Beep, beep, beep, beep.

"Listen, I can't stay long. Got to get to the debriefing. Seems the big brass want to sit in on this one. Should be interesting."

Beep, beep, beep, beep.

Jason pursed his lips. "Chimp. . .I'm running out of—"

"Don't call me that."

"Huh?"

"Don't call me 'Chimp,' like we're friends. Don't ever call me that."

Jason adjusted the gear on his belt. "Look, let's not talk about that right now. You're still, I don't know, in shock about the mission. I am, too. We all are. But—"

"Don't tell me how I am. You don't know."

"Doug, keep—"

"You want to know how I am, Kromer? You want to know how I feel all strapped down to this bed and locked in this cage like Frankenstein? Well, forget it. But I'll tell you what I *don't* feel: I don't feel my legs! Do you get it? I can't feel them. I can't move them. Nothing."

Jason nodded. "I know. The doctor said you—"

"They don't know!" Bigelow's arms thrashed against the restraints. "The doctor said this, the doctor said that. 'We'll have to wait and see.' 'It all depends.' 'We'll know in a week, a month, ten years!' Forget them, Kromer, and forget you. If it weren't for you, I wouldn't be here. You should've taken the shot, Jason. *You should've taken the shot!* But you hesitated because of some religion thing, and I took a grenade in the back. It should be you in this bed, not me!"

Jason heard voices in the ward behind him. Someone slid the curtain aside. Dr. Neal and four sailors moved toward Bigelow's bed.

"Your ride's here," Neal said to Bigelow. He grimaced knowingly at Jason. "You can help us take his bed if you want."

"I don't want to see him anymore, Doc. Get him out of my face."

Jason stepped aside to let the men work. They transferred the heart monitor and IV bags onto the bed railings and started wheeling the bed away.

"Chimp," Jason said, just loud enough to hear. "Doug, I'm sorry. Buddy, I'm so sorry. I wish it *was* me. Don't you know it? Don't you know I'm sorry?" He followed the bed toward the hallway, aware that he sounded pathetic but unable to help himself. "Chimp, I'll pray for you, Chimp. You'll be all right; you'll see."

Bigelow looked at Jason, seemed to struggle a moment with his words, and then told him where he could go. "And don't call me Chimp. Kromer, I'll never forgive you."

The sailors rolled the bed away.

As he stood in the pale green hallway, a simple truth coalesced in Jason's soul: *I'll never forgive myself, either.*

Five weeks later.

Jason stepped into the career counselor's office and shut the door on the San Diego heat. He blinked in the dim cube of painted concrete blocks that was the CC's office.

Chief Petty Officer Brian Artaud was a dark-haired SEAL with a large nose and a jutting forehead that seemed to be perpetually locked in thought, like he'd lost the remote control twenty years ago and had vowed to never give up the search. He was typing at his computer. "Have a seat."

Jason sat in a creaky wooden chair and studied the mounted

photos of Artaud's large family.

Artaud clicked his mouse and swiveled to face Jason. "Sending E-mail to my wife. Car's blowing blue smoke again." He shook his head. "It's a heap."

Jason nodded.

Artaud cleared his throat and opened a dark green folder on his desk. He whistled atonally as he studied the pages in the file. Without looking up, he said, "How are you doing, Jason?"

Jason watched him warily. "Good. How are you?"

Artaud's brow wrinkled, unwrinkled, and wrinkled again, reading the file. He hummed once, as if he'd noticed something interesting in the newspaper. Finally, he looked up.

"You thinking of staying in?"

"Nope."

Artaud nodded rapidly, like he'd just heard something he wanted to be seen to agree with. But his words didn't match: "So you've given your six years and you're out?"

"That's right."

Nodding. "Are you sure? I mean, you know about the reenlistment bonus, don't you?"

Jason winced. "Yeah, I know all about it."

"Thirty-five thousand dollars is nothing to just walk away from. Shoot, I could use that right now. Buy my wife a new car. Maybe take her for a nice vacation somewhere. You married, Jason?"

"No."

"Got a girlfriend?"

"No."

"Oh, a single man, huh? Loving the bachelor life. Yeah, I miss it myself. Hey, I bet you got a hobby, though, huh? What is it? Scuba? Guns? Fly-fishing? Man, what a guy could do in a sporting goods store with thirty-five grand, huh?"

Jason stretched his legs out and crossed them at the ankles. "You can save it, Chief. I'm getting out."

"Right, right. Bet you'll miss your buddies in the Team, though, huh? Bet that'll be tough, leaving them behind."

"Yeah, real tough. Hey, how'd you get this job, anyway? The more I talk to you the more I'm sure I want to quit."

Artaud lifted his hands in mock surrender. "Hey, now. I'm just supposed to ask you these things, that's all. So you're not a hundred percent sure you want to quit, then?"

Jason shook his head and chuckled. "Look, just bring up the papers and let me sign them, okay? I'll be out of your hair and you can go back to your E-mail."

The door opened and someone stepped in. Jason squinted against the bright morning. The door shut, but the man remained bright. Belatedly, Jason realized that the man was wearing a white uniform. It was Commander Dooley, SEAL Team Three's commanding officer.

Jason and Artaud stood.

Dooley took his hat off. "What do you know? I think I've found the only two SEALs in the Navy who will stand when an officer comes into a room. I've got to remember you guys. But you can sit down now."

"Um," Artaud said, sitting, "can I do something for you, sir?"

"No, no. I'm here for this meeting."

Jason smiled. "Is this good cop, bad cop? You guys are tag-teaming me, aren't you?"

Commander Dooley had an open face and a lopsided grin. His receding salt-and-pepper hairline retreated even more when he tried to look innocent. "Maybe a little." He reached for Jason's file. After a moment, he set it down. "Chief, where were you in the process when I came in?"

"I was just telling Mr. Kromer here all the bennies of staying in the navy, sir."

"The navy's a good life," Dooley said, a bit too loud. "And nothing beats life in the Teams. Am I right, gentlemen?"

"Absolutely, sir," Artaud said.

"Whatever you say, sir."

Dooley laughed heartily, an inviting sound, a sound that conjured up an image of warmth and good times. To Jason, it was the most appealing part of the reenlistment session so far. "Looks like your powers of enticement have failed to win over the client, Mr. Artaud."

"Oh, I'm just getting warmed up."

Dooley ticked his tongue. "Tell you what, Jason. Let's you and me go for a little walk, shall we?"

Jason stood. "All right."

"I'll send him by later, Brian," Dooley said.

They strolled across the SEAL compound at the Coronado Naval Base, walking by the black Zodiac inflatable rafts stacked three high. On their left, they passed the tall parachute loft with 'chutes hung out for packing. Finally, they left the entrance to the weight room behind and stepped out onto the hot sands of the beach. Two SEAL platoons were engaged in what appeared to be a to-the-death game of volleyball.

Dooley and Jason skirted the court and headed toward the obstacle course down the beach. On their left, seagulls sprinted after withdrawing waves. Over the horizon, Jason could see amphibious ships on maneuvers, and here and there a sailboat. A steady breeze filled his lungs with salt sea air.

"Been to see Bigelow lately?" Dooley asked as they walked.

"Nah. He doesn't want to see me. I've sent him some E-mails and called. I even sent him a snail mail letter. No answer to any of it. The guys say he's doing all right, considering."

Dooley nodded. "He is. I went by there last week. He's the same old Doug—attacking his rehab like he attacks everything else. They say he'll never walk again, though. And there's some question about his ability to father children." He chuckled. "Normally I'd make a joke about that not being any great loss, but it's different when it's real, isn't it?"

Jason's eyes were shut. "I didn't know that part of it. That's. . .

that's terrible." *So, I've taken that from him, too.*

"Oh, but like I said, he's the same old Doug. He's got a sweet young thing as his therapist. Shows off for her as much as anything else, I think. Not that I blame him. Hoo, she's a looker. From my observation, though, she doesn't seem to be much impressed."

Jason watched an F-14 making its final approach to North Island Naval Air Station, just two miles distant. "I miss him."

"I know you do, Jason. What happened to him is a crying shame. And taking it out on you like that is just crazy. I actually talked to him about that, said he ought to give you a break, that you were suffering, and all. You can imagine what he said."

"Yeah." Jason huffed out something that was supposed to be a laugh and turned away. "I can imagine."

They reached the obstacle course, a site loathed and revered in every SEAL's heart. The sixty-foot-tall cargo net dominated the course like a porous monolith. Dooley put his foot up on a horizontal telephone pole obstacle.

"Jason, I know it's been hard for you," he said. "Having a friend fall in battle like that—and then to lose the friendship on top of it. It'll take a man down." He smiled wistfully. "I love all those war movies that talk about how soldiers go out and die for the cause. You and I know that's only part of it. The real truth is you go out and fight and risk your life for your buddies, plain and simple. For the guy next to you. For the guy you've lived with and trained with and walked through leech-infested water with. That's what it's all about."

Jason felt something beginning to come unglued inside him. Maybe it was the compassion in Dooley's voice or the raw emotion evoked by being back in the obstacle course—or maybe it was just having some precious "father-son" time alone with his commanding officer. Whatever it was, it threatened to throw open a cage door Jason had kept double bolted. He clamped down on it hard.

"I know what you're trying to do, sir, and I appreciate it." Jason found he was clenching his jaw. "But I don't think I need it."

Dooley stared at him for half a minute without speaking. From up the beach came cheers from the volleyball game. Seagulls spun overhead.

"Jason," he said gently, "listen to me. What happened was not your fault."

Jason was staring at the surf. "I knew you were going to get to that. Look, I appreciate what you're saying and all, but can I just say that you're wrong? Dead wrong." He heard his voice rising. "Sir, forgive me, but you weren't there! It *was* my fault. Doug is paralyzed—and now I find out he can't have children—*because of me.* I should've taken the shot."

Dooley shook his head. "No, Jason, I know all about it. I know about your hesitation. I know that you didn't feel right about pulling the trigger. Believe me, I understand. It's a terrible thing to kill a man, to take a life. That's something they don't show in the movies, isn't it? They like to show soldiers blasting away with machine guns and tossing those stunt men through the air with movie blood exploding in little packets on their chest. And then what does the hero do afterwards? He takes a shower and goes dancing with the leading lady.

"Oh, sure, maybe the artillery guys can do it and the pilots with their fire-and-forget smart bombs. But when you have to look at a guy and see that maybe he's just a kid or maybe he's old enough to be a daddy, and when you see he's just as scared as you. . .it's different. To kill him then, when you've seen he's just like you—that doesn't feel like war; it feels like murder. But people just don't get that."

Dooley wasn't looking at Jason anymore. He was staring across the sand dunes. For several seconds he stood still, his eyes darting and his hands feebly gesturing, as if in waking REM sleep.

Then he shook out of it and stared at Jason. He chuckled and rubbed his eyes. "So you're in a Catch-22 when you get into combat. You shoot a guy and you've got blood on your hands for the rest of your life. You're haunted by the fact that you robbed a family of a father or a husband or a brother or a son. Or you don't shoot and you're hit by guilt again, because now you've failed your country and disobeyed your officer and maybe, just maybe, allowed a buddy to take a bullet instead. So if you shoot or if you don't shoot, you've got a situation on your hands.

"Is it any wonder that ninety-eight percent of all soldiers who engage in close combat end up as psych cases? Ninety-eight percent, Jason. The other two percent were psychos already.

"Now, you—you didn't shoot on that mission. Your intuition or your ethics or your upbringing or something else caused you to not take a life, even in self-defense. And your buddy got hurt bad. So now you're a traitor and a coward, or so 'they' would have you believe. But that's wrong. I think your instincts told you not to shoot and you didn't."

Jason walked away. He reached the cargo net obstacle and buried the heels of his hands into his eyes. There was a battle going on at that bolted cage door. Beast and keeper were going at it with fang and club.

Dooley's voice rose over the surf. "You can't let this get you down, Jason. You can't." He stepped close. "I'd be worried about you if you *weren't* having a hard time right now. And look: It's not like I don't know what it's like to lose a friend in combat. I lost five in Nam. And once. . .buddy, once it was one hundred percent my fault. My friend came home to his wife and baby in a body bag, and it was my fault. It tore the soul out of me, Jason. I'm still not over that one. When it happened, I was about to quit the navy, too."

He paused. Jason didn't look at him.

"But then someone told me what I'm about to tell you," Dooley said. "My CO took me for a little walk, like this one, and he said something I think that you of all people will understand. He said, 'Dooley, I'm not a religious man, but I do believe that there is a God in heaven who controls everything on earth. In combat, one man lives and another man dies. Why? No reason we can see. But it all works out.'

"Don't you see it, Jason? I know you're a Christian, so I know you know what I'm saying. Bigelow took the grenade because he was meant to take it. Now I ask you: Why didn't he die? He should have. But he didn't. Why? Because he wasn't meant to die. He's still got something left to take care of in this life. That's the way I see it. Now, you can't let Bigelow's anger take you out. You have to divorce yourself from it and go on with your life. Maybe he'll come out of it one day; maybe he won't. That's not your problem."

Part of Jason wanted to give in to what he was saying, to fall into the forgiveness he was holding out. But one mental image of Bigelow's shredded back, one memory of the hate in his best friend's eyes, were all it took to shout that part of him down. He decided to end the battle once and for all. He coiled all his guilt into a shape in his soul, the shape of the heaviest titanium padlock imaginable, and locked the cage shut.

Jason shook his head. "It's not just that, sir."

"So what else?"

"Stemper doesn't trust me, for one. He took me off the sniper team and won't put me on point anymore. He acts like he'd rather leave me behind. That last month of deployment was miserable."

"I'll have a word with him."

"Sir, meaning no disrespect, but what good would that do? You could make him use me, but you can't make him trust me again. I'm history as far as he's concerned." The venom in Jason's voice surprised him. "I'm no good for Team Three at all, sir, not since the rumor's out that I can't be trusted to do my job."

"I'm aware of that rumor, Kromer, and I'm on it."

Jason smiled. "I don't know why you're taking time with me, sir, but I appreciate it. Frankly, I don't think I'm worth the effort, but thanks."

"That talk's out of place, mister. Now listen to me: I'm not going to blow sunshine in your ear just to get you to stay in. All I'm trying to do is hang on to a first-rate operator. You guys aren't as common as the navy says you are."

Jason looked him in the eye. "Anyway, thanks. But there's one more thing, something that may actually be the main reason I have to quit the Team."

"Oh," Dooley said, folding his arms. "This ought to be good."

Jason swallowed and looked out across the beach. "I don't know, sir, but I think they may be right about me. I think I really am untrustworthy."

"Come again?"

"It's like this. All my life I've only wanted one thing: to be a Navy SEAL. These six years have been the happiest of my life. I could die today and still have lived more than ninety percent of the population. And happier, too. But then I found something that I never thought I'd find."

"All right, I'll bite. What did you find?"

"Something better. I know you don't believe like I do, but I have to tell you that Jesus Christ is the best thing that ever happened to me. It's like I've found something I didn't even know I was looking for.

"The problem is that when you get peace like a river you kind of start losing that fire in your gut. Do you see what I mean? I don't want to eat raw meat and destroy, maim, and widow like I used to. I'm not a rabid animal anymore. I. . .I don't really want to shoot people anymore, even if they do happen to work for the wrong government. I'd rather bring them into the kingdom of God with a gospel tract than send them there with my Remington .308. Does any of that make sense?"

Dooley had his poker face on, but his eyes were not unkind. "I see how it makes sense for you, Jason."

"The problem is that if I leave the navy, what will I do then?" Jason said. "All my passions and skills are for commando life. What am I supposed to do out there, flip burgers?"

Dooley shook his head sharply. "You don't go out there, Jason. That's the answer. You don't want to shoot people? Fine, no problem, you don't have to."

"You want to make me a boatswain's mate and send me to a tug?"

"Worse," he said, patting the cargo net's frame. "I want to make you a SEAL trainer and give you to BUD/S."

The thought struck Jason like a match lit in a cave. "I hadn't thought of that. A trainer." But just as quickly the flame blew out. "No, that won't work, either."

"Why not? It's perfect. I'll sign the papers today; you'll start next week."

"No, sir, it won't work. Because then I'd be training guys to go out and kill people, and I couldn't live with myself if I did that, either."

Dooley cursed. "You're pigheaded, you know that, Kromer? You've got the solution to your problem right in front of you, and you don't want it. I just don't see why being a Christian has to mean you can't be a SEAL anymore. Other guys do it. Why can't you?"

"I know, sir. I don't have a problem with anyone else doing it. Believe me, I've heard from guys all over the place about this. It seems like everybody wants to tell me how they've reconciled it in their heart. And some of their reasons are really good. The Bible even says that we're supposed to remain in the condition we were in when we got called and not just quit automatically. So I don't mean to be making a judgment on anyone else. It's just that. . .maybe my path is different from theirs.

"Yes, sir, I guess I am pigheaded. But I'm also certain that I'm right—for me. I have to lay down my guns and never kill another man as long as I live, if I can help it. Talking to you has only made me more sure of it."

Dooley shook his head. "I still think it would be a mistake for you not to reenlist, Jason. I think you would get out there and not know what to do."

"I understand, sir. And I know that you really do want the best for me."

"Ah, Kromer, I give up. The least you could do is fight me. Come on, make me mad."

"Nah. I've always liked you, sir. I've lost one SEAL friend—I don't want to lose another."

Dooley kicked at a pile of sand. "All right, you idiot. I'll tell Artaud to do the paperwork." He sighed heavily. "I'm sorry to lose you, Jason. Sorry as I can be."

"Thank you, sir."

A week later, Jason Kromer received an honorable discharge from the navy.

Part II

Afterlife

CHAPTER 4

CIVILIAN

SEA SCUM.

It was a fitting description of himself, Jason thought.

He focused his waterproof video camera at the slimy underside of the ship. It looked like a floating reef. The barnacles, mussels, tubeworms, weeds, and slime on the hull provided a virtual wildlife preserve for marine life but weren't doing the vessel itself much good. Jason shone his light on the parasites and zoomed in.

The water was murky from last night's rain. Jason surveyed the entire 146 feet of the *Spirit of Long Beach II,* staying close enough for his handheld spotlight to give the camera something to focus on.

The hull on this commercial excursion vessel was a mess. Fouling rating of four, at least, and probably five. Jason almost hoped the owner didn't hire him to clean it off. But it would pay well. And that was something he had to think about a lot these days.

He checked his air gauge. He'd need to head up in another ten minutes, but not just yet. He switched the camera and light off and let himself drift with the current.

Everything was quieter down here. Simpler. The multicolored world up above was here rendered in shades of blue only—or in this case, brown. The racket of his complex world was for a while reduced to bubbles and muffled hums. For nine minutes, he didn't try to figure anything out.

Finally he surfaced. The ship's owner was waiting for him on the pier.

"Well, what's it look like down there?" Oscar Clements's sweaty jowls waffled under his Ray-Bans.

Jason lifted his mask and climbed up the pier's wooden ladder. "It's not good, Mr. Clements. Looks like nobody's cleaned her in a year."

Clements swore. "I need it cleaned off, today!"

"No can do," Jason said, squaring away his gear. "Even if I could get my boat out here today, which I can't, it's going to take me a week to ten days to get that hull cleaned. You've got an ADR of three; your FR's at five; and I can't even see the paint to give you a PDC rating, but I'm guessing it's at a four or five."

"Talk English, boy," Clements said, his chins quivering. "What are you telling me?"

Jason popped the tape out of the camera. "I'm telling you that your boat's in about as bad a condition as I've ever seen; that it's in danger of splitting open; and that if an inspector saw it, you'd be grounded quicker than you can say 'Sorry, Charlie.' "

Clements swore some more. Then he seemed to fall into deep thought. At length his cheeks shuddered. "Can you start tomorrow?"

Jason sighed. "I suppose."

"Good. Be here at sunup. I will be by to make sure you're hard at work."

"You're the boss," Jason said, his voice almost free of sarcasm. "But it's going to cost you."

"You're charging me sixty bucks just to make a videotape. How much will it cost if you actually do any work?"

Jason blinked at him stoically. "I charge by the foot for ships like yours. I'm guessing 4 dollars a foot just for cleaning. That's 4 times 146. Close to 600. Plus you'll be needing zinc replacement, and I charge an additional 60 an hour for that. Then there's my own labor: 35 an hour. All told, I'm guessing it'll put you out 3,000 and take me 10 days."

"Three thousand *dollars?* Forget it. You think you can rip me off?"

Jason handed him the videotape. "And I haven't even told you about the shafts that need replacing. She's not seaworthy. I wouldn't take her out if I were you."

"Not take her out? Are you crazy? Do you have any idea what I—"

He stopped at the sound of footsteps on the wooden pier behind him. A man and woman—in their forties, slim, tanned, and exceptionally well-dressed—approached.

"Mr. and Mrs. Danworth-Myers!" Clements said, hurrying to them. "How wonderful to see you. Come to check her out before the reception, eh? Just look at her. Isn't she a beauty?"

"Yes, it's fine," Mr. Danworth-Myers said. "You're sure it'll accommodate five hundred? I don't want anyone left ashore tonight."

"Of course, of course. She's rated for up to 579, not counting crew. And if unexpected guests show up, I'm sure we can find a way to accommodate everyone."

"Well. . .we've been thinking that maybe a larger ship would—"

"Come, come," Clements said, leading them onto the boat. "Let me show you the interior. She has two climate-controlled decks, three full-service cocktail bars, and a 2,700 square foot observation deck. Mahogany and brass throughout. . ."

Jason shook his head. He unzipped his wetsuit and began to gather his gear. As he did, he felt someone looking at him. Mrs. Danworth-Myers was staring from *The Spirit of Long Beach II.*

Clements appeared again in the doorway. "I'm sorry, ma'am; did you ask about him? Oh, he's just a diver. He works for me. Got to keep the ship maintained, you know. Safety is a priority at Sunshine Charters."

She said something softly to Clements.

"I don't know; I'll ask," he said. To Jason he said, "Hey, what's your name, boy?"

Jason considered his answer. Finally he said, "Austin. Steve Austin. My friends call me Stone Cold."

Mr. Danworth-Myers reemerged on deck. "What's going on? Clements, show me the rest of the boat."

"Right, sir," Clements said. "I was just telling your wife about my diver. He's an ex-Navy SEAL, you know. Only the best for Sunshine Charters."

"I don't care if he's a navy blue sea otter. Get back in here and show me the cocktail bar."

"Right away, sir."

Clements scuttled in after Danworth-Myers, but the woman stayed behind, eyeing Jason. She licked her lips and looked him up and down. Jason gathered his gear and made for his pickup, feeling her eyes on him as he left.

At 6:15 P.M. Jason pulled his emerald green diesel four-by-four king cab pickup into the Island Grissom Air Apartments parking lot. He stowed his scuba gear in his storage space next to the laundry room and got his mail from the box.

Apartment 268 was on the corner of the fourth three-story building on the property. It was a one-bedroom efficiency with a separate bedroom and bath, living room/kitchen combination, and a four-by-eight balcony with a seaward view. In other words, it was a five hundred square foot dump with a narrow view of blocks and blocks of industrial park. He did get his fair share of seagull guano on the balcony, however, so he figured there was a bright side.

Jason closed the door behind him, dropping bills and credit card applications on the dining table. No messages on the machine. He turned on the air conditioner—just a little—and pulled dry clothes out of the plastic laundry basket. On his way to the kitchen he flipped on the TV. Almost time for *Wheel of Fortune.*

Inside the refrigerator, he found a giant jar of Sechler's genuine dill pickles with garlic. A block of cheddar cheese struggling with an embarrassing case of green acne. A covered bowl of something that used to be cantaloupe. An almost empty twelve-pack of Mountain Dew. He pulled a Jose Olé All Meat Burrito out of the freezer and stuck it into the microwave.

Five minutes later, he was sitting on the couch in the living room, chasing bites of burrito with swigs of his favorite green beverage.

If he'd been on with Pat Sajak that day, he would've walked away with forty thousand bucks. Not bad for thirty minutes of work.

He had a few moments before a rerun of *ER* would come on, so he pushed aside the wrappings his delicious dinner had come in and pawed through the mail.

Jason didn't even open the electric bill. What was the point? A note from the Island Grissom Air management told him he'd have to park his truck elsewhere for the next week so they could repave the parking lot. Then there were three notices of how he'd been pre-approved for credit cards and given a credit line upwards of twenty thousand dollars each. How was it that he could get approved for credit cards but not bank loans?

Heavy-duty bass thumped through the wall and reverberated along the floor. Russell must have been skipping out of his package deliveries again. Jason turned up the TV.

The last piece of mail was something he'd at first taken for junk, but now he saw had a real stamp on it. The envelope was heavy. He didn't recognize the outfit on the stationary: The Lord Is on His Throne Scripture Church. Akron, Ohio.

Inside the envelope was what appeared to be a bona fide round-trip plane ticket to Akron and a trifolded letter on The Lord Is on His Throne letterhead.

Dear Jason Kromer:

Greetings from The Lord Is on His Throne Scripture Church. The staff search committee has heard about you and would like to interview you regarding a position connected with our church.

Be assured that this is not a mistake. We are aware that you have not sought this position nor were previously even aware of it. However, you come to us highly recommended, and we feel that you may be just the candidate to fill this rather specialized position.

Please use the enclosed plane tickets to come visit us. When you arrive at Akron-Canton Regional Airport, a driver will meet you and take you to the Sheraton Inn, where a prepaid room is reserved in your name.

Spend that night, a Saturday, in the Sheraton, and in the morning please walk two blocks south to The Lord Is on His Throne Scripture Church. Service begins at ten in the morning. Afterward, please plan to stay for our all-church luncheon. We can discuss details of your interview when you arrive.

Thank you, Mr. Kromer. We look forward to meeting you.

The Staff Search Committee

"Leave your country and your people," God said, "and go to the land I will show you."

Acts 7:3

Jason studied the ticket in his hands. United Airlines all the way. Reserved seats. As far as he could tell, this was no elaborate junk mail deception. After six months of struggling to get work scrubbing barnacles off ship hulls to keep him in All Meat Burritos, someone was pursuing *him.* He found he was having difficulty keeping the ticket steady. He laid it down.

He looked around his apartment at the management-supplied

pastel seascapes on the wall, the cracks in the ceiling, the roach traps in the corners, the bills on the floor, and the remains of his frozen dinner in front of him. He thought about spending ten days cleaning the crud off *The Spirit of Long Beach II* so that the likes of Clements and the Danworth-Myerses could go on treating him like dirt.

And he decided then and there that whatever this church offered him, he was going to say *yes* to it.

CHAPTER 5

The Lord Is on His Throne Scripture Church

JASON was late. Service had already begun.

All morning he'd told himself he was intentionally delaying to gain the advantage of striking at a time of his own choosing. The truth was that he hated social gatherings in which he was the only outsider. He was hoping to miss the greet-the-visitors time.

The Lord Is on His Throne Scripture Church was an old brick building with a squarish bell tower and two rows of windows. It looked like a military academy built in the nineteenth century. Newer buildings adjoined the brick-red and white main structure and stretched down both streets of the corner it occupied. He could hear organ music coming from inside.

There was no one in the little entry area inside the glass double doors, so Jason helped himself to an order-of-service brochure from the marble counter and stepped into the sanctuary.

And stopped in his tracks.

One look into the congregation quickly revealed that his was the only white face inside the building. The man leading the singing stopped and stared. Seven hundred brown faces turned to look at Jason. The music had a seizure and died.

He felt like tar on Mother's white carpet.

Jason took a step backward but bumped into a round woman coming up behind him. "Excuse me!" he said, trying to disintegrate.

The woman wore a blue-and-white print dress and a white bow in her hair. "Come on, young man, let's see if any of these good people will make room for us on a pew."

She escorted him up the center aisle. He felt all fourteen hundred eyes on him. The only empty spot was front row center, of course. She sat down with a sigh and fanned herself, then patted the cushion next to her. Jason knew when to obey orders. He sat.

As if their processional had been an item on the order of service, the music leader went on with the singing. "Hymn number 431—'Great Is Thy Faithfulness.' Please stand."

The congregation stood and Jason followed suit, not making any sudden movements or loud sounds. He shared a hymnal with the woman next to him.

The song leader wore a long black robe and a gold print sash with golden fringe. His direction was stately and sure. He stood behind a dark wooden podium, the front of which was adorned with a green cloth bearing a yellow cross.

Behind him were wooden panels sectioning off the choir, thirty-six men and women wearing bright green or blue or pink kimonos with something like tie-die designs on them. They were the most outlandish choir robes Jason had ever seen, but he found he liked them tremendously.

A man in a black robe with wide golden cuffs sat in a chair in front of the choir, hunched over the Bible in his lap. He shook his shaved head back and forth, whether to the music, in the throes of worship, or in disgust at the depravity of mankind, Jason couldn't tell.

Set in the middle of the paneled wall at the very front of the church were three tall panels of stained glass. Each had an image of Jesus on it that looked as if it were drawn from a medieval illumination. In the left picture, Christ wore a white robe and held a book. Perhaps this was Christ the Savior with the Book of Life. In the center image, He wore brown and held a loaf of bread. Christ the man. The final image showed Christ with a crown and sword. Christ the conqueror.

It seemed like everyone in the church was a fantastic singer. The woman next to him, a full foot shorter than Jason, belted out the hymn with passion. Passion. The place seemed to be filled to the high white ceiling with it. Everywhere except inside Jason.

The organist, on the right, and the pianist, on the left, brought the song to a close. The song leader motioned everyone to sit, and he stepped off the platform.

The man in the chair stood and brought his Bible to the podium. He switched on a microphone clipped to the golden hem running up the front of his button-up robe top. His dark eyes scanned the crowd from left to right and back to front. With his gaze on Jason, he said, "Welcome one and all to the Lord's house. Let me hear you now: The Lord. . . ?"

The congregation spoke together. "The Lord is on His throne."

"That's right, my brothers and my sisters. The Lord *is* on His throne, and you that are here and you listening at home are gathered for worship in The Lord Is on His Throne Scripture Church. Welcome and God bless you."

People in the congregation spoke back. They said "Amen" or "Hallelujah" or "Praise the Lord!"

"Now, while you're turning to the book of Genesis, chapter thirteen, I want to remind you of what we've been talking about for the last seven Sundays. Some of you say, 'Pastor, why you always got to review what we done last time? We been here every week. Just get on with it!' I hear you; I hear you. But not everybody was here last week, amen?"

The woman next to Jason said, "That's right." Variations of that sentiment were echoed from elsewhere in the pews.

"And some of us just have a bad memory, amen?"

"Amen."

"And some of you rascals didn't listen last week so you have to get it again."

Jason laughed with the others. He dared a glance over his left shoulder and saw black men and women young and old, well-dressed and poorly dressed, excited and sleepy. The looks they returned—and his white face drew many—were curious, but not unkind.

"Now we're looking at Abraham and Lot," the pastor said, "because we're looking at the whole story of Abraham and how the consequences of the sins of the father will be visited to the third and fourth generation."

"Uh-huh, that's right," somebody said.

"Did I say the *sins* of the father?" the pastor asked.

"No way."

"No, I did not. I said the *consequences* of the sins of the fathers would be passed down. All right, you all are with me this morning. Maybe I'll preach it the way it ought to be preached. Are you with me that much?"

"Preach it!"

"All right, well, we'll see. Once I start preaching the Bible to you, you may change your tune. You say 'Give it to us, Pastor,' and maybe I will. But then when I start giving it to you, you say, 'Lighten up on us, Pastor. We can't take that.' That's the problem with Christians today, amen? They can't take the red meat of the Holy Scriptures. But I think maybe you're with me today."

"Amen."

"Still, I may have to run out of here anyway. I'll have my getaway car waiting for me on the curb, just in case. Because after what I have to say about Lot and what his sin means to us today, you may be after my hide. So I'll be ready.

"All right," he said, "let's review then."

If the letter hadn't said he needed to attend the all-church luncheon after the service, Jason never would've gone. During the sermon, he'd quickly become just one more worshiper in the congregation, but now he was the star attraction again.

The fellowship hall doubled as the gymnasium. The basketball backboards were winched to the ceiling, but the free throw stripes on the all-purpose green carpet remained. Round white tables occupied the floor, and down the center stood the line for food. Jason got in line, his hands shoved into the pockets of his blue jeans. He adopted what he hoped was an expression of quiet contentedness and watched the children chase each other around the tables.

Whatever information the staff search committee had received about him must've lacked one pertinent detail. Besides, even aside from the issue that he was the one slice of sourdough in a loaf of rye, what kind of minister were they thinking he could be? He had no formal Christian education, much less a full seminary degree. Maybe they wanted him to be their custodian. *"Rather specialized position," my foot.*

The pastor entered the fellowship hall along with the music leader and others Jason had seen in robes in the sanctuary. They were all in regular Sunday morning clothes now: suit and tie. Jason looked down at his jeans and tennis shoes, wishing for the trillionth time that he'd owned something nicer to wear to an interview.

The pastor's eyes found Jason in line, as every other set of eyes in the place had already done. He said something to the others and walked straight to Jason.

"Good morning," he said, extending his hand. "William Johnson."

Jason took his hand. "Jason Kromer. I enjoyed your sermon, Pastor."

"You did?" His eyebrows rose. "You're not supposed to enjoy it, my brother. If you enjoy it, I'm not doing my job. You're supposed to writhe in your pew and beg for mercy."

"Oh," Jason said. "In that case I didn't enjoy your sermon at all, Pastor. In fact, I hated it."

"That's more like it."

"My backside's raw from writhing, and I think the pew I was on will need to be reupholstered."

The pastor tilted his head back and laughed. "Oh, I've got to watch out for you, brother Jason. You're a sharp one, I perceive."

The line moved forward. Jason and the pastor advanced.

"You know, sometimes I see someone in the congregation, and I'm not sure whether I've met him or not. I go up to them after the sermon and ask if we've met before." He eyed Jason doubtfully. "With you, Jason, I had no problem figuring it out."

Jason smirked. "Are you saying I stick out, Pastor?"

"Like the sorest thumb I ever had, brother."

People in the line around them laughed. Jason caught a whiff of the lasagna at the front of the line. Tables were filling with people carrying their pasta, garlic bread, and salad. Jason's stomach rumbled.

"So what brings you to The Lord Is on His Throne?"

Jason stared at him. "Well. . .the letter."

"What kind of letter? Oh, you mean the letter to the editor I wrote? Now isn't that too much? That letter's gotten me more enemies than—"

"No, sir, the letter that came to me in the mail. The one with the plane tickets. It was from your ministry search committee." Jason looked at him through narrowed eyes. "You're pulling my leg, aren't you?"

The pastor smiled but shook his head. "No, son, I'm not. Not that it's not something I wouldn't do. What did the letter say? It was from the search committee, you say? The *ministry* search committee? We've never had such a thing, far as I know."

Jason pulled the folded letter from his back pocket and handed it over. The pastor read it, looking at it as if it were an article about a three-headed dog.

"Strange. 'Would like to interview you regarding a position

connected with our church.' A 'rather specialized position,' no less." He looked at Jason warily. "Now you're pulling *my* leg. Is this some crazy way to get an interview?"

"No, sir. I'm—"

The pastor walked across the gym to a cluster of men, at least one of whom was one of the ministers Jason had seen earlier. He said something to them, and they all crowded around the letter, glancing from it to Jason and back.

Jason grabbed a plate and held it out to the serving ladies. If they were going to send him packing, he'd at least get a meal out of it first.

He couldn't help noticing that all five ladies in the serving line were large maternal types in their fifties and up. They each smiled at him—and more than one put a double helping on his plate. At the food bar, at least, he was welcome.

He had to walk to the far end of the gym, but he finally found the last empty table. He wanted to sit alone. The only thing worse than having everyone stare at him as he passed would be having people trying to make polite conversation with him as he ate. He said a quick word of thanks and dug in.

About halfway through his generous slab of lasagna, someone approached his table. It was his front row buddy, the woman in the blue-and-white print dress who had brought him into the church. "May I join you?"

He stood. "Please do."

"Oh, such a gentleman." She set her salad and iced tea on the table and took off her apron before sitting. "Now quit fussing over an old woman and get back to your food before it gets cold."

"Yes, ma'am."

Up at the serving table, the line was gone. The ladies served up their own plates and then began appearing at Jason's table. He stood for them all, something that made them blush and giggle like middle schoolers.

"Tell us your name, young man," his front row buddy said.

"Jason, ma'am. Jason Kromer."

"Ladies, say hello to Jason."

"Hello, Jason."

Jason had never seen so many batting eyelids in one place. "It's a pleasure, ladies."

"This group of beautiful sisters around you is the widow's prayer group," his buddy said. "My sister beside me is Cheryl. Next to her is Celia, then Wilma and Ethel. And this glorious saint with the silver hair is Dorothy, our most mature member. I'm Eloise."

"I'm pleased to meet you all. And I have to say that I can't remember having such wonderful lasagna. My compliments to the chefs."

"Watch out, girls," Eloise said. "This one's got a smooth tongue."

The pastor and an older man approached the table. "Jason," the pastor said, "this is Millard Cuspert, chairman of our *pastor* search committee, back when we were looking to find a youth pastor. Millard, tell him what you told me."

Millard had gray hair cut almost to his scalp. He wore fashionable eyeglasses and a nice suit, the jacket of which even now remained buttoned. "Now I've read this letter," he said, his voice raspy. "And I never did send it. It's our letterhead all right, and Lord knows I've sent out more than my share of letters like this. But this ain't one of them. How it came to you, I can't say."

"It had a round-trip plane ticket in it," Jason said.

"So I read," Millard said. "And that's the strangest part of it. It's a mighty expensive prank, wouldn't you say, Pastor?"

"Absolutely. It's a mystery," the pastor said. "Where's Shaft when you need him?"

"So you aren't hiring for any position at the church?" Jason asked.

"No," the pastor said. "Unless you know something I don't and one of my men's about to take a new church somewhere."

The men stood a while in silence. Some people were taking their dishes to the kitchen window. Others were stacking chairs.

"Well," Jason said, sipping his iced tea, "it looks like a nice church, Pastor, even if I do stick out a little. I'm sorry you're not hiring." *Besides, now I have to go back and scrape off barnacles.*

"I'm sorry, too, Jason. I think it'd be nice to have a— You know, I've always wanted to have a *transethnic* congregation. Having you aboard might be the start of that. You say you've got a round-trip ticket, so you can get on home. I'll do some thinking about that, and at our next elder meeting, I'll bring it up. Maybe we'll give you a call. Give Millard your number." The pastor shook Jason's hand.

When Jason stepped onto the corner outside the church, the streets were mostly empty. The cars that had lined the curbs were gone. It was a beautiful, blue-sky day. He took a deep breath and headed off toward the Sheraton Inn.

Three steps later, he noticed a green bill fluttering on the ground, its edge pinned with a rock. It was a hundred dollar bill. He picked it up and looked around. Nobody. He straightened up and thought about it.

A hundred dollars would buy a month's worth of groceries—maybe he could branch out to tacos and enchiladas. Or he could pay a bill or two. It would certainly soften the blow of disappointment he'd received on this trip. Ten thousand pennies from heaven, right here on a city street, with no one coming to claim it.

He put it in his pocket.

And then he turned around to take it back into the church. He found an empty offering plate and put it in there instead.

He took his time returning to the hotel. He window-shopped and stepped into a few stores he'd noticed on his way to church. He decided that this part of Akron was nice.

When he arrived at his hotel room, there was a note sticking out from under his door.

Dear Jason:

Good interview. You're in.

Come to the First National Tower downtown tomorrow at 8:30 A.M. sharp. Twenty-eighth floor.

Your real interviewer

CHAPTER 6

The Interview

THE polished steel doors slid open quietly. Jason stepped out of the elevator onto the twenty-eighth floor of the First National Tower building. He'd been alone in the elevator from the seventeenth floor up and had received glances from the folks who got out there, glances that seemed to ask, *Are you somebody important, then?*

An attractive blonde stepped toward him, then almost stumbled when she saw him emerge. "Oh! You scared me."

He held the doors open for her. "Sorry."

She stepped by and pushed a button. A wave of sweet perfume followed in her wake. As the door closed, he saw her steal a glance at him.

Jason was standing before a wall of frosted glass. On the right side of the glass door in the middle was the company name: ABL Corporation. The logo was a blue globe with a red V flying upward and onward. He pushed through the silent door and stepped through.

The reception area was chic and open. White floors and walls, high ceiling, lots of glass and chrome and polished wood. On Jason's left was a gray counter, elevated slightly so that visitors spoke to the receptionist at eye level. A smartly dressed Asian woman sat at the receptionist's desk, a thin black microphone pointing down her cheek like a loose hair. She was engaged in a conversation with a burly UPS delivery man. A short stack of parcels sat on the gray marble countertop.

On the wall beside the receptionist was a ten-by-ten canvas that probably cost ABL a ton of lucre. It was all white except where it was streaked with black scratches. Jason could've done it in ten minutes, but he would have needed an art school diploma to collect any dough for it.

On the wall opposite the entryway, two columns of black-framed windows flanked a tall wooden door like sprocket holes in a strip of 35mm film. To Jason's right was a carpeted waiting area with smart-looking gray chairs that probably hurt to sit in and a chrome and glass coffee table. A super-clear HDTV panel hung on the wall here, showing *CNN Headline News.* Two ficus trees stood in just the right spots under pools of light from hidden bulbs. A tray of pastries sat beneath a plastic dome on the coffee table, next to a coffee pot and cups.

"Are you sure you don't want me to take it somewhere else?" the delivery man said. "It's pretty big. I don't know where you'll put it."

"No, thank you," the receptionist said. "I will—" A patient little tone tap-tapped on her desk. "Just a moment." She pressed a button. "ABL Corporate Headquarters, President Webster's office." She listened. "Yes, Mr. Hirabayashi, thank you for calling back. I'm sorry, but President Webster is in a meeting right now and is not available until after lunch. Would you like to leave voice mail?" She picked up a pen. "No, that's fine, sir. Go ahead."

Jason and the UPS guy traded a look. He was a good foot taller than Jason and was obviously into weightlifting. He had a bald head and a bristly orange goatee. He looked half-savage, like maybe on his days off he sailed aboard the pirate ship *Revenge.*

Jason wandered over to the waiting area. The glass coffee table held a neatly stacked array of magazines he'd never heard of: *The Defense Monitor, The Progressive, Government Executive,* and a newsletter from something called the Weapon Systems Technology Information Analysis Center. He also spotted a slick copy of ABL's latest annual report.

The CNN anchorwoman introduced an update on the revolution in Dagestan. The Russians were stalled in the cities, where Muslim rebels were fighting fiercely.

A male voice behind Jason expressed the thought that had formed in his mind: "It's Chechnya all over again."

Jason turned around. It was the UPS guy. "No kidding."

"Do not plot harm against your neighbor, who lives trustfully near you."

Jason looked at the big man. "Hey, isn't that from Proverbs?"

He winked.

Behind them the receptionist concluded her call. "Sir," she said to the delivery man, "do I need to sign for anything else?"

"Nah," the big man said. "I just wanted to be sure you really wanted me to deliver that beast up here instead of at a shipping dock or something."

"No," she said, "it will be fine. Please bring it up."

He shrugged. "All right." He nodded to Jason, grabbed his parcel stack, and went out the door.

She looked at Jason. "May I help you, sir?"

Jason stepped up to the counter. Upon closer look, he decided that the receptionist, in her mid-twenties, was truly lovely. Though her manner was professional and demure, nothing could hide her beautiful black hair and eyes, milky skin, and perfect smile.

"I hope so." He pulled the note from his blue jeans pocket. "It says I was supposed to be here at eight-thirty for an interview, but I don't—"

"Yes, Mr. Kromer," she said. "It's good to meet you. Please have a seat and I'll let President Webster know you're here."

"Oh, all right."

"Help yourself to coffee and a Danish. The cream cheese ones are my favorite."

"Okay, thanks. But I thought you said he was busy until lunch."

She didn't appear to hear him. She spoke into her headset. "Yes, Mr. Kromer is here." She listened, then looked up at Jason. "Very well." She pressed a button and spoke to Jason. "It will be just a few minutes, Mr. Kromer."

"Okay." Jason went to the plastic dome and selected a glistening cream cheese Danish. The coffee was piping, and the Styrofoam cups were large.

He'd just alighted on a fairly comfortable chair and opened the WSTIAC newsletter when the glass door opened. A wiry young man, probably not even out of his teens, came in carrying a laptop computer. His hair was shaved so close there were white nicks of skin where the barber must've glanced up at the TV. His head rotated as if on a turret, taking in Jason, the receptionist, and the Danishes. He walked strangely, bouncing with every step, as if his Achilles' tendons weren't quite long enough to allow him to stand flat on the floor.

"Hi, Tree-ooh," he said. At least that's what it sounded like he said. TREE-ooh.

"Well," the receptionist said, turning to him, "were you able to figure out what I did?"

"Oh, yeah, that was the easy part. The hard part was fixing it."

"Oh, sorry."

"For what? Actually, I thought it was kind of cool. You found something I hadn't when I coded it in the first place. So, really, you're playtesting for me."

"Playtesting?"

"Yeah, you know, beta testing? Never mind. Here, let me show you what I've done." He opened his laptop and the two of them leaned forward. "Used to, when you entered an appointment but had to change it to a time in the past—not exactly something I ever anticipated anyone doing, but that's OK—the thing would crash like an overclocked GeForce4 card. But now—"

"An over-whatted what?"

"Never mind. But now what I've done is allow you unlimited date-setting freedom. That's something I wish I had, but that's another story altogether. You can take the New Year's party for 2005 and put it in negative one billion B.C. if you want." He straightened up. "Go ahead, try it out."

Jason had seen this type before. He spent so much time programming that his skin had gone whiter than a shark's belly and his social skills made him about as popular as foot odor. Jason went back to his pastry and an interesting article on unmanned combat systems. He was going to have to subscribe to this newsletter.

"All right," the receptionist said, "that's better. Thank you, Lewis. When can I have it on my computer?"

"It's already there. Just exit out of the system and log back on."

She did. "And it's there?"

"What did you expect?" He snapped his laptop shut.

A new electronic tone sounded. The receptionist pressed a button and listened. "All right, I will." She looked at Jason. "Mr. Kromer, you may go in now."

Jason threw his trash away and went to the 35mm door. When he put his hand on the brass knob in the mahogany door, the receptionist pressed a button. Jason felt the door go slack in its frame. He pulled it open and went through.

There was a second secretary's desk behind a gray-carpeted partition on the other side of the door, but it was empty. A short-carpeted hallway led deeper into the bowels of the building. Jason heard a man's voice from that direction, so he went that way.

The hallway opened into a huge corner office suite at the top of the First National Tower. Floor to ceiling windows looked out over downtown Akron on two sides. The suite bore the same contemporary look as the reception area. A blond man sat behind an executive desk larger than the one Jason had seen on a childhood tour of the Oval Office, dictating a letter to a pretty brunette in the chair before him.

On Jason's right was a sitting area like the one in which he always saw the president sitting beside foreign heads of state. On his left was a long conference table with at least twenty chairs.

"Ah, Mr. Kromer," the executive said. "Come in and sit down. I'll just be a minute."

Jason nodded.

"Have a Danish."

"No thanks," Jason said.

He walked to the window behind the conference table and looked out. It was a clear, sunny day in Ohio. The rest of Akron wasn't much to look at, not compared to San Diego, anyway. But it was a nice "medium-sized" city. He felt he could do with a medium-sized pace of living for a change.

"All right," the exec said, "where were we?"

"The birding, I think."

The assistant's voice was low and pleasing. Jason looked at her—and his eyes widened involuntarily, as if he'd just recognized a movie star. She was beautiful. No, she was amazing. *Beauty must be a requirement for working at this place,* he thought amusedly. *Wonder why they want me?*

She had fair brown skin. Hispanic maybe? Or Native American? Or maybe she had just lightly toasted herself on the tanning bed? Straight, dark brown hair to her shoulder blades. Photo-shoot perfect eyebrows and makeup. Full lips, large brown eyes, and fit figure. She wore a white angora sweater with an asymmetrical collar that looked torn or stretched toward her left shoulder. It drew his eye to the skin of her shoulder, as perhaps it was meant to.

Jason decided he wanted to work here, if just for the babes.

She favored him with a look. He felt sweat pop out on his palms.

"Right!" the executive said. "Okay, let's say something like this: 'When you're out here, I'll take you to a place I know of. If we're very quiet and very lucky, we might get a glimpse of a brown-headed nuthatch! I saw one here last year and some friends of mine say they've already seen one this year.' "

He broke out of his epiphany and reentered the room. "Is that enough?"

"Sir?"

"Oh, just end it now. 'Sincerely. . .' yada yada yada."

She finished the note. "Will there be anything else, sir?"

"No, Rachel, that's all for now, thanks."

Rachel stood and walked toward the conference table next to Jason. If it had been a movie, she would've been in slow motion and had the Hallelujah Chorus playing in the background.

"Hi," she said.

She was wearing perfume that struck him like a stun grenade. He might've said *Hi* back, but he wasn't sure. His insides had turned to gelatin. She leaned close to him to collect her appointment calendar from the conference table. Then she disappeared down the hallway, taking with her half the bulb wattage from the room.

"Jason Kromer!" the executive said, crossing the room with his hand outstretched. "Great to meet you at last. Call me Chris."

The handshake was firm. This guy had obviously been working out, too. Babes and weightlifters. Had he stumbled onto a Hollywood film set by mistake?

The man could be a model. He was young, mid-twenties at the most, with the shiny-skinned, hair-gelled look of a magazine cover. A single blond curl dangled over his forehead like a signature beauty mark. His jaw was set and his blue eyes intense. But there was an animal ferocity in this guy, too, something that probably explained how he'd bagged this office before his thirtieth birthday. He wore a suit that looked like it cost more than Jason's truck.

"How was your flight?"

"Fine, fine. It was good."

He led Jason over to the sitting area. "Can I get you something?

Coffee? Soda? Juice?"

"Maybe in a while."

"All right. Why don't we sit."

The semipadded wooden furniture seemed designed to not let you get comfortable. They looked like chairs that ladies would sit in to take tea. He sat in one but couldn't make himself slump back into it.

Chris was watching him closely. "So how do you like life outside the navy?"

Jason thought about giving the canned spiel he usually gave at this juncture in such conversations: Oh, fine. Not as structured as I'm used to, but I like the freedom. Blah, blah, blah. But something about this guy's manner made Jason talk to him honestly.

"I hate it."

Chris laughed. "You hate it? Why?"

"Well. . .Chris. . .it's just that all I've ever wanted in my life was to be on the Teams. I mean, to be a Navy SEAL."

"Uh-huh."

"But now that I'm not on a team anymore, I. . .I don't really know what to do with myself. I'm kind of. . .drifting, I guess."

"Your hull-cleaning job isn't giving you satisfaction?"

Now it was Jason's turn to laugh. "Hardly. I'm only doing that to pay the bills. It uses some of my skills and gives me the chance to get wet, but. . .Well, it's no way to make a living."

Chris stared at Jason in silence, blinking rapidly as if doing mental calculations. Finally, he folded his arms and placed one hand to his lips. He looked like a man who had just decided to buy a grand piano and was now trying to figure out how to get it into the car.

"Do you know what ABL does, Jason?"

"Uh, not a clue. But if I had to guess from what I've seen this morning, I'd say that you were a defense contractor of some sort or maybe one of those computer outsourcing companies that runs everything from the Olympics to the Stock Exchange."

Chris's eyes twinkled. "And, just for the sake of conversation, what if you were right? What use would a company like that have for someone like you?"

"I don't know. Personal security for you? Weapons tester? Crash test dummy? Maybe your yacht's gotten all nasty below the waterline?"

Chris walked to his desk and pushed a button. A large flat-screen monitor set in the wall behind Jason came to life. Hidden speakers boomed out generic corporate music. The new Joint Strike Fighter zoomed past the camera on full afterburners. Then a platoon of Abrams M1A2 tanks raced across a desert plateau, firing their 120mm M256 smoothbore cannons. Next came a flyby shot over a DD-21 stealth destroyer launching a cruise missile. Next came a space-based image of a spy satellite orbiting overhead. No-nonsense white text flashed onto the screen: "ABL Corporation: For a Peaceful Planet."

A well-paid voiceover announcer began to rave about the virtues of ABL and its contribution to world peace through superior fire-power. Chris muted the audio.

"So you're a defense contractor, then?" Jason said.

"You could say that. We're not actually building the stealth destroyer or the JSF or the rest, but we are providing, let us say, *useful* technology that makes them extraspecial. But your other guess, about us providing the infrastructure for large projects such as the Olympics, wasn't far off, either. ABL has its fingers in lots of pies. We like to say that ABL is the cerebral cortex for any system or platform we're involved with—we make it all work together."

Jason looked at the screen, which was now showing behind-the-scenes footage of *Monday Night Football.* A technician was talking with Al Michaels and gesturing toward a row of computers.

"Jason," Chris said, "a career with ABL is a very good thing."

"I can see that."

"It would certainly pay better than de-fouling tugs and scrubbing barnacles."

"Are you trying to convince me? Why don't you just show me where to sign?"

Chris returned to his chair. He looked like he needed to say something unpleasant. "There's just one thing I want to ask you. There's the matter of your. . .religion. Certain information has reached us indicating that your personal religious preferences may have interfered with the performance of your duty. Indeed, there is some indication that if you had not left the navy voluntarily that you might've been transferred to a less sensitive post for the remainder of your duty."

Jason wondered who this guy's connections were. "Yes, sir, that is correct."

"So," Chris said, facing Jason squarely, "I put it to you now: Is your religion still a hindrance to you? If asked to do something that might violate, say, one of the Ten Commandments, would you do it?"

Jason looked at the screen again. It was showing an interview with a bigwig at George Lucas's special effects company, Industrial Light & Magic. Everything about this place said money.

"No, sir."

Chris blinked. "What?"

Jason stood up. "I left the Teams for a lot of reasons, but one was that I realized I couldn't live with myself if I had to do anything that violated my faith in Jesus Christ. I'm sorry. I don't know what you were wanting me to do, and I realize I'm throwing away a lot of money here, but no amount of money can help you if you've gone against your conscience. My Christianity isn't a *hindrance* to me, Chris—it's all I have. If I violate that, I've lost everything." Jason turned and made for the hallway. "Thanks for the Danish."

Jason thought he heard a door open behind him, but he kept going. Near the door there was another nice-looking woman, this one with dyed red hair and large hoop earrings, making copies at the machine beside the secretary's desk. She smiled politely. Jason put his hand on the brass knob and pulled.

The door was magnetically locked.

"Hey, can you open this for me?"

The girl was about to answer when someone called to Jason from back in the large office. It was a woman's voice.

"Jason, come on back in here."

The voice was deep and kind, and seemed vaguely familiar to him. Jason walked down the hallway.

It was Eloise, his front-row buddy from The Lord Is on His Throne Scripture Church.

CHAPTER 7

A Proposal

THE large black woman, this time wearing a white-and-yellow dress and white shoes, stood in front of the desk. Chris stood beside her.

"Hey, I know you," Jason said. "You're. . .Eloise. Isn't that right?"

She beamed. "What a memory. That's right, Jason. Eloise Webster, chairperson of the widow's prayer group."

"Wait a minute. Webster? As in President Webster, CEO of ABL?"

"The very same," she said, smiling. She walked around the desk. "Chris, that'll be all for now."

"Yes, ma'am," Chris said. He passed Jason and flashed his million-dollar smile.

Eloise sat in the chair behind the desk. "Take a load off, Jason. Sit yourself down."

Jason sat.

She laughed suddenly. "What's the matter, son, ain't you never seen a black woman who is a billionaire before?"

"Um, no, ma'am, I haven't."

"Oh, there's lots of us. Well, I know of one other, anyway." Dimples appeared in each cheek as she grinned. "I suppose you're wanting to know what kind of game I'm playing with you?"

"That would be nice."

"Listen to him. 'That would be nice.' Loosen up, Jason, you're with family now."

Jason leaned stiffly back in his chair. "I'm loose."

"All right. Here's your history lesson for the day." She took a deep breath. "My husband, Charles, and I built ABL up from a little niche industry after the Korean War. Charlie figured out a way to improve the range of certain kinds of radar arrays. That's what he was, a radar man. I won't go into what it was he did, exactly, since it would bore you and I don't get all that technical babble, anyhow. But the short of it is that everybody wanted my Charlie's new radar. Radar led to sonar, which led to infrared, microwave, and a bunch of other stuff.

"Before the Lord took my Charlie, back in seventy-eight, he handed the reins over to me. Back then we were doing lots of production work, building the FLIRs and towed sonar arrays and the rest. But he told me to lead the corporation the way I thought best, under God, and that's what I've done.

"I moved ABL to more of a research and development outfit, and outsourced most of the manufacturing to subcontractors. I got us into the development and application of new technologies. We figure things out, prototype them, just like my Charlie did. But then I'm glad to let someone else build what we design. And we also do a lot of infrastructure work with computers. Mostly system design. Again, we figure it out and let someone else build and operate it.

"That video you watched showed some of our contributions to the United States military, our primary client. But we also sell our technology internationally—under certain restrictions. The last thing I want is some other American woman's husband shot down with something I built. I'll sell to foreign airlines and media networks and such. But if I ever get wind that someone else is using our technology for military purposes, I pull their licenses so fast it'd fry your eyeballs. They have to renew their licenses with us every year."

She looked at a photo frame on her desk. When she spoke again, her voice was quieter. "Have you ever felt that there was something more you ought to be doing with your life, Jason?"

"Ma'am?"

"Have you ever felt like the Lord wanted more from you than what you were doing, even though there wasn't nothing wrong with what you were doing? Like maybe there was a higher path He wanted you to take, and suddenly the thing you'd been doing all of a sudden didn't seem so important. Am I coming through to you?"

"Yes, ma'am. I know exactly what you're talking about."

"I know you do, Jason. That's one of the things I like about you." She folded her hands on her lap and rocked in her chair, studying him. "Would you like to know why I flew you out here?"

Jason's eyebrows rose. "Absolutely."

"Jason, because of who I am and what ABL does, I get briefed on things the average person has no clue about. That's on the official side. Unofficially, I hear a lot. And I'm a smart girl. I put things together.

"This is not a nice world, Jason. Not at all. Men do things to each other that ought never be done on God's green earth. Women, too. Governments? They're the worst of all. Sometimes I think that the world would be better off without them. It's not that the people in government are any viler than anyone else. It's just the nature of government to rule selfishly and cruelly. It's right there in the Bible, from King Saul on down. My pastor says that before Saul, the children of Israel had God as their king. They were a theocracy. Do you think we could ever go back to a theocracy? Can you imagine it?"

She stared over his right shoulder. "It's human nature, Jason, that's all it is. The old devil, along with your flesh and mine, having a heyday. So what's an old woman going to do to stamp out human nature? What am I to do when governments do what governments do and innocent people get hurt, when babies get hurt? Can I put an end to that? Still, one ought to do something, shouldn't she, if it's in her power? Yes, I believe she should."

Her eyes snapped onto his. "And it *is* in my power."

Jason shook his head slowly. "I'm not sure I—"

"I know you don't, sugar. Keep your shoes on. I'm getting to it."

She leaned forward so that her elbows rested on the desk. She had such a pleasant face. "Jason, I know you can keep a secret. Your SEAL training made sure of that. I know you're a mighty man of valor, if I may speak biblically. I've seen today with my little test that you're a godly man who would rather suffer the loss of great income than dishonor his Lord. Everything that has gone before now has been to assure me of these things. I also know you're strapped for cash, living in a roach motel, and about as miserable as a frog in a hot springs."

Jason winced. "You have a delicate way of putting things, ma'am."

"Did I get it wrong?"

He shook his head.

"Then hush and let an old woman talk." She gave him the same look his mother used to when he was misbehaving.

"Yes, ma'am."

"About two years ago, during an especially good sermon from my pastor—hoo, the Spirit was moving that day—the Lord spoke to my heart. 'Ellie,' He said, 'I've put you in this position at ABL for a purpose. I've raised you up for just such a time as this. Not to enjoy the passing pleasures of sin. Not to provide weapons of war so that godless men can do wicked things to good people. Not to stand by like a dead June bug when the world goes down the toilet. I've raised you up, Ellie, to do a good work. I have a high calling for you, girl, and we can get on with it anytime you're ready.'

"I said, 'I'm ready, Lord. Send me. Here am I.' And right there in church He began unfolding His plan to me. I spent upwards of a month on my hands and knees listening to that still, small voice, letting Him refine the vision in me. Do you know what a vision is like, Jason?"

"W—"

"A vision is like a rope. One end of it is in heaven, tied onto the thing He's promised. The other end dangles down here on earth, and any that see it may grab hold and pull. If you pull hard enough and in the right way, you can pull that blessing down to earth. The Lord wants it down, you see, but He's not going to just push it off the edge and let it fall. He waits for someone to give her a yank. Colaborers with Christ, my brother.

"Well, two years ago I started pulling on that rope. You're sitting here right now because of my pulling. The vision's almost here, Jason. It's right at the lip of heaven. But I think you're a part of it. I think you're supposed to grab onto this rope with me and give it all you've got."

Eloise rolled a pen back and forth. Then she placed it in its stand. "Jason, I'm putting together a special little group that I want you to consider being part of."

He raised an eyebrow.

"Go on, young man. Ask."

"Okay. What kind of group?"

"A group that you might be well-suited for. In fact, I know you're well-suited for it. It's a small group—six, counting you—made up of Christian young people who have. . .special talents. Talents that would be necessary to conduct the kind of. . .tasks that I intend to set before them." Her eyebrows leapt. "Interested?"

He smiled. "You seem to know me pretty well, ma'am. What do you think?"

The dimples returned. "All right, then, I'll lay it on the line for you. I'm putting together a team of ex-special forces types, people like yourself, along with some others with special skills, to go into flashpoints around the world to conduct high-tech, covert, absolutely deniable missions of mercy. Assigned by me. Using only nonlethal weapons. And not really within any government's jurisdiction."

She watched his face like a nurse waiting for the patient to pass out. "Still with me?"

His finger rose and his mouth opened. But then he sat back and dropped his hands to his lap. "You wanna run that by me again?"

"I'm—"

"Slow," he said. "One piece of it at a time. You're putting together a group of ex-special forces types? Like who?"

"Like you, for one. Like a former Green Beret. Like a former Force Recon man."

"Okay, that's good." He scratched his ear. "But that's only three out of six. Don't tell me: The others are civilians, aren't they?"

"They are."

"Oh, no. This is one of those *A-Team* things, like on TV, isn't it? Some kind of cutesy gimmick with a token American Indian, an Asian, a black, a white, a Hispanic, and a little crippled boy genius?"

That look was back in Eloise's eyes. "If you mean 'Is there racial diversity in the group?' yes, there is. But that was done to allow the team to operate in a variety of cultures, not for the sake of political correctness. You know, if I didn't like you so much—and if I thought I could catch you—I'd have you over my lap for a paddling. It may surprise you to learn that there are no African-Americans on the team, at present. As you well know, a black man in the SEALs is about as common as a white man at a Black Panthers meeting."

"Negative buoyancy."

"If you mean that my strong black brothers' muscle mass is so dense that he tends to sink in water, you are correct. The other special forces outfits don't require so much underwater work, and they have more black men in them. But believe it or not, I have been screening potential team members based on skill and character, not to have a 'token' member of every race. It just so happens that there are three full-blooded white boys on my team right now, not counting you."

"I. . .I'm sorry I said that about the *A-Team.*"

"What? Do you think I'm upset? You haven't seen me upset yet. Now let's get back to the Firebrand team."

"Firebrand?"

"Didn't I say that before? It's taken from the book of Amos in the Bible: 'And you were like a firebrand snatched from a blaze.' Because, you know, that's what this team is going to go around doing, snatching innocents out of danger before they can get burned up. Anyway, if I may continue?"

"Well," he said, matching the sass in her tone, "who's stopping you?"

A look of slight surprise registered on her face, but it didn't slow her down. If anything, she accelerated.

"And before you ask, yes, there is a woman on the team, too. Two, I'll have you know. But no, that wasn't for political correctness, either. You may not know it, and I know they never taught you this in the navy, but there really are some things that a woman can do better than a man. And I'm not talking about birthin' no babies, neither. One of the women on the team is our language specialist; the other is our sniper. Both are as good or better at what they do than any man you could pony up—and, as a special bonus, they're both of diverse ethnicity."

"You've got a sniper? I thought you said you only used nonlethals."

She wagged her head. "Hold on! Look who thinks he knows it all. Mr. Peabody himself, as I live and breathe. I see you're not up to date on the latest in nonlethal weaponry. Well, let me catch you up. My sniper fires protein bullets out of an Dragunov SVD. The bullet penetrates muscle tissue and disintegrates instantly, releasing sedatives that render the target unconscious in thirteen seconds flat. I also have aerosol anesthetics, dimethylsulfoxide topical agents, neuroelectric pulse generators, and a host of other goodies that I'll save for later. Trust me on this one: My babies will not go out there unarmed."

"All right, all right. I see I'm behind the times," Jason said. "Let's get back to that part about this not being within any government's jurisdiction. What do you mean by that?"

She shook her head. "It's a gray area, Jason, I won't kid you. Private citizens are not supposed to go around forming little militia groups, and they're sure not supposed to go sending them off to other countries to do things that other governments might not approve of. It's a good way to get yourself arrested, fined, and barred from international travel."

"Not to mention killed."

She regarded him soberly. "Not to mention killed. Look, I've pursued you for this team because I think you are right for it. In fact, I believe you are supposed to *lead* this team. It never occurred to me that you might be afraid of a little danger. Yes, I'm sending my babies into harm's way. That's the whole point of Firebrand. But the innocents we're going after are already in harm's way. It's my idea to send a group of highly trained, well-armed specialists into those areas to try to pluck those little ones to safety. But if you're more concerned about protecting your own hide, then I guess I've been wrong about you all along." She stood up and pointed. "The door is that way."

"I—"

"Go on. I've got work to do."

He didn't move. "Mrs. Webster, I know you're pushing me. This is another test. I—"

She sighed. "No, it's not a test. I gave you an opportunity to change the world, but you didn't want it. So go on and leave. We'll be better off without you."

"I'm not leaving."

"I could call security."

He sneered. "Try it."

"Why won't you leave?"

"I'll leave if you want me to. But not until you've understood me."

Her hands flew open. "Lay it on me then, baby. I'm all ears." She sat back down.

He gave her what he hoped was a steely-eyed glare. "I'm not afraid to go into danger. If you know me as well as you say, then you know I was point man in my squad. I was first into danger, and I wouldn't have had it any other way. SEALs are always chomping at the bit to get where the action is, and the point man's the razor tip of the spear, okay, so no more casting doubts on my courage."

She shrugged dismissively.

"What I meant was that you're putting your people, your *babies,* into more danger than you know. If you really think I'm cut out for this team, and especially if you think I'm the one to lead it, then you have to listen to me. If the man on the ground has to obey orders from somebody sitting in some air-conditioned office somewhere calling the shots, that man gets in trouble real quick-like. And most likely his team comes home in little black bags, get it?

"Are you really serious about this nonlethal weapon thing? You'd really send them in without real guns?"

"That's what this whole team is founded on," she said. "No more killing. Not in the name of saving lives. No way."

Jason shook his head. "Ma'am, sending any team, even a SEAL team, into a combat zone with only tranquilizer darts and crossed fingers is just plain crazy. That's a real good way to get them all killed. And you're doing it with civvies on the team? No thank you. Maybe the best thing I can do for you on this trip is to tell you *no* and tell you not to send your people out.

"I'm sorry about the innocents in the world who get hurt. I really am. I'd like to do something about that. But getting shot isn't exactly what I had in mind—because I'd be dead and they'd still be in trouble. Maybe I'll mail in a donation to UNICEF instead."

They sat there quietly, staring at one another across the desk, pushing wills back and forth. A helicopter flew across the Akron skyline. Clouds rolled by.

Finally, Eloise leaned back in her chair. "Jason, I think you and I will get on just fine."

"I like you, too, ma'am. But I don't know if we'll be getting on about anything. I think I'll be heading to the airport and going home."

She shook her head. "You're that pigheaded?"

"As pigheaded as you are, ma'am."

She chuckled. "I imagine you're right. Well, before you give your final answer, I want you to see our little toys. And I want you to meet someone. Come on."

He followed her into the hallway. "You mean the team's here now?"

"The team? Of course they're here. You've already met them. Where you been?"

"What, the widow's prayer group?"

She laughed so hard she had to lean against the wall. "Oh, gracious, I think we need to stop by the ladies' room before we go for our ride."

"Who then?"

"Chris Page, for one." She led them back into the office toward a narrow door in the inner wall.

"You mean your junior executive boy?"

"That's right. Former Force Recon. He's point man for Firebrand. Also a crazed bird-watcher. You'll have to keep an eye on that one, or he'll lead you way out of your way just to get a glimpse of a blue-bellied sapsucker."

"Who else?"

"The UPS delivery man."

"No way!" Now Jason was smiling in disbelief. "He's the Green Beret."

"That's right. Heavy weapons specialist, demolitions, escape and evasion, booby traps, and all-around Mister Fixit. Drives a Harley."

"No doubt. Who else?"

"My receptionist, Trieu."

"This is too much. What's she?"

"Sniper. Olympic sharpshooter, silver medallist, 2000 games in Sydney. She's also the team doctor."

"A doctor and sniper? First she shoots them then she heals them? Isn't that kind of against the Hippocratic Oath or something?"

"She's special, that's for sure. She's also in charge of mixing the cocktails for the various sedative delivery mechanisms."

"She fills the dart guns?"

"Right. Pardon me a minute." She stepped inside the bathroom.

Jason leaned against the wall, enjoying the game in spite of himself. He felt like he'd stumbled onto his own surprise party. He could not stop grinning. He was ready for her when she emerged. "Who else?"

"Maybe you saw a young man come out and help Trieu with her computer?"

"The computer nerd? Oh, no. I thought you said no crippled boy genius."

"What are you talking about? Lewis's only disability is in his social skills. But he's a hacker, inventor, and communications maniac. When he's not flying one of his robot planes or rewriting the elevator software, he's rigging a way to talk to the astronauts on the space station. I swear, that boy has some kind of supernatural connection with anything that travels through the air. Now if I could only get him to grow his hair out and get some sun, maybe we could get him hooked up with some nice girl."

Jason half smiled. "Okay, whatever."

She led him by the copy girl's vacant desk, then through the miraculously unlocked door into the receptionist area. A dark-skinned woman Jason hadn't seen before was at the receptionist desk.

"Wait a minute," he said. "Where is everybody?"

"Oh, they left as soon as you went through."

"You guys are too much. Okay, but you're still missing one. A female."

"That would be Rachel Levy."

Judging by how she looked at him, he must've had some kind of visible reaction to that news. "Close your mouth," she said, "before a fly gets in there."

"She's your language specialist?"

"Yep. That girl speaks nine languages at last count, not counting dialects, accents, and sign language. But her real specialty is distraction tactics. From the way you've lost control of your saliva, I can tell that she's still all that and a bag of chips. Watch out for her, Jason. She's a sweet girl, but she can eat you for a midnight snack. And if you ever hurt her," she said, suddenly pressing him against the wall, "I'll put the hurt on you."

He nodded quickly.

"And she's a sorceress with costumes and disguise," she said, backing off. "You met her three times this morning."

"What?"

"The girl you almost bumped into in the elevator. That's one. Chris's assistant is two. And my copy machine girl is three. It was a little experiment she wanted to try. In fact that whole thing with the team meeting you in disguise was a little prank Rachel thought up. She's our practical joker. Behind that pretty face, she's always thinking. Anyway, they all wanted to get a look at you, and I wanted you to see a little of them in action. Hope you're not bothered."

"Nah."

Not only was he not bothered, he was more intrigued than ever. He couldn't ignore the obvious benefit that if he did sign on to this crazy team, he'd get lots of time with Rachel. Something to think about.

"Come on," Eloise said, pushing through the frosted glass door. "Let's go see my toys."

CHAPTER 8

Toys for Big Boys

JASON followed Eloise into the elevator. As the doors closed, she opened a panel below the buttons and typed a code on a little keypad.

"Changing the elevator music?"

"Huh," she said, "even I don't have that much power. No, just making sure we have some privacy while we get to where we're going. Relax, son, this is going to take a minute."

Jason watched the numbers as they counted down.

Ah, to be on a team again. He couldn't deny how nice the idea sounded. And though he'd never officially commanded a SEAL squad, he knew how. Every man in the platoon had been trained to do every job the platoon required.

Having a Green Beret and a Force Recon Marine around would be a real plus. He knew he could count on them in combat. *If* he took the job, that is. But a SEAL was the natural choice to lead such a team, if he did say so himself, because if anyone got incapacitated, he could step in and do that person's job.

What was he doing? It was crazy to even think about it. There were plenty of reasons why he wouldn't take the job—plenty of reasons why the team shouldn't exist at all.

Still, to be an operator again! *Once more unto the breach, dear friends, once more.* To do it for humanitarian causes, taking no life, and, on top of it all, to be led by a Christian and surrounded by fellow believers in the team. Wasn't this the story he would've crafted for himself if he'd been able to write out his life?

There was something else behind his reluctance. He knew it as surely as the elevator was descending, as surely as the illuminated ten turned into a nine. And it didn't have anything to do with danger or weapons or even his faith.

It had to do with a man in San Diego. A man who would never walk again.

The elevator didn't stop at 1. It didn't stop at LL. It didn't even stop at G. He looked over at Eloise, whose eyebrows bounced twice. The display read B1, B2, and B3. When it read B5, it finally slowed.

Ding.

The doors opened and Eloise stepped into the white-floored vestibule. No one was in the small room, but a camera watched them from the corner. Three keypad-locked doors were set into the plain white wall before them. One was marked Plasma Lab; the middle one was marked Prototyping; and the door on the right was marked Research. She took him to the third door and punched in her code.

"Jason, my boy, get ready to be James Bonded."

She led him into what looked like a hospital ward with no beds. A large white room lined with squarish devices and consoles, operated by men and women in pale blue scrubs. He even imagined he smelled rubbing alcohol. High-speed computers whirred and chirped, their sounds hushed by the gentle roar of a host of cooling fans. A laser printer spat out pages for three collated copies of some document the size of the Akron Yellow Pages. In the middle of it all sat a small, glass-enclosed room that looked like a gondola car. A technician with goggles on had slid open a glass panel and was doing something inside.

"This is one of our microengineering labs," Eloise said. "Here we make itty bitty things that cause great big explosions." She crossed the floor toward a door in the far wall. "But I'm taking you to a product packaging room because it's got a big table."

He followed her past a bank of what looked like huge microwave ovens, or maybe baby incubators. No babies ready to hatch, though. The next door had no keypad. She indicated that he should go in first. He did.

And promptly got shot.

Three times. In the chest. He hit the deck, half out of pain and half from instinct. Before he'd reached the linoleum, he'd been hit twice more in the back. Some part of his mind recorded a *click-click-click* sound coordinated with the impacts. It sounded like two rulers smacking together. His airway was suddenly constricting and his eyes were tearing up. He coughed and gasped, writhing on the floor, his brain only now registering the white powder that had exploded off his chest from whatever had hit him.

"Should I get him again?" a man's voice asked.

"No!" It was Eloise, stepping over Jason into the room. "I think you've made your point."

It was about then that Jason realized he wasn't going to die. His breathing was labored, but at least air was getting through. And he wasn't bleeding. He rolled onto his side and looked up through bleary eyes.

Six or seven people blobs formed a semicircle around him, looking down.

"What—" he croaked, followed by a coughing spasm. "What-w—" More coughing.

"Listen to him," another male voice said. "He sounds like he's goth a berry bad code in hid nose."

Everyone laughed.

Except Jason. He got to his knees and tried to stand but decided all fours was a bit more stable for now. Gentle hands supported him under his arm and lifted him up. He leaned heavily on a large wooden table.

His eyes were clearing a bit. Now he could see that the wide table filled most of the room. Metal shelves lined one long wall. The table was covered with weapons—rifles, shotguns, grenades, mines, though they were all slightly modified—and an array of gadgets and gizmos the likes of which he'd never seen.

He wiped his eyes and turned back to the group in the room. He recognized them: the UPS guy with his buccaneer beard; the Asian receptionist; the computer nerd, his laptop still in tow; Chris, placing what looked like some kind of submachine gun back on the table; and Rachel, shaming the fluorescent tubes in the ceiling. Of the three personas she'd shown him today, right now she looked most like the executive assistant character. They all wore casual clothes, making Jason feel at home in his blue jeans.

Eloise was standing off to Jason's right, next to a classic scientist type: A small, bespectacled man with a high glossy forehead and very short Grecian Formula hair. He wore a white lab coat and carried an array of black markers in his pocket. He blinked with his whole face.

Jason rubbed at the chalky powder on his shirt. He could feel welts forming underneath. "What did you hit me with?" His voice was still wheezy.

"Just a little chili pepper, boy," the hulking buccaneer said. "A little cayenne to spice up your day."

"Pepper spray?"

"Technically," the scientist next to Eloise said, "it's oleoresin capsicum, a natural resin derived from dried cayenne peppers. Those pellets pack an SHU rating of somewhere upwards of two million. Hehehe."

Jason looked at him dubiously. "Meaning. . . ?"

"Meaning it's not pepper spray; it's pepper *powder,"* the scientist said. "The powder is an excellent delivery mechanism for the debilitating agent and can be applied to the target in capsule form. Something that could never be done with an aerosol. Hehehe."

Jason noticed Chris and the buccaneer stifling a laugh. "Okay. . . Well, ma'am, I have to ask you: Is this how you treat all your guests?"

"No," Rachel said, tilting her head at Jason, "only the ones we like."

Chris and the buccaneer hooted and slapped hands like middle school boys.

"In that case," Jason said directly to Rachel, "I don't want to know what you do to people you love."

"Well," Rachel said, "then I don't think you've got anything to worry about."

More hooting and slapping.

"All right, children," Eloise said. "That's enough nonsense. Jason, I'm sorry about our little ambush, but I thought you might need a little convincing about the effectiveness of our nonlethals."

"Yeah, but it hasn't even been five minutes, and I'm back on my feet."

"Yeah," Chris mimicked, "id hadden bid fibe bidits, and I'm back od my feet."

"You may be able to stand now," the Asian woman said, "but you were completely incapacitated for at least thirty seconds."

"Oh, yeah," the computer nerd said. "Plenty of time for us to tie you up with your own bootstrings."

"Or knock you out with this," the buccaneer said, brandishing a metal baton.

"Or inject you with a sedative," the Asian woman said.

"Or taze you with this," Chris said, pointing what looked like a cattle prod.

Jason looked at Rachel. "Well. . . ? What would *you* do to me if I was incapacitated?"

"Oooh," sang the all-male chorus.

Rachel tore off a strip of duct tape from a roll and placed it firmly over his mouth. "This."

Everybody laughed. Except Jason. Instead, he yanked the tape off, eliciting from the crowd the sound heard at every swimming pool after somebody did a belly flop. He smiled at Rachel roguishly.

"I declare," Eloise said, "you all are worse than children. My seventeen nieces and nephews act more mature than you. Bunch of full-grown adults. Ought to be ashamed. Now everybody leave poor Jason alone and let Dr. Furness get on with his presentation."

"Yes, Mother," the buccaneer said.

Jason sidled up to the table. "First, though, could I ask something?"

"What is it, sugar?"

"I think I've earned the right to at least learn everybody's name, haven't I?"

"Oh, dear!"

"I mean, how many more of these things do you have to shoot me with before I get introduced?"

"Oh, I can answer that one," Rachel said to Jason. "One name per weapon. And since you've already heard mine, I ought to get to shoot you for free."

"Land's sake," Eloise said, "where are my manners? Y'all's nonsense has upset my cart. Babies, introduce yourselves. Lewis, you start."

The computer nerd put down the night vision goggles he'd put on his head. "Hm? Oh, okay. Name's Lewis Griswold. I'm nineteen, but I really act much younger. That's a joke." He ran his hand over his buzz haircut and swiveled his head left and right. "I'm into computers, pretty much. And radios and robots and just about anything with a microchip."

Jason tried to imagine this kid deployed on a mission somewhere. He was fit enough, tall and lanky, and there was no questioning his enthusiasm. And if Eloise were to be believed, he was pretty good with electronics. But Jason didn't need to point out the razor scrapes on his scalp to know that Lewis was a prime candidate to freak out once the bullets started flying. Sorry, but if Jason were even going to think about joining this group, this kid would have to stay home.

Chris shoved Lewis. "Don't forget your games. Kid plays so many games on that computer I'm surprised his body hasn't atrophied." He pushed him again. "Get a life, kid."

"Oh, yeah, birdbreath?" Lewis answered. "You spend so much time looking for your dumb birds I'm surprised you don't start molting."

"Children!" Eloise shouted. "Enough, already. Trieu, I know I can trust you to talk nice. You next."

The Asian woman flicked her eyes onto Jason's. Intelligence roiled within that gaze. "My name is spelled T-R-I-E-U, Jason. You pronounce it TREE-yew. Trieu Nguyen, which is not spelled W-I-N as it sounds, but it's enough that you say it right. I am a physician. Also, for many years I have been a competition sharpshooter. In the winters, I competed in the biathlon. In the summers, I was a sharp-shooter. First for Vietnam, then the United States. I am thrilled to be part of the Firebrand team. It is nice to meet you, Jason."

Jason listened to her sweet, gentle voice. How would this woman do on a mission? How would any woman do on a mission? There were many reasons why there were no female Navy SEALs, but one was pure physical endurance. Trieu participated in the biathlon at the championship level, so she was in shape. The lithe figure under her modest blouse was evidence that she was still in top form. And having a full-fledged physician on the team would be a huge plus.

Not that he would be given the choice. Since this whole team was predicated on the idea of nonlethal weapons and because Trieu evidently mixed the sedative cocktails herself, she was probably an intractable component of the team, whatever hesitancy he might have.

Something about Trieu was appealing to Jason, beyond her pretty face and obvious intelligence. There was a calmness about her, a serenity. She didn't call out brashly like the others in the room. She wasn't flirtatious. She was just Trieu, quiet and stable.

Still, given the option, he'd leave her behind. If he were forced to take a woman along, she'd be on his short list. But he wasn't being forced to take her, because he wasn't being forced to join the team at all. Why not let her stay behind and be safe to shoot in the next Olympics?

"Nice to meet you, too, Trieu," he said.

"There," Eloise said. "You see, children: You can talk nice. Garth, you next."

Garth was the UPS buccaneer's name. He rubbed his bald head repeatedly, like polishing a bowling ball. "Garth Fisher, former special forces engineer sergeant. Served in Kuwait, Bosnia, Afghanistan, and a few other places I can't tell you about. I ride a hawg and I got me a tattoo. Wanna see it?" He rolled up his left sleeve to reveal an intricate snake-woman-knife design, all blue and green.

Jason nodded. "Nice."

"Mostly I like to blow stuff up. But I can also build things from time to time, and I've been told I'm decent at making things work. My specialty's e-and-e—that's escape and evasion for you civvies. And I'm always thinking of new and nasty things to do to bad guys. All in a harmless, not-permanently-debilitating kind of way, of course. Right, Big Mama?"

"You keep that Big Mama talk to yourself, boy," Eloise said.

Garth shook his head at Jason. "She loves it."

Jason smiled. What about this guy? He was a monster, more like a defensive tackle than a soldier. He looked like Howie Long and Terry Bradshaw and Stone Cold Steve Austin rolled into one. He wore ripped blue jeans and a black T-shirt, but Jason couldn't shake the image of this guy climbing up the rigging of a fast galley, bandana on his head, gold earrings in both ears, nasty dagger in his mouth.

The Green Berets were solid operators. Sure, there was rivalry between them and the SEALs, but that didn't mean there wasn't respect, too. SEALs were better at some things, like underwater work, whereas Green Berets had the edge in military hardware. Here, at least, was a solid member of the squad Eloise had in mind. Too bad he was probably going to get himself killed on the first mission.

"Chris," Eloise said. "You next."

Chris managed to look as good in his Audubon polo shirt and jeans as he did in his expensive suit. That single curl continued to dangle over his forehead. Jason wondered if he spent hours each morning getting it to coil just right.

"Sergeant Christopher Page, retired. Five years on point with Force Recon, Camp Pendleton. Total of three years in the Gulf. Married, divorced. No kids. Triathlete, rock climber, card-carrying ornithologist. Cleveland Browns dawg. Any questions? Oh, and I once snuck through an Iraqi platoon while they were having their midday prayers."

Jason nodded, impressed. Chris fit the classic commando body type: not too tall, stout but not bulky. He was cocky like a spec-ops boy, too. His posture and bearing exuded confidence. Jason had a feeling that if this man ever went cruising for chicks, it would be a short cruise. And if his boast about the Iraqis were true, then he was a skilled scout, on par maybe with Jason himself. The bird-watching thing was no biggie. Despite the fact that Chris had just shot him with a peppergun, Jason would be glad to have this guy next to him on patrol.

Jason tipped his head toward Chris. "Pleasure."

"The same."

"All right, Rachel," Eloise said, "your turn. And tell it *right.*"

Jason was glad to see someone else getting That Look for a change.

Rachel seemed to be staring at Jason's forehead. Thinking how he'd look with a dangling curl? Looking at some embarrassing mark? Eyes that didn't quite focus? But then she dropped her gaze onto his eyes, and he felt his higher brain functions shut down.

When she spoke, it was in an emotionless voice he hadn't heard her use before. "My name is Rachel Levy. I was born in the city of Tiberias, on the Sea of Galilee. My father managed a hotel popular with tourists. In 1984, he was murdered by a Palestinian suicide bomber, along with seven Jewish pilgrims. When we were old enough, my brothers and I all applied to the Mossad, but I was the only one accepted. I spent six years as a case agent, operating in various places around the Middle East. And. . . ," she paused, looking away, "I did a brief tour with Komemiute."

Jason knew about Komemiute, the Mossad's special operations unit. They were tasked with the most sensitive assassination and sabotage ops. *Wonder what went wrong.*

He was fighting to think clearly—but it didn't have anything to do with the pepper dust. Rachel was electrifying, like what an artist would create if he sat down to depict the ideal female. Her face was almost angular, like a straight-sided heart, but soft. Her dark brown hair was pulled off her forehead and clipped behind her head. Again he was struck by her dark, perfectly formed eyebrows. Large brown eyes with curving lashes. Sumptuous lips, red lipstick expertly applied.

She wore a gray sweater over a scoop-neck shirt. A black stone hung on a golden chain low on her neck, drawing his eyes to where they should not go. She wore black pants that seemed to be made of windbreaker material, and those tall shoes currently in fashion. Her overall look was so smart he thought she was either the result of a team of Hollywood costume and makeup artists or the master of those artists herself.

Eloise had said Rachel did distraction work. No kidding. This girl was a distraction just walking in the door. She could've picked Jason's pockets, shaved his head, and stolen his shoes, and he wouldn't have noticed. Or minded.

He had to force himself to listen to what she was saying.

". . .was when I became a Christian. After that, I knew I didn't really belong in the Mossad anymore. And I sure didn't belong in Komemiute. So I quit." She shrugged. "I did a little work for a modeling agency in Tel Aviv. Worked at a TV station for a while, then as a translator at l'Ambassade d'Israël en France, in Paris. Just kind of floated. That's when I met Eloise. And. . .here I am."

Jason knew there had to be a lot glossed over in that last sentence. Oh, well. If this trip served no other purpose, he had at least been able to bask in the presence of a goddess.

Every time he tried to evaluate Rachel's potential for special ops, his cerebellum did wheelies. Could she pack it in and out with fifty pounds of gear on her back? She was obviously fit, but could something so delicate endure ten days of jungle or tundra or desert—far away from bath oil and makeup mirrors? Still, he had a very healthy respect for the Mossad. If she'd been an operative for them, she must have some useful skills. An image flashed into his mind of a *Get Smart* episode in which the KAOS agent kisses our hero with poisoned lipstick.

This girl knew how to use disguise and take on different personalities. She could probably infiltrate just about any Third World village on the planet. What was it Eloise had said—nine languages? Yikes. That would be useful. But there were lots of questions remaining: Did she know her way around a weapon? How would she react under fire? Was she a whiner, a liar, a slacker?

Would she go out to dinner with him?

That was a concern, too. If she was distracting *him* as much as the enemy, they could all get blown up real good.

Not that he had to worry about such things, of course, since he wasn't going to agree to joining the team.

"Thank you, Rachel," Eloise said. "That's probably enough for now. Jason, you already know all about me. And they all know about you."

"Oh?"

"Oh, my, yes. You've been the most popular topic of conversation with this lot since we heard about you."

Jason surveyed the group. Some were watching him; some were looking bored. Lewis had the night vision goggles on again and was crawling around under the table.

"Exactly how did you hear about me?"

"Oh, let's not talk about that now," Eloise said. "Come on, Dr. Furness, show us something."

"All right," the scientist said, settling his glasses on his nose. "Mrs. Webster asked me to pull together a sample of the paraphernalia we're thinking of equipping the team with. But don't think for one minute that ABL makes all of these devices. Goodness, no. That would be even harder than achieving parabolic velocity from the earth's gravitational attraction using only an ion drive and a solar sail! Hehehe."

He cleared his throat and pulled at the lapels of his lab coat. "Well, anyway, we make only a few of these. The rest are from competitors. All right, let's get started."

He picked up the gun Chris had used to shoot Jason. It looked like a CAR-15 assault rifle, but parts of it were made of plastic. It was black and elongated. It had a short clip on the bottom, just like an M-16. "This is the pepperball launcher, developed by Jaycor. This version can fire in single-shot, three-shot, and full auto modes. The clip holds twenty-five pepperballs."

Furness rolled out what appeared to be brightly colored marbles. There were red ones, purple ones, yellow ones, clear ones, and white ones. He picked up a red one. "This is what you got shot with. It's a live round containing oleoresin capsicum powder irritant. Just like a paintball, but with a little surprise.

"The purples are target rounds. They have powder in them but no pepper. They smell nice, though. The clear ones are trainers, too, but with liquid. That's to train you to use the yellow ones, which contain indelible liquid dye. The whites are solid rounds, used for breaking windshields and such. Be glad Chris didn't hit you with those."

"Let me see that," Jason said. He hefted the gun in his hand, then swiftly turned it on the rest of the team.

Lots of eyes got very wide. Lewis bumped his head under the table.

"You guys want to see something funny?" Jason asked, looking through the sights.

No one answered.

Jason put the gun down. "Just joshin'."

Everyone began breathing again.

"Hey, Doc," Jason said, "why does it sound like a toy gun when it fires?"

"It's just the mechanism used to fire the pellets. There are no explosives used, no firing cap, so there's no bang."

"What's the range?" Jason asked.

"Effective from point blank out to about thirty feet."

"Thirty feet!"

"A hundred feet if you're going for area saturation."

Jason looked at Chris and Garth. "Doesn't this bother you two? Thirty feet? That's the length of this room! You seriously want to walk that close to a guy and his AK-47 before you can do anything to him? You guys are just asking for it."

"Calm down, baby," Eloise said. "Let the man finish."

"Hey, tadpole," Chris said, "some of us aren't scared of the bad guys. Some of us know how to move real quietlike."

"You cut that out, Chris," Jason said, his finger jabbing the air with a will of its own. "This isn't about courage or skill. It's about survivability. Look, I'm not telling you two anything you don't already know. I'm surprised you're still sitting here seriously considering joining this team if all they're going out with is pop guns that you have to be thirty feet from the guy to use! And you!" he said to Trieu. "You're used to firing from fifty meters. You're trading that for this toy?"

She looked at him calmly. "Jason, you're overreacting. I will not carry that weapon with me when we are on a mission. I will carry my Dragunov SVD—"

"As I've already told you," Eloise said.

"—that fires a protein bullet. I will continue to fire at ranges up to one thousand meters."

Jason felt the rage seeping out his tennis shoes. "Oh."

Furness had in his hand what appeared to be a regular paintball pistol. "This is the sidearm pepperball launch system. Fires eight rounds at up to six rounds a second. Comes with ten speed loader tubes like this." He held up a plastic tube with ten red balls stacked inside, capped by a green lid.

He set the tube down and picked up what appeared to be a travel-sized aerosol canister.

"Don't have to tell me what that is," Jason said.

"Yes," Furness said, "I'm sure you're quite familiar with the traditional acoustic and optical diversionary device—"

Lewis popped his head up. "That's *flashbang* to you and me."

"Lewis," Eloise said, "stand up straight and take those goggles off your head before I flashbang your backside."

He took them off sheepishly. "Yes, ma'am."

"As I was saying," Furness said, "I know you know what these are. But you may not have seen one mixed with dimethylsulfoxide and fentanyls! Hehehe."

Jason looked around the room for help.

"He means," Garth said, "that it's got some chump juice in it that'll make you go night-night."

"Oh."

"Yes," Furness said, "in addition to the optical and aural disorientation, the DMSO introduces a calmative through the epidermis at a rate one thousand times faster than normal."

"Cool." Jason picked up something that looked like a blow drier. It was a black off-center T, like the junction of two PVC pipes. It had a red button as a trigger and a long coiled cord leading to a box the size of a small guitar amp. "What's this?"

Furness took it from him. "I'll show you." He worked some switches on the "amp" and put the short end of the "blow drier" to his lips. "This really works better outdoors."

Jason saw the man's lips move, and he heard his voice, but the voice didn't come from the same place where the lips were. The sound came from the other side of the room.

"How'd you do that?"

"It's an acoustic deference tone projector," Furness said.

"It throws your voice?"

"Exactly. The sound appears to originate from the target location."

"Cool. Let me see that." Jason brought it to his lips. From across the room he heard his voice, as if through a speaker over there: "Can you make the amp thing smaller, Doc?"

Furness switched the amp off. "I suppose."

"It's just a bit big to be lugging around in the field on top of everything else."

"Well, I could—"

Lewis grabbed the amp and hair drier and opened the door to the lab. "Watch this." He worked the dials and spoke.

Jason could faintly hear Lewis's voice out in the big room but couldn't pick up what he said. All the workers in the room made a sudden rush for the exit.

"Child!" Eloise said. "What did you do? If you called a fire drill, I'll have your hide."

"Nah," Lewis said, bringing the device back to the table. "I just said there were hot doughnuts in the break room."

Over the next hour, Furness displayed a dizzying variety of weapons and gear. Jason found himself organizing them into six categories: Very Cool, Interesting, Dumb, Risky, Untried, and Whacked. Several fit into more than one category, like the "optical munitions mine," a packet of inert gas that could be remotely ignited when illuminated by a targeting laser. Interesting but Untried. Or the superglue that could be painted onto the floor or doorknobs to immobilize bad guys. Risky and a little Whacked.

Atop his Very Cool list, though, was the chameleon camouflage. Color and light sensors detected the soldier's background and a tiny computer adjusted the pixel array in the gel within the plastic raincoatlike jacket and pants. Jason had it in the Whacked category until Lewis put the thing on and basically vanished. All they could see clearly was his head, floating in space, and his shadow on the floor. Too bad it wasn't in production yet.

He was introduced to a device that could generate false targets to fool smart bombs, an acoustic curdler unit that created a "voodoo effect" on groups of people, and an air bag mine that would inflate to immobilize a passing vehicle. He saw a laser-infrared carbon dioxide gun that could heat a target's skin—like the skin on the hand he might be holding a grenade in—but would not burn, a "dazzle rifle" that disoriented enemies with an eye-safe argon-ion laser, and a human net mine that fired an entangling net at the passing soldier.

He saw a device that could project a hologram of just about anyone or anything to a distance of thirty yards. He saw a beanbag projectile that could be shot out of a twelve-gauge shotgun. He saw a glorified water pistol that carried an electrical current to the target. And he saw a nonlethal claymore mine that dispersed blunt impact ordnance to disperse crowds.

Of course there was the assortment of nonlethals he'd been expecting, like tear gas and tranquilizer darts. And there were the "normal" high-tech goodies such as night vision goggles and GPS systems keyed to hyperrealistic topo maps.

Furness deferred to Lewis for the discussion of remote drones. Jason got the feeling that Lewis was down here a lot. At a certain point in his narration, Lewis took out a palm-sized helicopter and flew it around the room. While Trieu pointed some kind of gun at it and Lewis remote piloted the buzzing plane, Jason and the others watched its video output on a monitor.

All in all, it was an impressive display of weird stuff. Jason was almost sorry he was going to walk away from the whole thing.

"Hey, Mom," Garth said to Eloise when the presentation was done. "I need food."

"Yeah!" Lewis said.

"Oh, right," Chris said. "Tell us the truth, Lewis. You need to use the ladies' room, don't you?"

Lewis swiveled his head toward him, paused, and then made a face. Chris clutched his heart as if he'd been stabbed.

"Well, I know I could use the ladies' room," Eloise said, *"and* a snack." She looked at her watch. "How about we reconvene in the VIP lounge on B2 in fifteen minutes?"

CHAPTER 9

We Must Have Hope

THE sea is dead.

Aleshbaye Kudratkhodzhayev stood atop the earthwork dike, looking across the North Aral Sea. It glistened and heaved and roared as it had for millennia. Seagulls dipped and wheeled overhead. A steady breeze brought the briny smell to his nose. As long as he looked this direction, he could imagine that all was well.

Behind him was desert. Beached fishing vessels and exposed piers marked what used to be the perimeter of the Aral Sea proper. Ships that had settled on the seabed years ago were now curious aquatic junk on the desert floor, looking like toys that had fallen out of a titan child's pockets on his way to the lake. Far away south somewhere, some of the greater Aral Sea remained.

But really, the sea was dead.

The only hope was to save the north part.

Aleshbaye stood at the narrowest part of the dike. Ten feet below him the saltwater struck the packed earth. As he watched, another large chunk of dirt fell into the water. He measured off the width of what five months ago had been a twenty-five-foot dike. In this spot, it was now fifteen.

"How long will it hold, Mayor?"

Aleshbaye looked up to see four men approaching. His old friend, Askar, the port authority of Aralsk, led them. Behind him came Mukhtar, who owned many of the ships now rusting on their sides. Then came the two Mujahadeen from Iran. They appeared to be in an even fouler mood than usual.

"I don't know, Askar," Aleshbaye said. "A month, maybe less."

The Mujahadeen wore long sleeve shirts, suit vests, and tightly coiled turbans. Both were young, their black eyes full of fire. Apparently, they had been convinced to leave their assault rifles in the car for once.

"This lake," the lead Mujahadeen said, struggling with his Russian, "it is all that is remaining of Aral Sea?"

"You see?" Mukhtar said to him. "This is what the Soviet Union did to us."

The Mujahadeen spat. "Russian vipers."

"It is only Mayor Kudratkhodzhayev's dike that preserves what remains," Mukhtar said. "The fish return. The rain comes more often. The grass grows. My boats sail again."

"Thanks be to Allah," the younger Mujahadeen said.

"For how long?" the lead Mujahadeen said testily, walking to look over the edge. "Spring comes. Snow melt. Lake rise." He made a sweeping motion with his arm. "This whole. . ." he indicated the dike. . ."be moved from its place. Lake spill into desert and go back to Allah. All from Russian vipers!"

"Not this time," Askar said. "We have installed sluices this time. Overflow will prevent—"

"Your sluices will not save you," the lead Mujahadeen said. "Only Allah can save. If Allah, bless His name, decide to raise sea to the sky, it will be done. Yet even if this false earth does not burst, still you must remember sickness of your people. Moulana, tell what you are seeing today."

The younger Mujahadeen, whose beard was not long, faced Aleshbaye squarely. "Today I walked the streets of your village. I see many people coughing very hard. Old women, young men, children. I see women so white and weak they cannot rise from their mats. I see children without arms—only hands. I see children with no eyes—only skin. Allah forbid I should ever see such things again."

Aleshbaye thought the young man was going to throw up. As for himself, he had been beyond illness for years. He looked at his narrow earthworks, the ever-slimmer manifestation of his hopes to save his people. On the dry seabed below was the town's only working bulldozer. He should be on it, bringing up more earth.

He found that the lead Mujahadeen was peering at him, his thick eyebrows lowered. "It is the Russians that are doing this to your mothers and children. The Russians who do this and make themselves fat with cotton and rice grown in Kazakh fields, stealing Kazakh water, and making poison for Kazakh children. If this being traditional Islamic state, we would not allow Russians to do this. Russian people all through your land, placed by Russian government to draw you away from Allah! The more up this river you go, richer the Russians being. All the way to Baikonur Spaceport." He spat. "Most unholy scourge of Allah."

"No, no," Askar said. "Kazakhstan's government wants to remain a secular state. Meaning no offense, but they don't trust the more. . . radical strain of Islam."

"I have prayed to Allah," the lead Mujahadeen said, still staring at Aleshbaye, "that He allow me bring invincible jihad young men—and very many weapons—to your help. Moulana and me send word today. Mujahadeen army arrive in five days."

Aleshbaye and Askar exchanged an incredulous look. "An army?" Aleshbaye asked. "Why do I need an army with weapons? If they will come and help me shore up my dike, I welcome them in the name of Allah. But if they are coming to fight against my neighbors, they can stay in Iran or Afghanistan or wherever they are."

"But the Russians—" the lead Mujahadeen said.

"The Russians are as sick as we are! They drink the same water. They die of the same diseases. They are not to blame."

"Now, Mayor," Mukhtar said. "You must admit that it was the Soviet planners who left us in this situation. The people in town have been—" He stopped himself.

Aleshbaye looked at him. "What about the people in town, Mukhtar?"

Mukhtar looked to the Mujahadeen leader, who simply stared back at him. "It's only a few people. No, it's more than a few. I won't say their names. But they have been listening to our Iranian friends here and the others like them. And it's not only me who thinks that those upstream, who have siphoned off the river feeding our sea, are to blame for our troubles. Especially," he added belatedly, "the ones of Russian descent."

Aleshbaye could've silenced him with a word. But he'd heard the talk himself. He couldn't remember when the first Mujahadeen had begun visiting his town, talking of revolution, but it had been decades ago. They presented an attractively simple worldview to his bewildered people: Everything is Russia's fault. It would be so easy to give in to it.

"No," he said softly, watching a sailboat skim the horizon. "We will not look back for someone to blame. We will look forward for something to save us. Come, Mukhtar, Askar: We have built this dam with our own hands, is it not so? The sea heals itself. When the prime minister settles in his post, he will approve the aid to make our dike permanent. We have only to hold on until then. We must not give in to the fear that. . ." he swallowed. . ."that the sea is dead. We must have hope."

Askar pointed. "Look!"

Five pickup trucks were speeding across the dry seabed, lurching with every sandy pothole. The trucks were packed with men. They stopped at the base of the dike amid a cloud of the toxic sand. Prominent businessmen and assorted young ruffians from Aralsk spilled out of the trucks and ran shouting toward Aleshbaye. Each one carried a gun of some kind.

"The radio! The radio!"

"What?" Aleshbaye said, walking down the hillside toward them. "What about the radio?"

Bekzal Dzamalutdinov, Aralsk's transportation official, grabbed Aleshbaye by the shoulders. "Our money, Aleshbaye, our money for our dike. It is gone! They said it on the radio!"

Aleshbaye stepped away. "Gone? What do you mean it is gone?"

"The new prime minister," Bekzal said. "He has cancelled the project! He is diverting the money elsewhere. It is a catastrophe!"

"Where? Where else?" Aleshbaye was having trouble thinking. "No, it cannot be. Where is the money being diverted to?"

Bekzal and the others said it as one: "To the Russians!"

"The money to save our children and our livelihoods, Aleshbaye," Bekzal said. "It is to be used to remodel apartment buildings in the Russian north of Kazakhstan. It is a catastrophe!"

Aleshbaye could feel the Mujahadeen's stares in his back. He did not look at them.

The young men from the trucks shouted and shot their weapons into the air.

Aleshbaye launched himself at them. "What are you doing? Stop that right now. Your bullets will come down and murder your families. What are you thinking? Go home, all of you. Put your weapons away. We will. . .we will think of something. We will bring the sunken ships and make them part of our dike. We will install metal plates to the sides. We will do this ourselves! Bekzal, bring the backhoe. Hurry."

No one moved.

Finally, the lead Mujahadeen walked down the dike. "No," he said to the group, "time for vain hoping is ended. Time for action now. Come, unconquerable Muslims, rise up with anger from Allah, and let us put wicked to the sword!"

The men shouted and fired their guns. The Mujahadeen vaulted into a truck. They all piled in—even Mukhtar—and sped away across the sand, the lead Mujahadeen shouting "Death to Russians! Death to Baikonur City!"

Askar watched them go. He blinked against the blowing sand. "What will happen, Aleshbaye?"

Aleshbaye turned toward the dike, imagining he could hear whole sections of it falling away. "They will come to no good end, Askar." He looked at him. "Will you help me, my friend? Will you help me with the dike?"

"Even if no one remains in town to be saved?"

"Yes."

"Even if you are not mayor when we return?"

"Yes."

"Even if we are standing here in the gap when it fails?"

Aleshbaye smiled grimly. "Even then."

"I would rather be nowhere else."

Aleshbaye laughed and pounded his friend on the back. "Come, then. To the bulldozer. The prime minister be cursed. I will never believe that our sea is dead!"

CHAPTER 10

No

THE VIP lounge was evidently where Eloise brought her fat-cat government and corporate executives to wow their designer socks off. It was a sumptuously appointed, dimly lit room with a wet bar at the back and a chef-prepared buffet under glass domes. Four semicircles of overstuffed furniture stood around the dark, plush carpet, ready for discussions of billion-dollar deals.

But the real high point of the room was the bank of slanted windows that overlooked the ABL control room below. Jason looked through them onto a scene right out of *War Games.* Scores of men and women sat at rows and rows of computer terminals on the floor below. Everyone faced the two-story wall, which was alive with intricate maps, animated charts, and crystal clear video feeds. He could hear no sound through the thick glass, just the constant rush of an air conditioner in the lounge.

Eloise appeared beside him. "You like my TVs?"

Jason smiled. "I always wondered if there were really places like this. You see them in the movies and all, but. . .yikes."

"I know. We've certainly come a long way from the early days. My Charlie died before this thing was finished. He would've loved it. But he'd have always been down there crawling all under everything if anybody got their wires crossed." She chuckled softly. "He was a terrible manager. Always wanted to do it himself." She rubbed Jason's back affectionately. "As you've already figured out, I don't have that problem."

"So this is where you run all your infrastructure, your outsourcing and all?"

"Uh-huh. This is where the action is. I've got a smaller room on another level for more private showings. But down there is where half my money is made or lost."

The team members were gathering behind them in the lounge. Chris was serving out wedges of French bread with cheese melted on top. The smell of the hot cheese made Jason's stomach growl. Garth was serving up ice in Styrofoam cups, into which Rachel was pouring fruit smoothies from a blender. Finally they all converged on one of the furniture sets and passed food and napkins around.

"I know we're not having a real meal," Eloise said, "but I just can't sit down to eat without saying grace." Immediately she was in prayer. "Dear God, I thank Thee that Thou hast brought these children together today here in this place. We thank Thee that our brother Jason has made the trip safely. And now, Dear God, we beseech Thee that Thou wouldst guide us to make right decisions and take right roads. We thank Thee for this, Thy provision for our bodies. Use us in Thy service. Amen."

Jason was tempted to ask Rachel what language that prayer had been prayed in but thought better of it and instead joined the rest as they chorused, "Amen."

Everybody took a bite. For a minute, the only sound was of

chewing and the occasional moan of culinary appreciation.

"So," Garth finally said to Jason, "what did you think of Furness's toys?"

Jason wiped his mouth with a napkin and surveyed the group. He was sitting in a plush chair at one edge of the semicircle. On his left was Eloise, also in a chair. Garth, Rachel, and Chris sat on the big couch. Trieu and Lewis sat in a loveseat at the other end of the semicircle. The hors d'oeuvres sat on a coffee table in the middle.

"I liked a lot of what I saw," Jason said. "I didn't see the point of some of it. And some of it would be great if it didn't weigh five thousand pounds or need a continuous power supply or cause everyone for a mile around to throw up. Did anyone else notice how many of those things he showed us made people throw up? Flashing lights, gas bombs, ultrasound. . .Nonlethals may not kill you, but you can sure get sick of them."

"Ooh, Jason," Trieu said. "Was that a joke?"

"Rachel," Lewis said, "pass me the pizza, would you?"

"Unh-uh," Chris said, his mouth full. "Make him get it himself."

Rachel flicked him hard on the head. "Cut that out, you bully. Here you go, sweetie."

"Ow," Chris said, bringing his hand up to his head to look for blood. "That hurt!"

Lewis's smile was wide. "Thank you, m'lady."

Garth grabbed his cup. "My favorite ray gun is the sticky stinger."

"Which?" Jason asked.

"The little shock cartridge you shoot out of a shotgun. Oh, yeah, that'll make you get off our tail in a hurry."

Jason laughed. "Always thinking escape and evasion, aren't you?"

"Better believe it."

"Mm," Lewis said. "Rachel, this smoothie is delish."

"Why, thank you, Lewis, you charmer."

Chris rolled his eyes. "Oh, brother."

"Now Christopher," Rachel said, swirling Chris's curl around her finger. "You never know how far a little manners might get you, too."

"All right," Eloise said, setting her plate down. "Jason, we've done a lot of showing off today. But now it's time for you to give us your answer. I am officially offering you the once-in-a lifetime opportunity to be leader of the Firebrand team. What do you think?"

Every eye turned to him. People paused in mid-chew. Jason found he was holding his breath. He let it out deliberately.

"So, we finally come to it, huh?" He paused to collect his thoughts. "Eloise, are you sure you want to do this here? You know. . .with everyone?"

"Who, them?" she said, taking in the team members with a glance. "I think this concerns everyone present, don't you?"

"Well. . ."

"He's going to say *no,*" Lewis said.

"Oh," Chris said, "like you know."

Rachel nodded. "No, he's right. Why would he want privacy to say what he knows we all want him to say?"

Did she look at him shyly, or was it just his imagination?

"Well, sugar," Eloise said, "if you're going to say *no* or you're going to say *yes,* get on with it. And yes, I want them here either way."

"All right." Jason set his cup down. "I'm sorry, everyone, but Lewis and Rachel are right. I'm going to say *no.*"

"Ah, nuts," Lewis said.

Rachel smiled thinly. "I hoped I was wrong."

Trieu and Eloise were silent.

Garth crushed his cup against his forehead. "Figures."

"Are you serious?" Lewis asked.

"Yeah," Jason said. "Afraid so."

"Why?" Chris said, suddenly irritable. "I don't get it, man. You'd rather go back to your pathetic apartment—to your pathetic *life*—than have the chance to go out in the field again? To go out with some heavy duty bad news gear and do some good? That's just crazy." He stood up and moved behind the couch. "But hey, if you'd rather splash around eating boat crud all day instead of being with us, we understand, don't we, gang?"

"All right, Chris," Eloise said soothingly. "Come on, you all, let's hear the man out."

Jason leaned forward, elbows on knees. "Look, I won't tell you that what you are offering me isn't appealing, that it doesn't interest me. Because it does. I mean, when I look at you guys, I feel, I don't know, a kind of a connection already. You seem like a fun group. And I won't lie to you and say that I'm just being overrun with friends back in California.

"And I'll tell you something else. Chris, you're absolutely right: There's nothing I wouldn't give to be an operator again. To be out there where the action is. . .I miss it. And this would be even better than being in the Teams, in a way, because it's a Christian outfit doing Christian-style missions. That's something I could sink my teeth into."

"Then what's your problem?" Chris said, his hands clenching the back of the couch. "Just nod your head and let's go!"

"That's what I'm telling you, Chris. I want to. Everything in me wants to do this. But—"

"Then what's your—"

"But, there's more to it than that. Being in a spec-ops team again is one thing, like if I was to get back in the SEALs and not have any hesitation about the job. But this isn't the same as that. The Teams have the whole U.S. military behind them. The squad gets in trouble, no problem, they just call in the air strikes and wait for the fireworks. A mission goes south, just make the call and wait for the gunship. We don't set foot in-country without a fire support plan.

"But you guys, if you get in trouble, there's *nobody* coming to your side. Now I bet Eloise could sit here," he said, gesturing toward the windows, "and maybe see you get in trouble from the satellite, but what's she gonna do about it? Call the embassy? Pay some local warlord to have your bodies sent home to your loved ones?

"You guys, Chris and Garth, you ought to be saying this, not me. You shouldn't be sitting here already having joined the team. You know what it's like to be under fire. These guys don't, so I can understand that they don't get it, but you do. How many stories do the three of us know about guys who got cut off behind enemy lines and no air support or exfil could come? What happens to those guys? They end up with their heads on stakes outside some dude's stronghold, that's what."

He turned to Eloise. "I mean, if you could promise an AC-130 orbiting around or a Pave Low on call, or even another platoon of guys to back the team up, then maybe I'd think about it. But you're not. Ma'am, you're not thinking straight. All I can think is you've got a big heart and you want to do something about it because you've got the cash. Well, that's cool, but I just can't see how sending these people—these good Christian young people—out to die is going to get you what you're wanting.

"And don't give me that garbage about sneaking in and sneaking out, either," he said, looking at Chris. "No plan ever survives contact with the enemy, you know that. Worst-case scenario is what you've got the best chance of getting. Going out without backup is what's crazy, Chris, not saying *no thank you* to it."

Jason's heart was pounding. His hands were shaking. Something in his chest was shuddering. He'd gotten more worked up about this than he realized. Everything he was saying was true, wasn't it? So why did he feel like he might break down into a blubbering idiot?

Eloise pursed her lips. "Anything else?"

"Well, actually, yes, if you really want to know. Lots more. I think I'd better tell you everything, too, because it may just be that God has sent me here today to talk you guys out of this. You're all mad at me now, but who knows if I'm not saving your lives?"

In truth, no one really looked mad. Chris had returned to the couch—and gotten an affectionate hug from Rachel, curse him. Garth and Lewis were reaching for more pizza. Trieu was unreadable.

"Go on," Eloise said.

"Okay. Using those nonlethal weapons. . .that's insane. No way would I go up against bad guys with assault weapons if all I had were these ray guns and powder puff balls and superglue. Forget it. This isn't a game, folks. Those people *will shoot you,* and I can guarantee they won't be using bean bag bullets."

He looked at the edge of the coffee table. "I had a mission go bad once. Bad guys all around, shooting at us." As he narrated, he could almost hear the gunfire all over again. In his mind's eye he saw Bigelow's body landing into the mud. "We barely got out of it. One of us didn't, almost. It was the most scared I've ever been in my life. I wish. . ."

Then he seemed to break out of it. He looked up at the others. "And we were loaded for bear, armed to the teeth, firing back like crazy. We had live ammunition, months of teamwork, and a whole support network backing us up. And look what happened to us.

"I'm telling you," he said to Eloise, "that if you send them out with these squirt guns, they are not coming home. You know what else? I think that if they really understood what you were asking them to do, they'd be out of here so fast you wouldn't believe it."

She looked at him tolerantly. "You done?"

"Not quite. I mentioned teamwork. SEAL teams train together, live together, fight together, work out together, eat together, and play together. You can't ask six people who don't know each other from Adam to go out into the field and work together as a team. I mean, you have to know what the other guy's gonna do without asking, and he has to know what you're going to do.

"That's why the NFL's Pro Bowl is such a boring game every year: Those guys have never played together. They get a couple day's practice to hike the ball a few times, but out on the field they play it real safe and boring. They can't do what a team that's played and practiced together for nine months can do.

"With lack of teamwork goes lack of trust. These guys don't

trust me, Eloise, because they don't know me. They don't know what I'm going to do under pressure. They don't know if I can really lead a team or not. They don't know if I'm going to crack or send them all into an ambush or what. And you know what else? I don't trust them.

"I mean, I'm sorry, but I just don't trust that every one of them is going to be able to hack it in the field. Garth and Chris have solid combat experience, but even with them I don't know what they're like under fire. And as for Rachel and Lewis and Trieu. . ." He lifted his palms. "I'm sure they're amazingly good at what they do, but to me they're unknowns. And frankly, I'm afraid they'd be a liability to the team. Taking civvies along on a military mission is a good way to get everybody killed—them because they don't know what they're doing, and us because we're trying to protect them."

He looked at Rachel and Trieu and Lewis. "I know I've probably offended you guys, and I'm sorry. But you have to understand I'm trying to save your lives.

"And, since I've already offended, I might as well go all the way. I don't think it's a good idea to take women on military missions. Sorry, ladies. I know, I'm a total male chauvinist pig—so sue me. But Trieu could tell you this: She's a physician and an Olympic athlete. She knows that some things, especially physical things, can't be done by women at the same level as men. Are these other guys going to have to carry more than their share of gear because the girls can't hack it? Are they going to slow us down? Sorry, they're a liability.

"You asked me to lead this team, but there's no way I could if I've got to be coddling people the whole time. It's suicide enough to send your spec-ops men out without support and real weapons. But to bring women and civvies along, too? No way."

He rubbed his face. "I'm very sorry to offend you all. I really am. And I'm sorry to be refusing something that I'd really like to do. But I just can't get around everything I've said. I think it's a great idea,

Eloise, a fine idea. But don't do it like this."

He sighed. "Okay, I guess that's it. Thank you for honoring me by asking me to be part of something with you all. I really would like to get to know you better. But I guess I'd just better leave." He stood. "Good-bye."

CHAPTER 11

MAYBE

"JASON," Eloise said. "Sit down."

"Ma'am, what's talking going to do?"

The woman gave him a look that communicated clearly she wasn't accustomed to disobedience. Then she smiled serenely. "Son, you can't even get on the elevator without me, so you may as well hear me out. Fact is, you're right about some of what you said. But you're also wrong, and you need to know it. So sit your skinny backside down and listen."

Jason sat.

Others got up. Chris headed back behind the bar and began stacking plates as noisily as possible. Lewis went to look out onto the *War Games* floor, mumbling something about now being hungrier than ever. Garth stretched out his long legs and appeared to fall instantly to sleep. Rachel pulled her legs under her on the couch. Trieu took a dainty bite from her piece of French bread pizza.

"For one thing," Eloise said, "you need to hush about not taking civilians along, because unless you've gone off and joined the Coast Guard in the last two minutes, you're a civilian, too."

"Well, yeah. But you know what I m—"

"For another, that part about nonlethal weapons not being able to hack it? You're wrong. It may not be what you're used to, but that's saying something else entirely. I happen to know that the senior staffs of all the armed forces are fully engaged in late stages of development and deployment of nonlethals.

"Here's why: Used to be, you had no choice when you went into battle. You either carried guns that killed people or you went with billy clubs. Then when you got there, you had no choice between using those guns—which would most likely kill or maim—or sitting there and not using them while the other men shot at you. Your rules of engagement were strict because we can't go around shooting children and old people. But what it came to was that many of our own boys were getting killed with their loaded weapons in their hands.

"But with nonlethals, oh, honey, you get a range of choices between *kill* and *do nothing.* You can go in there and shoot up the joint and walk out without having ever caused any permanent injuries, yet your team would be safe.

"Now, you and I know that from now on warfare is going to be fought in cities and other places where there are innocent people. Rachel can tell you about the Intifada, when the Israeli military started answering the Palestinians' rocks with live ammunition. When they did, well, you know the TV started showing dead grandmothers and children. And world opinion left Israel like a dog caught in the trash can. So, on the one side, you just can't go shooting people up, but on the other, you've got to have a way to protect your people.

"I'm not making anything up here, son. I may be using nonlethal weapons in a way no one else has yet, but that don't mean I'm the only one using them. If you'd stayed in the Navy for another six years, by the end of it you'd have been toting a whole mess of these weapons with you every time you went out. It's a new world, baby.

Get with it or get left behind."

Now that she mentioned it, Jason could recall reading some articles supporting what she was saying. "If the future of warfare is urban," one article had said, "then the future belongs to the less-than-lethals we can put in our soldiers' hands."

"I have no intention of sending anyone out just to get killed," Eloise said. "If I didn't believe they could accomplish their missions using these guns, I wouldn't even be working on this team. I'd still be waiting for the right time. And I'd be funding the research to get us there. But as it is, Jason, the Lord's timing is perfect. The time for such a team as this is now. And whether you're with us or not, baby, this team is going forward.

"You don't have access to some of the things I do, son, so you don't know what I've seen. But I've seen these weapons at work. I've seen videos of them in real combat and hostage takedowns and in riot control. I'm telling you that in the moment, some of these things are even worse than their lethal cousins—louder, brighter, scarier. All that psychological impact. Only when the smoke clears, everybody gets up and lives another day. Rest assured, son, I won't send my babies out like lambs to be slaughtered.

"Now, about the air support and all: You're right. I don't have a fleet of gunships to come to the rescue, and I don't have fighter jets to drop napalm if you get in trouble. Oh, I've got some boats with a few surprises, and I've got some helicopters and small planes that might be fitted with tear gas launchers or whatever. But you're right: I'm asking this team to go on these missions without the kind of fire support you're used to. And yes, I've explained this to them, and they've still volunteered.

"Now, the good news is that you won't be going after your usual military targets. You won't be trying to knock out any missile sites or blow up munitions depots. You'll be going for targets far away from the front lines, typically. In some cases, you may do the whole mission without ever seeing a soldier with a gun. And anyways—you know this—when you're behind enemy lines, if you fire your weapon, you've probably done something wrong."

The team members were drawing back toward them. Garth quit pretending to sleep. Lewis took the last piece of pizza. Eloise took a sip of smoothie and wiped her lips with a napkin.

"Here's another thing you're right about," she said. "Trust and teamwork. Of course you don't trust them yet and they don't trust you—yet. You've only just met them. But these five have been training together for weeks. Among themselves, they're building the kind of trust you're looking for. If you were to join, you'd start building that trust, too. As far as whether or not they would follow you. . ." She shrugged. "Lord only knows.

"Now, what was your other thing? Trieu, honey, I know you know. What am I forgetting?"

Trieu answered evenly, "About what a bad idea it is to have women on the team."

"That's it! I knew there was something else."

Jason cringed. Trieu gave him a half smile. Was she being polite or had she just decided which mood-altering drug she was going to put into his next smoothie?

"Now," Eloise said, "I'm not going to debate you about how much weight a woman can carry over how long a distance. And I certainly won't bring up what a woman goes through to give birth and that if a man had to do it he'd soil his PJs. The Father didn't make women for no lifting; he made them for being smart and for making the men do the lifting. Am I right, sisters?"

"Amen, honey!" Rachel said, arching a perfect eyebrow at Garth.

"That's why we've worked so hard on making the gear lighter," Eloise said. "Everyone will carry his or her fair share. Most of the time you'll be taking two hours to crawl a hundred yards, anyways, so don't talk to me about no woman getting left behind. When it comes down to it, what these kinds of missions takes is grit. And I'm here to tell you that men ain't yet cornered the market on grit. Back in my old neighborhood, 'bout the only folks left to have grit or not was the womenfolk.

"My sisters here are part of the team. Before it's over, you will be praising Almighty God that they're with you. These two dear sisters come from lands where the fight came to their very doorstep. Where they come from, the women fight right alongside the men, just as they do here in the inner cities. You may not like them being there, Jason, and you can just decide to walk away from the team. But whether you come along or not, they're coming.

"I'll tell you something else that'll wax your surfboard. If I'd have been able to find six women with all the skills I needed, I would've filled the team that way. Do you doubt me? Women know how to be versatile. But I made myself be color-blind and gender blind and everything else but Spirit blind when I picked this team. Lord, forgive me.

"Now, Jason, I believe you're supposed to be on this team. I believe you were *made* to lead the Firebrand team. I believe one of the reasons God called you to Himself at all was to lead it. I believe He soured your heart on killing so's you'd be primed and ready to join us. I know that's putting a lot of pressure on you, saying it's God's will and all, and I'm sorry for that. But sometimes we need a kick in the backside to do what we know we're supposed to do."

She raised her hand. "Don't answer me! You've heard me out, and I thank you for it. But whether you've changed your mind or not, there's one more thing I want to show you." She stood. "Children, y'all behave. Jason, come with me."

She led Jason out of the lounge and to the elevators. They got on and she punched the code for B1. This was a floor of offices and workshops. She brought him through three keycode doors into a room marked "Operations." It was probably the room she'd mentioned earlier: the smaller version of the *War Games* room.

Moments later they were in a single-story room the size of an interactive distance-learning classroom. Light blue carpet, white walls, track lighting on the ceiling. A large flat screen panel occupied the far wall. It was blank now except for a digital clock in the bottom right-hand corner. Three rows of countertops faced the screen. Flat screen displays were set into the countertops at regular intervals.

At the center of the back row was what looked like the teacher's seat. Arrayed around it were a triad of flat screens, two keyboards, two printers, two telephones, and a professional quality radio microphone.

Along the back wall of the room ran a row of metal lockers. From their look, the exhaust coming out of vents at floor level, and the sound of a fleet of fans coming from behind the metal doors, Jason knew there were a bunch of computers back there doing something very serious.

Three doors led off the sidewall. One was open. Jason could see metal shelves on either side of the narrow passage, stacked with office supplies. Someone was clattering around inside, muttering.

"This is where I show the matinees," Eloise said to Jason. "By invitation only. Hey," she said louder, "anybody running this place for me or do I have to do everything myself?"

The clanking in the side room stopped. "Huh?"

"Get out here and show yourself. I got someone here for you to meet."

"All right, all right," the man's voice said. "But I'm not wearing my tie."

Eloise winked at Jason. "This one's something else. I think you'll like him."

After more clanking Jason heard the sound of someone approaching the door of the room. The man's shadow fell on the carpet before him. Something was odd about it. Too short. Finally, a wheelchair rolled into view.

Jason's mouth opened involuntarily.

"Chimp?"

CHAPTER 12

YULIA

A MAP of Central Asia appeared over the newscaster's shoulder. A section labeled *Kazakhstan* was outlined in red. With an apparently unflappable aplomb, the woman at the desk looked directly into the camera and spoke:

"The secretary of state announced today a new travel warning for the nation of Kazakhstan. Widespread poverty and political unrest in the former Soviet republic has triggered rioting and armed uprisings in numerous provinces in the beleaguered nation. The state department's travel warning advises all American citizens to 'consider their personal security in light of recent events' because 'during an emergency, departure options may be limited.' CNN's Vic Tomlinson is in southern Kazakhstan. He files this report."

The picture cut to a thin, blond man in a blue windbreaker. He was standing in a desert. Flatbed trucks rolled past behind him, filled with Asian and Slavic-looking men waving at the camera. Some had guns. The reporter spoke into a handheld microphone.

"The trucks you see behind me are ferrying revolutionary fighters from southwestern Kazakhstan—around the Caspian and Aral Seas, mainly—east along the ancient Silk Road.

"These people are angry. For decades, the Soviet Union depleted their land of resources in order to fuel the Iron Curtain's machinery. Since the fall of Communism, their situation has not improved. They say their government has mismanaged funding that was supposed to come to them, funneling it to other parts of the country or simply pocketing it.

"It is not only here in the southwest that Kazakhs are angry. In the northeast, too, where Soviet-era nuclear waste still causes severe health problems, armed mobs have threatened locals. In the central west, where Russian rockets bearing nuclear materials have crashed, students and militants have seized buildings and are making demands for restitution from the government.

"Last night, hundreds of people from the group passing behind me—peasants, farmers, shepherds—put twenty-one homes and businesses to the torch. Today, they're continuing their march up the Syr Darya River, which you can perhaps see beyond the road. As they go, they burn.

"When will it stop? One grandfather told me that they would stop burning and looting when someone in the government finally hears the braying of their sheep.

"Vic Tomlinson, CNN News, in Kazakhstan."

I wonder what Max is doing right now.

Yulia Bazhanova stirred a giant pot of lamb and water broth and looked out the window to where the girls were playing.

Maxim Mukanova hadn't known she was even alive last year. What made her think he would grow fonder of her during her year off from school? He was probably surrounded by adoring girls right now. He'd spare no thought for that quiet girl who once returned his sweater to him.

Yulia looked down into the pot. The meat was beginning to separate from the bones nicely. She covered it and went back to rolling the noodle dough into circles. Besh barmak was Yulia's specialty. One day she would like to fix it for Max.

Katie Strickland came into the kitchen while Yulia worked, closely followed by Damira and Roza, two of the oldest orphans in the home.

"Hello, Katie," Yulia said in English.

Katie smiled. "Hello, Yulia. How are you this afternoon?"

Yulia scrunched up her face. " 'After-noon'?"

The American translated it into Russian for her.

"Ah," Yulia said. "Afternoon good very!"

"Oh, Yulia, the lamb smells wonderful," Katie said, sticking to Russian. "When my tour is up, I'm going to have to publish a book of Kazakh cooking so that all the folks in South Dakota can taste what they're missing."

Roza tugged on Katie's sleeve. "Please, Miss Katie, will you play volleyball with us?"

"Why don't you girls play together?"

"No!" Roza and Damira said together. They were both nine, thin but full of life.

"The little ones play wrong," Roza said. "And Luda always knocks the ball over the fence."

"Please, Miss Katie," Damira said. "No one else can teach us the right way to play."

Katie looked reluctantly pleased. "Oh, all right."

"Yea!"

"Go get the ball pumped up and I'll be there in a minute."

The girls ran outside and shut the door.

Yulia used tongs to pull out the lamb bones, watching the meat fall away and rest in the pot. "What will the girls do without you,

Katie? I wish you would never go back to America."

Katie hesitated, then came close to Yulia and looked around conspiratorially. "Yulia, I've just heard something on Voice of America."

Something about Katie's tone worried Yulia. She put the tongs down. "What is it?"

"You know the troubles in Semipalatinsk?"

Yulia nodded.

"They've gotten worse," Katie said. "Not only that, they're spreading. People in Karaganda—from the Karbushevka and Salamalkol villages, where the rockets crashed—have joined. And in Almaty and Astana there are demonstrations."

"Oh," Yulia said, "there are always demonstrations in Almaty. Probably some of my friends from the university. I wouldn't worry about it."

"There's more," Katie said. "People from the Aral Sea have joined the uprisings. They say that anyone living on the Syr Darya River is a thief. They blame the people upstream for diverting their water and dumping poisons into it."

Yulia turned down the heat on the stove. "Well, of course they are right. But they are also wrong. How many of them eat the rice grown with that water?"

Katie caught Yulia's wrist. "You don't understand. They're saying that *everyone* living on the Syr Darya is their enemy. They've burned whole villages, Yulia. And they're marching this way. If they don't turn back, it will be only weeks before they reach Baikonur City—maybe less. Of course they will think we have been made rich from their water, because of the Cosmodrome."

The threat finally registered in Yulia's mind. "They would come here?"

"They might."

"Burning?"

"It's possible."

Yulia noticed Damira standing at the door. "Um. . .I think this will be the best besh barmak I have ever made. Don't you agree, Katie?"

"Oh. . .oh, yes. Definitely. Hi, Damira. You girls ready?"

Damira nodded. "Are you talking about something bad?"

Katie smiled brightly. "Of course not, dear. Come on," she said, walking to the door. "Let's play some volleyball."

Yulia sliced the lamb into chunks. The Aral Sea was a long way from Baikonur. They would not come here. Even if they did, Katie was with the American Peace Corps. The Americans would keep her safe. And surely no one would dare hurt anyone at an all-girl orphanage. What had these poor girls ever done to them, anyway? No, no. They were completely safe.

Still, she wished Max were there.

CHAPTER 13

YES

IT ISN'T often that three emotions hit you all at once. But when Jason saw Doug Bigelow wheel into the room, he got hit by elation, sorrow, and—most powerful of all—something that felt exactly like self-loathing. All of a sudden, Jason didn't want to be in his own skin.

"Doug! Wh–what are. . . ? I mean, how did you. . . ? You're in a. . ."

"Jace, dude, relax. Sit down before you throw a breaker."

Jason pulled a chair from behind one of the long countertops and sat. He couldn't take his eyes off Bigelow's legs, strapped to the leg rests at the ankle and knee. His friend was wearing blue jeans and a San Diego Padres baseball shirt.

Behind Jason, Eloise cleared her throat. "I think I'll let the two of you catch up for a while. Doug, when y'all are finished, bring him on down to the lounge."

"Gotcha, boss."

Eloise gave Jason's shoulder a reassuring squeeze, then left the room.

"Well," Bigelow said, spinning his wheelchair around like a pro, "how do you like my wheels?"

"Um. . .They're. . .they're nice, Doug. Real nice."

"Liar. I could always tell when you were lying. Do you remember when you stole that girlie magazine from my locker and then tried to tell me Lemke had taken it? Right, as if. Then I found it a few days later under your mattress?"

Jason blushed. "That was a long time ago. That was before I. . ."

Bigelow watched him closely. "Yes. . . ?"

"Before I became a Christian. You know that. Speaking of which, what are you doing here, working for her? Do you do some kind of weapons testing for her or something?"

"You mean, what is someone like me doing working for *a Christian?*"

Jason held up his hands. "Don't get me wrong, Chimp— I mean, Doug. It's just that—"

"Why'd you do that?"

"Huh?"

"Why'd you just correct yourself?"

"Well. . ." Jason found it difficult to swallow. "Doug, I don't guess you remember much about the last time we talked, but—"

"I remember everything."

"Okay, then you remember you told me never to call you Chimp again. You said I shouldn't call you that 'like we were friends,' or something."

The two men's eyes met. They held the gaze, as if trying to telepathically communicate something their mouths were having trouble with.

There was a hardness glinting inside the man's eyes at first, as if tempting the rest of the face to release some inner rage or sorrow. Sorrow finally won out as Bigelow shook his head sadly. "I know," he said quietly, letting his gaze fall toward the floor. "Listen, Jace, I'm sorry

I said that to you." He sighed. "I was. . .I don't know. Messed up."

"Well, you were injured. You were being flown off for major surgery on your spinal cord. They were saying you might never walk again. You were scared. You. . .you were pretty mad at me, too, as I recall."

"Yeah, yeah. But I was wrong to say that to you."

"No," Jason said quickly. "No, you were absolutely right. I deserved it." *Still do.* "Besides, you were the one who was hurt, and there I was walking around fine. And now you're. . .Well, look at you."

"What are you trying to say? That I'm *crippled?* That I'm no good because I can't line dance anymore? Crip! Lamo! Rollerboy. Go ahead, call me something. I'll have you know that disabled people are some of the finest—"

"Okay, okay. Doug, I'm sorry."

Bigelow's face finally broke into a wide, familiar grin. "Aw, I'm just messing with you, dude. As if I was into all that PC stuff. If there's one thing I've learned since that day, it's that if you don't have a sense of humor, being a paraplegic will take you out. Sorry about the crip humor, though. It can get a bit sadistic." He shrugged. "It's a survival tactic."

Jason shook his head back and forth.

"What?" Bigelow asked.

"Oh, nothing. I just feel like I'm riding Space Mountain today."

"Boss lady keeping you guessing?"

"You could say that."

Bigelow nodded. "She does like to hold all the cards."

"What are you even doing here, Doug? *Chimp.* You're supposed to be in San Diego doing rehab or whatever."

"I was. Now I'm here. Been here for about four months."

"So you're done with rehab?"

"Ha. It's never-ending, Jace. I brought my physical therapist with me. Rehab—yeah, right. For a while they call it that. Then, when it doesn't look like you're going to get any better, they kick you out and you start what they call occupational therapy. Guess I'll be doing that 'til I die—which, for paraplegics, is usually about half as long as for the rest of the world. When you're half a man I guess you only rate half a life."

"Don't talk like that."

"Sorry. Crip humor."

Jason looked around the operations room, seeing it now as his friend's daily environment. "So what do you do for ABL?"

"Come on, I'll show you."

Bigelow wheeled himself back to the "commander's chair." He locked his wheels, unbolted his leg restraints, and hoisted himself into the seat.

"Shouldn't they let you just drive your chair right under that?" Jason asked.

"Oh, they would," Bigelow said, lifting his legs under the counter, one at a time. "But I like the swivel chair. Besides, sometimes it's nice to stretch my legs."

Jason looked at him suspiciously. "That's crip humor again, isn't it?"

"Now you're getting it." Bigelow pushed buttons on the keyboards and monitors. The big screen on the wall came to life. He slid the microphone stand toward him. Into it he said, "Alpha."

The wall screen shifted into a multiwindow view. The largest window showed a slowly moving aerial shot of open ocean. The digital clock display was now in the upper left hand corner, superimposed over the blue water.

The other three windows were much smaller. In the bottom right was a detailed depiction of the globe, with a red dot on a spot over the Pacific Ocean, just east of Indonesia. A wide, short window stretched across the bottom of the screen. In it were an array of icons—some red, some blinking, some ghosted—the meanings of which Jason could only guess at. A small window in the bottom left-hand corner gave a continually updated latitude and longitude report. Along the right-hand side of the main window, Jason could see status messages overlaid on the ocean image.

"This is Icarus," Bigelow said. "One of my pet birds."

"So I see. Since when did you become Mr. Wizard?"

"Since I landed in that chair. You'd be surprised what you can do with remote control these days. And you know, sometimes I'm just too lazy to get up on my own two feet and go see what I want to see. So I get this baby to go do the looking for me."

"Icarus," Jason said. "Wasn't that the Greek dude who basically crashed and burned into the ocean? You sure you want to name your satellite that?"

"I don't know. I just like the name. Besides, that's just what I call it. It's real name is made up of letters and numbers and dashes. Mine's better."

Jason sat down beside him. "So you can look around with your satellite, so what?"

"So what? You got a satellite you can task to do whatever you ask it to do?"

"Well, no."

"Then shut your mouth. Listen to him, 'So what'? So what is that I can sit here and zoom in on whatever I want. If I wanted to, I could tilt this thing around and find a beach filled with bikini-clad babes. . . . Not that I would."

"Yeah, right."

"But the point is that I can see what I want. Which means *I'm* the operations guy for your little Firebrand team. *I'm* the guy you'll be talking to when you're in-country and you call for help. *I'm* the one who'll be sitting right here watching the bad guys cut off your retreat." He leaned back, folding his hands behind his head. "Oh, yes, we'll be having some good times."

"Doug," Jason said, "I'm not on the team."

"Shut up. You're what?"

"I'm not on the team. I told her *no.*"

Bigelow looked at him like he'd just said *I like to eat camera batteries.* "Are you whacked? This thing is perfect for you. It's got your two favorite things: guns and God. As soon as I heard of it, I thought of you. You're the poster child for this group. Why would *you* say no?"

Jason was staring at Bigelow's wheelchair. "So you're how they got my name."

"Duh. She says, 'Do you know of anyone else who might fit what I'm looking for?' 'Do I know anybody else? Do I ever.' And here you are."

Jason shrugged. "Sorry to disappoint. It's just not for me, Chimp."

"No," Bigelow said, shaking his head resolutely. "I don't buy it. There's got to be some reason you're holding out. Because anybody could see you were made for this job. Why in the world would you turn it down?"

Jason told him his reasons. On this time through it, though, he wasn't sounding quite as convinced. He kept remembering Eloise's corrections. Still, he tried to make it sound persuasive for Bigelow. When Jason was done, his friend summed up how successful Jason had been.

"What a load of hooey."

"Which?"

"None of it. All of it, whatever. That's not your real reason for saying no."

"It isn't?"

"No way. Don't you think that if I had the chance to go out with this team that I would take it? I want to be *out there* again, man, kicking tail and taking names. But to be stuck here watching it like a mutant coach potato? Now that's something that could drive a crip to drink. So I've come as close to it as I can. I got this job and this room, which ain't half bad. I like to think of myself as the seventh member of the team. But it's nowhere near as good as what you're getting the chance to do."

"There's no way she would even pick you, Chimp. Didn't you know that Eloise 'got religion,' too, just like me? I'm surprised she's letting you do this much of it, you being you and all."

"Ah," Bigelow said, wagging a finger at Jason, "that's where you'd be wrong."

"Huh?"

"Haven't you been hearing what I've been saying, Jace? I got Jesus myself, brother—hallelujah."

Jason looked at him dubiously. "Yeah, right. You mean you pretended to so you could get this job."

"No, really! Jason, dude, listen to me. After that mission, I had a lot of time to think about things. Believe me, a *lot* of time. Mostly, I thought about you and how I was going to kill you. But whenever I thought of you I ended up thinking about God. I have to say I was pretty ticked at both of you. Still, I couldn't deny that it seemed like you'd found The Answer. You know, the answer to that ultimate question. There was a change in you. I don't know—a shift. You got more peaceful or something. Settled. And you didn't need to be going out with the ladies or kicking back the kegs to 'have fun.'

"Then there was also this girl: Jamie. She was my physical therapist in San Diego." He reached into his blue jeans pocket. "Here's a picture. Ain't she something?"

Jason looked. Jamie was a striking young woman with long, gently curling sandy blond hair and a magnificent smile. "Wow."

"Yeah, that's what I thought, too." Bigelow put the picture away. "She's a Christian, just like you. Every day she'd come in and tell me some Bible verse or sing me some worship song while we were working. And she was always playing Christian music CDs: Kim Hill or Point of Grace or Stephen Curtis Chapman. This girl was a walking Christian environment.

"After a while, I had to deal with how bitter I was at everything. It's one of those turning points every cripple comes to. I really fought it out, but I'll save you the blow-by-blow. Bottom line: I either had to surrender to this Jesus, who was, like, hounding me, or I had to just curl up and die. So I chose Jesus Christ. He's my CO now, dude. Oh, and also I got to date Jamie. Ha! You probably still think I'm faking it so that I could date her. Don't you?"

"What else?"

"Well, there's nothing I can do about that. You'll just have to watch and see if it's true. But the fact that I'm here talking to you right now without trying to rip out your liver ought to say something. Think about, Jace. How could I even begin to forgive you if I hadn't experienced the power of God's forgiveness myself?"

Jason thought about that for a moment, then allowed himself a small glimmer of hope. "You know, Chimp. I don't think you could."

"Anyway, I'm going to marry that girl. Jamie and me are tying the knot in about five weeks. Wanna be in the wedding?"

"Is she out here with you?"

"Yeah. I told you I brought my therapist with me. We don't live together or anything. That ought to be more proof that I've changed! For now, she rooms with Rachel and Trieu. Anyway, that's that. I'm a Christian, I'm engaged to my physical therapist, and I'm team Firebrand's operational manager. And you *are* going to join this team, or I'm going to roll on your carotid until you do."

Jason wiped some dust off the countertop in front of him. "Doug, can we go back for a minute? This is. . .going a little too fast for me. I mean, the last time I saw you you said you'd never forgive me. Do you remember that?"

"I was a basket case, J—"

"So you remember?"

"Of course I r—"

"You said I should've taken the shot instead of you. Remember that?"

Bigelow looked into space. "I do."

"You said that it was my fault that you'd been injured. You said that if I hadn't hesitated that we'd have avoided the ambush and you'd still be on your feet. Remember?"

"I do. But you should know there's some new information coming in about that mission. Intel's investigating Ibnu's r—"

"I don't care about that, Doug. Would you just listen to me?"

"Okay, but—"

Jason opened his hands. "So, buddy, what I'm saying is that's where I'm still at. Back with you saying you'd never forgive me. And now you come rolling back into my life saying you're a Christian now and all is forgiven? Which am I supposed to believe?"

"You're su—"

"Because I've had time to do a lot of thinking, too. Ever since you left me on the *Stennis,* I've been replaying what you said. And you know what? You were right. It *was* my fault that you took that grenade. And it *is* my fault that you're in that chair. It's my fault that you can't have kids or whatever else." Jason heard his voice quivering.

"No, they say I can still have—"

"So when you say there's something else behind all my other reasons for not joining the team, you're absolutely right. You want to know what it is? You want to know the real reason why I said *no;* why I left the Teams; why I live in a dive and peel tubeworms off ships?"

Jason's mouth was going on its own now. It was like a shaken-up can of Coke that somebody finally popped open. "You want to know why I work myself to death in my physical conditioning and stay away from relationships and spend most of my time alone? You want to know?"

"Yes, you lunatic, I want to know!"

"All right, I'll tell you. I do all that because you were right! Because I hesitated on a mission and it cost my best friend his legs. And not only that. It cost him his legs, his career, his chance to have a family. I stole your life, Doug. It *should've* been me. You were right. I should've taken the bullet."

Oh, dear Lord, it should've been me! Why wasn't it me?

Against his will, tears threatened to leap out of Jason's eyes. That beast in the titanium-padlocked cage was rattling the bars like a gorilla. But the lock held.

Jason saw his friend reaching for him, and he knocked his hand away. "Don't touch me. Just–just stay away. For a minute."

"Jace, I—"

"So, *yeah,* Doug, you're right: I guess there is another reason. I'm not going to join this team because I don't deserve to. You should be on it, Chimp. You should be the team leader. What I deserve is that life back in Long Beach, that stupid, pointless life. You're here. That's great. You're doing well. You've got the love of a beautiful woman. You've adjusted to your chair. You've dealt with your anger or whatever. Great. I'm happy for you. But maybe I'm just not ready for it, okay? You be part of this team, Chimp. You've earned it. But just let me go back to my pathetic life like I should, okay?"

Bigelow was watching him, his arms folded. "Are you done?"

Jason didn't answer.

"Oh, you're a beauty, aren't you? 'I'm such a bad person. Oh, I'm no good.' Buddy, I think I need to teach you a little song Jamie taught me in rehab. But first, you need to know that the doctors say there ain't nothing wrong with my. . .ability to have children. Okay? So you can just let that one drop. Now, listen up. The song goes like this: 'Nobody likes me, everybody hates me, I'm gonna eat some wor-rr-rms.' Come on, buddy, try it."

Jason smiled in spite of himself. "No, I'm not going—"

Bigelow wrapped his arm around Jason's shoulders. "Come on, now, here we go."

"Nobody likes me, everybody hates me, I'm gonna eat some wor-rr-rrms."

On the third time through, Jason joined in. They sang it—shouted it, really—once more, with feeling.

"That's it, Jace. See? Now doesn't that feel better?"

Jason shook his head, but inside he was feeling a little lighter.

And just like that, he saw what he had to do.

It was going to be almost impossible not to join this team; he could see that now. They were all so sure he was "the chosen one" that they'd probably physically restrain him until he agreed. So why fight it?

The plan he saw with HDTV clarity in his mind frightened him. It was horrible and perfect. It met all of his requirements and tied them off elegantly. If he had the guts to go through with it.

But it would require a lot of acting skill. He'd have to make them believe he was really on board with them, that he'd really come around to their way of thinking. He couldn't just flip a switch and say he was suddenly with them. Then he'd have to go through with the training. He'd have to play the part of the responsible team leader to the hilt. He'd have to pick the weapons and outfit the squad and plan whatever their first mission would be. He'd have to fool Eloise—with that all-knowing motherly look of hers—and he'd have to fool Doug.

In a way, he wouldn't be acting deceptively at all, since he did care about the team members' survivability. He wanted them trained well. He could enjoy being part of the team, for a while. This awful, wonderful plan would allow him to give in to that part of himself that wanted desperately to be an operator again. But then, at a crucial point, there would be one difference.

It was no more than he deserved.

Jason looked at his friend—his brother in Christ?—and started the great game. "You're not going to let this thing go, are you?"

"Absolutely not. Not until you sign on the dotted line."

"And if I say *no* and go back to California today?"

"Then I'll hunt you down. I'll sic Garth on you. He'll tie you to his Harley and haul you back here. Your face'll be all bug-gut-splattered, but you'll be here. Oh, you're going to join us, Jace, have no fear."

"If it's like that," Jason said, sighing dramatically, "then I guess it's no use fighting it."

Bigelow looked at him cannily. "Uh, Jace, are you saying what I think you're saying?"

"Well, with you threatening me with physical violence and Eloise telling me it's God's will—and me not having much of anything holding me to California—I guess there's no reason why I shouldn't say yes."

"Are you pulling a crippled man's leg?"

Jason met his gaze brazenly. "No."

"Well, all right!"

"I mean, it would be great to be an operator again, wouldn't it?"

"Oh, what I wouldn't give."

"And those funky weapons were kinda cool, weren't they?"

"Sure. And you should see some of the designs I've been cooking up."

"And I don't guess it would be so terrible to spend time alone and in danger with a couple of beautiful damsels in distress."

"Now you're talking. But I'm not sure they're going to need rescuing."

"And to lead my own team," Jason said, staring at the ceiling tiles. The wistful tone in his voice wasn't a show.

"I know you'll be great, Jace."

"So what are we waiting for?" Let's go tell them the good news."

"Oh, man," Bigelow said. "Chris is going to wet his pants."

They didn't have far to go. The whole group was waiting for them just outside the Operations Room, sitting in a semicircle facing the door.

"Whoa," Bigelow said, wheeling through the door. "You guys after my autograph *again?*"

"That's right, baby," Garth said. "Would you sign my head?"

Jason noticed that not everybody met his eyes. Trieu and Eloise and Lewis seemed to be locked onto his face like SAM radar. But Chris and Rachel seemed more interested in the carpet. Garth was just Garth.

"Well?" Lewis asked.

Jason started to answer, but Bigelow did it for him. "You guys even have to ask? You sent him to me, didn't you? I'm da closer, baby."

"So you're in?" Chris said, his eyes homing in.

The smile formed on Jason's lips all by itself. "I'm in."

They cheered. Even Trieu looked pleased.

Eloise raised her hands to the sky: "Thank You, Lord. Oh, Lord-a-mercy, thank You! Halleluia!" She broke into song, a marvelous booming alto.

"Amazing grace,
How sweet the sound
That saved a wretch like me."

They all joined in.

"I once was lost,
But now am found,
Was blind, but now I see."

As they sang about being in heaven ten thousand years, Jason merged his voice gently into the chorus. He looked around the circle and saw not strangers nor civilians nor gender nor race, but a family. His family, for a while. For three full verses of "Amazing Grace," he forgot his guilt, forgot his bitterness, forgot his loneliness—even forgot his plan for a moment—and allowed himself to become one with these seven people.

"Praise the Lord!" Eloise said when the song was done. The group was giving out hugs all around. "Say, any of y'all hungry for lunch? My treat."

"Oh, yeah!" Lewis said. "Lanning's, please, Mrs. Webster, please?"

"Come here, you hoodlum with those puppy-dog eyes. Yes, we can go to Lanning's."

"All right!" Lewis said. "New York strip, here I come!"

Eloise enveloped Jason in a great embrace. She whispered into his ear, "What made you change your mind?"

"Oh, lots of things. I guess mostly I didn't want to miss out on what you're doing with this group."

She smiled knowingly. The others were rolling office chairs back to wherever they'd come from.

"But you may want to make it a dinner instead of a lunch," Jason said.

"Why's that?" she said.

"Because, if it's all right with you, I'd like to take these guys out and see what they can do."

"Today?"

"Sure. My flight doesn't leave until morning. I might as well take this group out for a test drive. Kick the tires a little. See what I've got to work with. You just let me know where there's a firing range and a track and maybe a weight room, and I'll put them through their paces."

"If you do too much, they might be too sore to enjoy dinner."

"Why not do both? You've got some bank, don't you? Light lunch, so they don't puke all over the place this afternoon, and then a nice dinner somewhere quiet. Maybe someplace where there's dancing?"

"All right, you smooth talking man. You know, I'm going to have to keep a special watch on you, aren't I? Okay, you can have 'em. Just. . .take it easy on Lewis. He's the one I worry about."

"Cross my heart."

"Ha."

Part III

Team Firebrand

CHAPTER 14

Fight Club

THE loss of lunch at Lanning's didn't go over very well, and the Schlotzsky's soup and bread Jason offered them instead was little appreciated. But with the promise of Akron City Club for dinner held out before them and the chance to show their new boss what they could do, they got through it fine.

They headed to Green High School in nearby Green, Ohio, to use its track and gym. Jason rode in Bigelow's specialized van—the Lamoloader—along with Lewis and Trieu and all the weapons for the firing range. Chris followed in his mud-caked Jeep Renegade (he claimed it was black under all the tan mud) with Rachel in the passenger seat and Garth sprawled in the back. Eloise had opted out of their little outing.

"So what are you going to do to them, boss?" Bigelow asked, accelerating by rotating the motorcycle-style handle beside the steering column. "Something sadistic, I hope."

"Nah," Jason said. "I just want to see what they can do."

"Like whether or not they've got the guts to stay underwater so long they'll black out?"

Jason smiled. "Oh, glory days, huh? Nah, Doug, this isn't the Teams."

"Still, it'd be fun, though. I bet Chris'd do it. He's a maniac."

Bigelow pulled into a school parking lot. "Here we are, ladies. Everybody out."

The van door opened, and the ramp extended automatically. Bigelow rolled from the driver's position and out onto the grass to follow the six members of the Firebrand team as they headed to the track. It was suprisingly warm for January, but there was still a chilly wind blowing. About twenty teenage girls trotted around the track in T-shirts and green sweats, looking like they'd rather be doing anything—even cleaning toilets—than doing laps. There were no coaches in sight.

Garth wore gray cotton shorts and a black tank top with "House of Pain" emblazoned on the front. The sight of him in all his bald massiveness was impressive. His latissimus dorsi muscles bulged behind his arms. Jason was glad to be on the same field with him.

Trieu wore dark blue biker shorts and matching half-top. It looked like what she probably wore in summer biathlons. Between the top of the shorts and the bottom of the half-top there was not even a hint of body fat.

Chris wore brown government issue shorts, a tan T-shirt, white crew socks, and expensive tennis shoes. His forehead curl was present and accounted for. He looked sweaty already. Correction, he glistened. What a bunch of studs.

Lewis was the only one who didn't look like he'd been frequenting the gym—or at least paying attention to what people were wearing at the gym. He wore long gold basketball shorts and a white basketball jersey with red numbers. Black hightops with no socks. Jason pitied his feet.

Rachel wore a cobalt blue sleeveless one-piece that zippered up the front. The color alone would've attracted any eye that happened to glance at their group. It fit too tightly to keep any secrets. It was apparent, however, that this wasn't one of Rachel's primary concerns. Jason had to keep his eyes on a short leash.

Jason wore his beach volleyball duds: Navy blue jersey knit shorts, navy and red USA tank top. To that he added his New Balance X-treme cross trainer shoes and his runner's wristwatch.

Lewis bounced up and down. "What's first, chief?"

"You might want to stretch, Lewis," Jason said. "You're going to be doing quite a bit of running."

"Nah, I'm all right."

"Lewis," Jason said seriously, "stretch out. Your body will thank me later."

Lewis dropped to the ground and joined the others in some stretches.

Bigelow wheeled across the grass. "You want me to hold your watch for you, Jace?"

Rachel looked up. She had to shield her eyes against the sun. "You mean you're going to run with us?"

"Course," Jason said, handing his watch to Bigelow. "What good's a leader who doesn't lead?" He began to stretch out. "You did get us permission to use the track, didn't you, Chimp?"

"You betcha."

After they'd all had enough time to get loose, Jason showed Bigelow how to work his stopwatch. "Okay, everybody: On the track."

They lined up on the brick-colored track, leaving room for the high school girls to trot by. It was springy under their feet. Chris stood next to Jason. They were about the same height and build. Chris looked like he was about to run for the gold medal.

"How far are we going to run?" Trieu asked.

"We'll start with five," Jason said. "Chimp, you ready?"

"Ready, boss."

"Count us down, then."

"Five, four, three. . ."

"You mean five laps?" Lewis asked.

"Two. . ."

"No, Lewis," Jason said, "five miles."

"Five m—?"

"Go!"

They ran. Chris shot forward and claimed the inside lane, glancing over his back. Lewis surged ahead, too, but soon fell back with the pack. Jason lost track of Trieu behind him, but he knew she might be able to beat them all. The race was on.

After the second lap, the spread widened. Chris up front; Jason, Trieu, Rachel, and Garth in the pack; Lewis dropping behind, but not as badly as Jason had feared. They lapped the teenage joggers like Indy cars passing bicyclists.

Jason kept himself in front of Rachel. She probably thought he was doing it to show off. The real reason was so that her body wouldn't be right there in front of his eyes.

Entering the fourth lap, Garth was still breathing easily, running an exceptionally disciplined race. Jason had expected no less from a Green Beret, but it was still surprising to see a big man move so well over distance.

Bigelow shouted out times as they finished their first mile. Chris made it in 5:26. The pack crossed at 5:37. Lewis was coming along fine at 6:10.

With a mile left to go, Trieu made her move. She came alongside Jason—almost perfectly silent. He saw a sheen of sweat on her face, but she was running easily, as if she could do this for another twenty miles. As she broke away from the pack, Jason went with her, slipstreaming.

Ahead of them, Chris was still going strong, but he'd lost a step from his earlier miles. A dark brown stripe ran down the back of his T-shirt. He glanced over his shoulder and saw Trieu and Jason closing the distance. He faced forward again and for a lap Trieu and

Jason couldn't gain on him. But then he started looming larger in their sights.

Jason noticed that the high schoolers were walking off toward the school buildings in a pack. If they were impressed by the "grownups," they didn't show it.

As Jason approached Bigelow on the bell lap, he saw an attractive blond woman standing beside him, her hand in his. What was her name again? Oh, right: Jamie. She must've tracked them down somehow. Jason was glad for his friend. The thought occurred to him that if he'd never had his accident he would never have met her.

But there was no time for that kind of nonsense right now.

He and Trieu were fifteen feet behind Chris, but Jason could tell by the way he ran that the man was spent. He would beat the rest of the pack and have a great run time, but he wasn't going to beat Trieu. Or him.

Coming down the back stretch, they passed Chris shoulder to shoulder. Then Trieu hit the afterburners. Jason couldn't believe her acceleration this late in the run. He stayed with her.

Twenty yards from the finish she was still a leg ahead of him. But he touched a wire to that fire in his gut and flat-out ran.

He beat her by two seconds.

The difference was that when they finished, he went down to one knee to catch his breath, and she kept running, jogging along as if she were just beginning her run.

Next came Chris, who probably would've collapsed in a heap if Jason hadn't been there. A few seconds later Rachel came across. People were supposed to get less attractive when they got tired, not the other way around. When Garth crossed, he hooted, heaved a few big breaths, and then fell into casual conversation with Jamie and Bigelow.

When Lewis rounded the last turn, they all turned to cheer.

Bigelow counted out his last mile's time: "Seven-twenty, seven-twenty-one. Come on, Lewis, beat seven-thirty."

"Come on, Lewis!"

"You can do it!"

Lewis dropped his head and hurried, his gangly arms flapping and his skinny legs lost under the massive gold shorts.

He made it across at 7:29.99.

And promptly passed out.

When they filed out of the track headed for the gym, a couple of middle-aged joggers with sizable paunches stood ogling them.

"Look, Gene," one said, "it's the cast of Baywatch."

Gene elbowed his friend. "Say," he said to Garth, "that was amazing. You guys some kind of *American Gladiators* team or something?"

Garth smiled. "Absolutely."

The joggers hurried after them, staying close to Rachel and Jamie. "Well, where are you going now?"

"To the gym," Jason answered.

Lewis groaned, having just regained the use of his legs.

The joggers exchanged a look. "Can we come?"

"I don't believe this," Chris muttered.

"I won't stop you," Jason said, "so long as you stay out of our way."

There was a P.E. class going on in the main gym, but the school's "small gym" was available. This white-walled room was not much bigger than a racquetball court, but it was perfect for Jason's use. The team entered, their footfalls echoing endlessly off the wood floor and smooth concrete walls. A volleyball net was set up in the center. Stacks of blue tumbling mats stood along the far wall. It smelled of teenage work ethic.

"All right," Jason said, "let's get those mats out. Everybody choose a partner. Same gender, please, Chris. Spread out, too. Use both sides of the net."

There were enough mats to pretty much cover the whole gym, so that's what they did.

When Rachel teamed up with Trieu, Chris was bereft of his first choice, so he went to Garth. That left Lewis with Jason.

"I'm always last on these things," Lewis confided to Jason. "Tell me we're going to do something today that I won't be last in."

"Sorry about that, bud," Jason said. "But I gotta know what you guys can do."

"Hey, chief," Garth said, "I already know how to square dance."

The two joggers, sitting on the floor by the entrance, laughed. Jamie sat on the floor next to Bigelow's chair.

"All right," Jason said, "we're going to do a little hand-to-hand stuff here. Take turns immobilizing your partner. First exercise will be with the target facing away from you. Start whenever you're ready."

As the others discussed who would go first, Jason turned to Lewis. "Do you think you can do this?"

"Sure—if I had a few of my tools with me."

"I mean now, unarmed. You can't always count on computers and gizmos."

"Huh. Shows what you know."

Jason waited. "Well?"

"I'll try," he said.

Jason noticed that when Lewis got nervous, the kid's heels bounced even more than usual.

"Turn around," Lewis said.

"Okay." Jason turned to face the rest of the group.

As he waited for Lewis's attack, he saw Rachel grab Trieu's left hand and flip her over her back. And though Chris gave away seventy-five pounds to Garth, he had the big man pinned in nothing flat.

"Hiya!"

Jason was hit by a giant flying monkey. He staggered forward, regaining his balance. Though Lewis grunted and squeezed and encircled Jason's neck with his forearm, Jason pretty much just stood there indulgently.

"Are you immobilized?"

"Only out of boredom." Jason bent at the waist and Lewis went flailing to the mat.

The concrete walls made the group's laughter that much harsher in Jason's ears. He saw Lewis's face redden. He helped him up. "Don't worry, bro. I'll teach you a good move in a sec." To the others he said, "You guys go on. Let the other one take a turn."

Garth put a meaty arm around Chris's neck—and then found himself on his back staring up at the ceiling. Chris helped him up and turned around again. Garth came at him lower, reaching for a leg and his torso, trying to upend him. Chris twisted and fell on Garth and rolled over to achieve a scissors lock on Garth's neck. On the third try, Garth just lifted Chris over his head and held him there.

"All right," Jason said, laughing. "That's enough for now, you two. Good work."

Trieu simply walked up to Rachel, grabbed one arm, and kicked her legs out from under her. The instant Rachel hit the mat, Trieu's knee was in her ribs and her fist cocked to go to the face. Rachel flinched, but the blow didn't come. Trieu helped her up.

"Good," Jason said. "Just right. Okay, you guys take five while I work with my partner for a minute."

He turned to Lewis. "Okay, buddy, I'm going to teach you 'the sleeper.' You'll like it. The best way to immobilize someone from behind is to come around his neck with the right arm, like this. Center the inside of your elbow at the throat. See?"

He released Lewis. "When I've got you in the V, I'm going to lock my hand on my left bicep, like this. You do it, just in the air. That's it. Okay, now bring your left hand up. That's going to go up against the back of my head to push my throat into your elbow."

He got Lewis in the hold again. "You feel that?"

"Yeth."

Jason released him. "That cuts off your carotid artery. Ten seconds of that and you're taking a nice little nap. Try it on me."

He did. When he didn't let loose after seven seconds, Jason gave him a jab to the ribs. Lewis released.

"Now," Jason said, "if you're going up against somebody big, like Garth over there, you're going to have to take him to the ground for this to work. Otherwise he'll get out of your grip before lights out. If you have surprise on your side, he'll come down easy. Watch this."

Jason began to move out of Garth's field of vision while the big man was talking to Chris. As he did he noticed that the audience had grown. Apparently word had gotten out that something was going on in the small gym. Now there were about ten newcomers, high school students and coaches, crowding in the doorway beside the two joggers. Bigelow and Jamie had scooted over. The group fell silent as they saw Jason stalking.

Jason sprang at Garth from behind. He landed his foot on the back of the big man's knees at the same moment that his arm came around his throat. Garth folded like a towel, and Jason had him on his chest, interrupting the flow of blood to the brain.

After a five count, Jason released him and backed out of range quickly. "Sorry, big guy, but it wouldn't have worked if you'd been ready for me."

Garth rubbed his neck. "You guys are too rough for me. I'm gonna have to find some kids who don't play so mean."

He and Jason slapped hands.

"Now," Jason said to the team, "get with your partners again and give yourselves some space. I want you to face each other. No taking turns now. You're both trying to take the other person down."

As he spoke, Jason predicted that Chris would take down Garth, Rachel would overcome Trieu, and he would make quick work of Lewis.

He was right, except that Trieu and Rachel ended up in a kind of double-pin. The crowd cheered at each takedown. He heard Gene's friend say, "Better than live mud wrestling!"

"Okay," Jason said, "that's good, everybody. Chimp, I think we're ready to head over to—"

"Wait a minute." It was Chris, jutting his jaw at Jason. "I want a piece of you."

Garth hooted, and Lewis hollered. More people surged into the gym.

"You do, huh?"

Chris tore his shoes and socks off and threw the mats aside. He began circling Jason. "In eight years in the Marines I've never been beaten. Undefeated, baby. Kickboxing champion. What do you got?"

Jason watched him warily, expecting him to be using the trash talk to unbalance him. *Kickboxer, huh? This is going to be fun.*

Whatever invisible force that had been keeping the crowd bunched up at the doorway suddenly failed, and twenty wide-eyed fans ran in to form a circle around Jason and Chris. Jason caught a glimpse of Bigelow in the circle, smiling and shaking his head at him.

Chris bounced lightly, shifting his weight forward and back, disguising whether his kick would come off the front leg or the back. His hands, open, were in front of him defensively.

His first kick was a jumper that began like a rear kick but ended with a high side kick from the front. Jason sprang backward. Chris's kick snapped smartly in the air.

"You got somebody here taking action photos of you?" Jason asked. " 'Cause I'm way over here."

"I see you, little rabbit."

His second attack was another crowd-pleaser: a leaping side kick. He gained impressive height and landed his kick right on. . .

Nothing. Jason simply stepped aside. Chris was getting winded and Jason hadn't done more than bob.

"I thought you wanted a piece of me," Jason taunted. "So far it looks like you're just putting on an exhibition."

"Come on, Chris," Rachel said. "Hurt him!"

Chris shuffled forward in his stance, closing the distance rapidly. When he was in range, he launched a combination of straight punches and kicks. His fourth punch connected with Jason's cheek with a *crack*. Jason's head snapped back, and the crowd cheered.

Chris pressed his advantage, kicking high and low with his front leg. Then he reached for Jason's shirt to pull him close for a punch.

Jason flicked Chris's hand away and bolted straight into his body. Chris backpedaled to try to regain his balance, but Jason kept shoving forward. The crowd shouted.

Finally Jason got the angle he needed and sent Chris to the boards. Jason landed astride Chris's chest.

Chris punched up at Jason's reddening cheek, but he didn't have any force from this angle. He struggled to get Jason off, but it wasn't working. The crowd urged each of them on. They flowed around the fight like mercury. Chris reached up with rabbit punches at Jason's kidneys, but they were glancing blows.

Jason, on the other hand, did have the angle. He gave Chris a measured shot to his left cheek at the base of the nose. Chris's head bounced on the floor, and the audience groaned.

When Jason looked like he was going to give him another headshot, Chris rolled to his stomach. That was what Jason had been waiting for. He slid Chris into "the sleeper."

"Here it comes, baby!" Lewis shouted.

Chris clawed at Jason's hands and rolled frantically. The crowd shouted for him to get up.

Jason gave him a gouge to the midsection with his heel, like kicking a horse to gallop. On the second kick, Chris brought his hands down to protect his stomach. After that it was all over but the shouting.

Chris went limp, signaling defeat. But Jason didn't let go.

Chris tapped on Jason's arm, signaling surrender.

But Jason didn't let go.

He held it for another two seconds, demonstrating his mastery.

Then he let go.

The whole crowd took a breath together, as if helping Chris take in some oxygen. Then they fell into excited chatter. Jason heard somebody say *bloodsport*.

He leaned to Chris. "You okay?"

Chris nodded but didn't look him in the eye.

Jason reached out his hand and helped Chris to his feet. The circle the crowd had maintained collapsed as everyone stretched to touch Jason or Chris.

"Okay," Jason said. "Show's over."

"Aw!"

"Sorry. We're moving to another location now. Guys, get your things. Chimp, let's roll."

"Okay, boss."

"Where you headed to next?" someone asked.

"Like I said," Jason said, "the show's over."

"Thanks for coming," Garth said. "Don't forget to buy a T-shirt on your way out."

Doug cupped his hands. "All donations accepted here. Come on, help a crippled veteran buy a hamburger."

Jamie slapped his shoulder. "Stop that."

CHAPTER 15

FIRING SQUAD

THIS time no one rode with Chris. He took off before anyone could catch him. As Bigelow drove, he said he thought he could see Chris's Jeep on the highway ahead. Rachel and Trieu were riding with their roomie, Jamie, in her white Toyota Camry. While Bigelow sought technical advice from Lewis, Jason turned in his bench seat to speak to Garth, who appeared to be sleeping again.

"Hey Beret, you awake?"

"No."

"Good. So, tell me how you came to get out of the army."

Garth put his long arm on the back of the bench seat. "I didn't."

"Come again?"

"Technically, I'm still in."

"Okay. . ." Jason looked out the window. "Are you talking about the reserves?"

"Kinda. There's those three levels of reserves: ready, standby, and retired."

"Yeah?"

"The ready reserve is what's called up whenever there's a flood or war or whatever. That's not me. I'm in the standby reserves. And there's two kind of standbys: active and inactive. Couple years ago I applied for a hardship discharge. My mom had got real bad, and there wasn't nobody but me. She tried to kill somebody at the old folks' home.

"But the army didn't want to let loose of me. Said they'd put too much into me to let me out before serving my time. So they transferred me to active standbys. It was a temporary reassignment, the way they saw it. Wait 'til the old girl kicks the can and then get that boy back in a uniform.

"You know they can activate the standbys, even the inactive standbys, if the secretary of defense approves it. Thought I was gonna get called up after 9/11, but Ma managed to hang on long enough to keep me out of that one. She finally keeled over a year ago."

"So," Jason said slowly, "you're still in? You could get called up anytime?"

"That's a fact. And I'm all out of demented relatives, unless you count Butch, my hound dog, but stupid ain't the same as crazy."

"Doesn't it have a statute of limitations or something? I mean, can they call you up anytime as long as you're still alive?"

"Nah, just until my service obligation's up. Another fourteen months."

"So you could go tell them that your mom's died, right? You could ask to be put on ready reserve or even back on a team."

"Yessir."

"Then why don't you?"

"Well, that goes back to Miss Eloise. She found me—don't ask me how—and talked me into looking at this 'new thing' she was brewing up. When Ma finally went, I was kinda interested in what Miss Eloise had going, so I just never bothered to tell the army."

"You dog."

He grinned. "Woof."

Outside the van windows the terrain was getting more lush. "How we doing, Chimp?"

"About ten more minutes, chief." Then he turned to Lewis: "But how do you gain administrator rights in the target computer if the company's got both kinds of firewalls?"

Jason smiled. Lewis might not be a great commando, but he sure knew tech stuff. If they ever needed to subdue *virtual* soldiers, the kid might come in handy. It struck him that with Bigelow and Lewis together, they had their crippled boy genius after all. *Great, we really are the A-Team.*

He looked over Garth's shoulder and saw the white Camry out the back window. The girls appeared to be jamming to some tunes. Trieu and Rachel had put windbreaker warm-ups on over their running clothes.

"You still see Chris up there, Chimp?"

"Yeah, he's there. He's going to have to get behind us in a minute, unless he knows the way to the range."

Jason turned back to Garth. "What about Chris? Why did he leave the marines?"

Garth stroked his goatee. "Trying to save his marriage. He'd been a jerk to the girl the whole time. Married her because it was what he'd set his mind to do. Then he set his mind on Force Recon. Special forces are full of guys like that. After he got back from one tour in the Gulf, his enlistment was up. His wife drew a line in the sand, said it's me or the marines. He chose the marines, of course. Idiot. But he didn't actually reenlist. When he got served papers he changed his mind and tried to patch things up. But she was long gone. He did it to himself.

"That, my good man," Garth said in a terrible British accent, "is why Squire Fisher will not get married until he is sure he's ready to settle down with a woman."

"Here we are," Bigelow said, pulling into a parking lot.

When Jason got out, Chris's Jeep and Jamie's Camry were just pulling in—along with ten carloads of fans from the high school. "Oh, great. They followed us! That's nuts."

"Are you kidding?" Lewis said. "This is Akron, remember? There's not that much to do here."

"Jace," Bigelow called from the back of the van, "help me get these weapons inside."

"Coming."

"Sorry, boys," Garth said, arms outstretched to the crowd, "I'm all out of trading cards. But I can tell you one thing for sure," he said in his best WWF challenge voice, jabbing his finger in the air, "that the Scorpion King—if he has the little bug guts to step into the ring with me—is gonna find he's lost his sting! I'm gonna pluck that tail of his right out and feed it to him up his nose! Now, excuse me, gents, but I gotta get ready to rumble."

He headed toward the entrance of the indoor firing range, a mass of groupies in his wake.

Jason recognized Gene and his jogging buddy. Gene's friend hurried up to Jason. "Who are you guys *really?*"

"Just regular citizens like yourself."

"That's right," Lewis said, pushing the crowd back. "Now please step aside to let the ring card girls through."

Gene and his friend's eyes bugged out as they watched Rachel and Trieu and Jamie walk to the entrance.

The crowd began funneling toward the door.

Jason hurried to block the way. "Hang on. Look, you people followed us out here, which I think is crazy. I mean, don't you guys have jobs or classes or something?"

Gene only had eyes for the ladies. "Not today, buddy. Not today."

The crowd laughed.

"Well, I'm sorry, but I can't allow you to come along."

"Aw!"

"Hey," Gene's friend said, "it's a free country. We can go where we please."

"Yeah."

"True," Jason said, walking next to Garth, "but my large friend here is also free to—"

"Jace," Bigelow said quickly. He shook his head at Jason. "Don't."

Jason sighed. "All right, we'll just find us another range."

"There's not that many firing ranges in this whole area," Gene said. "We'll find you."

In the end, Jason settled for getting his people and gear through the door and having Garth hold the door against the riffraff.

Inside the door was a showroom. It looked like a typical army/navy surplus store, with flags mounted like posters all over the walls, along with stuffed big game trophies, patches from various military and law enforcement units, and signs with messages like "Trespassers must carry ID—the morgue will need to know who you were." Racks of ammunition belts, hats, MREs, ear muffs, and camo T-shirts stood around the glossy white linoleum floor. Glass cases lined three walls displaying handguns, shotguns, compound bows, scopes, and consumer night-vision gear.

A checkout booth stood in front of the door to the indoor range. Behind it sat a stunned clerk and his manager.

"What is he doing holding the door shut?" the manager asked.

"Can we lock your door?" Jason asked.

"Why?"

"Hey, Doug," Garth called over his shoulder. "Flash the plastic, baby."

The manager had a tall face with slicked over black hair and a large mole under his left eye. He wore a yellow windbreaker under which Jason was confident there was a handgun of some kind. "You guys some kind of rock band or something?"

"Sir," Jason said, "we'd like to buy out your range for a few hours. First the indoor, then the outdoor." He took the credit card from

Bigelow and *snicked* it down on the glass counter. "Charge enough to make it worth your while."

"Gee, Jason," Rachel said. "You sure are generous with other people's money."

He looked at her large eyes and beautiful lips and tried to remember his name. He was desperately trying to think of something clever to say when Rachel reached up as if to caress his face.

"What's this?" she said, pressing his cheek.

"Ouch!"

"A wound? Oh, how the mighty have fallen."

The manager cleared his throat. "What's with them out there?"

"They, uh. . ." Jason said.

"They won't pay you as much as we will," Bigelow said. "Now give that boy your keys so we can get shooting."

Rachel smiled at the man and leaned onto the counter. "Please?"

His eye twitched, and he rubbed his forehead. He produced the keys and tossed them to Garth. He did some quick calculations and then charged the credit card. He distributed eye and ear protectors to the team, put a *Closed* sign on the door, and joined the party.

Through the door was another white linoleum floored room. It appeared to be a preparation area and a viewing gallery. A wooden shelf lined the walls all the way around. It was just wide enough to lay out ammunition or glasses. Windows along the far wall looked out into the indoor firing range beyond. Jason led the team in there, along with Bigelow, Jamie, and the manager.

The range smelled of gunpowder and disinfectant. Up against the windows on this side was a row of folding metal chairs. Twelve metal wheels were mounted on the wall at waist height, with steel cables reaching up onto pulleys at the ceiling. It looked like the "pirate ship" area at a nice playground. Black runners stretched across the ceiling from the pulleys to the targets at the far end of the range. The floor in here was gray concrete. A white wooden table, divided into eighteen shooter stalls, stood fifteen feet from the gallery wall.

As the team came in and sat down, Jason handed a stack of silhouette targets to Bigelow. "Let's start at ten yards." Then Bigelow, Jamie, and the manager started clipping them to the holders and cranking them back down the line.

"Now I know we're going to be using nonlethals when we deploy," Jason said to the group. "But today I want to see you shoot what I'm used to." He opened up a rifle case and hefted an MP-5 submachine gun. "Anyone not fired one of these before?"

He studied each of their reactions. Garth looked at it like he'd never seen such a thing before, which was obviously a joke. Rachel's eyes flared tauntingly. Chris—his nose and cheek an angry red—made no sign but at least met Jason's eyes. And if Trieu had made any reaction to the gun, he'd missed it. Only Lewis raised his hand.

"Okay," Jason said. "I'll show you, Lewis. Don't worry. Nothing to it. You ever fired a gun before?"

"I'm not a total dweeb."

Chris coughed.

"Good, then this won't be hard for you," Jason said. "We'll take turns at first because I want to watch you each shoot. Later we'll do some magazine changing drills and stuff when you can all shoot together. Who's first?"

Rachel stood up. Jason handed her the gun and a loaded magazine. "What do you want me to do?" she said.

"Switch to semiauto. Give me two body shots and one head shot." He turned to the group. "Eyes and ears, people." He put on his plastic goggles and the earmuffs.

Rachel chambered a round, brought the gun to her shoulder, and fired a couplet followed by a single higher shot. She switched the gun to safety and laid it on the table. "Anything else?"

Jason brought the ear muffs down. "Hang on." The target was close enough that he could verify her marksmanship from where he stood. Light streamed through two holes in the human silhouette's heart and one through his cerebrum. "Try it at twenty-five."

Bigelow cranked the target to the far wall.

Rachel fired another three rounds and tabled the weapon. When the target creaked close, Jason could see a nice group of holes in the heart and a dyad in the head. An image entered his mind of her taking down a room full of bad guys with this little gun.

"Wow," he said. "You're good. Nice work, Rachel."

He expected some smart remark, but instead a little girl smile broke on her face. She looked away awkwardly and walked back to the chairs.

The rest of the team shot as Jason would've predicted. Garth, Chris, and Trieu were dead-on at ten and twenty-five. Lewis had to get the feel of the gun, but before long he was hitting the target consistently, if not exactly where Jason had asked. He saw lots of time at the range in this boy's future.

By now it was expected for Jason to show his stuff, too. So he nailed the target at both distances. He capped his performance by hitting the target three times, quick changing magazines, and hitting it three more times. When his target cranked into view, there was a respectful silence.

After more drills and some pistol shooting, Jason led them outdoors to the rifle range. Some of the crowd had remained. There wasn't much he could do to clear them out. Thankfully, they stayed back without being told. Jason saw the occasional flash of a reflected binocular lens, but it was better than having them thronging the shooting line.

At the hundred-yard range, they shot with twelve gauge shotguns (at twenty yards) and CAR-15s, the M-16's little brother (at one hundred yards). By this time, Lewis was getting into it, and his accuracy increased with his confidence.

Finally, Jason broke out the sniper rifles, a .308 Remington Model 700 rifle like he had preferred as a SEAL sniper, and Trieu's Dragunov SVD, a gas-operated wood and steel beauty with range-finder scope and ten-round magazine. As he led the team to the range's thousand- yard area, Bigelow carried a spotter scope in his lap.

It was a déjà vu moment for Jason.

Perhaps sensing another competition, the crowd seemed to be drawn forward. Jason kept expecting a TV truck to roll up.

The long-range area had steel silhouette targets at 100, 300, 600, and 1,000 yards. Jason's intention was to let everyone shoot at 300 yards, and then to test Trieu at 1,000. The manager provided mats for them to sit or lie on.

Garth and especially Chris produced nice groupings at three hundred yards with the Remington. Trieu and Jason scored at championship level at that distance. Rachel was actually less accurate here than Lewis, who was starting to swagger a bit. Bigelow fired a few from his chair and convinced Jamie to take one shot.

From behind them, Jason could hear Gene's voice talking to the crowd. The whole group had crept closer. Gene was using binoculars to describe where each shot hit the targets: "Left shoulder," "Eyeball," or "Whiff." The small audience oohed and ahed like it was the Fourth of July.

"Okay, everyone," Jason said, "good shooting. Anybody besides Trieu want to take a try at a thousand yards?"

Everybody looked across the range. A thousand yards was a long way, over half a mile. The row of targets on the downrange hillside was fuzzy with distance. Between the shooters and the targets a creek ran by at the bottom of the hillside, with bushes and small trees growing along it. Windsocks every hundred yards hung mostly limp today.

"I do!" Lewis said. He took the Remington from Jason and brought it to his shoulder.

"No, Lewis," Jason said. "At this distance you have to shoot prone."

Lewis got down on a mat.

"Don't forget to account for wind," Chris said. "And gravity."

"Yeah," Garth said, "and the torque of the rifle. The Model 700's famous for that."

"And the humidity," Chris said.

"Right, right," Jason said, "and the rotation of the earth and the proximity of the moon. Lewis, they're just trying to throw you off. Take aim, lift your crosshairs some to account for the distance, and squeeze off your best shot."

"Okay, Jason, thanks."

"Eyes and ears, people," Jason said.

Lewis took his time aiming but finally fired. The rifle rose off the ground with the recoil. "Whoa!" He rolled over to look at Bigelow. "Did I hit it?"

From behind them, they heard Gene's voice: "Whiff!"

The crowd chuckled.

"Don't listen to them, Lewis," Jason said. "None of them could hit it, either. Chimp, could you see where he hit?"

"Looked low and to the right to me, boss."

"Okay, Lewis, take another shot. This time shoot higher and off to the left to account for the wind."

"I'll try."

His second shot hit something. The faint sound of steel hitting steel floated back to them as the rifle's report was still echoing around the field.

"Another whiff!" Gene said.

"No," Bigelow said, squinting through his spotter's scope. "You nicked the right edge of the target. Congratulations, kid, that was quite a shot."

Lewis looked like he'd won the raffle at the company picnic.

After that, everyone else wanted to take their two shots, too. Chris hit once, but Garth and Rachel missed both times. At Bigelow's insistence, Jamie and Jason got him down to take a prone shot. He nailed the target's chest with his first shot, then decided to waive his other one. The crowd cheered as he got back into his wheelchair.

When he was done, Jason walked over to Trieu, who stared back quietly, her poker face on. "What do you say, champ?" he asked. "Want to give her a go?"

"Against you or with you?"

He smiled. "Good question. No, no competition. I only want to see what you can do."

Bigelow blew through his lips. "Yeah, right. Who'll put money down that the little lady smokes our hero like yesterday's newspaper?"

"I gotcha right here," Gene's friend said, leading the crowd even closer.

"Doug!" Jamie said. "Gambling?"

"Honey, it's only a—"

"No!"

"Oh, all right. Who'll put *Monopoly* money down? Remember, Miss Trieu is a national champion sharpshooter, Silver medallist at the Sydney games, Olympic biathlete in '94 and '98. Smart money's on her. Smart *pretend* money, I mean."

"No, no," Lewis said, facing the crowd. "Don't count our fearless leader out. Champion sniper for SEAL Team Three for six years running. I'll bet you Boardwalk and Park Place that he'll take the prize today."

They waited as the manager rode a three-wheeler out to put out paper circle targets. By the time he'd returned, the fans—plus every member of the team—had placed themselves firmly in either Trieu's or Jason's camp. Rachel and Bigelow were the anti-Jason cheerleaders.

"Shh!" Chris said, a finger in the air and his eyes scanning the range. "Shh."

Jason turned to him. "What is it?"

"Ah, it's gone," Chris said, looking crestfallen. "I was sure I'd heard a yellow-rumped warbler. Never mind."

"A yellow-rumped what?" Garth said over the tittering crowd.

"Warbler," Chris said peevishly. "Extremely rare in this part of Ohio in January."

"Oh, well," Garth said, "then it really is an emergency. Everybody keep an eye out for anything with a yellow rump."

"Oops," Bigelow said, half rising out of his wheelchair, "that would be me. Sorry."

Jason and Trieu walked to the firing line. "You ever do anything but prone at this distance?" he asked.

"Not usually. If I think I'm going to be exposed sometimes I lay back."

"You ever seen the one where you look through the scope upside down?"

"I don't like it," she said. "It's stable out to about seven hundred yards, but not at this distance. Besides, if the target moves your adjustments are backwards."

They went to the mats.

"How many are we shooting?" Trieu asked. "One? Five? Ten?"

"Let's do a ten-shot string in forty-five seconds. That's what you're used to, isn't it?"

"For free rifle, yes. But not at this distance."

"Okay, then what?"

"How about best score in sixty seconds?"

"Any number of shots?" Jason asked.

"As many as you can shoot. Standard scoring."

"Let's do it." He chambered a bullet. He poured out some other bullets on the mat for easy reach. "Doug, give us a sixty second countdown, please."

"You betcha, loser."

Trieu cocked an eyebrow at him. "You want to make this more interesting?"

"Whoa," Jason said, "I thought we weren't competing."

"Well, if you don't think you can shoot with me. . ."

"Oh, no you don't. What did you have in mind?"

"Loser buys five cases of the winner's favorite drink."

He smiled. "You would buy all that Mountain Dew for lil' ol' me?"

"I drink strawberry carrot Sobe," she said, calmly chambering a round. "I can show you where to get the best price on cases."

"You lovers ready to shoot?" Bigelow asked.

"Give us ten-second updates, Chimp, and then count down the last ten."

"Come on little boot," Bigelow said. "Make me some money and do not go to jail!"

"Eyes and ears, everybody," Jason said. He pulled his earmuffs on and brought the Leupold scope to his eye.

Bigelow held Jason's wristwatch in his hand. "Ready, set, go."

The earmuffs helped Jason block out the distractions. It was almost like going underwater. The bright image of the target, crossed by thin black hairs, simplified the world to an array of concentric circles. He'd been assessing the wind and other factors since he'd cracked the guns out of their cases, but now he made a final determination. He quieted his mind, eased his grip, and flipped the rifle off safety. Behind him, he heard Bigelow say *Fifty.*

Beside him, Trieu fired. He resisted the urge to swing over and check her shot. He concentrated on his target. But now he saw an image in his mind's eye. There wasn't a beige paper target before him, but the broad nose and dark features of a man whose black hair was swept back over a high, wrinkled forehead. It was the man Jason had been assigned to shoot in Indonesia.

Jason rolled over to look at Bigelow. His friend looked emaciated all of a sudden. His useless legs lay clamped into the metal contraption that branded him an invalid. All his brave talk was just a front, Jason knew. Half a life for half a man, isn't that what he'd said? *What am I doing here? I don't deserve to be leading this team. I deserve to be dead—or worse, like Doug.*

He saw that his friend was watching him. Though aware that Trieu had fired again, maybe multiple times, and that the crowd was cheering for Trieu or urging him on, all of it disappeared. Only Bigelow's eyes existed. What was back there? How deep did his hatred go? When would it finally come to the surface? *Yes, my plan is the right thing to do. If only to even the score.*

Jason heard Bigelow say *Twenty.* He rolled back to his stomach and found the target in his scope. He fired. The hole was a little high. He loaded another round, adjusted, and fired again. Perfect. He was running on autopilot. Aim, shoot, work the bolt, repeat. Some part of his mind told him he was moving way too fast. By the time Bigelow reached *Zero,* eight shell casings lay on the mat beside him.

Jason got to his knees and took his earmuffs down. Gene and Bigelow and a few others were trying to determine the winner through their optics. Apparently, it wasn't immediately obvious. The range manager roared out on his three-wheeler.

Trieu reached out her hand and Jason shook it. "Strange style, Jason. I thought you weren't going to shoot at all. It threw me off a little."

"Yeah," he said, rubbing his hand down his face. "Me, too. I guess I. . ." He sighed. "Maybe I've still got some things to work through."

She held his gaze. She appeared to be looking for something, as if trying to see whom she was talking to at a masquerade party. Finally she smiled, a gentle expression on her face. She touched his shoulder and began picking up shell casings.

When the manager returned with the targets, Chris and Garth and Bigelow crowded around to score them. Aided by "helpful" comments from the cheap seats, they finally determined that Jason had hit the target more times than Trieu—eight to her six—but that her shots were better, thus giving her the edge in total score.

"Food for Less on Kelly Street," she told Jason with a wink. "Best prices in town."

The crowd razzed Jason mercilessly.

"Okay, you gangsters," Jason said, "show's over here. Let's get these weapons back in their cases."

"What's next on the world tour?" Gene's friend asked.

"You guys don't get it, do you?" Jason asked. "We'd like to have some privacy, okay?"

"Sure, sure," Gene's friend said. "Gene, get in the car. We'll follow them again."

CHAPTER 16

Wheelchair Accessibility

"YOU want to tell me what happened out there on the range?"

Bigelow shifted his eyes from the road and the rearview mirror to see if Jason were going to answer his question.

Jason was sitting in the passenger seat this time. "You mean with Trieu?"

"I mean when you looked back at me instead of shooting."

Jason's eyes unfocused. "Yeah, that was a little weird, wasn't it?"

"Tell me about it. I thought you were having one of those 'I'm back in 'Nam' flashbacks like they show in the movies. Thought you were gonna go postal on us."

They were alone in the Lamoloader. Garth was riding with Chris this time, and Lewis had elected to ride with the girls.

"You're not far off," Jason said. "I dunno, Chimp. When I looked through that scope. . .I think it was the first time I'd looked through one since that day. Something about that black circle and the way the occlusion disappeared at the edges and those crosshairs. . .combined with having to shoot fast and under pressure. I guess it just brought it all back to me. Then when I turned and saw you there in your chair. . ." He blew out a sigh. "I guess maybe I'm not as 'over it' as I thought I was. I'm surprised I hit the target at all."

They rode in silence for a while. Finally Bigelow changed lanes. "I think we've lost our groupies. We'll double back a few more times to be sure, but I think we may finally be on our own. You want me to go to a pool or an obstacle course?"

Jason looked at the sun. It was low in the sky. "Let's skip the pool this time. I'd like to put 'em through an endurance swim to see who's going to give up and who's going to stick it out, but I don't think we have time. The o-course, then."

"Oh, man," Bigelow said, "I was hoping to go for a dip."

"Can you swim?"

"What? Of course I can swim. Once upon a time I was a Navy SEAL, remember?"

"Right. Well, I guess the water would kind of offset your disability some, wouldn't it? I hadn't thought of that. Do you swim much?"

"Sure. Whenever Jamie makes me, which is about twice a month. I get my water wings on and I'm ready for beach infils again."

"I'll bet."

"I'm trying to get her to let me roll my chair off the high dive, but so far no luck."

"Well, we could go by the pool if you want. We'll rig your chair with ropes and haul you up," Jason said. "Garth'll even give you a running push."

"No doubt."

"And I'll bet you could still get up there on your own, Chimp. You earned that name for a reason, remember."

Bigelow nodded slowly. "Maybe I could, in a pinch."

"Well," Jason said, "when we start training, we'll be swimming a lot. You'll have your chance then."

As they came into a busier part of town. Bigelow slowed down.

"Hey, I was thinking: Since me and Jamie will be getting married in five weeks, why don't you just move in with me and the boys until then? After the wedding, they'll have an open spot for you."

"You live with those guys?"

"Sure," Bigelow said. "That's something I advised Eloise to do. Comrades in arms, and all. Believe me, if I could've figured out a way to do it and still be respectable, I'd have had all of us living together, even the ladies."

"I'll bet you thought about that long and hard, didn't you?"

"You know it."

"Well, we'll see," Jason said. "I want to talk to Eloise about where we'll train, so maybe the living situation will take care of itself."

Bigelow turned right.

"Chris and Jamie still with us?" Jason asked.

"Right behind."

Jason watched the town of Green go by. "I think I just want to do one team drill at the o-course."

"Okay. What evil thing were you thinking?"

"I don't know. Something where we have to problem solve and work together for it to work. Maybe when we get to the course I'll have us run laps while you think of something sinister."

"Oh, baby, now you're talking."

"Welcome to Fantasy Island."

Bigelow spread his arms wide and tried to sound like Ricardo Montalban.

The six members of Team Firebrand found him sitting alone at the base of a climbing tower, surrounded by an array of poles, ropes, and harnesses.

"So," Jason said, "have you had enough time to come up with some devilry for us, or should we go run a few more laps?"

"No!" Lewis said. "Please, no."

"Nah, I've had time," Bigelow said.

Jason looked around. "Where's Jamie?"

"Aw, she's mad at me right now," Bigelow said. "She burned rubber out of the parking lot a minute ago."

Rachel folded her arms. "Douglas Bigelow, what did you do that girl? If you made her cry I'm going to make you bleed."

His mouth opened. "Why is it always me? Maybe she did something wrong for a change."

Nobody looked too convinced.

"Okay, it was me. She didn't like my idea for your team challenge."

Chris was already five holds up the face of the wall. "What's not to like about it?"

The YMCA obstacle course consisted of both a high ropes and a low ropes element. The platforms and rope bridges disappeared into the trees on Jason's left and down the hill on his right.

"Okay, Chimp," he said, "what's the drill?"

Bigelow tilted his head toward the tower. "Jace here gave me the idea. He said that one day you guys could rig me up with ropes to get me and my chair up to the high dive so I could roll off into the pool. Garth, he said you would give me a running push."

"No way, baby," Garth said, a black bandana on his head now. "I'd be in your lap all the way down."

Jason looked at the top of the tower. It was a brown wooden beast with wooden climbing holds of various colors dotting its sides like chewing gum on the underside of a school desk. "No, Chimp. Not if you're thinking what I think you're thinking."

The others looked at Jason, at the top of the tower, down at Bigelow, and then at the tower again. Garth whistled in awe.

"Now at least we know why Jamie left," Trieu said.

"Using only what you find lying around," Bigelow said dramatically, like an illusionist describing his next trick, "you must elevate me, my chair, and all six of you to the top of this tower."

"We all have to be there at the same time?" Lewis asked.

"At some point, all of us have to be up there at the same time. But you don't have to arrive there at the same instant."

Garth lifted up a fence post and a jump rope. "With just this stuff?"

"Whatever you find lying around," Bigelow said.

"Trieu, what about it?" Jason asked. "Is this safe? I mean, could we end up really hurting Doug worse than he is now?"

"What are you worried about?" Bigelow asked. "That I'll fall and become paralyzed, chained to a wheelchair the rest of my— Hey, wait a minute. . ."

"Yuk, yuk," Jason said. "But if we drop you, Jamie's going to have all our hides."

"There is no greater danger to him than to the rest of us," Trieu said. "A paraplegic is at no greater risk than anyone else for additional injury. What's done is done."

"All right, then," Jason said. "Let's get to it. How are we going to get this cantankerous cripple to the top of that tower?"

"I've been rock climbing for ten years," Chris said. "I'll just go up and. . ."

"And what?" Lewis asked. "Pull him up? All we have got is a jump rope."

"I'd say that the first thing we need to do," Jason said, walking to the pile of equipment, "is see what we've got to work with."

A careful search of the area yielded a seven-foot jump rope, two six-foot wooden planks, one harness for the high ropes course, a five-foot fence post and a ten-foot pole, two metal carabiners, a two-pound jogging barbell, and a three-foot bungie cord. Plus a pile of sticks, rocks, and soda cans.

Lewis grabbed one of the planks. "What if we used this as a stretcher? We strap him to it with the bungee and lift him hand-to-hand with the rope."

"Are you crazy?" Chris said. "You'd have to have two people at least carrying the board. You'd drop him at the first handoff."

"Then let's hear your great idea," Lewis said.

Chris nodded irritably. "I'm working on it."

"Come on, you two," Rachel said. "Let's work together."

"Jason," Trieu said, looking up. "See how close that platform is?"

"The one from the high ropes course?"

"Yes. And do you see the trapeze?"

Jason followed her pointed finger. "You mean swing him off of that? He'd have to fly twenty feet through the air—at forty feet up. I'm surprised you'd even mention it."

"I wasn't suggesting we swing anyone through the air," she said evenly. "I'm only pointing out our assets."

Jason realized that he'd gotten into a rut already, only looking at what he knew, not looking for opportunities around him. "Okay, Trieu, good thought. Keep looking around. Maybe something will come together. Garth, you're the booby trap man. What would you do to get him up there?"

"Hmm." Garth scratched his chin whiskers. "You ever see *Princess Bride?*"

"Yeah."

"Remember the cliffs of insanity?"

Lewis spoke in a faux Spanish accent: "Hello. My name is Inigo Montoya. You killed my father. Prepare to die."

"In-con-theev-able," Jason said.

"So you want to strap him onto you and you just climb up?" Rachel asked.

Garth flashed his best pirate smile.

"Anybody see why that wouldn't work?" Jason asked.

Lewis was looking up. "But how are the rest of us getting up there? I'm not climbing way up there without some kind of safety rope or something. We don't even have helmets. Aren't you supposed to wear helmets on these?"

Garth grabbed Lewis under the armpits and lifted him over his head. "I'll just come back down and get ya."

"Okay, Garth," Lewis said. "Ha ha. Can I get down now?"

Garth put him down. "Kid, the name of the Lord is a strong tower; the righteous run to it and are safe."

"Uh, okay," Lewis said. "I'll try to remember that."

Trieu pointed up. "What are those wires?"

"For the spotters," Chris said. "Normally you have got a guy holding onto your safety line. If you fall, he has got the rope, and you fly."

"Like a bird, Chris?" Lewis asked, almost innocently. "Seriously, though. Trieu, this isn't safe, is it? Tell them it isn't safe."

"No, it isn't safe," Trieu said. "But neither is going into a war zone, and we've all signed on for that, haven't we?"

"Maybe we should all have our heads examined," Lewis said.

Bigelow cleared his throat. "Hello. You know, I'm starting to get hungry. The sooner you get me up there, the sooner we get to City Club."

"Well, let's get to it," Chris said.

"Wait a minute," Jason said. "Let's be sure there's not a better plan."

They all thought about it. Chris walked a distance into the woods, his ear cocked.

"Are we sure we've looked everywhere?" Trieu asked. "It would be just like Mr. Bigelow to hide a rope ladder under a rock or something."

Bigelow tried, unsuccessfully, to look innocent.

"Let's do another look around," Jason said. "Meanwhile, Chris, you and Garth get Doug rigged up. Take him up first. We'll bring the chair later. Until we have a better plan, we'll go with this one. The sun's almost down."

The search turned up a broken hair bow and twenty-two cents in change.

Garth took his shirt off. He coiled it around the jump rope and slung it across one shoulder. Chris and Trieu put the harness on Bigelow. Jason affixed the jump rope to the harness. Just as Garth was about to lift him out of his wheelchair, Bigelow spoke.

"Oh, there is one other thing. We're on a ship, and it's sinking.

We're climbing to the tower to stay above water. But no one can stay behind, because they'll be swept away."

"What?" Chris said.

"So we can't do our multiple trips?" Jason said.

"Nope."

"You're just making that up!" Lewis said. "You're changing the game because you know I don't want to go up without the harness."

Bigelow spread his hands. "My mistake. Sorry. You're just going to have to figure out how to all get up there together."

"Let's just go!" Chris said. "I'm tired of sitting around. Come on, Rachel. You and me."

"What about me?" Lewis said. "I was going to ride the Garth-evator, too."

"Relax, everybody," Jason said. "Mission objectives change in the field all the time. We've got to be flexible. Come on, we'll get through this. Garth, why don't you get going now? Rachel can climb with Chris. Lewis, you and Trieu can go in front of me. We'll go nice and easy."

Garth lifted Bigelow out of his chair, which promptly fell backward. "Who's going to bring that?" Garth asked.

"I will," Chris said.

"No," Jason said. "I will. You concentrate on Rachel."

As he collapsed the wheelchair down, he heard the echo of his own words. *What did I just tell that rascal to do?* He shook his head and concentrated on using the carabiners and the bungee cord to hang the wheelchair off his waist like a swinging fanny pack.

"Okay, people," he said, "the ship's going down. Everybody at least get on the bottom hold. Get off the ground. And let's spread out. Use all four sides of this thing."

Garth was a monster. His body bulged under the strain of lifting Bigelow, revealing muscles Jason never knew existed. He looked like a medical school anatomy picture in which the muscles had been enlarged for the purpose of illustration. As he ascended the wall,

Bigelow's legs dangled below Garth's feet.

The last Jason saw of Chris and Rachel, they were disappearing around the back of the tower. Trieu decided to climb up on the same side as Garth. That left Lewis and Jason on a side to themselves. The wheelchair swung beneath Jason like Godzilla's tail.

About halfway up the wall, just when things were getting interesting, Lewis froze. Jason could hear Bigelow smarting off to Garth and, on the far side, Chris and Rachel trading flirtatious banter. But Lewis was his responsibility now.

"Talk to me, Lewis."

Lewis's knuckles were even whiter than his skin. Both hands were on holds at his shoulders and his feet were firmly planted. Technically, he was doing fine. But telling him that wouldn't have helped. "I'm gonna fall! Jason! I'm too high. I—I can't do this."

"Okay, buddy," Jason said, climbing up next to him. "You're doing great."

"No, I'm going to fall." He pulled himself as close to the wall as possible. "My leg's got a cramp, Jason!"

"Just think of this as a ladder," Jason said. "You're in a library somewhere and you have to use the ladder to reach the top shelf. The physics of climbing at this height are no different than they were for the steps you've already taken."

"Yeah, but if I fell down there, it wouldn't hurt!"

Jason looked over Lewis's head. "Are you ready for your next hold?"

"Jason! I don't want to go up. I want to go down."

"But the ship is s—"

"Forget about the stupid ship. We're not on a ship, all right, and I'm not playing this game anymore."

Jason grabbed Lewis by the tricep. "No, Lewis. You think this is a game, but it isn't. You think that if you were really in danger you'd make the climb. But let me tell you something: You will fight like you train. If you squirrel out in training, you will squirrel out in combat. And I'm not taking you on any mission if I think you're going to cheese on me, understand?"

Lewis answered by swallowing and looking up—and then down. His frantic eyes turned again on Jason.

"Let me tell you something else," Jason said, trading volume for intensity. "You told me you didn't want to be last at everything today. Well, here's your chance. I have to tell you, Lewis, that right now when I look at you, I see the weakest link in the chain."

That got Lewis's attention. Now he looked mad.

"I know you're a wiz on computers. That's great. You can stay at home and help Doug. But to be honest, I don't really see the point in taking along a kid who can't even climb a flat wall with nice little ergonomic holds laid out just perfectly for him. You're right, Lewis, you should go down. Go on down and I'll consider you out of the team."

"You can't do that. Eloise wouldn't—"

"You wanna bet? And even if she made me take you with me, that doesn't mean I would have to use you. You could hide at the extraction site and wait for us to get back. Take it from me, kid, a team leader can make his people's lives miserable if he wants to."

With that, Jason climbed away quickly. He made the wheelchair bump the wall next to Lewis, just to point out that he was conquering the climb with an added burden and Lewis wasn't even hacking it unencumbered.

At the top of the tower, the corner posts rose above the platform. When Jason pulled himself up, Garth, Bigelow, and Trieu were already there. Bigelow was leaning back on one elbow as if reclining in front of the TV. It was breezy up there.

"Ah, my ride!" Bigelow said. "Set her up and I'll do a wheelie."

"No way," Jason said. "That wasn't part of the mission. You said get you and your chair up here, and that's what we've done. Garth's worked too hard to have you go rolling off because you're fooling around. You just sit there until everybody else makes it."

Trieu sat cross-legged on the platform, as calm as if she were waiting for a bus. "Look," she said, reaching behind her, "we found this at the top."

It was a rappelling rope. Jason looked at Bigelow. "You did this."

He shrugged. "I said you could use whatever you found lying around. I didn't specify lying around *on the ground only.*"

Jason hit him upside the head. "How'd you get it up here?"

"Threw it."

From over the side they heard Chris's voice. "Almost there, sweetie. Almost there."

Chris's hand appeared first, followed by Rachel's head. She grabbed Garth's hand and let him slide her up. Chris released his hand from the back of Rachel's zipper suit and then climbed the rest of the way up. Rachel sat down and leaned against Garth's chest.

Jason held out his hand for Chris to slap. "Welcome to the top, dude."

Chris's nose had almost returned to flesh color. He slapped Jason's hand and looked at him tentatively. "Thanks."

Garth looked around. "Where's little buddy?"

"Oh," Jason said, "I'd better explain that. I'm afraid that from now on I think we should consider Lewis off—"

"I'm right here!" Lewis said, appearing suddenly. "Somebody give me a hand."

Jason and Garth hauled him up.

"Well!" Jason said, laughing. "I didn't think I'd see you up here." He grabbed Lewis's head and gave him a noogy. "Way to go, kid."

"I can't believe I did it!"

"Man," Garth said, looking over the countryside, "this is some view."

Down in the parking lot, Jason spotted a white Camry next to the Lamoloader and Chris's Jeep. A woman was standing beside the car, looking toward them. "Hey, Doug, I think you have a visitor."

Bigelow pulled himself to the edge and waved. "Hi, sweetie!"

Jamie waved back and walked toward the tower.

Trieu was checking Bigelow's pulse. "How are you feeling?"

"Fine. But you're going to have to take my pulse again in a minute. Now that my baby's back my blood pressure will go way down."

"Speaking of down," Lewis said, "let's get down. It's getting dark, and we've got miles to go before I get my Chicken Wellington."

"I thought you wanted New York strip," Rachel said.

"That was when we were going to Lanning's."

Chris tied his shoe firmly. "Well, let's do it."

"Can we use the rope this time?" Bigelow asked. "Garth's starting to stink."

"A rope?" Chris said. "Where'd you get that?"

"Hang on," Jason said. "Let's just take a minute. We've accomplished something here. Let's savor this moment."

They sat silently. Rachel held Garth's hand. Chris cocked his ear.

"This is the first time we've done anything as a team," Jason said. "God willing, it won't be the last. I want to say that I have seen something special in each one of you today, and I want to thank you for working so hard for me. For this moment at least, we're all safe, together, and united."

Jason's skin tingled. He wouldn't have believed that he could feel all googly to be part of a team again, but he did.

"Couldn't we. . .I don't know. . .sing a song or something?" he said. "That's corny, isn't it?"

"I think it's sweet," Rachel said. She began to sing "God Is So Good."

They all joined hands and sang along.

That moment stuck like a snapshot in Jason's mind. The whole team, atop their first conquered challenge, holding hands and singing of God's goodness as the sun dropped beneath the Ohio horizon.

For the first time, Jason wondered if he could go through with his plan.

CHAPTER 17

Akron City Club

"AND then Jason says, 'Don't you guys have jobs?' "

Eloise laughed so hard at Chris's story she bounced in her chair. "You didn't!"

Jason shrugged.

"I swear those guys followed us everywhere," Chris said. "I think I even saw one of them in the lobby downstairs just a minute ago."

The team—plus Eloise, Bigelow, and Jamie—sat at a round table next to the window. Below them, downtown Akron glittered in the night. The Akron City Club was on the top floor of the Bank One building. This part of the restaurant was called the Grille. It was a more casual area than the main dining room down the hall. Though the Grille was officially closed in the evenings, the restaurant had opened it for "Miss Eloise."

A blues quartet—sax, drums, guitar, bass—played by some of Eloise's friends from church, sat in the corner playing something smooth.

Jason smelled the last spanikopita hors d'oeuvre before eating it. It was a spinach and mushroom pastry with feta cheese and onions. He never would've ordered it in a million years, but it smelled amazing and melted on his tongue. He could've eaten another plate full of them.

Everybody looked clean and shiny after time off for showers and dressing up. Trieu sat on his right, elegant in a black velvet gown. Her hair was loose and straight. Though Rachel had stolen his heart—stolen something, anyway—Trieu was a beauty to be reckoned with. He looked at the young ladies around the table. Definite babe-age.

Next to Trieu was Bigelow in a navy coat and tie that Jamie had made him wear. She sat next to him wearing a red spaghetti strap dress and looking ravishing. On her right was Garth in a black suit and green tie. The man could clean up real well, except now he looked like Jesse Ventura. Eloise sat next to him wearing a bright magenta dress and wrap. Next to her sat Chris, looking like a total lady-killer in a perfectly fitted gray suit and silver tie. His hair had been freshly styled, so the trademark curl was in its proper place.

Then came Rachel. She wore a short white dress that fit close enough to hint at the near-perfect form beneath it, but not so close as to give anything away either. It had a scoop neck and white straps. She had her hair down. Dark locks came over her shoulders to frame her angular jaw line. Black stone earrings. Makeup masterfully applied. Very high heels.

It was all Jason could do to keep from staring at her all night long. But even when he looked away, she remained in his periphery. What a chump he was. Could he command a woman like this in a military squad? Could he send her into harm's way? Could he keep from taking stupid risks in order to win her from Chris and Garth? This was something he'd not had to deal with as a SEAL.

Then between Rachel and Jason was Lewis. He wore a black tuxedo exactly like the maitre d's. Despite his unfortunate haircut, he managed to look pretty sharp.

Jason had to say that he was looking fine himself. They'd gone back to the guys' apartment to change, and Chris had let him try on his pick of James Bond quality suits. He chose a handsome brown worsted wool suit that probably looked better on Chris but that fit Jason well and saved him from having to wear his sneakers and blue jeans.

"So you took them to the firing range, Jason?" Eloise asked.

"Yes, ma'am."

"I had a notion you might. What did you find out?"

"More of what I'd seen on the track and in the gym. And what I saw again at the tower."

"And what was that?" Eloise watched him over her last bite of Caesar's salad.

Jason noticed that everyone's eyes were on him. "That you have assembled a very fine team. A team with the potential to actually pull off some of the missions you might have in mind for them to attempt."

"Hmm," Eloise said, smiling. "Then I guess they've shown you a good time today?"

"Let's see," Jason said. "In one day, I've been shot with a pepperball gun, deceived by a bunch of play actors—I'm gonna have to talk to you, Rachel, about your split personalities—reunited with a church lady, given a chance to join a team again, and taken to Q's secret weapon's lab. I've seen Trieu beat me in sniping, Chris punch me in the eye, Garth tell me about how his mom died at just the right time to keep him out of the army, Doug dangling from a climbing wall, and Lewis deciding he really likes guns after all. I'd say it's been a pretty full day."

"And hey," Bigelow said, "the night is young!"

"What about me?" Jamie asked. "You skipped what you saw me do today."

"Hmm," Jason said. "Well, I saw the black marks you left on the YMCA parking lot. I saw that you swerve your car to the music on the radio. And I see how you hold my best friend's hand whenever you can."

"Oh, my," she said, blushing. "You were watching, after all."

"Hey now," Bigelow said. "Just you pay attention to some of these other fine looking women and keep your eyes off of my fiancée."

"Oh, that's rich coming from you," Garth said.

"What's that supposed to—"

Their waiter arrived with their food. "Very hot plates, everyone." Using a cloth napkin as a hot pad, he laid the dishes out.

Jason got the chicken breast stuffed with sun dried tomato and boursin cheese. He had no idea what boursin cheese was, but he figured it must be edible or they wouldn't be serving it. He'd eaten grasshoppers before, so no matter what, this wouldn't be the worst thing he'd ever eaten.

"All right, children," Eloise said. "Who wants to lead us in prayer? Trieu, how about you this time?"

Trieu lifted her chin. "Very well, Mrs. Webster. Let us pray. Dear Lord, thank You for bringing these men and women together and for the task You have set before us. We can do nothing apart from You. Lord, we dedicate ourselves to You. Thank You for this food and this time of fellowship. Amen."

"Amen."

For a while, all conversation ceased. The quartet played *Born for Bad Luck*. The guitar player sang directly to Eloise, or so it seemed. Jason's chicken was fantastic, juicy and tender. The boursin turned out to be a creamy spread flavored with garlic and pepper.

"So, Jason," Eloise said, dabbing her mouth with a white cloth napkin, "when can you move out here?"

"Well, let's see. It will take at least a month to clean out my seven-bedroom home and help the servants find other employment. Then another two weeks for the summer home. Not to mention having the yacht delivered. And my collection of Fabergé Eggs can't be moved by any old moving company. Ooh, we're looking at a good three months, I'd say."

"Chris," Eloise said, "you hit him before. Care to do it again?"

"With pleasure, ma'am."

"Okay, okay," Jason said. "Hoo, I don't know—a day? The biggest problem would be selling my boat or getting a trailer for it. And getting my truck out here. If I started packing tomorrow when I got back. . .I'd need a day, I guess, to get out of my apartment, check out of my bank, and—maybe if I got an advance on my salary?—pay off a few debts and buy a boat trailer. I think I could be in the truck Thursday morning on my way out east. I could be here by the weekend."

The waiter came with a new basket of bread and refilled everyone's water.

"What kind of training do you have in mind?" Eloise asked. "And how long before you think my babies will be ready for a mission? There are several *situations* brewing right now."

Jason swallowed a bite of chicken. "Ah, I need to talk to you about that. We need to find someplace else to train."

"What?" Lewis said.

Rachel and Eloise looked surprised, too. Jamie looked alarmed. The ex-special forces guys nodded and kept chewing.

"Why?" Eloise asked. "What's wrong with Akron? Didn't you just find everything you needed today? I was thinking of renting out that firing range indefinitely."

"The main thing wrong with Akron, ma'am, is the altitude. What are we here, a thousand feet above sea level? Fifteen hundred feet?"

Bigelow carved his filet. "Twelve hundred."

"So?"

"So, if you train low you can't operate at high altitude. But if you train high, like between eight and twelve thousand feet, you can operate anywhere, high or low."

Eloise stared into space over Jason's shoulder, as if there were a map of the United States floating there. "But where would you go?"

Jason reached for some bread. "I was thinking Idaho or Utah. Anywhere over eight thousand."

Eloise clicked her tongue. "Well, I declare. Trieu, honey, is there any sense in what this boy is saying?"

"Definitely. If we were to be acclimated to somewhere low, say around here, and then try to conduct a mission anywhere higher, we'd be dealing with altitude sickness instead of conducting the mission. Acute mountain sickness could incapacitate the whole team within forty-eight hours."

"Didn't you train at altitude for biathlon?" Garth asked her.

"Always."

Eloise swirled the iced tea in her glass. "Somewhere high, he says."

"But as for training time before we're ready to even think about a mission," Jason said, "I'd guess six months. We've got to—"

"Six months?" Eloise said. "No, I want you out saving lives in four weeks, tops! I've waited and planned for this for years. Getting you to see sense was the last piece of the puzzle. Now you all need to get out there and start making good things happen. The world's falling apart, and some of these situations I'm watching will not wait six weeks, much less six months."

She started mumbling. "Oh, no. Uh-uh. Six months, he says. Ha! I'll give him six months of the back of my hand. Those babies need help now, is what I'm saying. Not in no six months."

Jason waited for her to stop. When it didn't look like she was going to, he interrupted. "No, ma'am. No can do. Look, even a fully trained SEAL team needs two months from mission assignment to execution. You need at least six weeks to gather intel and plan and train for that specific mission. Then you need another two weeks to acclimate to the location. And this group is not anywhere near that level of readiness.

"Eloise," Jason continued, "for centuries, people have been in need of the kind of help you're wanting to provide. You're putting together a team that can help. That's wonderful! Praise God for you.

But trust me: There will still be the need for such a team in eight months to a year. Bad guys will keep being bad, and good people will keep getting hurt by them. I'm sorry about the people we can't help in the meantime, but people like them have been without hope for a long time. We'll get the next ones, don't worry."

She looked like she was either about to cry or dump the table over. "Get the next ones? Am I paying for this team or am I not?"

"You are. But I'm telling you that if you send these people out too early, you won't be helping anybody. Those 'situations' you keep talking about will only get worse—and you will have thrown away the best chance for helping them or others like them.

"No, ma'am. People like you've got here at this table are not easy to replace. It's like what Jesus said about new wine in old wineskins. You do that and you'll lose both the skins and the wine. You send this team out and you may not only *not* help the people you want to save, you may lose your team, too. Am I getting through to you?"

Her eyes flared. She looked like a bull about to skewer a toreador.

"Big Mama," Garth said in as gentle a voice as Jason had ever heard him use.

"What!"

"Now, I know your heart, and I know all you want to do is get out there and help people. Don't get mad at me, but I do think you need to listen to what the man's saying."

She turned on him. "You think what?"

"No, Miss Eloise," Chris said. "He's right."

"You, too?"

"Special forces units are constantly training," Chris said. "All military units are. To ask them to go into battle before they're ready is to basically hand them over to be massacred."

"Look around the table, Eloise," Jason said. "These are your babies, remember? Well, if you put a baby behind the wheel of a moving car, would you expect him to do fine?"

Eloise pushed her plate away and mumbled. Jason heard "big for his britches" at least once.

"So you want six months and you want someplace higher? Ohio ain't good enough for you now. Anything else you want? Maybe you want to study over in Spain for a few years to think about it?"

"No," Jason said. "Nothing else. Except for everything I ask of you in training."

"Oh, just everything you ask of me."

"Uh-huh. And it's not six months, it's eight."

"Eight!"

"Six before we're ready to think about a mission. Two more to train and plan for that mission and to get over there and get acclimated."

"Eight months! I'll be an old woman in eight months!" She turned to Rachel and Trieu. "Come on, girls, back me up here. What you think about this *eight months?"*

Jason noticed Trieu cover a smile. Apparently he wasn't the only one amused by the way Eloise could wag her head.

"I think," Rachel said, glancing quickly at Jason, "that we all want to be out there as fast as we can so we can start helping people who are getting hurt."

General nodding around the table.

"But I also think that what we're going to do is dangerous. And anytime you're facing something dangerous, you ought to be as prepared for it as you can be." She stared into her iced tea. "I went on missions that we'd trained ten months on before executing. And even then we could've used more."

Eloise raised her eyebrows at Trieu. "And you?"

"I don't know how long it would take to train us for a military mission. Maybe six months is too long. Maybe it's not long enough. But when I agreed to help you, I knew there would be some training time. There has to be. If I'm going to be using scuba gear or jumping out of an airplane, I certainly want to know what I'm doing before I enter a dangerous place where people might be shooting at me."

Eloise looked deflated. "All right, all right. Eight months. That seems too long. And I'll look for someplace higher for you to train. And, yes, you hoodlum," she said to Jason, "I'll give you whatever you want for training. Within reason! I'm not a trillionaire, you know."

The jazz quartet launched into an upbeat tune. The guitarist announced it was called "Here to Stay."

Garth pushed back from the table and stood. "Come on, Big Mama, let's cut a rug."

Eloise smiled and shooed him away with her hand. But then she stood and went with him to an open spot on the beige and burgundy carpet. There he took her hand and they commenced to boogie the old-fashioned way.

"Sweetie," Chris said to Rachel. "May I have this dance?"

She drained her glass and stood. "Why, Christopher, I would be delighted."

"Hey, baby," Bigelow said to Jamie. "Let's show 'em what this rig can do."

Jamie giggled and walked with him to the floor. Bigelow did a complete double spin and then did figure eights around Jamie while she kept a hand on his shoulder.

Jason looked at Trieu and Lewis. "Trieu, I'd ask you to dance, but I don't want to leave Lewis alone at the table. Plus, I'm not really any good."

"Ah, I don't mind," Lewis said. "I'm no good, either."

"What a sad story you two have," Trieu said. "Come on, Lewis, I'll show you some steps. And then on the next song you can steal Rachel away from Chris."

"Oh, okay"

Jason watched his friends cavort on the dance floor. Garth was surprisingly graceful and Eloise surprisingly nimble. Aside from the Laurel and Hardy size mismatch, they made a pretty good dance pair. Chris and Rachel looked like the prom king and queen. Next to Chris, Jason felt like a buck-toothed freshman. How could he compete?

Even Lewis managed to look less dorky than usual when paired with Trieu, his heel-bounce actually making him look light on his feet. But Jason was pretty sure it was Trieu's presence that made the difference. She exuded dignity the way Rachel overflowed with pizzazz.

It was fitting that he was on the outside looking in, he thought. *If you're planning to leave someone, in your heart, haven't you already stepped on the outside?*

When the song ended, the band segued into a lilting slow blues number called "Buddy's Blues."

Chris pulled Rachel close. She seemed to like it, but Lewis was right there, tapping on his shoulder. Jamie sat on Bigelow's lap and laid her cheek on his forehead. Garth escorted Eloise back to her chair and sat down with a whoop.

As Trieu returned to the table, Jason stood. "May I have this dance, my lady?"

She smiled. "Certainly, gentle knight."

He took her hand and put his other hand on her back, trying to be debonair. He led her in a simple step, the only one he knew.

Smitten as he'd become with Rachel, there was no denying the impact of Trieu's closeness. She wore a perfume that reminded Jason of apricots. She moved easily in his arms. He'd danced with girls who'd made him feel like a klutz. With Trieu he felt like Astaire.

How long had it been since he'd been this close to a girl? He realized that this was the closest he'd been to a woman since he'd come to Christ. No wonder he was so puddin-headed around them: All he had were bad habits and bad memories. But these were nice girls. He didn't know how to act. It was sure going to be a shame to leave them.

He looked into Trieu's black eyes. "So how does a nice Vietnamese sniper like you come to be in a place like this?"

"You mean on the Firebrand team?"

"That, and shooting for America, and not in the Olympics anymore. All of it."

"Oh, dear. I don't think this song is long enough for that story."

"Then maybe we should dance to another. As many as it takes." *What are you saying, meathead?*

She looked at him mischievously, "Why, Jason Kromer, did you just make a pass at me?"

He felt the rhythm drain out of him as quickly as the blood was probably draining from his face. Rather than stomp on her expensive shoes, he just stopped moving. "I don't know. I think maybe I did. I'm sorry."

She laughed and got him moving again. "Oh, never mind. I think it's nice. Besides, I know what you've got in your crosshairs."

He sputtered. "Well, I. . .You see. . .When you. . ."

She smiled. "Dance, silly."

He danced.

"To answer your question, I never was a sniper for Vietnam. I was an air gun shooter for their Olympic team. My mother, on the other hand, was a very successful sniper during the war. Legendary in my province. She shot for Vietnam's team, too. From the time I was very small, she was putting air rifles in my hand. I made the team somewhat by default."

Jason humphed. "I don't think that's all it was, young lady. You shoot like nobody's business."

"Thank you, Jason," she said, seeming genuinely flattered. "But I wanted out of it. Out of Vietnam, out of the pressure of the Olympics, out of the politics of international sports. At the competitions, they kept very close watch on us, but I was able to make contacts with one of the American coaches. It took years, but we were finally able to change my citizenship to this country. My mother would've died, but she was already dead.

"I shot for America for a while. As payment, I suppose. But I found that the politics and pressure were the same no matter who I was shooting for. While I was on the Olympic team, one of my teammates introduced me to Jesus Christ. My mother would've died about that, too."

"Is this a common theme?" Jason asked. "Upsetting your mother?"

She smiled. "You are perceptive."

"What about becoming a doctor? Did you do that to upset your mom, too?"

"No," she said quietly. "That was something I did for me."

For a moment, they simply danced. Jason didn't know if she was enjoying being close to him, but he knew he was sure enjoying himself. There was something invigorating about the mix of her closeness, the day's rollercoaster, and the bass guitar resonating inside his chest. Who needed alcohol to be intoxicated?

"Anyway," she said finally, "as soon as the Sydney games were over, I dropped out of the team. Now it was my coach's turn to die, almost." She shrugged slightly. "Who knows? Maybe I'll shoot in competition again."

"And the biathlon?"

"I picked that up when I became an American. Seemed like a good way to stay in shape in winter and keep my skills up."

The band was in what sounded like a final time through the chorus.

"So how did you come to join this team?"

"Mrs. Webster heard about me somehow. I think it was one of the articles that came out about me not repeating in the biathlon for Salt Lake City. She flew me out here and we had a long talk. A very long talk. At the end of it, I joined the team. In a way, even after all that I've done, I think it wasn't until I joined that I finally found my purpose." She looked at him seriously. "Do you know what I mean, Jason?"

He smiled. "I think I do."

The song ended and everyone clapped.

"Thank you for dancing with me," Jason said. "I enjoy talking with you, Trieu."

Her smile came more from her eyes than her mouth. "I enjoyed dancing with you, as well."

The band went into a jazzy song with lots of saxophone. Jason led Trieu back toward the table but was intercepted by Bigelow. Somehow Jamie had allowed him to dance with someone else. Garth—curse him, too—spun Rachel out to the carpet. And Lewis danced with Jamie. Eloise went to stand with the band.

That left Chris and Jason alone at the table.

"Your eye's looking all right," Chris said. "It may not go black after all."

Jason touched his cheekbone gingerly. "I don't know. I'll bet it does. And your nose looks fine."

Chris munched on a piece of bread. "You know, I've never been beaten before."

"I know."

"It's not an easy thing to get over."

Jason nodded.

Bigelow was riding a wheelie and spinning, showing off for Trieu—and, it seemed, for Rachel. Jamie was countering by seriously getting down with Lewis. The poor kid was trying to get the groove but lacked the genetic sequencing for true rhythm. Garth and Rachel looked like they could be on an MTV dance show.

Jason looked at Chris. "So you were married and then divorced?"

"That's right. Biggest mistake of my life."

"Which? Getting married or getting divorced?"

"Both. Stupid to get married when I wasn't really ready for it. Jennifer deserved better than me. Oh, we got into some fights that made that little tussle today between you and me seem like the Romper Room. But she was a good woman, and I had no right to leave her alone like I did."

He took a deep drink from his water glass. "And then I was stupid to let her get away."

"Any chance of getting her back?"

Chris smiled ruefully. "No way. She's married to a missionary now. They've got five kids and are living in Tanzania. Besides, she'd rather eat road kill than talk to me."

"Tanzania, huh? Maybe we'll run into her on a mission."

He laughed unexpectedly hard at that. "Maybe so."

"It sounds like it's still unresolved."

"Yeah, you could say that."

"Then you need to at least get that fixed. I'll pray that you have the chance."

Chris looked at him curiously. "Uh, thanks, I guess."

"As long as you've got something unresolved, it's like a tether holding you to it. You won't ever be able to move on until you do." Jason wasn't so much counseling Chris as trying to formulate something for himself.

"Hmph. Maybe you're right. But for now," he said, sweeping his hand toward the dance floor, "I'm loving life."

The song ended. The waiter and a busboy came in to clear dishes.

"All right," the guitarist said. "We're gonna play one more song for you folks tonight. By special request," he said, looking at Eloise, "a nice slow dance tune by a woman named Sade. It's called 'No Ordinary Love.' "

Somehow Jason found himself standing in front of Rachel. The others might've been sitting or dancing or gone, he didn't know. All he knew was that this was a moment they'd had coming since she first ran into him on the elevator. From the way her huge eyes stared back at him and did not look away, it looked like she felt it, too.

He slid an arm behind her and pulled her close. As the band sang about a spectacular love—slipping away—she leaned in to him and brought her head to rest on his shoulder.

"I wondered if you'd ever ask me to dance," she said.

He swallowed. Her dress felt like gauze to his touch. She smelled like roses. He was exquisitely aware of every place their bodies touched. In a minute, he was going to have to dump ice water over his head.

He found his voice after a century's absence. "I've wanted to be this close to you since the moment I laid eyes on you."

She looked up at him. "I thought you didn't like me."

He almost laughed. "Are you kidding? I've been thinking about you all day. And watching you."

"But you never sat by me. You hardly ever spoke to me. You never challenged me to any kind of duel or anything like you did the others. You kept pairing me up with Chris."

"Huh, he did that one all by himself. Anyway, what about you? You've been flirting with Chris and Garth and Lewis all day. Even the firing range manager got it better from you than I did. All you did to me was cut me down: 'Do you treat everyone this way?' 'No, only the ones we don't like.' Duct tape over the mouth. Remember? What was all that about?"

"I was only teasing you." She looked away. "It's. . .one of the ways I know how to talk to men."

"Oh," he said, amazed at his own eloquence.

She kept her eyes averted. "Back at the firing range, when you said I'd done a good job. Did you mean it?"

"Well, yeah. I mean, you really surprised me." He licked his lips. "But Rachel, it seems to me that you, with your. . .you know. . .and your. . .I mean, I just think that there's probably not much you can't do if you put your mind to it. I mean, look at you. You're beautiful, you're smart, you're a talented actress. Oh, my. The world's got to be your oyster."

She smiled softly. Not the usual saucy smile, but a tenuous thing that she probably wore when she was six. She put her head on his chest. "You're something else, you know that, Jason Kromer?"

What did that mean? Something else good or something else bad? Something else like not a person but really a space alien? Something else like no one she'd ever met before? His mind would play Twister if he let it, so he didn't. Judging from her body language he had to conclude that *something else* was a good thing. Rachel was in his arms, laying her cheek against his chest. Her dress felt like gauze, and she smelled like roses. Forget everything else.

"Rachel, tell me about what happened with the Komemiute," he said. "And how you came from the embassy in Paris to be working with—"

"Shh." Her finger touched his lips. "Shut up and dance."

He shut up and danced.

When the song began to wind down, she lifted her head and spoke to him in a language he didn't know. It sounded like an Asian tongue at first, like maybe Korean, but it had many guttural *sch* sounds, which Rachel somehow managed to make sound pleasant. He decided it must be Hebrew. She spoke softly for what seemed like a full minute. The whole time her eyes watched his nervously. Somehow he knew that she was telling him something very close to her heart. She stopped when the music did.

"Rachel, I have no idea—"

Her finger was on his lips again. A tantalizing smile. "One day I'll tell you. Maybe."

Then everyone was gathering coats and purses. The band was packing up. Lights were going out. Rachel disengaged from him and went to get her wrap.

As everyone filed out toward the elevators, Jason found himself in the rear of the pack, walking next to Eloise. She took his arm and rubbed it.

"You've been on a long road, haven't you, baby?" she said softly. "Welcome home."

Part IV

Dry Tears of the Earth

CHAPTER 18

DAMIRA

WHY are they all sleeping on the ground?

Damira woke from the dream confused and anxious. Fear was just around the corner of her mind. Any moment it would leap at her.

She decided that she must not have cried out because none of the other girls had awakened. Luda was snoring, as usual. They'd finally convinced Miss Ashirova to put Luda in the corner at night, but now it sounded even louder. All around Damira was a lumpy sea of sleeping girls. It brought back an image from her dream that troubled her, so she got up.

There was no way she could make it to the door without waking somebody up, so she headed for the window behind Saule's bed. She pulled the curtain aside gently, careful not to tear off any more rings, and looked into the Kazakhstani night.

Damira had heard of cities with so much electricity glowing that you couldn't tell the difference between night and day. That wasn't a problem in Baikonur City. The lights were always on at the Sputnik Hotel, of course, and certainly out at the Cosmodrome they had every convenience. But the rest of the residents used candles at night or went without.

The window was cold, and it seemed like she never really got warm during the winter. At the right edge of her vision she could see a deeper blackness where the Syr Darya—the river of life—flowed by. The steppe pulsated faintly. Perhaps she would hear a rocket launch tonight. She thought she caught a popping sound, like fireworks, but she didn't hear it again.

Yelena's feet were sticking out sideways from her bed. Damira moved the little girl's body back onto her mattress and covered her up. Then she went back to her own bed.

She was awakened some time later by a commotion at the door. Natalya and Ainura were peeking out into the hall. Damira heard bare feet slapping in the concrete hallway. *Clank.* The stairwell door! Feet slapped louder, and Roza appeared and collided with Natalya. All three of them ran back into the room and dove onto their beds.

Several girls woke up.

"Roza, what is it?" Damira hissed in Russian.

"There are men downstairs!" Roza said.

"Oh," Ainura said, sounding disappointed. "Only a delivery."

"No!" Roza said. "They were dressed as peasants. Villagers. I even saw an Egyptian, I think!"

"How close did you get, Roza?" Natalya asked.

"All the way to the bottom of the stairs. And," she said, making sure her audience was with her, "they all had guns."

The girls gasped. Renata started to whine piteously. Damira went to sit on Renata's bed.

"Are they soldiers?" someone asked.

"Is there a war?"

"Maybe they're robbers."

"My father was killed in a war."

"Don't get worked up," Ainura said. "Nothing exciting ever happens around here."

The chatter got so loud that even Luda woke up. "What, breakfast already?"

"Shh!" Damira said. "Miss Petrova will come with her stick."

That hushed all forty girls. But when there was no sound of anyone coming, the chatter rose again.

Behind them, Yelena screamed. She was looking out the window, pointing and screaming. She seemed to have lost the ability to speak.

The girls bounded from bed to bed, mostly avoiding the few girls still lying down, and crowded around the window.

Where before Damira had seen dark flatland, now there was a horde of people and trucks. The people, bundled against the cold, carried torches and rifles. The trucks were full of villagers gawking up at the buildings, including the orphanage. The firelight revealed faces made ugly by anger. Anger at what?

"Look!" Roza shouted.

As they watched, the two-story apartment house down the street leapt into flame. Men ran up the street tossing torches onto roofs. Others broke windows and tossed the torches inside. Smoke poured out of windows. Families straggled outside in their bedclothes and fell to the ground coughing.

Most of the girls were screaming.

Still the people kept coming, swarming around the orphanage and into the city. Headlights stretched down the Syr Darya as far as Damira could see. Four houses were on fire.

Two police cars and the fire truck screamed onto the scene, but the people didn't make way for them. A police car, its lights flashing, tried to push against the sea of people. But the people pushed back. They climbed onto the hood. They began rocking the car.

As the girls watched, the mob gathered at one side of the police car and flipped it over. They kicked at it and bashed it with sticks and shot at it. A policeman crawled out of the car and tried to retreat to the other car and the fire truck, both of which were already backing away. But the people held onto him. They beat him with their fists and kicked him when he fell. Then someone raised a rifle and shot him.

With that, a line was crossed. The mob went into a frenzy, destroying and burning and shrieking so loudly that Damira could hear it through the glass. The girls screamed and bolted for the hallway.

Damira and Roza passed the others as they went down the frigid, echoing stairwell. Together they threw open the door to the downstairs living room.

Seven adult faces turned toward them. Four of the five ladies who worked at the orphanage were standing against the wall, crying. Three men stood in a line in front of them, frightening looking weapons in their hands. Miss Ashirova lay on the brown carpet, not moving.

Damira didn't recognize the men. Two wore the traditional wool coat, earth tone breeches, and billed chapeau of ethnic Kazakhs. Except for the guns, they looked like fishermen. The third must have been the one Roza said was an Egyptian. His face seemed very white and his beard and eyebrows very dark. He was dressed in a long beige tunic and unbuttoned brown vest, and he wore a gray turban.

He said something in a language Damira didn't know.

One of the fishermen translated into Russian. "How many children are there?"

Damira noticed that the women—Miss Petrova, Mrs. Ignatenko, and Yulia, the young university student volunteer—were staring at the ground. Only Katie, the Peace Corps volunteer from America, looked the men in the eye. She'd never seen Katie look scared before. Finally, it occurred to Damira that they weren't safe. She backed away, but the press of girls behind prevented her escape.

The Egyptian took Katie's chin in his hand and shouted at her.

Katie struggled against his hand. "We have forty-two girls in this house."

The fisherman translated, and the Egyptian asked another question. "How old? And where are the boys?"

"Three to nine," Katie said. "We send the boys to Almaty."

The fisherman translated. Then he said, "He wants to know if you are an American."

She nodded.

"You others," he said, "you look Russian to me."

The three other women didn't look up.

"They're Kazakhs," Katie said, "just like you."

"No!" the other fisherman said, brandishing his rifle. "Not like us. You live in a nice building. You have lights and heat and shoes. You are not sick. You have our Syr Darya. You are not like us!"

Then the Egyptian walked toward the girls. They screamed and ran for the stairs. But he caught Damira by the arm.

"Leave her alone!" Katie said, pulling at his hand.

He backhanded her to the face. She hit her head against the wall and slid to the floor, momentarily stunned. The women wailed. Yulia dropped down to cradle Katie's head. The front door was open, letting in an icy wind and the sounds of mayhem.

"Please," Yulia said, her Slavic eyes downcast, "do not hurt our girls. Please leave us in peace. You can have whatever you want, but leave our—"

One of the fishermen shot a bullet into the ceiling.

The Egyptian let Damira go. She went to Katie and they hugged. It appeared that the men were disagreeing about something. They gestured to the women, the stairwell, and the door to the street. Finally they reached an agreement.

The Egyptian grabbed Katie by the arm and brought her to her feet. He pried Damira away and shoved her toward the stairwell. With his other hand, he yanked Yulia to her feet.

The fishermen lifted their weapons. "Death to Russians." Then they shot the other two women.

Katie and Yulia screamed and thrashed against the Egyptian. Damira couldn't move. She couldn't tear her eyes from the bodies of her caretakers or the lines of blood sliding like raindrops down the wall.

Why were they all sleeping on the ground?

One of the fishermen grabbed Katie and dragged her outside.

The Egyptian pulled Yulia to himself and pawed at her hair. He said something to her that sounded mean and yanked her toward the door to the street.

"Damira!" Katie shouted from the street, fighting against her captor. "Oh, dear Lord, the children! Damira!"

And then they were gone. The door slammed shut. Damira found herself alone with three dead bodies. It seemed as though she were still in her dream. Maybe she could just wake up.

She heard the sound of breaking glass. From the stairwell she heard the girls scream again. They came rushing down the stairs, running blindly like startled sheep. They saw the workers on the floor and screamed again. The near ones tried to flee back up the stairs and the far ones pushed into the room.

"Fire!" someone shouted. "There is fire upstairs!"

Outside something exploded. Shadows jabbed across the curtains of the living room windows. Fire and shouts and sirens and gunshots raged beyond the wall of the orphanage.

Luda came down the stairs coughing. "Yelena and Liliya!" she shouted. "They're upstairs. They won't come down. The fire is coming closer to them!"

That broke Damira out of her daze. "Roza, take the—Roza, look at me. Get the girls outside."

"No, we can't go outsi—"

"The building is on fire, Roza! We have to get out. You have to get the girls outside. Go to the church. Natalya, get all the coats and shoes from the closet and bring them outside. You and Ainura. Go now!"

Damira pushed past the girls and ran up the stairs.

Already smoke was thick at the ceiling. She ducked her head and ran toward their bedroom. She could hear the fire crackling.

In their bedroom, the curtains were blazing, billowing in the cold wind blowing through the broken window. The beds beside the window were churning with gray smoke and orange flame.

"Yelena!" she shouted. "Liliya! Where are you?"

No answer.

She put her arm to her nose and breathed through her sleeve. The room that never warmed up was finally too hot for her. She waded through the beds, her eyes watering uncontrollably.

She added real tears when she couldn't find the two little girls. The fire reached across the ceiling and up the walls. She crawled into the hallway, every breath stinging and her eyes blurry. As she passed the bathroom, she heard a tiny cough.

There in the bathtub were Yelena and Liliya, holding each other and waiting to die.

Somehow Damira managed to pull them onto the tile and into the hallway. When she got to the stairway, the two girls ran down on their own. Damira watched their little bodies recede and was glad they would be all right.

Then she decided it wasn't such a bad thing after all to sleep on the ground. She laid her head down on the cool floor. Once, she thought that strong arms were carrying her up to heaven. But it was probably only a dream.

CHAPTER 19

Live Fire

Lewis kept his MP-5 pointed at the ground. He crept up to where Chris crouched behind a bush, his peppergun rifle held at the ready.

"Librarian, this is Bookworm," Lewis whispered into his microphone. "How copy?"

"Copy fine, Bookworm." Jason's voice was hushed as if he were trying not to spook an elk.

"Librarian, Bookworm is in position."

"Copy, Bookworm. Hang tight."

"Copy."

Lewis raised his left fist to tell Chris to stay put. Chris saw the signal but appeared not to like the idea.

Lewis checked the MP-5 in his hand. The safety was on, and the thirty-round clip of tranquilizer darts was ready to roll. He settled into a waiting crouch and wondered what everyone else was doing. If he'd been allowed to use his gear, he would know.

Jason watched the enemy camp through binoculars. Forty yards of dense white fir stood between him and the objective, but he and Trieu had found a small mountain lake to look across. They had a clear view of the target.

"Do you have a shot?" he asked Trieu.

She was flat on the ground staring through the scope on a CAR-15. "Yes. I count four hostiles. Can't tell if there are more. Maybe some inside the tent. I've got the leader in my sights."

Jason keyed his microphone. "All units, this is Librarian. Count at least four hostiles at objective. How copy?"

Lewis and Rachel both said they'd received the message.

"Patron," he said to Rachel, "where are you? Your books are overdue. Over."

"Copy, Librarian," Rachel said softly. "Coming into position now. Had to avoid a. . .a snake. Over."

Jason and Trieu shared a smile. "Understood, Patron. Report when you're in position."

"Copy, Librarian."

"And everybody remember: We still have to get out of here when we're done," Jason said. "Don't forget the possibility of hostiles in our exfil zone."

He heard Garth's comment over Rachel's headset: "Yeah, right."

"Chris!" Lewis hissed. "What are you doing? We're supposed to wait for Trieu to hit the paper tar—"

Chris brought a finger up. His face was lined horizontally with green and black camouflage paint. Lewis almost couldn't tell where his makeup ended and his camo uniform began. He shuffled close to Lewis, his white eyes fierce through the greasepaint.

"Come on, partner," he said, managing not to choke on the word. "Let's show them how it's done. We'll take down the whole camp before the other team's even in position."

"I don't know. . ."

"Lewis, we can do this. You've gotten pretty good with that thing. We'll do it just like we practiced. I'll knock 'em down; you knock 'em out."

"But what about—?"

Too late. Chris was already rounding the bush. Lewis followed.

They sprang into the enemy camp like Bengal tigers. The enemy didn't even seem to react. Chris plugged the nearest target with a three-shot burst of the peppergun and was on to the others before Lewis could follow up with the tranquilizer darts that would take them out of commission for the duration.

Lewis swung around to tranq the others, but something struck him in the neck and he heard a high-pitched *tcht.* "Ow!" Even as he felt at his neck he heard the projectile fall to the ground. Trieu's tranquilizer dart. "Chris. Chris!"

Chris was shooting at something inside the enemy's tent and didn't respond.

Lewis finished tranquilizing the other soldiers, but his thoughts were getting sticky. From across the lake behind him, he thought he heard someone shout. Jason seemed to be speaking Japanese in the speaker in his ear. Garth and Rachel burst out of the trees on the other side of the camp. They looked at him in surprise.

Then, for some reason, Lewis was lying down, staring up through the treetops at the nice blue sky.

"Man down! Man down!" Garth shouted.

Jason held the headset away from his ear. He and Trieu were running toward the site. "Stay calm, everybody. Stick with the op. Is the objective neutralized? Over."

"Check!" Chris said, punctuating it with a short burst from his gun. "They're history."

"Understood," Jason said. "Then let's grab the intel and extract."

Trieu reached Lewis first. He was on the ground between three pepperballed and tranquilized department store mannequins. She checked his pulse. "He's all right."

Chris returned to the camp. "What's wrong with him?"

"He was hit by a dart," Trieu said.

Chris shook his head and looked at Garth. "One of yours, buddy?"

"Excuse me?" Garth said. With his baldness under his floppy camo hat, he looked less odd and more huge. "You guys went before the order. I don't know how he got hit."

"He was hit by my dart," Trieu said, standing. "No one was supposed to move until I hit the paper target."

"Well, I didn't know you were going to—"

Jason cut Chris off. "Forget it for now. Treat this like a real op. We still have to exfil, and we might just take a casualty on a mission. So stow it for now. Rachel, search the tent for the documents. Garth, set the charges. Chris, you carry Lewis. Trieu, make sure nobody leaves before my command this time. I'll take point and scout ahead. Trieu will report to me when you're ready to move out."

Ten minutes later they were a safe distance away from the enemy camp. Chris was grumbling about having to carry Lewis and his pack, but Jason wasn't inclined toward sympathy. They were skirting the mountain lake.

"Okay, Patron," Jason said over the radio. "Touch it off."

Jason made an explosion sound with his mouth to substitute for the sound that would've been there had they been using real explosives.

Except there really was an explosion.

CAAAOW!

Water birds took off. Frogs jumped into the water. Turtles slid off rocks. And everybody in the team shrank about two feet. Echoes bounced off the trees ringing the lake.

"What was that?"

"Is there a fire?"

"Something blew up."

"Oh, man!"

Jason shushed them all. "Knock it off, people. Are you crazy, shouting on an op? Come on. Let's get to the extraction site." He wagged a finger at Garth, who was doing a terrible job of trying to look nonchalant.

Two steps later, Trieu cried out. Jason turned. *What is it this time?* was already on his lips.

But as he looked, Chris and Garth were struck by something. They fell with a surprised shout. Chris dumped Lewis to the ground and lifted his weapon. He had a bright yellow splotch on his chest. Jason was just figuring it out when something cracked on his head like a Coke bottle. He brought his hand up and it came down wet and red. But not blood red.

He almost smiled as he saw movement in the brush above them. Rachel was still standing, looking confused, when a red paintball exploded on her midsection.

Chris fired into the bushes, and someone cried out. But Jason lifted Chris's gun. "Stop, Chris. You're dead."

"What?"

Jason pointed at the yellow paint. "You're dead. You can not shoot back."

Chris looked like a cornered cat. "What is going on?"

"It's okay," Jason called toward their attackers. "Mission accomplished, you guys. You got us all."

Five young men Lewis's age emerged from the bushes. They all wore plastic goggles and carried paintball guns with massive plastic hoppers on top. They whooped and high-fived each other as they came down the bank.

"So much for ex-special forces," an extremely tall and thin teenager with long red hair said. "You guys are llamas!"

"Dude," a kid with a nose ring said. "What happened to the Lewd? Get it? Dude, Lewd."

"*Lewis* will be all right," Jason said, taking off his headset. "He was hit by a tranquilizer dart by mistake."

"No way," Nose Ring said. "You guys shot one of your own guys? Whoa. Remind me not to be on your side."

The paintballers laughed. Even Jason had to chuckle.

"Okay, guys," he said. "That's enough for today, I think. I'll have Lewis call you up if we need you again."

"Sure, man," the redhead said. "Tell the Lewd we'll come frag you noobs any time."

"Dudes," Nose Ring said to his friends, "Legion of Doom Clan totally rules!"

"Yeah!"

They walked off toward their cars, laughing and looking over their shoulders.

The Firebrand team, decorated in bright paint, stood in a semicircle and watched them go.

"Dude," Garth said, "they totally waxed us."

Lewis stirred and moaned.

Trieu went to him. "How do you feel?"

He shook his head. "Burdy gooood."

"Okay," Jason said. "Let's hoof it back to the enemy camp to be sure Garth didn't start a forest fire. We can debrief there."

"So," Jason said, looking around the circle. "Who wants to go first?"

Lewis raised his hand.

"Go ahead," Jason said.

"If I get it right and all at once, can I show you some of my tools?"

"What tools?"

"Back at the compound," Lewis said. "Give me just one hour to show you what me and my tools can do for this team."

Jason rolled his eyes. "Lewis, we've been through this."

"Forty-five minutes, then. Look, I've played nice up till now and tried to be Mr. Soldier Boy. I even took a dart in the neck trying to play army. But I'm no good at it."

"Sure you are, L—"

"No, look!" he said, standing up. He went over to a mannequin and knocked it off its post. "Would you just listen to me?"

Jason was ready to shout him down, but something made him hold his tongue. "Okay, Lewis. I'm listening."

Lewis implored with open hands. "I don't even know why you're bringing me along if you don't let me use my things. I'm no soldier. Get someone else if that's all you want. But I was picked for this team because I know tech stuff. And I can use it to help us if you'd just let me show you. What happened here today would not have happened if I'd been on my computer."

"No," Rachel said, "what happened here today didn't have anything to do with a computer. It had to do with someone not following the plan."

Jason was pleased to hear her say it. It saved him from having to.

"I'm just saying," Lewis said, "that I can help you guys a lot better doing it my way than I ever could trying to be something I'm not. So what is it going to be, Jason? Will you give me forty-five minutes of your time, or do you just want me to be one of your G. I. Joes? Because I won't do that."

Jason thought about it. Everyone stared at him. "Okay, Lewis," he said at last. "If you can knock your mission summary out of the park, I'll give you forty-five minutes."

Lewis's body relaxed so much Jason was almost afraid he was going to pass out again. "All right!"

"So let's hear it. What went wrong today?"

"That's easy," Lewis said, taking his place on the ground of the dusty campsite. He pointed at Chris. "First, Rambo here decides he's going to be an army of one and attacks the target before he's supposed to. Probably to impress a certain young lady."

Chris kicked him. Rachel just arched an eyebrow.

"Being the good squaddie I am," Lewis said, "I followed my fearless leader into the breach to finish off Plastic Jim and his gang of nogoodniks. But because we'd gone in early, I walked behind the paper target and took the tranq after it passed through. Thanks a lot, Rambo. And Trieu: Good shooting." He rubbed his neck.

"Then, as I understand it," he said, "Mr. Clean here decided he wanted to really blow something up for a change."

Garth shrugged and grinned.

"Which, I should point out," Lewis said, looking pointedly at Jason, "is completely understandable when a guy isn't allowed to do the thing he signed on to do. But I digress. Then while everyone was apparently admiring his scorched earth policy at the top of their lungs, my *Quake* clan buddies found you and turned you all into splatter art."

He smiled at Jason. "Can I show you my stuff now?"

Jason rubbed his chin. "In just a minute. First, does anybody want to add to the commentary provided by The Lewd? Chris, are you listening?"

"Hmm? Oh, sorry. Do you hear that piping? It's a Townsend's solitaire." He whistled a single note over and over.

"Chris, focus here for a minute, okay?" Jason said, clasping his hands around his knees. "There are many things I could bring up about that mission: the dangers of disobeying orders, the foolishness of going it alone, the fact that you will act in a mission the way you train—and how that's really scaring me today, how to react when we get a casualty, or the unauthorized use of explosives. Not to mention that stunts like this tell me that we're not training seriously and we're not exactly jelling as a team."

He looked at his people, their clothes and faces stained by primary colors, their faces downcast. On the outside, at least, they looked sufficiently remorseful.

"But I think you will be doing plenty of thinking about those things on your own. Especially when we spend *all* of tomorrow running."

They groaned.

"Ten mile run and o-course in the morning. Followed by a full-gear conditioning run in the afternoon."

"Both?" Lewis said, aghast.

"Both."

"But Trieu and Lewis and I don't have to run, right?" Rachel asked. "We didn't do anything wrong."

"No, but we're all part of a team that allowed it to happen. We created a climate on a mission that on a real op would've gotten us all killed."

"Oh, now, Jason," Rachel said, walking to him with her hips in full swing. She laid her head against his arm. "I know we were very naughty. We're all sorry, aren't we, everyone? But let's just forget it now, okay, Jasie-wasie? We'll be good from now on, won't we?"

Jason pulled away. "Jasie-wasie?"

She smiled imploringly.

"Forget it," he said. "The whole team runs."

"You're part of the team, too," Chris said.

Jason nodded. "I'll be running right beside you. If we were in the navy, I'd be held responsible for the failure of my team. I'll call Chimp and let him think up some kind of nasty punishment for me in addition to the running."

"Yeah!" Lewis said. "Oops. Sorry."

"Hey, I've got a question," Garth said. "Why do you call him that?"

"What: Chimp?" Jason said. "Because he's so good at— Because he *used to be* so good at climbing. Nobody in our training class could keep up with him, whether it was going over walls or up trees or over ropes. I could've sworn he could grip stuff with his feet."

Oh, nice. I've taken away the reason he even has that nickname.

He found himself staring at the dirt. Finally, he felt the eyes on him. He looked up and clapped once.

"Okay, anyway, like I was saying, I could talk about any one of those things you guys did wrong. But I'm going to restrict myself to just one, and then we'll get back for Lewis's fireworks show.

"I don't know what you guys were thinking, shouting like that on an op. Yeah, you were surprised. So what? If you get surprised in-country, are you going to just shout out, 'Here I am! I'm not supposed to be here in your country, but I am. Would somebody please come shoot me'?

"You guys," he said, leaning forward, "stealth is the commando's best weapon. Without stealth, you are dead. Commandos must not be compromised. That means *seen or heard* to you and me. You think these hot little guns we've got are your best weapons, but I'm here to tell you that invisibility is a boatload better than any weapon you can carry. That's why snipers are so deadly.

"I think those movies are so funny that show the commando walking in and blowing everything up, getting into these massive firefights and then walking away undead. But I don't care how you see 'Ahnold' or Sly or Steven Seagal do it, I'm telling you that when we're behind enemy lines, we're going to take very few chances. And stealth is what's going to bring you back home every time, not going in guns-a-blazing.

"From now on," he said, "if an engagement lasts more than one minute, I'm going to see it as a failure. Understand? Okay. End of sermonette. Let's go home."

CHAPTER 20

BANSHEE

"HERE, put these on."

Jason took the boots Lewis handed him. They were tan lace-ups that looked exactly like the ones he'd worn in the Teams.

"What's wrong with mine?"

Lewis was on the ground fiddling with a camouflaged Kevlar helmet. "These, my Stone Age friend, will recharge your radio batteries as you walk."

Jason turned them over. "How?"

"The magic of piezoelectricity."

"Pie-eezo-what?"

Lewis put the helmet on his own head and flipped down a small black panel over one eye. It looked like he was blocking one eye to read an eye chart with the other. A black cable snaked around to the back of the helmet.

"Piezoelectricity," he said. "Never mind. It just means that we've rigged your shoes with a special material that generates an electric charge when mechanically deformed. In other words, when your heel hits or the ball of your foot bends, your battery is happy."

Jason was sitting in a folding camp chair at the edge of their training compound in the Utah mountains, changing his boots. Trieu and Rachel were already suited up in Lewis's modified helmets and gear. Garth and Chris were hiding in the woods, waiting for their chance to be aggressors in the demonstration.

Bigelow had heard about this compound through some mercenary types—it used to be an Aryan Nation complex—and had talked Eloise into buying it. It had lots of room for live fire training and orienteering, a brutal obstacle course and ropes course, barracks, kitchen, indoor pool, track, and firing ranges. It even had a short airstrip and a helipad. Best of all, it was extremely remote.

Lewis went to put the helmet on Jason, but Jason stopped him.

"I don't wear helmets."

"Are you kidding?" Lewis said. "This is the upgraded Kevlar with the seven-pad suspension system and the slow memory impact foam. It can actually stop a 9mm bullet. Why wouldn't you want to wear it?"

Jason shook his head. "They're too bulky and restricting. They keep me from hearing everything. Forget it."

"Tough," Lewis said. "For this you have to wear one. Besides, when you see what it can do for you, you may change your mind."

He put it on Jason and stepped around behind him to plug something in. Then he helped Jason into the load-bearing vest with its camouflaged components evenly distributed around his body. Lewis pointed out a narrow black box on the chest strap. Three black buttons in a row.

"This is your mouse."

"What do I need a mouse for?"

Lewis smiled. "You'll see." He stepped back. "Ah, you look mah-velous."

"So this is it? I carry all this gear and I wear a helmet. Big whoop."

"Oh, baby," Lewis said. "You ain't seen nothing yet." He reached up and flipped the panel over Jason's right eye.

Suddenly Jason understood. His eyepiece was a tiny computer monitor. In it he saw a top-down topographical map of the compound. Three green dots were superimposed on the map, gathered at the northeastern edge of the camp. With his left eye he saw Lewis instruct Rachel and Trieu to walk in opposite directions. And with his right eye he saw the dots disperse.

"Oh." The word came out slowly, as if he'd just had a delicate situation explained to him after he'd already offended everyone.

"Exactly," Lewis said. "And watch this. Ladies, illumine me."

Jason watched as both girls pointed their CAR-15s at Lewis. He noticed the strange optics on top of the weapons. Suddenly a red dot appeared on the helmet display, exactly over the spot where Lewis was standing.

"Oh."

"Now, Jason, press the top button on your mouse."

Jason reached up and found the big button. When he pressed it, the view changed to a satellite image of the compound, again with the green and red dots.

"No way," Jason said. "Is this a live shot?"

"No, just a photo. We might be able to get a nearly-live feed on missions, but this is just for show. Even so, because the system is coordinated to GPS data, it can show your position on a map, satellite feed, or reconnaissance photo."

"Cool."

"And if you ever lose GPS for any reason, it can estimate your position based on how far you've moved from the last known position."

"Cool."

"But that degrades the longer you go without GPS. Okay, now hit your mouse again."

The image became live video.

"What am I looking at?"

Then the image swerved around, and he saw Lewis and himself, standing there looking like a cyborg.

"That's Rachel's gun cam," Lewis said. "Hit the button again to see Trieu's. And again to see your own."

"Why would I need to see something on video I can see with my own eyes?"

"Because," Lewis said, picking up Jason's modified gun and holding it at arm's length, "with this you can see what's around the corner without getting your face blown off."

"Oh."

"You can shoot around the corner, too."

Jason nodded as he cycled the mouse through the different views. "I'm impressed, Lewis."

"If you like that, you're going to love the rest. You see, you three form a walking LAN—local area network. You can share information with each other silently."

"What kind of information?"

"Like where you are and where they are and what they see."

"Hmm."

"You've got the leader unit on," Lewis said. "With your mouse, you can place waypoints on the map for everyone to see in real time. You can give orders, change orders, and identify targets. Best of all, you know where you are on the map, and everyone knows where everyone else is."

Jason wagged his head to jostle the helmet. "Don't know if it'll make me wear a helmet, but I can see how it might have potential. Okay, is that it?"

"No way. One more thing to get going."

Lewis knelt down over a suitcase and produced something with four black metal arms, a clear plastic dome, and black rotors. He started unfolding the arms. They locked out in roughly the shape of an office chair's wheel assembly.

"Knowledge is power, right?" Lewis asked as he worked.

"So they say."

"And on the battlefield the one with more knowledge has more power."

"That's the theory."

"No, that's the fact," Lewis said. "Why else do we put all these spy satellites in orbit? Why do we fly AWACS planes? Why do we listen in on their radio traffic? So we can have superior knowledge. It's the same reason we jam their electronics and take out their radars when we're about to attack. Because we want to deny them knowledge while hoarding it for ourselves. We're really not very nice when it comes to fighting."

Jason smiled. "Whatever it takes."

It was clear now that Lewis was working on a small flying device. It looked like a bubblegum dispenser with four spindly arms, each with a three-bladed rotor at the end. From the end of one arm to the end of its opposite, the whole thing was four feet wide.

"What is it?"

"I call her the banshee." Lewis was fitting himself with his own vest and helmet.

A fourth dot appeared in Jason's viewfinder. "What does it do?"

"It's our eye in the sky, baby. Real-time bird's-eye view of the mission area. Unmanned stealth recon drone."

Lewis pressed a button on his chest strap mouse and the banshee's rotors squealed to life. Almost instantly it was aloft. Jason took a step back. The thing shrieked like a leaky window on a 747 at thirty thousand feet.

"You call that stealth?" he shouted.

But it shot up quickly, and in five seconds it was two hundred feet up, invisible unless you were looking for it, and completely silent.

"Whoa."

Lewis sent it sprinting around the sky, diving and turning it through sharp aerobatic maneuvers. Finally he sent it back up to two hundred feet and looked at Jason.

"Cycle through your views again."

He did. Suddenly he was looking down at live video of himself. He waved his hand at the camera. "Nice."

"She's locked into synchronous hover over you," Lewis said, "but you can move her wherever you want."

"You mean I'm supposed to be flying it?"

"No, she flies herself. I've got her on auto right now. The radio signal keeps her over you, and GPS data can keep her on station wherever you want her. Blizzards and tornadoes tend to have a detrimental effect on her, but otherwise she's as stable a platform as you could hope for."

"Very nice."

"She's fitted with thermal imaging optics and a laser viewfinder accurate enough to call in artillery strikes—if we had any artillery. She can even lift small objects or knock things over. How about flying in and snatching a map right out of the bad guy's hands? She also screams like a banshee up close, as you've noticed, which can have a psyops effect on Third World villagers."

Jason chuckled. "Okay, Lewis, you've got me on board. Let's try this thing out."

Lewis showed Jason where his microphone bar was on his helmet. "Key the second mouse button to transmit to the whole team."

Jason had the team fan out in a line. His instinct was to put them in two teams of two, but he realized that one of the rationales for that formation was to make sure people knew where each other were. With these moving green dots, he saw that he could spread his people out, maybe even make the enemy think he was a company-sized force instead of merely a squad. Gideon's battle with the Midianites came to mind.

"Wait a minute." He keyed his mic. "Halt. Everybody hold up. Lewis, how can I make your banshee fly around?"

"Tell you what," Lewis said, "for the demo why don't you just tell me what you want to do, and I'll do it for you? Later I'll show you how to do it yourself."

"Check. Seems to me that if we've got this asset we ought to use it. Let's scan the forest in the grid square where the aggressors are supposed to be."

Jason felt kind of silly sitting against a tree watching TV when he was supposed to be conducting an op, but he couldn't argue with his own logic. At the very edge of his hearing, sometimes he thought he detected a high-pitched whine, like a mosquito hovering by his ear.

"Wait a minute, Lewis. Hold right there. Can we zoom in with this thing?"

"Absolutely. What do you want to see?"

"Over by that fallen tree. No the other one. Right. There at the base." He smiled. "Hello, Mt. Baldy."

Trieu's voice came through the speakers. "We'll have to remind Garth to keep his hat on."

"Lewis, is there any way to mark his position on our map with the little dots?"

"It's already there."

Sure enough, there was a red dot on the map about seventy yards to the right of Rachel's position in the line.

"Now that won't move if he does, will it?" Jason asked.

"No. Our green dots move because we're constantly transmitting our location to each other. But his won't update if he leaves, unless we follow him around updating him with the rangefinder."

"All right. Zoom back out and look for Chris. But I'm guessing that they've split up. In the meantime, we'll advance on Garth. Lewis, can you fly that thing and walk?"

"Uh, I'd better hang back if you want me actually searching for something. If you just want her to keep pace with us, then I can come with you."

"Yeah, lock it back into hover mode. Let's shift over toward Garth. Lewis, you take the right flank and watch for Chris. Then Rachel, then Trieu. I'll take left flank. Let's move."

Five steps later, Jason keyed his mic again. "Oh, and Lewis, good job. I'm impressed."

"Thanks, boss."

They had crossed half the distance to Garth's last known position when the high-frequency whine increased.

"Lewis, your banshee losing power or something?"

"It's not me, Jason."

"Look," Rachel said.

Jason quickly called up her gun cam. There he saw a real live helicopter approaching the camp. "Okay, somebody's here. Break off the op. You guys tag Chris and Garth and get back to barracks. I'll go meet the chopper."

Jason jogged back toward the compound, the helmet jostling awkwardly on his head. When he broke out of the woods, he saw that it was one of the ABL corporate jetcopters Bigelow had flown out in before. He hurried toward the helipad.

Bigelow waved at him from the window. But it wasn't Bigelow who got out first. It was Eloise.

"Jason," she shouted over the rotor's noise, "where is everybody?"

"They're coming." He led her out from under the blades. "I didn't expect to see you out here. Out for a weekend in the woods?"

"No." She was doing all she could to keep the rotor wash from lifting her black and white skirt over her legs. But her expression was grim. "Jason, something's happened. I need your team to do a mission."

"What? When? I think in another two months we could—"

"No, Jason. Listen to me: You fly out tomorrow."

CHAPTER 21

NO WAY

"YOU'RE not listening to me."

Eloise's eyes flared. "No, son, you're not listening to *me.* Now hush up and get in there with the rest of them."

"Not until you've listened to sense," Jason said.

"What are you going to say that you haven't said already?" She sat down on one of the long polished benches in the lodge. "You've told me you're not ready. Uh-huh. I hear you. You've told me I'm crazy. Got that, too. You've told me they messed up on an exercise just now. I heard you. You've told me you need weeks to plan and acclimate to the weather and get your head from out your rump roast. You've told me, child. I've done heard it all."

"But you're not—"

"Now you listen to me. These babies are in real trouble, and nobody cares about them but Miss Eloise. This is exactly why I formed this team, so listen up. Firebrand is *going.* I'd go myself if I thought I could. And if that's what it takes to get you to go, I will, too. You watch.

"Now, Jason, honey, I know your heart's in the right place. We've had this talk before. You're thinking about getting your team back in one piece. That's good, baby. That's what I want from you. But I also expect you to take the missions I assign you. I'll hear your complaints and your why-nots, but after that, if I still want you to go, you go. Got it?"

Jason clenched his jaw. "It's a mistake."

"I hear ya. Believe me, I hear you. Look, I've given you a month of training, Jason. I've bought this here place in the sticks for you—and don't think I didn't enjoy paying cash money to boot those white supremacists off the block. I've given you the best equipment, the best food, and the best supplies. I've let you train these people the way you want, without any interference from me. But now it's time to pay the piper, honey. It's time to give a little back."

"You're a black woman Godfather, aren't you?"

"Honey, I'll be the Queen of Sheba if it'll get you to sit your self down and listen. And guess what? Where you're going ain't even five hundred feet above sea level. You happy now?"

"Thrilled."

"Good, now get in there and take some notes."

The lodge was fabulous, more what you'd expect to see at a ski resort than at a survivalist compound. Vaulted dark wood ceilings, dark red brick fireplace, polished wooden tables, polished wooden stools, and polished wooden rafters.

The team sat in the fireside room, lounging on the tan sofas and passing bags of chips across the polished wooden coffee table. Garth had started a fire. Except for Lewis, who was helping Bigelow set up a video projector, they had all changed into sweats or blue jeans.

Rachel, wearing giant fluffy koala bear slippers, was sitting across Chris's lap, the punk. Faint black and green lines on Chris's face had survived a scrubbing. Trieu sat next to Rachel. Jason moved the love seat to face the screen on the wall. Garth pulled up a chair for Eloise and then came to sit beside Jason, bringing the chips and salsa.

"Do we get any previews?" he asked. "Or is it just straight into the movie?"

Bigelow swiveled in his wheelchair. "You get previews. But no changing theaters. I'm watching you guys."

Lewis handed the remote control to Bigelow and then sat beside Trieu and pulled Rachel's legs onto his lap. Smartest one of the bunch.

"All right, class," Bigelow said, "pop quiz time. Anyone know the name of the largest republic to break off from the Soviet Union?"

"Ooh," Garth said, shooting his hand up.

"My, you are an enthusiastic student. Yes?"

"Belarus!"

Bigelow made the *Family Feud* X buzzer sound. "Nope. Anyone else?"

"The Ukraine?"

Buzzer.

"Russia?"

"Oh, good guess, Chris. Russia is the largest remaining part of the Soviet Union. But I mean a country that's broken off from Russia."

"Kazakhstan," Trieu said.

Bigelow pointed at her. "Very good, young lady. Here." He tossed her a Hershey bar.

"Hey," Garth said, "you didn't say there were prizes."

"Sorry. I don't have any more, either." He pointed the remote at the laptop computer next to the projector and a map of Kazakhstan appeared on the screen.

A red laser pointer dot zipped around the canvas.

Bigelow wheeled over to Chris. "Give me that."

"Hey!"

"You'll get it back after class." Bigelow used it to point at things as he mentioned them. "You can't tell from this map, but Kazakhstan is basically a big flat hunk of nothing. The fancy name for it is steppe, but that just means desert or prairie. Now, we don't have time to go into it all, but Kazakhstan has had it bad most of its life. It was born a poor black stepchild. No offense, Miss Eloise."

She waved a "go away" hand at him.

"In World War II, the Soviets used Kazakhstan as a dumping ground for all its undesirables. Then, during the Cold War, they used Kazakhstan as a testing ground for nuclear weapons. People are still having two-headed babies in the area today. Then Khrushchev decided to plow up the steppe to plant grain to feed Mother Russia. And they developed Kazakhstan's mineral resources to provide raw materials and heavy machinery for the motherland. Everything for the good of the people. Meanwhile, Kazakhstan was left pretty much poor and abused. Communism at its finest.

"There are only sixteen million people living there, most of them in cities. Sixteen million is nothing, folks. There's eight million in New York City alone. Double that and spread them out over the ninth largest country in the world, and you've got lots of wide open nothing with nobody but vipers and wild camels for company.

"Now let me jump to the current crisis. Some of you may have heard something about the troubles in the Caspian and Aral Sea regions." Bigelow pointed to the inland sea on the screen. "That's the Caspian Sea there, and next to it is the Aral.

"Thanks to Soviet central planners back in the day, both seas are now drying up. The Aral Sea has dropped by sixty percent since the sixties. The two rivers feeding it—the Syr Darya in Kazakhstan and the Amu Darya in Uzbekistan—have been diverted to irrigate the fields to grow grain and cotton. Whole industries along the Aral shore have vanished. As you can imagine, the folks there are a little put out."

He used the remote control to cycle through photos of desert, rotting cattle carcasses, and ships sitting in very dry-dock.

"But that's not the worst of it. As the Aral Sea receded, it exposed a seabed encrusted with toxic fertilizers and pesticides, including

DDT. The people are finally beginning to understand why there's so much cancer in their area and why they're having so many birth defects. DDT in the water! But now that these poisons are exposed on the seabed, dust storms come and whip it up into the air. They call it the 'dry tears of the earth.' They breathe it and end up with all kinds of respiratory diseases.

"But the last straw for these people seems to have been this plan to build a dike to save the north part of the Aral Sea. The locals had built a couple of dikes before, just with whatever things they could find. Their hope was to save all the towns at this dog's head part of the sea because that's the part fed by the Syr Darya. But every time the sea rose a little, their dikes got washed away.

"They were hanging on for money from the government to turn their latest makeshift dike into a real one. But then the prime minister—who had promised them the cash—resigned. By Kazakh law, when the PM resigns, his whole cabinet has to resign, too. When the new group got in power, they announced that they were diverting the dike money to stimulate the economy in the mostly Russian north.

"The dike thing probably would have been enough to push the Aral Sea people over the edge by itself. But there was more. Don't know if you know, but right about here, along the Syr Darya, is one of the most famous spaceports on the earth: the Baikonur Cosmodrome. In the red hammer's glory days, this was the place to be if you wanted to catch a shooting star. Sputnik was launched from here. Yuri Gagarin blasted off from here. And all those space tourists, includig Dennis Tito and Mark Shuttleworth, go on their pleasure cruises from here. It's still a working facility, rented by the Russian government. But a few years ago, two Proton rockets launched from Baikonur—help me out with pronunciation, Rachel."

"Bye-ka-noor," she said, suddenly sounding Slavic.

"Thanks. Two rockets from Baikonur crashed right in here somewhere, spilling their radioactive materials out and causing yet more two-headed babies. So the people there are ticked, too.

"So you've got the Aral Sea people mad at the Soviets—only now there's no Soviets so they settle for being mad at Russians—the Caspian Sea people mad at the Russians, the Aral Sea people on the Uzbeki side mad at the Russians, the people who had a rocket dropped on their heads mad at the Russians, and the people up in the northeast here still mad at the Russians for using their backyards as a nuke test site.

"Plus you've got all the ethnic groups that were deported here by the Russians. Some of them have still not been allowed to go home. *And* you've got the fact that there are basically two countries here: the industrialized north and the rural south. *And* interracial conflict because until recently the ethnic Kazakhs were outnumbered by ethnic Russians and Slavs, whom the Kazakhs see as usurpers.

"In all, it's a powder keg waiting for a dry summer night. It's amazing the place hasn't blown up before now.

"So for whatever reason, all of these groups have basically decided that enough is enough. There've been riots in the northeast, in the central area where the rockets crashed, along the Caspian Sea, and all along the Aral Sea. The country's pretty much caving in on itself.

"Now, the president of Kazakhstan, Nursultan Nazarbayev—don't help me, Rachel, I'm on a roll—is no dummy. Even though his people are seriously ticked at Russia and Russians, he knows that his only chance of keeping his landlocked country alive is by being nice and cozy with Moscow. So to keep those subsidies coming, he's using what military he has to try to quash this little uprising before it gets out of hand. Trouble is, it was way out of hand the minute it started.

"Now we come to the interesting part for those of us in the room."

Bigelow changed the PowerPoint slide to a regional map of the Syr Darya east of the Aral Sea. There were only three black dots on the map: Baikonur City, Bainkonur Cosmodrome, and Kyzylorda.

"The folks in the Aral Sea area decided they were going to go upstream and deal with the idiots who were stealing and poisoning their water, something that killed off their way of life in less than one generation and was quite literally killing them off even faster than that. So they came up this way, burning and looting. Trouble is, the people they were burning weren't any better off than them. Overirrigation has raised the salinity of the soil and now nothing grows upstream, either. And they've got the same high incidence of birth defects and health problems. So these people either fought the mob or joined in with them.

"Probably the real destination for this lot has been Baikonur all along. Here is the biggest, closest, wealthiest reminder of the Soviet Union they've ever known. It's like the epicenter of their anger. Like that, Trieu? *Epicenter.*"

"Very nice, Doug," she said.

"Yes," Rachel said, "Jamie will be so proud."

"I try. Anyway, these people—around three thousand of them is the best guess, along with their trucks and cows and stuff—have congregated at Baikonur and are burning it to the ground.

"Oh, I should say that there's been some evidence," he glanced at Eloise, "that these farmers and fishermen aren't alone. It seems their ranks have been swelled by certain undesirables, like radical Muslim cats from the Middle East—guys who want to turn Kazakhstan into another Afghanistan, and maybe some Chechen fighter types or guys moving here from that scrap in Dagestan. That's the trouble with revolution: It attracts all kinds of people, not all of them believers in your cause."

He changed slides to a photo of a very Western looking hotel.

"This is the Sputnik Hotel. It's pretty much the only modern building in Baikonur City. French-built. It's where you stay if you go on a tour to see the Cosmodrome. It was built to attract Western tourists and to house Western investors in the Russian space program. Here is where what's left of Baikonur's police and military forces have fallen back to. It's all they can do to hold the hotel until reinforcements arrive. The rest of the town they've pretty much written off."

He switched to a black and white satellite photo of a dilapidated post-industrial city. Two buildings were ringed with red circles.

"This is Baikonur City. The Cosmodrome's not in this shot because it's about twenty-five miles to the north. The top circle on the photo is showing the Sputnik Hotel. The bottom circle, that smoldering ruin, is where there used to be a girls' orphanage."

Bigelow paused and looked at Eloise. "You want to take it from here?"

"You're doing fine, baby."

"All right." He shone the laser dot on the orphanage. "Not long ago the mob went through the town attacking everything that looked rich or Russian, including this orphanage. They killed the Russian workers and kicked the girls—forty of them, all between three and nine years old—out into the cold."

He turned the PowerPoint presentation off and cued up the VCR. He paused it with a shot of a young woman speaking to the camera.

"The reason we know about these kids is this woman here. Her name is Katie Strickland. She's a Peace Corps volunteer from Sioux Falls and, until recently, was a volunteer at the girls' orphanage in question. She was captured by the rebels and then released. This is the videotape she made for them, probably at gunpoint."

He played the tape. Katie looked subdued and sullen. She said she'd been treated well and that the Families for the Aral Sea Association only wanted justice: medical help, the North Dike rebuilt, promised subsidies, and international aid. There was a jump cut in the tape, and Katie was back. The lighting was different on her now, and she kept glancing off to the right of the camera. She said that the Families for the Aral Sea Association also wanted Russia to pay to clean up their water and soil, deport all ethnic Slavs from Kazakhstan, and institute a conservative Islamic state as the official government of Kazakhstan. The screen went black.

Bigelow stopped the VCR. "She was turned over to the troops at the Sputnik Hotel and allowed to leave the city under escort. She's now at the embassy in Almaty being debriefed by State."

Chris whistled. "How did you get that tape?"

"It's a copy, of course," Bigelow said. "Eloise got it overnight from. . .someone who thought she might be interested."

Jason looked at Eloise. Whatever secrets she had, her expression wasn't giving any of them away.

"So you've been in touch with this girl?" he asked her.

"I spoke with her on the phone," she said. "She said she saw these men burn the town and murder her coworkers in cold blood. Except for one, a college girl named Yulia, who they took probably for their own wickedness. Katie is worried sick about her.

"But mostly she's worried about the girls from the orphanage. The poor girl's beside herself with grief. They have to post a guard at the door to keep her from trying to get back out to the city to help those poor babies. She didn't know me from Eve, but I believe the Holy Spirit prompted her to say what she said: 'Eloise, if you know of some way to get help to my girls, then I beg you in God's name to use it.' Now, she probably couldn't have been thinking I could do more than write a letter to my congressman. But you and I know different."

Chris transferred Rachel to Lewis's lap and sat up in the couch. "Uh, ma'am, are you saying you want us to go halfway around the world with zero preparation, go into this unstable situation of mass hysteria, try to find forty orphan girls who could be anywhere, get them out somehow, and get ourselves out, too, in the middle of the Russian winter, using only nonlethal weapons?"

Jason chuckled, glad to have an ally.

"That's what I'm asking you," Eloise said.

Chris stood up and rubbed his hands together. "When do we leave?"

Rachel let out a whoop. Lewis set her aside and leapt up, karate chopping the air.

Jason turned to Garth. "You're smarter than that, aren't you?"

"Me? You bet." He stood and pounded his chest. "Bring it on, you orphanage-burning, Chechen bozos. Come and get some right here, baby." He high-fived Lewis and Chris and lifted Trieu onto his shoulder. "Kazakhstan, here we come!"

"You know the best part of this?" Lewis asked. "It's going to get us out of Jason's runs tomorrow!"

They cheered and laughed and cavorted like teenagers.

Jason watched in disbelief. He probably couldn't have reined them in if he'd tried. But as he saw their joy, he felt the rush of impending battle sweep over him, too. And then another thought settled in his heart.

He'd almost forgotten about his little plan. But now it occurred to him that this mission would be the perfect way to pull off what he was planning. Surely an opportunity would present itself on the op. If they wanted to rush into danger—perhaps their own deaths—before their training was done, that wasn't his concern. He'd done his bit to try to sway Eloise from sending them and to increase the team's survivability.

Now instead of having to wait six months or more, it seemed he was going to have his. . .resolution. . .within the week.

He sat back and watched them dance.

CHAPTER 22

Planning the Op

"You're not getting out of the wedding, so don't even think it."

Jason looked at his friend. "Doug, why would I not want to be in your wedding?"

"I don't know. Maybe it gives you the heebie-jeebies to stand so close to a crip."

Jason spread his hands over the map-strewn table where he and Bigelow were sitting almost shoulder to shoulder. "What do you call this?"

"I mean in public."

"Oh. Well, in that case, maybe you're right."

"Too bad," Bigelow said. "You're in."

"I don't know. We're not in the Teams anymore. These guys haven't sworn to never leave a guy behind. You might have to get Lewis to be your best man."

"Lewis? Look, if I have to come out there and scrape your sorry carcass off the dirt, I will. I'll prop your road-killed-zombie body against the piano and pass out nose plugs."

Jason couldn't keep the smile from his face. "Chimp, I don't get you, man."

"What?"

"I mean, if it wasn't for me, you would still be walking around on two legs. If it wasn't for me, you'd still be hoofing it across some desert or jungle or arctic wasteland or something."

"Yeah, glory days. But if it wasn't for you, I wouldn't be getting married to a hot, foxy mama with a mean streak the size of Cleveland, either."

Jason heard the wheelchair creak as Bigelow gestured. "Still. . ."

An old wooden clock on the mantelpiece of the fireplace chimed eleven o'clock. Jason stretched and got up from the polished table. He put another log on the embers, then stood staring into the fire.

Bigelow wheeled over to him. "Speaking of which," he said, "how are things with you and Rachel? You guys were looking pretty serious back at the City Club, but you haven't said a word about her since. What's up with that?"

Jason smiled feebly. "Oh, that. Well, you know Rachel. She just flirts with people to get her way."

"Un-uh," Bigelow said. "There was more than that going on in that slow dance."

Jason sighed. "Doug, I had to fly back to California that next day to get my apartment cleaned up and all. I didn't see her again until a week later, and then we were never alone. The first chance I got to talk to her was when we were moving in here at the compound."

The new log shifted down on the embers, sending up a cluster of yellow sparks. "We had a long talk. She says she still likes me and all but that she just wants to move slow. And that's cool, you know, because we're working together. It's actually helped me cool my jets. Don't know if you noticed, but there are two very fine women on this team."

"Uh, *yeah,* I noticed."

"So it's helped that Rachel's put the brakes on. Plus, now that I've spent more time with her and gotten to know her, some of that goddess worship stuff has worn off. She only looks *amazing* now, instead of jaw-drop-drool-spill-carry-me-away unbelievable, like at first. Besides, it's given me the chance to take a second look at Trieu. She gets blown away by Rachel's star power, but there's something nice and stable about that girl. I kind of like that, too."

He shrugged. "It was a jolt to go from that dance to basically nothing. But now that we're about to get ourselves killed, it's probably best that we're not romantically involved, you know?"

"You're not going to get killed on this mission," Bigelow said.

Jason looked at him sharply. He clamped his mouth shut and looked at the fire. "I'm just saying that we shouldn't get too close. Isn't that what they always told us in the Teams?"

"Yeah, and I remember us disregarding that the same as we disregarded most everything else."

Jason smiled. "We were arrogant punks, weren't we?"

"What do you mean *were?* I'm still as arrogant as ever."

"Still as much of a punk, too."

Bigelow shook a finger at him. "You're lucky you can run fast, chump."

Jason poked at the fire with the iron. "It's just that I've never had to command someone I really cared about—romantically—to maybe charge a machinegun nest or fall on a grenade or whatever."

"If you're going to command your team to do that, I'm relieving you of duty."

"You know what I'm trying to say."

Bigelow rolled his front wheels side to side. "I'm sorry, Jace. I know what you're saying. If I had to send Jamie into combat. . .No, there's no way could do that."

"Exactly."

Bigelow shrugged. "So you'll go on this mission and you'll get captured and she'll come rescue you. You can be her damsel in distress!"

Jason shook his head. "You are one sick individual."

"The point is that you'll find out on this mission whether you two are good for each other or not. That's one thing combat will do for you: It'll show you what people are really like at their core. Almost wish me and Jamie could do something like that before we tie the knot. You think I should fake a car wreck in the mountains so we can go on some kind of survival adventure thing to see if we bond?"

"Yeah, Doug. Definitely."

"I'll work on that." Then his eyes lit up. "Oh! Did I tell you about Ibnu?"

Jason shook his head. "Just what you told me last month, that they were checking into it or something."

"Yeah. Got E-mail yesterday from a buddy in intel. Met him in rehab if you can believe it. Blew out his hip surfing. He's the one who's been keeping me in the loop. He says that they've made some kind of breakthrough in that case. Says he can't tell me until it's verified, but that it might be pretty big."

Jason rubbed his eyes. "Cool. Okay, so, now that we've covered my lack of a love life and gotten an update on world affairs, can we please get back to planning this disaster of a mission?"

Bigelow turned his chair around. "You were the one who left the table."

"Only because you were giving me the heebie-jeebies."

They came back to the table. Jason pulled the largest map of Kazakhstan from the stack and put it on top.

Kazakhstan. Until now it had been "just another one of those –istans" to Jason. Now it was engraved in his soul because he was leading a team into battle there. This time he wasn't going to take lives, but to save them. He couldn't deny the thrill of it, even if this blocky fish-shaped country was going to be his launch pad to eternity.

"So you still think jumping is better than swimming?" Jason asked.

Bigelow rolled up to the table. "Absolutely. It's all about speed, Jace. These kids aren't going to last long in that cold, if any of them are still there anyway."

"I know," Jason said. "I've thought of that. What if we get all the way out there and there's nobody to save?"

"Oh, I'm sure you'll have plenty of people needing saving if that's what you're after. But if you turn the place upside down and you can't find our girls, I say you exfil and come back here to get fitted for your tux."

"Okay."

"Plus, the latest word out of Almaty is that the Trans-Aral Railroad is out from the Aral Sea to Baiknour. Seems our friends have been pulling a William Tecumseh Sherman and tearing up the railroad as they've gone along. Russian reinforcements have to dismount and come by foot or head back to get on airplanes. And the Kazakh military's got its hands full, too, with uprisings all over the country. Still, you can't count on more than seventy-two hours before the whole situation is radically different. Maybe that's good for our girls, maybe not.

"Here's something else you'll find interesting. Russian jets are patrolling overhead, firing at clear targets when there are any, which isn't often. But pilots are reporting being fired on from civilian buildings—and even having shoulder-launched missiles fired at them from schools and apartment buildings. Now where did fishermen get surface-to-air missiles? The shooters are hiding behind their human shield, just begging the planes to shoot back."

Jason pursed his lips. "Just like Chechnya or Iraq or Afghanistan. If you hit a plane, you show that on TV. If you miss and the plane hits you, you show *that* on TV. Either way, you gain public opinion points."

"You see why we're thinking this isn't just a bunch of farmers with pitchforks?" Bigelow asked.

"No kidding."

"Anyway, watch yourself," Bigelow said. "And keep an eye out for Spetsnaz."

"You think we'll see any?"

"If you were Russia and one of your main rocket sites was about to go up like Smoky Bear and your main forces were delayed, would you keep your special forces where they were? Or would you get them there even if you can't get anything else there?"

"Gotcha," Jason said. "Whew, that ups the ante, doesn't it?"

"Just keep your nose clean, pal." Bigelow took a drink from his water bottle. "Like I said, it's all about speed."

"Okay," Jason said, looking at the map. "I just don't see how I'm going to get Lewis and Rachel and Trieu out of an airplane and onto the ground without breaking their legs. Don't suppose just me and Chris and Garth could go, huh?"

Bigelow smiled. "I already asked. No way. So you don't think any of them are freefall qualified?"

"Are you kidding? Lewis froze up on a forty-foot tower, remember? You think he's going to gladly jump out at thirty thousand—and freefall for ninety-five percent of that?"

"Hmm. I hadn't thought of that. No time to get them HALO qualified."

"And we couldn't do a standard low altitude jump, either. Even if there weren't Russian fighters in the skies, Baikonur Cosmodrome's got the best radar within a thousand miles—and SAM missile sites, to match. We'll have to jump high and open low if we're going in by air."

Bigelow tapped his lips with a pencil. "I just don't see you getting there in time if you infil any other way." He looked at Jason. "You think tandem rigs then?"

"Yeah. One of us with one of them. Three pairs."

Bigelow pointed his water bottle at Jason. "You with Rachel, of course."

"Well, rank's got to have some privileges."

"Absolutely."

"Aw, but I'll probably have to put Rachel with Garth, just to not stress the big guy's chute too much."

"What? No way. You jump with Rachel if that's what you want. Put Trieu with Garth and you take any extra gear he would've had.

That'll keep your loads balanced."

Jason smiled. "I like the way you think, cowboy. Okay, I'll do it. Me with Rachel, Garth with Trieu, and Chris with Lewis. He'll hate me for it. He'll think I'm using my position to gain an unfair advantage with Rachel."

"Which you are."

"Which I am. But he'll still hate me for it."

"Tough."

Jason tapped his fingers on the table. "You know, I think we're going to have to slip Lewis a mickey or something to get him out of that plane."

"Mmm. Talk to Trieu about that. She's a devious chick."

"Okay. You think she's done with her paperwork yet?"

"Probably," Bigelow said. "It doesn't take that long to update a will."

"I'll go by her room later."

"So, HALO jumping in tandem rigs. What fun you're going to have."

"I think we'd better do combat equipment lines, too," Jason said.

"You've got that much extra gear? What are you planning to take?"

"Oh, not too much extra. Maybe some blankets and shoes for the kids if we do find them. Plus, Lewis did a presentation for me today with this little screen that pops down over the helmet."

"Yeah," Bigelow said. "It's his version of the army's Land Warrior system. Very cool. So you're going to use it?"

"I think I will. We're supposed to have an eye out for whatever works best, aren't we? Chimp, I could see the bennies of this thing right away. But you know, if it crashes we'll just ditch it and let Garth blow it up. Plus I liked Lewis's little toy airplane." He shook his head. "I dunno, Chimp, that kid might prove to be worth something, after all."

Bigelow smiled. "Don't act so surprised. I knew it all along."

"Well, that's because you're a cripple and God gave you extra knowledge to compensate for your lack of leg strength."

Bigelow's mouth locked into a wide O. "What's this? You sassing me, boy? Come here. I oughtta take you backside the barn and whoop you."

"Yeah, right. Settle down, Chimp, and let's finish this plan. Answer me this: How're you going to get us over the target anyway? And where are you going to get six HALO rigs? And you will get *new* chutes, won't you? MT1-X chutes only. They ought to handle a tandem rig with extra gear. And once we get in, how are we supposed to find the girls? And even if we find them, which we won't, what are we supposed to do with them? And then when we figure out what to do with them, how are we supposed to get out of there so I can come back and steal your bride out from under your nose?"

Bigelow smirked. "Are you done?"

"For now."

"Of course we'll use new MT1-Xs," Bigelow said. "What am I, a moron? Don't answer that. And as for the plane, don't worry about it. Your girl Rachel has a number of. . .helpful contacts that we can tap. We'll get your plane, loverboy."

The clock chimed eleven fifteen.

"What were your other little ulcers?" Bigelow asked. "Oh, tandem rigs. No problem. I know a guy.

"As for what you should do when you find the girls, that's easy: Get 'em out of there! Find some way to put them on train cars or buses or goats or something. You'll have Rachel to talk for you, and I'll be sure the boss lady sends you out with lots of *tenge*—the local money—to talk even louder."

He traced his finger on the map along the Syr Darya River. "The Trans-Aral runs along the river all the way to the Chinese border, so look for a train going your way. I'm thinking that if you get away east, you won't have any more problems. Let's see, what's the nearest airport away from the action? If you could just get them to the Kyzylorda airport, I'll have the jump plane waiting there for you. That's. . .about 125 miles. Load them in and fly to Novosibirsk or somewhere. I'll have it arranged. From there you escort them to France or Germany or wherever the boss lady feels good about you dropping them. Then you and the rest of Hogan's Heroes get back here to watch me get hitched."

Jason stared at the map. "Sounds good, Chimp. Still, I hate rushing into this." He rubbed his chin. "That's not the way we trained."

Bigelow leaned back in his chair. "I know. But your team's better off now than they were when you started, aren't they?"

"I guess."

"You've had them shooting nothing but the weapons they're going to use, haven't you?"

"They're at the line every day. Trieu's still missing her Dragunov, but until we can fit it with a power control valve—"

"And I know you've been running them through PT," Bigelow said. "Even Lewis looks buff."

"Yeah, I guess I work them pretty hard."

"You've got good people and good equipment. You've got surprise on your side. You've got a fairly well-defined and achievable mission. You've got the technological edge with Lewis's toys. You've got—"

"But don't forget they totally blew it just a few hours ago. Chimp, they're not jelling as a team. I'm afraid we're going to lose more from blue on blue than from enemy fire."

"Maybe," Bigelow said. "Maybe not. You're also forgetting your biggest asset of all?"

"What, that you're going to be sitting in your air-conditioned room watching us get surrounded?"

"Well, that'll be nice, but it's not what I was thinking of."

"Oh, you mean that I'll get to die next to a couple of beautiful women?"

"There could be worse ways to go. But wrong again."

"I give up. What's our biggest asset?"

Bigelow opened his hands. "Duh! God. You guys have Jesus Christ on your side, or have you forgotten what this whole thing is about? Defending the defenseless. Rescuing the widow and orphan, dude. Plucking the firebrand out of the fire. This is God-territory, bud." He picked up the pencil and a pad of sticky notes. "Here, keep this with you."

Defend the cause of the weak and fatherless; maintain the rights of the poor and oppressed. Rescue the weak and needy; deliver them from the hand of the wicked (Psalm 82:3–4).

Jason read it. "What's this?"

"Kind of my theme verse for this team. Thought it might help you remember." Bigelow rolled the pencil away. "I'm surprised at you, Jace. You were always the one giving me Scriptures about this and that. Making me sick." The gaze he leveled on Jason was as bright and focused as a laser pointer. "How's your walk with the Lord, bro?"

Jason didn't answer. He tried to meet Bigelow's gaze but found himself looking at the table. Then he walked over and put another log on the fire. He grabbed the poker and fussed over the logs.

Bigelow followed him to the hearth. "You gonna tell me how long you and God haven't been on speaking terms, or are you gonna make me guess?"

Jason didn't take his eyes off the fire. "It's not that we're not speaking, Doug. It's just that. . .it's been a while since we've seen eye to eye."

Even though Bigelow was silent, Jason felt his friend's eyes on him. Jason tried to look too involved with the fire to be bothered with conversation.

"Jace," Bigelow finally said, "this is bad. Of all the reasons you've given for why the team shouldn't go on this mission, this is the most serious. It's like taking the Lord's Supper if your heart isn't prepared for it. I don't know, Jace. You're scaring me." He wheeled closer. "Come on, let's talk about it."

"I don't want to, Doug, okay? Let's just leave it be for now. We'll go on this thing and. . .when we come back we can have a nice long chat. But I'm busy now. I haven't started packing and I don't even know where my will is."

"Un-uh, no way." He moved to block Jason's escape. "We settle it now."

Jason shoved the poker back on the rack. "Look, Doug. . . Chimp. I'm fine. My walk with God is fine."

"Liar."

"Okay, what about this? I'll take some time tonight to deal with a few things that have been bothering me lately, and it'll all be fine." He met his friend's gaze. "I'm going to lead this mission, Doug. God's fine and I'm fine, okay? Now get your sorry wheelchair out of my way before I push you over."

Bigelow blinked at him. "Jace, what's got into you? I've never seen you like this."

"I don't have time for this." Jason hopped over the back of the couch and headed for his room. "I'll see you at the pad at 0200."

CHAPTER 23

Pigs in Space

"I'M GOING to die. I'm going to die. Oh. . .Oh. . .I'm going to die. I'm going to die. Oh. . .Oh. . ."

Rachel leaned down over Lewis, who had gone fetal in a spot as far away from the plane's cargo ramp as possible. "Lewis, honey, you're not going to die." Her voice was muted by the oxygen mask.

She looked out the window of the big cargo plane. "Oh, there's clouds below us. We're going to be falling through clouds?" She sat down next to Lewis. "Maybe you're right. You *are* going to die, and me with you."

Garth and Chris looked up from the weapons they were retooling. With their green continuous breathing masks and suspended plastic bags, they looked like they were expecting the plane to go down at any moment. They looked at each other and rolled their eyes.

"You guys," Garth said disparagingly, shouting over the mask and the noise of the four massive propellers. "You make it sound like jumping out of an airplane five miles up is a bad idea."

"Yeah," Chris said, "and you act like the fact that we're not going to open our chutes until we're about two thousand feet off the ground is dangerous and might result in nothing but a Lewis-shaped hole in the ground."

"Chris!" Rachel said.

Jason was sitting in the rear of the plane, near the ramp that would open up and spit them out into the void. Like the others, he was prebreathing aviator's oxygen to flush the nitrogen from his bloodstream so that he didn't get the bends. Their tandem rigs and heavy rucksacks were laid out carefully on the metal floor in front of him atop the nonslip strips and cargo rollers.

The C-130's cargo hold was big enough to park a bus inside. The white padded walls and intricate network of white metal bars along the arching ceiling made Jason feel like Jonah in the belly of the whale. Trieu was sleeping on one of the stretcher shelves on the side of the hold.

Jason held a yellow square of paper in his polypropylene glove.

Defend the cause of the weak and fatherless; maintain the rights of the poor and oppressed. Rescue the weak and needy; deliver them from the hand of the wicked (Psalm 82:3–4).

It wasn't the content of the verse that troubled him so much as its author. He'd known there was a problem between him and God, but until Bigelow's question he hadn't realized how severe it was. And now he was about to go into harm's way—without his spiritual armor.

Lord, I. . .

The words wouldn't come. How does one tell God that he's mad at Him? And when he is mad at God, how does one pray?

He flipped through the pint-sized Bible in his fingers. It reminded him of countless quiet times in the field as a SEAL. Even now, he was still keeping his appointed time with the Word every day. It was just that for months someone had been missing from the relationship. And he was pretty sure it wasn't God who had moved.

He put the sticky note in a pocket of his desert fatigues and stood up. Might as well check those chutes one more time.

He heard a heavy thump from the front of the plane. The forward crew door slid open and a paunchy Slav in a brown flight suit poked his head out. He spoke to Rachel in Russian, then looked at Lewis and laughed. Rachel's eyes found Jason's. She motioned him forward.

"He says we're about fifteen minutes out," she said.

Jason nodded to the man. "Ask him if we're at thirty thousand and on the course we logged on the flight plan. I don't want those SAM sites at the Cosmodrome thinking we're anything but a cargo plane headed to Almaty."

Rachel interpreted and the man answered in the affirmative.

"Ask him for wind speed and direction."

She did. The man spoke disapprovingly and left through the crew door. Jason heard him stamping up the ladder to the flight deck.

"He's going to ask the pilot," Rachel said.

Jason watched her eyes. There was something intriguing about how the mask took away all facial expression except what those deep brown oases could convey. The straight-on look she gave him now meant more, somehow, than it would've had her full face been showing. He smiled, hoping it would communicate beyond his own mask.

Jason turned to his team and noted that Trieu had awakened and joined them. "Okay, people, listen up. We're about fifteen minutes out. Let's go ahead and switch to our jump helmets so we can talk on radio. But remember, nobody take even one breath of this air. One, it stinks from all our outgassing—especially yours, Garth—and two, it will totally erase everything the prebreathing has done for you."

Just like they tell you in the airlines, Jason, Chris, and Garth fixed their own masks before they helped their dependents. Jason stood before Rachel with her jump mask and helmet in his hand. "Ready?" he asked.

For the first time since that dance weeks before, she seemed uncertain in his presence. "Jason, are we really going to do this?"

He dared a quick stroke of her cheek with the back of his glove. "I think we really are."

She embraced him suddenly, burrowing her face into his shoulder. Even with fatigues and hoses and parachute harnesses between them, she still felt mighty good.

"This is my first time back," she said.

"You've been to Kazakhstan?"

"No, silly: back in the field. The first time I've actually done a mission since. . ." She shut her eyes, but a tear leaked out. She looked back into his eyes. "Will you protect me?"

"Rachel, I. . ."

"I know you can't do special favors for me. I just mean will you be as sure as you can that. . .*all of us* get out of this all right?"

He smiled behind his mask. "Of course."

"Even you?"

Jason didn't answer.

"Even you?"

He nodded and shrugged and shook his head all at once.

"Promise?" she said.

He was glad she couldn't see his mouth opening and closing. "I'm. . .it's. . .I guess we'll have to see what God has in store for us all."

Her eyes narrowed and she tilted her head. "Jason."

"Mmm?"

"I know you'll do the right thing."

His throat was very dry, and it wasn't just from the bottled oxygen.

Chris's voice came through Jason's helmet speakers. "If you two want to be alone, the rest of us are about to leave."

"All right, all right," Jason said into his microphone.

"I'm ready to change masks now," Rachel said.

For a half-second eternity, she entrusted herself to him fully. It was an unexpectedly intimate moment. He took the prebreathing mask away and put her dive mask and helmet on. In just a few minutes, she was going to put herself fully into his care in a big way.

He turned to the team. All of them were putting themselves in his care. What a hypocrite he was.

"Let's do a radio check," he said. "Everybody sound off."

The radios and masks were working fine. The air from their bailout bottles was cooler and smelled of rubber with a metallic tinge. It was actually refreshing, like a splash of cold water on a hot day.

"Okay," Jason said, "is everybody clear on the mission?"

They nodded their heads.

"What about the jump? Lewis, are you okay about the jump?"

"Do I look okay?"

Jason pursed his lips. He glanced at Trieu—who looked especially Asian with only her eyes exposed—and nodded. She walked to her rucksack.

"Anybody else?" Jason asked. "Rachel, have you had enough time with your language tapes?"

"No way. But that's okay, since pretty much everybody down there speaks Russian."

Trieu approached Lewis with a syringe.

"What's that?" he said, falling backward. Garth held him.

"Relax, Lewis," Jason said. "This is just a little something to calm you down."

"Yeah," Chris said, "we're going to knock you out and chuck you out the back of the plane."

"What!"

"Don't listen to him," Trieu said. "It's called Versed. It's like valium but doesn't knock you out as long. It will help you relax."

"Oh. . .it's kind of funny," he said, trying to get away, "but I don't really like needles very much."

"Hey, Lewis," Rachel said, running a finger from his forehead to his chin. "Have I told you how handsome you look in your uniform?"

"Oh, baby, you really think s— OW!"

Chris slapped Jason on the back. "What'd we tell you about her? Queen of distraction."

Lewis rubbed his rump and looked at them like the dog back from the vet. "You guys are dorks. That hurt."

"Sorry, Lewis," Jason said, "but I think it will help. Okay, people, let's suit up."

"And you!" Lewis said to Trieu. "You're always sticking me with needles and making me pass out!"

Trieu shrugged and headed back to her rucksack.

Garth stopped her. "You did use a clean needle, didn't you?"

Lewis's eyes went wider still. "What!"

The Slav reemerged through the crew door and spoke to Rachel.

"Five minutes out," she said and then translated wind speed numbers for Jason.

The crewman evaluated the team skeptically and pronounced his verdict with a word Rachel didn't bother translating. He stepped to the rear of the plane and strapped himself into his safety harness.

"Oh. . ." Lewis said. "I'm going to die!" There was a little slur between his words now.

"Wait!" Trieu said. "I think we should pray before we do this, don't you?"

Chris groaned but gathered with the others in a tight ring. They joined hands.

"Who wants to lead us?" Rachel said, staring at the metal floor.

"The leader leads," Garth said, looking at Jason.

Jason nodded slowly. "Oh, okay. Lord, I. . ." He swallowed. "Father, we're about to go do a bunch of crazy things. But the people in this circle are doing them in Your name. They're going out to. . . rescue the needy and defend the cause of the fatherless. Would You please help us accomplish Your will? And Lord, as team leader, I pray that You would take care of each one of these people. Because I can't do it. Just. . .bring them all back home safe. Thank You, Jesus. Amen."

"Amen."

"Okay," Chris said, "let's get this show on the road. Lewis, get yourself over here, boy."

Garth bowed to Trieu. "My lady, may I assist thee with thine silk parasol?"

"Yes, please."

Jason stepped into the chute's harness and pulled it onto his shoulders. He clipped it down and checked the bag of equipment between his legs. The oversize altimeter on his wrist said 31,000 feet above ground level. He attached his peppergun to his leg and a short chemical glow-stick to his altimeter. All the while, the crewman was standing by the ramp release, ogling Rachel.

Jason came to Garth and Trieu, who were connected with her back against his front. He checked their fasteners. "You guys ready?"

"Aaaaaaaaaaaagggggggghhhhhhhhh!"

Jason looked from Garth to Trieu. "What about you, are you ready?"

"Not especially," she said.

He gripped her hand. "You're going to be fine." He whacked Garth on the shoulder. "Okay, you two, put your goggles on and break your lightsticks."

They brought their goggles down over their eyes. Then they squeezed the vials inside the narrow gel tubes on their helmets and on Garth's ripcord. The released chemicals mixed together and soon the tubes were glowing bright green.

Jason made sure their harnesses were secured before moving to Chris and Lewis. "You guys good to go?"

"Let's party, baby!" Chris said, giving Jason a head-butt. "Man, I still can't believe I let you go with Rachel while I'm stuck here with bonehead."

"You'll live. Lewis, what about you? You ready?"

"Jason," he said, his eyes not quite opened all the way, "will you call my mother if I die?"

"Yes, Lewis, I'll call her. Okay, you two, goggles on and lightsticks broken."

Rachel was sitting against the wall in a cannonball position. Jason knelt in front of her. "You ready to do this?"

She looked up. "Aren't you scared at all?"

"Are you kidding? I can't tell because of my polypropylene long johns, but I think I've wet myself."

"Ha."

"Seriously, I am freaking out. No matter how many times you do it, to jump out of an airplane you still have to override a bunch of your brain's warnings." He stood and extended his hand to her. "Come on, let's go do something stupid together. It'll be like our first date."

She took his hand and stood. "Is this your idea of showing a girl a good time?"

"You got it, sweetheart."

Now came the part he'd been simultaneously longing for and dreading. With a last look into his eyes, Rachel turned her back toward him and snuggled into his chest. Her body felt very very nice against him. He reached around her waist, not exactly avoiding feeling the curve of her hips, and grabbed the straps of her harness. It had to be a Jedi mind trick or something, but he could swear he smelled roses.

He got them connected and had Garth check them out.

"Okay, Rachel, goggles down. Now let's break those glow sticks. Good." He led her to their spot between the two other pairs. "We go out at the same time. Is everybody ready?"

"Aaaaaaaaaaggggggghhhhhhhhh!"

"Okay," he said, motioning to the crewman. "Open her up."

The crewman yanked the lever and the cargo door began to clank open. The wind howled louder than Lewis's banshee. And, since they were higher than Mt. Everest, the air was just as cold. Loose paper whirled around the cargo bay as the door dropped open like a puppet's mouth. Stars twinkled in the thin atmosphere.

"I'm going to die. I'm going to die. Oh. . .Oh. . ."

Then the door was all the way open.

Jason felt his pulse rate triple. *Oh, dear Lord, what am I doing?*

He wrapped one arm around Rachel's waist. "On three, everybody! One. . ."

"No. . ." Lewis said.

"Two. . ."

"No, no, no, no, no, no!"

"Three! Go, go, go!"

Three two-man teams scurried forward—back legs working with more determination than front legs. The wind swept behind them, scooping them out.

And then the plane was gone.

"I'm going to diiiiiiiiiiie!"

CHAPTER 24

Kazakhstan or Bust

As always, Jason felt more like he was body surfing than falling. His leap out the back of an airplane flying at over two hundred miles an hour made it feel as though he were drifting out into a wash of air. For the first three seconds, he felt incredible peacefulness, the wind rushing against his body in a gentle massage.

Still, adrenaline shot through his body faster than any syringe could force it. Their speed increased to terminal velocity and they plummeted toward a bank of high cumulus clouds. The wind roared deep in his ears.

Rachel wasn't moving much, but she maintained the proper arch and her head moved from side to side.

Pinpricks of green light showed that the other two teams were nearby. Jason steered toward them. He could faintly see Chris holding Lewis's wrists out, Chris's altimeter stick glowing weakly. They looked like a radioactive dragonfly. Garth and Trieu were in perfect position. Garth was steering them back toward Jason and Rachel.

Jason glanced upward but knew he could never spot the C-130

high above him. In his mind he could see the crewman laughing at them. *Here's hoping they're waiting for us upstream.*

Just about the time they sliced holes in the cumulus, Jason no longer felt the sensation of falling. Now he was just floating. He had ten seconds of gray fog, during which he felt that same sense of simplicity he enjoyed while scuba diving. Then they popped through the cloudbank, and suddenly Kazakhstan stretched out beneath them.

Two clusters of lights speckled the desert floor: the Cosmodrome and Baikonur City. Jason identified the brighter cluster as the city because of its proximity to the black thread that had to be the Syr Darya. For now at least the electricity was on in most of the city.

"I'm a birdie!"

It was Lewis's voice over the radio. Jason spotted Lewis and Chris on his right. Garth and Trieu were close behind.

"Flap, flap, flap."

"Can't tell we're falling, can you?" Jason said.

"Trust me, kid," Chris said, "that nice little aerial photo you see down there is the floor of an elevator coming up to you at a hundred and twenty mph."

"Everybody okay?" Jason asked.

"Doing fine, boss," Garth said.

"Sure," Chris said.

"Let's link up," Jason said. "Chris, you and me first."

They maneuvered together carefully and clasped onto each other's wrists.

"Okay, Garth," Jason said, "come on in."

They formed an Esther Williams water dancing shape in the dark sky. Their green tubes lit them like kids with glowing necklaces at Six Flags.

"Rachel," Garth said. "Open your eyes, girl."

"Th–they're open. I'm just in sh–shock. And cold!"

"Trieu," Jason said, "you okay?"

"I'm fine, Jason. I do this all the time."

"Yeah, right."

"You guys," Lewis said, his words slurring, "does anybody else think this is strange?"

"What," Rachel asked, "that we're falling through the air like idiots?"

"Hey," Garth chided. "The proper term is 'meat bombs.' "

"No," Lewis said slowly, "that we're having a nice conversation while we're doing it."

Jason's altimeter read ten thousand feet. On the horizon, the sky was beginning to turn pink. Two MiG-29s in formation patrolled below them.

"Okay," Jason said, "looks like our primary landing zone to the east of town is still good. We'll try to touch down together, but if the wind blows us off, we'll regroup at the LZ, check?"

"Check."

"Look," Trieu said, "some of the buildings are still burning."

Not all the lights twinkling beneath them were electric. Orange flashes and bright orange beacons reminded them that they weren't dropping in on Phoenix or some other well-behaved desert city. The dispersed buildings of the Cosmodrome covered an area fifty miles wide and twenty-five miles long. Baikonur City was a speck in comparison.

"Don't the astronauts always talk about how peaceful the earth seems from space?" Rachel asked.

"You guys," Lewis said, now sounding almost as if he were talking in his sleep. "Would it boil your brains if I told you I kinda like this?"

They laughed as the earth sucked them toward certain death.

"We're at three thousand," Jason said. "Pull at two thousand. See ya on the hardtop."

They broke out of their ring and separated.

Chris pulled his cord first. The chute tumbled upwards and he and

Lewis were suddenly no longer next to them. Garth pulled his, too. Then Jason pulled hard on the D-shaped cord at his chest. He felt a solid yank on his back and heard the parachute flooding with air. He looked up. The canopy had deployed perfectly.

"You all right, Rachel?"

She sighed audibly. "Does this mean we're safe?"

"Yes, sweetie," Chris said over the radio. "We're now safe to float gently down to a nice little combat zone where crazy people with guns will try to kill us."

As the three chutes descended, they began to encounter the wind blowing over the steppes. It was stronger than expected. The fifteen mile-an-hour forward velocity their military performance chutes gave them was only enough to minimize how far south of the city they were being pushed. Garth was faring better. He and Trieu were tacking into the wind. They were going to come down on the north side of the train tracks. It was all Jason and Chris could do to stay north of the river.

"Just watch those power lines, Garth."

"I'm on it, boss."

Jason could make out details of Baikonur City now. He saw the twin stacks from the central heating plant, belching out steam like retro rockets steering the earth. Soviet-style apartment buildings, looking ancient when they were new, comprised the downtown area. A few cars moved about, but it looked almost deserted. The city was more run-down than he'd expected. Even from here, he could see collapsed structures, bricked-up windows, and old car frames that had been cannibalized and gone to rust.

"This doesn't look like a foreign country," Lewis said.

"What are you talking about, boy?" Chris said. His voice sounded less muffled. Jason guessed he had stripped his mask away.

"Nah, this is somewhere in America, isn't it? It just looks like anyplace I've ever been. I see clouds and ground and a city with cars and apartment buildings. Why isn't the sky green? And where are the two suns?"

"Trieu," Garth said, "next time not so much valium, okay?"

"There's shrubs and streetlights and birds and stuff," Lewis said thickly. "All the colors are right. I thought everything would be different on the other side of the world."

"Don't get out much, do you, Lewis?" Rachel asked.

"It's just. . ." Lewis's voice trailed away.

"Um, Lewis," Chris said, "what did the birds look like? Lewis? Lewis, man, wake up."

Despite the fact that the icy wind was blowing down from Siberia, it felt warmer here. Compared to the minus-fifty degree temperatures of the C-130, the five degree wind chill down here felt positively toasty.

"Okay, campers," Jason said, "we're coming up on three hundred feet. At two-fifty, drop the packs."

"Gotcha, skipper," Garth said.

"Two-fifty."

Jason pulled a quick release cord and his extra combat gear descended on a twenty-foot cable. It reminded him of going up the climbing tower with Bigelow's wheelchair dangling behind him. Always something holding him down.

At fifty feet, Jason turned square into the wind. "Here we go, Rachel. You ready?"

"Ready or not, here it comes."

At twenty feet, he pulled down on both toggles to bring them to a stall. The equipment pack touched down nicely and dragged behind them. At this height, the ground always seemed to rush toward him too fast. But they lifted their feet and with a shock touched the ground.

Jason unhooked himself from the parachute and, reluctantly, from Rachel. She took a few steps and then promptly fell on her face. In the dim light, he could see Chris and Lewis touch down—in a heap—and Garth and Trieu going down farther north.

When they were all down, Jason adopted his best Russian accent and said, "Velcome to Kazakhstan, Comrades. Ve hope you vill enjoy your stay."

"CPU, this is Monitor. How copy? Over."

Jason looked at the satellite radio. "You sure this thing can reach the bird, Lewis?"

Lewis was still out cold, his head pillowed on his rucksack.

"Never mind," Jason said.

The hide was almost finished. There wasn't much of a riverbank to dig into, but it was better than digging straight down, and they had between them and the city the only bush for five hundred yards. Chris and Trieu were down at the river scavenging for driftwood to cover their little home away from home. Garth was still digging, muttering about having to dig in frozen ground. Rachel was at one side of the hole trying to change clothes under a camo blanket. At least this little burrow would give them a break from the Central Asian wind machine.

"Man, this place is even brown at night," Garth said. "I thought we might be getting in a little skiing on this trip."

Dawn was almost upon them. The growing light was exposing more and more endless nothing. They were in the middle of a windswept wasteland where no person in his right mind would want to go, much less live. The sound of jet engines rumbled at the edge of their hearing.

"What does it tell you," Garth said, dumping out a spade full of dirt, "if a river can't even support plant life right at its edge?"

"It says," Jason said, "that we don't drink the water."

Lewis began to stir. His leg moved like a puppy having a chasing dream. Jason wondered if the kid's Achilles' tendons were too short even in his dreams.

"Wake up, Lewis," he said. "I need you to help me with the

radio. I can't get anything."

Lewis sat up groggily. "Where am I?" Then it seemed to come to him. "I thought we were going to jump. Did we land instead?"

"Lewis, dude, wake up," Jason said. "You jumped out of the airplane. Don't you remember?"

He sat up. "No, I didn't."

"Yes, you did. And you said you were starting to like it. Didn't he, Trieu?"

Trieu smiled. "He may not remember."

"What?"

"It's one of the side-effects of the Versed."

"I did not jump," Lewis said. "You guys are pulling my leg. Come on, tell the truth. We landed." He went to the bushes by the entrance and pushed them away. "See. This is Utah. . .or. . .someplace." He looked doubtfully at Trieu. "Isn't it?"

Static hissed from the radio. "Monitor, Monitor, this is CPU. We've gotcha now." It was Bigelow's voice. "How copy? Over."

Jason raised the phone. "Copy fine, CPU. Good to hear your voice, Chimp. Report successful delivery and installation of all components and. . .peripherals. Over."

Lewis stared out into the night. "You mean, this is, like, Kazakhstan?"

Trieu nodded.

Bigelow's voice came through the speaker. "Copy safe delivery and install, Monitor. Good to hear it. What is your status? Over."

"CPU, Monitor. Settling in for the daytime. Incriminating evidence disposed of. Concealment almost complete. Everybody up and at 'em—finally. Preparing to send out. . .Scanner and WebCam. Over."

During the communications delay, Lewis pointed eastward up the river. "Ooh, camels!"

"Monitor, this is CPU. Copy your status and plans, and approve. Bad news on my pet bird, Icarus: He can't see you guys very well from where he flies. Maybe next time. Also, need to report problem with your. . .upload. Seems your ride decided to make a little side trip into the Far East. How copy? Over."

"Great," Chris said, approaching with a load of gnarled, bone-white sticks and a dead shrub. "Always something."

"CPU, Monitor. Copy side trip. Over."

"Chris," Lewis said, "we didn't jump out of the airplane, did we?"

Chris looked at him irritably. "Duh."

"Monitor, CPU," Bigelow's voice said. "Don't worry, though: It will be at your designated exfil facility when you need it. Over."

"Copy, CPU," Jason said. "That's good to know. Settling in for day shift now, CPU. Over."

Trieu brought a couple of tumbleweeds, which Garth and Chris added to the stack.

"Isn't anyone going to notice this shrub convention?" Lewis asked. "It's like the mouth of a black hole for dead bushes."

"Monitor, this is CPU," Bigelow said. "Copy day shift. Will call later with update. Over and out."

Jason switched off the radio and handed it to Lewis.

"Sun's coming up, folks," he said. "Let's get inside."

"Wait." It was Rachel's voice, but it wasn't Rachel who stepped out of the hide onto the scorched steppe. Instead, it was a poor Kazakh woman with a white turban on her head, a soiled tan robe with dirty red shoulder stripes, a simple ankle-length print dress that used to be beige, and brown fur-lined moccasins. Four nasty moles crowded her nose and cheeks, and a dark birthmark stretched down her jawline onto her neck.

"Ew," Lewis said. "What slimy hole did you crawl out of?

Garth smacked him upside the head. "Lay off, Lewis. She came out of the slimy hole you're about to spend the day in. Besides," he said, taking her hand to his lips, "I find old hags sexy."

"Ew."

"All right, Romeo," Jason said, pulling Rachel away. "Let's just hope the locals find her as uninteresting as Lewis does." He looked into her eyes, the only part of her face that looked familiar. "This is a new look for you, isn't it? You look. . .um. . .awful. Congratulations."

"Thank you."

"Are you sure about this?" he asked.

"Relax, Jason. I love it. I'm going to tell you a little secret. Promise you won't make fun of me?"

Jason pulled her down beside the bush for camouflage. "I promise."

"Well," she said, pressing her warts on tighter, "it's really not all that fun being. . .well. . .looking like I look all the time. You'll laugh, but it's actually a lot of pressure being the one who turns everybody's head. See, I told you you'd laugh. I knew you wouldn't understand." She stood.

Jason pulled her back down to a crouch. "I'm sorry. I just. . .I guess I just never thought it would be a bad thing to get every man's motor running when you walked into a room."

"It's not bad," she said. "I didn't say it was bad. Lord knows I count on it. I just said it was hard. Look, God made me this way, and I've mastered what He's given me. But sometimes it's nice to jump out of my skin and be somebody else, somebody that people ignore. Sometimes I find a character that I think I could be for a long time."

She stood and tucked a strand of hair under her turban. "Who knows, Jason? Maybe I'll become a kazakh goatherder's wife and you'll never hear from me again."

Jason stood, too. "Not funny. Lewis," he said over his shoulder, "where's Rachel's tracker from the Land Warrior thing? I want to know where she is all the time, in case she decides to take up goat herding."

"Already got it on," Rachel said. "Underneath."

"Jason," Trieu said, looking at the eastern horizon, "the sun."

"Right. Everybody inside. I'll cover the hole and climb in. Lewis, get the banshee going."

Rachel adjusted her dress and looked toward the awakening city.

"You sure you want to go alone?" Jason asked her. "I could throw something on and come with you."

Her eyes twinkled above the moles. "Hey, I used to do this for a living, remember? No problem." She winked. "Be good."

She hurried up the embankment toward the railroad leading into town. Jason watched her go, then hurried to cover their hide. Finally, he climbed in, bringing the last tumbleweed up into place.

The brown earth of their hole seemed to seep their warmth away, but it was better than the alternative. Chris posted himself as first lookout. Trieu had her helmet on with the eyepiece down. Her right eye was lit pale blue from the monitor. Garth was holding a light while Lewis unfolded his toy airplane. They all had chemical heat packs at their feet or under their rumps. The hole was probably the warmest spot for fifty miles around.

"How long can that thing stay up?" Jason asked.

Lewis brought his load bearing vest into his lap and located the mouse on the chest strap. "Usually, about forty minutes. But with this wind and the cold, I'll be lucky to get twenty out of it."

"And then how long to recharge?"

Lewis keyed the mouse to test the plane's propellers. They all whined to life.

"Hey," Chris said, not turning from his vantage through the brush. "Keep it down, would you?"

"I've brought two other batteries," Lewis said. "Takes about an hour to charge one back at home with a wall socket. Here, all we have is solar—except I didn't bring any panels—and shoe squish power."

"You mean we've got to jump around all day to charge your little birdie?" Garth said.

Lewis shrugged. "At least we've got some way to charge them."

"Should've used wind power," Chris said. "Got plenty of that. Ooh!" he said, craning his neck. "Something just flew by! I think it was an eagle owl. What's the subspecies for this area? *Bubo bubo turcomanus?*"

"Boobo-what?" Garth said.

"Shut up, barbarian. That's a lifer for me."

"A what?"

"Forget it."

Jason duck-walked over to Trieu. Even in desert fatigues and a cyborg Kevlar helmet, she managed to look refined. "Where is Rachel?"

Trieu lifted her helmet off and offered it to Jason. Her hair, which for the jump had been pinned down mercilessly, now spilled down gently over one shoulder. He put the helmet on.

The eyepiece showed the satellite photo of Baikonur City that he and Bigelow had planned the mission from. Five green dots clustered in a spot directly east of the city, next to the river. He found the sixth green dot in the southeast portion of downtown, near the new hotel.

He used Trieu's mouse to zoom in on the dot. It didn't show him anything else and the photo pixilated like crazy, but somehow seeing that fuzzy green dot that much larger made him feel like he was a little closer to Rachel. The hag.

"Jason?" Lewis said.

He handed the helmet back to Trieu. "You guys ready?"

"Yeah."

"How's it look, Chris?" Jason asked.

"Pretty good." He was using a small set of binoculars now. "Got some activity downriver about three miles. Looks like small horses or mules. And I've been hearing traffic noise picking up on the highway—though where anyone would want to drive to, I have no idea. I heard the MiGs a few minutes ago but haven't seen them. And no sign of the eagle owl. But there's nobody even breathing in our general direction right now. Can't see behind us, though."

"That's a problem," Jason said.

Garth rubbed his chin. "I'll start working on a periscope or something."

"Good idea, big guy," Jason said. "But for now, I'll just go out and take a look around."

He eased out of the hide and did a careful three-sixty. The clouds were pushing off to the south, revealing the dirty blue desert sky. In the purple smudge of the northern horizon, Jason could see low square buildings and a few satellite dishes pointing straight up. Nothing moved on the train tracks a mile away or the highway two miles beyond that.

"Bring it out, Lewis. You're clear."

Lewis crawled out of the hole with the banshee, its four legs and plastic dome looking even more alien in this wasteland. He keyed his mouse. The rotors screamed to life like shrieking eels, and he launched it straight from his hand. It cleared the embankment and was immediately swept toward the river by the airstream. Lewis leaned it into the wind and sent it upward.

"You want her stationed at two hundred?" he asked Jason.

"You think that's high enough? Can you go up to four just for starters? We'll get it over the city and then bring it down some if we need to."

"Sure."

"But let's get out of sight."

They went back in and covered the hole. It smelled musty and wet, like an old cave. Except for Chris, they all put on their helmets and flipped down their eye panels.

"Aw, man," Garth said, flipping through views with his mouse. "You mean I don't get ESPN on this thing?"

The images beamed into their helmets from the banshee revealed a depressed post-Soviet boomtown that didn't even appear to be fighting for life. It looked like an abandoned Mars colony. Though reports said ten thousand people lived here, even with the Aral Sea mob in town it was hard to find any evidence of current human habitation. A few buildings smoked blackly, and here and there were overturned cars, but nothing new seemed to be happening in town.

"How are we going to find anyone from this height?" Lewis asked. "Even at full zoom we can't tell a kid from a grownup."

"A 'grownup'?" Chris said incredulously. "Lewis, what do you want to be when you grow up? Maybe a fireman or an astronaut?"

"I didn't think we'd spot the girls from here," Jason said. "I just wanted to get the lay of the land. How we doing on battery?"

Lewis checked his watch. "Got another five minutes before I better start her back. Have to save some for loitering in case we've got company when she gets here."

"Okay," Jason said. "Well, let's use those five to try to find Rachel." He flipped his view over to the green dot map. "Looks like she's on main street there by the hotels. Everybody keep an eye out for school buses or semis just sitting around."

"Whoa, look at that," Lewis said. "That's a nice building."

"Sputnik Hotel," Jason said. "That's where all the police are supposedly holed up. Wonder where everybody is."

"Yeah," Garth said. "We ordered a bloodthirsty mob, and I'm not leaving here until I get one."

"Well. . ." Lewis said slowly. "I don't think I'm going to be able to spot Rachel from this altitude. I think she's there by those long tables or whatever they are."

"Looks like an open air market," Jason said.

"Wonder who they sell to," Lewis said. "Not tourists."

"They sell to each other," Trieu said. "They need each other to survive."

Jason looked at Trieu in the darkness and tried to picture her on the streets of Hai Duoung. He smiled and concentrated again on his eyepiece.

"Man, they did the damage quick, didn't they?" Chris said. "After just a few days of craziness, parts of this town look like Grozny after months of war. Hoo, they got after it."

"Yeah," Lewis said, "and how is it that these people can be having their little market day when the place is basically in chaos?"

"I guess it's like Trieu said," Jason said. "They need each other to live. And now that the action seems to have moved off somewhere else—anybody else think the spaceport?—I guess they're coming out of hiding to trade turnips."

"I'd better get the banshee back here," Lewis said. "We can launch her again with the new battery if you want."

"Nah," Jason said. "We'll save 'em for later."

"So you didn't see truckloads of angry villagers looting and pillaging?" Chris asked.

"Nope," Lewis said. "We're fresh out of lootage."

"Before you land, Lewis," Jason said, "can you point north again? I thought I saw smoke on the horizon."

The image rotated to the left. At the edge of the banshee's visual range there appeared to be a dark cloud close to the ground.

"Could be smoke," Jason said.

"Or a rain cloud," Trieu said.

"Or a dust storm," Lewis said.

"Or a flock of dim-witted runny-nosed heron gulls!" Garth said.

Chris didn't even blink. "Ha ha."

"Okay," Jason said, "when you get overhead, point down to scan the area. Then bring her down."

"Got somebody coming up along the riverbank," Garth said, peering through his makeshift periscope—the binoculars, two mirrors, and a stick.

"And we've got one green dot coming toward our position on the map," Trieu said, stretching from her nap.

Jason and Chris dropped their heat packs and grabbed their weapons.

"Is she alone?" Jason asked.

Garth squatted around the dirt in a circle. "It's getting darker out there, but I think so."

A hunched old woman appeared at the entrance to their hide.

Garth nodded to Jason. "It's clear."

Jason pulled the bushes aside and helped Rachel inside. She

looked even dirtier than when she'd left. She pulled off her turban and scratched through her hair.

"Here you go," Garth said, offering something to Rachel in his fingers. "One of your warts hit me in the face."

"Ew," Lewis said.

Jason handed her some water and she drank it all down. Makeup ran down her chin and dripped onto her dress. She gave the container back to Jason and then climbed into Trieu's lap.

"If you guys don't mind," Rachel said, "I'd like a little quiet time, okay? Just. . .let me rest a little before I have to be me again."

The four men exchanged looks.

"Rachel," Jason said, "are you—"

Trieu shushed him. She held Rachel's head to her chest and rocked gently. Lewis brought the camo blanket and put it over Rachel.

"Well," Jason said to the air, "anyone hungry?"

"Always," Garth said, digging through his rucksack. He brought out his night vision goggles and peered through his periscope again.

Jason brought out the MREs—meals, ready-to-eat. He read the packet labels by the light of a hooded flashlight. "Okay, I've got beef teriyaki, chicken strips in salsa, cheese tortellini. . ."

"I'll take the teriyaki," Chris said.

Jason tossed it to him and went on with the distribution. Rachel sat up and grabbed one packet for Trieu and one for herself. Soon, they were all enjoying the finest cuisine the American military could produce—with a three-year shelf life, to boot.

As the last Frito crunched in Rachel's mouth, the fatigue faded from her face. She primped at her hair, and it seemed to Jason that her aura swelled again to its usual size of five times bigger than the average person's.

"You guys," she said, "I don't know why anyone would ever want to live in this place. I mean, it's not like you can just run in to civilization when you want something. It's some kind of outpost on the edge of the earth. No wonder people blast off into space from here—anything's better than being stuck in this place." She eyed Chris's MRE package. "You going to eat your granola bar, Chris, honey?"

Chris handed it to her. "It's yours, sweetie."

She tore it open and took a fifth of it in one bite. "Sorry," she said over her chewing, "I skipped lunch and dinner. Jason said not to drink the water, but I figured the food wouldn't be any safer."

They waited as she consumed the bar, the last bites of which were accompanied by contented moans.

"If you want anything else," Garth said, "I spotted a dead camel across the river."

She punched his arm playfully.

"Okay," she said, wiping her mouth, "you probably want to hear what I found out there, huh?"

They laughed.

"What?"

"Never mind," Jason said. "Yes, do tell."

She sighed. "Well, for one thing, I could've used a lot more time with those Kazakh tapes. Maybe they speak Russian everywhere else in this country, but here there's an awful lot of people who don't. But I just acted hard of hearing to those people and gravitated to the Russian speakers.

"I can tell you that people are confused by the mob that came here. Most of them were ethnic Kazakhs, but most everybody in the city is, too. They came hunting Russians but found only people like them. Plus, most of the people here are mad at the Russians, too. Seems they don't always pay their rent for the launch pads.

"Guys, did you know there's two mayors in this city? One appointed by the president of Kazakhstan, the other by the president of Russia. There's also two police forces and two court systems. Weird.

"Anyway, people don't know whether to fight the mob or join them. I thought I was going to run into some pretty crazy stuff, but everything was kind of normal, except for the fires and crumbled buildings everywhere. The bazaar was open just like usual."

"Where'd everybody go?" Chris asked.

"Oh," she said, after a sip of water, "if any of you guys go out there, we're going to have to get you one of these beanies they wear. Just about every man I saw was wearing something on his head, either like a yamika or these pointed white ones that looked like boats you make out of a sheet of paper."

"Rachel," Jason said.

"And did I tell you about the children? They're so cute. Trieu, I saw this one little boy who—"

"Rachel."

"Huh?"

"That crazed mob we were sent here to rescue orphans from," Jason said. "Where are they?"

"Oh, at the Cosmodrome."

"Everybody?" Chris asked. "Even the people whose houses got burned down?"

"I don't know," Rachel said. "Maybe they left for the next town upriver or something."

Jason nodded. "Well, the ones from the Cosmodrome should be back soon, then. They'll be turned away by the soldiers."

"Ha," Rachel said with a snort. "From what I hear, there aren't that many soldiers there. One person said he's never seen more than thirty in one place. And, those 'soldiers' are all conscripts, teenagers pulled off the streets of Moscow and given the worst post in history. They don't get paid most of the time, and their living conditions are terrible. A few years ago, they mutinied. And," she said, beginning to pick moles off her nose, "the barriers at the entrances are supposedly flimsy or not even there."

"Well," Chris said, kicking Garth in the rump, "so much for the runny-nosed heron gull theory."

Rachel rummaged for her fatigues. "The what theory?"

"Never mind," Jason said. "So the smoke we saw may've been smoke after all." He whistled softly. "You gotta know there's Spetznaz on the ground here, or will be soon. And the Russian army's probably landing troop transports at the airport right now."

"That may not be all the players here," Garth said. "If I were China or Japan or somebody else trying to become a big-time space nation, I'd have my spec-ops guys in here taking advantage of the ruckus, wouldn't you?"

"Don't count out the U.S. of A, either," Chris said. "They'd want their piece of the action."

"Great," Lewis said, "ringside seats to the start of World War Three."

"Wouldn't miss it," Garth said, giving Chris a high-five.

"Perhaps it will be to our advantage," Trieu said, holding the blanket up so Rachel could change clothes.

"What do you mean?" Jason asked.

"I mean, with everything focused on the space port, perhaps no one will mind if we leave town with a group of children in buses."

Jason nodded. "Good point."

"Ooh," Rachel said, wrapping the blanket around her. Even in the darkness certain shapes were visible. "I heard something. Don't know if we can use it or not."

Jason looked at the dirt. "Yes?"

"The woman selling cabbages said there's a train stuck in Zhosaly, about fifty miles east of here. They were headed through to Moscow, but then they got word that the rebels had torn up the track. So there they sit. They may have to go backwards all the way to Almaty. But Kyzylorda is on the way to Almaty, so maybe we could hitch a ride."

"Hmm," Jason said. "Sounds like a possibility. We'd still have to get them across the fifty miles, though. Maybe tomorrow you can go to the train station and find out if it's still there."

"Oh, man!" Chris said. "I don't want to spend another day here. Let's find those kids and get out of here."

"What do you think we're trying to do, Chris?" Jason asked.

"You mean we might be leaving tomorrow?" Lewis asked.

"I'd like to be out of here tonight," Jason said.

Lewis's mouth hung open. "How could we do that?"

"What were you wanting to do," Chris asked, "stay here for your whole summer vacation?"

"It's kind of like how you thought the sky would be green, kid," Garth said. "You're thinking we've got to stay here for a week or a month or something. But this is a bona fide FedEx mission: Pick up the package and drop it off at its destination. Got your tracking numbers right here."

"But we don't even know where the kids are."

"Exactly," Jason said. "Which is why we'll probably still be here tomorrow for Rachel to go to the train station. But they're right, Lewis: We're not set up for anything over two or three days. We've got to get out soon."

"Then why'd you make us run so much?" Lewis said. "I thought we were gonna be doing something hard—or at least long. Man, think of all the computer gaming I gave up to run laps around that stupid compound."

"Lewis," Chris said, "man, you are such a dweeb!"

"Cool it, you guys," Garth said, the night vision goggles on again.

"All right, look," Jason said, checking his watch. "It should be totally dark in an hour or so. Rachel, why don't you try to get some sleep? The rest of us have napped."

"Yeah," Lewis said, "like most of the day."

"Oh," Rachel said with a yawn, "I'm fine."

"No way. Finish getting dressed and—"

"Yeah," Chris said, *"please."*

"What's the matter, Chris?" Garth said. "Are you distracted having a partially nude beautiful woman three feet away from you in the dark, clad only with the blanket you took your nappy in? Come on, dude, get a grip!"

"Why, Garth," Rachel said coyly, "you big pretender. I thought you never noticed."

"Huh."

"Rachel," Jason said, grinning in spite of his best efforts not to, "please finish getting dressed and at least lie down with your eyes closed. Trieu will protect you from any shenanigans. Then in about three hours we'll suit up and go see what we can see."

Lewis craned his neck toward Rachel. "You're nude?"

Chris threw an MRE at him.

CHAPTER 25

JERBOA

"NOW *this* is what a foreign country is supposed to look like."

Lewis looked at the other team members through his night vision goggles. "You guys all look like glowing green slime mutants."

"Lewis," Jason said, standing beside him inside their hide, "for next time, see if you can work out a way for the night vision to integrate with the other views. I don't like having to take the NV goggles off to flip down my eye panel. I want to be able to cycle through it just like anything else."

"Oh, ho-ho," Lewis said. "How quickly we come to rely on technology."

"Just work on it, okay?"

Lewis gave him a thumbs up, then proceeded to stare at his hand through his goggles.

Jason brought his night vision goggles down to see his team in the total dark. Their warm bodies stood out like green neon in the thermal and infrared-enhanced image. Six little mutants nestled in their pod.

"Everybody set?"

Before they could answer the radio hissed. "Monitor, this is CPU. How copy? Over."

Jason reached onto Lewis's backpack and grabbed the handset. "CPU, this is Monitor. Read you Lima Charlie. Over."

Lewis looked at Garth. "Lima Charlie?"

Garth leaned toward him. "Loud and clear."

"Oh."

"Monitor, CPU," Bigelow's voice said after the delay. "Report status. Over."

"CPU, this is Monitor. We have passed the day fine. WebCam and Scanner have given us good data. We are about to do a little Web surfing. Over."

During the delay, Jason strapped the NV goggles onto his helmet in order to operate the radio hands free.

"Copy Web surfing, Monitor. Any luck finding our little lost links? Over."

"Negative, CPU, negative. Hoping to find them now. Over."

"Copy, Monitor. Motherboard wants to know if you've found the other member of the staff. How copy? Over."

"CPU, Monitor. Copy fine. No luck on finding the missing staffer. Over."

"Copy, Monitor. Man, wish I were there with you, bro. Wish I could tell you if I was starting to get that feeling in my gut. Over."

Jason squeezed his eyes shut. "I wish you were here, too."

"Now don't get all mushy on me, Monitor. Listen up, I've got an update on your ride home. The bird is back in its original nest. No worries. Repeat, your ride is waiting. How copy? Over."

"Copy bird in original nest, CPU. Thanks. Will update you at zero hundred hours zulu. Over."

"Copy, Monitor. Happy hunting. Over and out."

Jason put the handset back. When he did, Lewis caught his arm. "Can I. . .have a word with you?"

"Sure. Chris, keep an eye out for a minute."

There wasn't exactly a side room they could go into for privacy, but Lewis led Jason as far away from the others as he could, and crouched with his back to them.

"Um. . .I'm a little unclear about something, Jason."

Jason nodded. "Shoot."

"Right, well. . .it's this whole shooting people thing. And them shooting back."

"Ah."

"I mean, up until now it's been this little game. We've been playing army. But now we're about to go out and sneak around where people have real guns with real bullets. And they don't want us to be here." He resettled himself on the dirt. "I'm just a little, um, concerned about that, is all."

Jason smiled. It struck him as a trifle odd to be having a counseling session in the middle of Kazakhstan in a dirt hole artificially lit by cyborg goggles. At least nobody else could see how silly they looked.

"Lewis," he said, "let me let you in on a little secret: They won't shoot you."

"Excuse me?"

"Hear me out," Jason said. "Bottom line: People don't like to kill other people. If you give the average guy a gun and tell him to shoot someone else, he won't do it. Would you? I read a paper once that said that in the Civil War, both sides reported an eighty to eighty-five percent non-firing rate. In other words, eight or nine out of every ten soldiers didn't even *fire* his weapon, let alone point it at anyone. The World Wars were the same.

"It wasn't until Vietnam that we figured out how to overcome that reluctance. That's when professional soldiers began to get deadly. It's also when we started hearing about this little thing called post-traumatic stress disorder and when we started seeing epidemic psych problems among combat vets. The two are related."

Jason didn't need high-tech goggles to pick up Lewis's skepticism. "You're making this up."

"No, I'm dead serious. I don't know what it is, Lewis. I think it's that we know that we're all connected somehow, that the guy on the other end of my barrel isn't that different from me. He's got kids, a wife, a favorite way to eat chicken. Whatever. 'What's he ever done to me?' So long as we're talking about civilians, when it comes time to open fire, it's usually only the mentally unstable who draw a bead on the other guy. Fortunately, there aren't as many psychos out there as the movies show.

"I'm telling you, Lewis: These peasants and farmers and fishermen we're going up against *will not* fire at you. And if they do shoot, it's just to keep their leaders off their backs. But they won't aim to try to kill you. Trust me, Lewis: In a fight like this, the safest place on the battlefield will be right in front of the guns.

"Another good thing is that the six of us don't have to overcome that aversion to killing. Why? Because our weapons don't kill. We're just using smelly paintball guns and sneaky dartguns. We can aim right at their bodies and not worry about actually killing anybody."

He put his hand on Lewis's shoulder. "You're going to be fine, Lewis. Don't worry about it. You'd have a better chance of getting shot if they were aiming at something besides you.

"Now let me tell you something else: You've helped us be even safer out there because of your green dot tech stuff and your little helicopter." He grabbed Lewis's helmet with both hands and looked him lens to lens. "Lewis, you are a solid part of this team. I'm glad you're here with me."

Jason could see his toothy smile even in the dark.

"All right, people," Jason said, moving out to the others. "Everybody got everything? We may not be coming back here."

Garth held up a plastic bag weighted with stones. "Just have to drop this trash where the chutes are swimming with the fishes."

"Check. Chris, are we clear?"

“Clear as Bachman’s Sparrow birdsong, baby.”

“Then let’s go find us some orphans.”

“Two more coming in from the northwest,” Chris said, pointing.

As the team watched through their night vision goggles, two military jets appeared on the horizon and roared eastward toward the Cosmodrome.

“That’s six MiGs in the area,” Garth said over the squad radio.

Jason nodded in the darkness. “Must be about to get serious in Sputnik City.”

As if on cue, they saw two white flashes—very light green in their goggles—from the direction of the spaceport. Several seconds later, they heard and felt the explosions. There was a loud *BAM!* followed by a quick sparkle of popping.

“Cluster bombs,” Garth said. “A lot of people just died.”

“Or wished they had,” Chris said.

“All right, people,” Jason said. “Let’s keep our minds on our own mission. Powerstrip, you and Scanner take up an overwatch position at the corner one block up to our right. Printer, you and Mouse do the same one block up to our left. When you’re set, Keyboard and I will check out what’s left of the orphanage.”

“Printer, copy,” Chris said.

“Powerstrip, copy,” Garth said.

As Jason and Trieu scanned the ruined homes and apartment complexes, watching for any people at all, the other two teams advanced away diagonally. Chris and Lewis ran toward the left, Garth and Rachel to the right.

Besides the green globs of the other team members, the only heat sources in Jason’s NV goggles were beds of embers in some of the gutted buildings. Streetlight poles, bereft of their light fixtures, poked out of the ground like giant soda straws. The Siberian wind whipped between buildings and accelerated over any flat space—of which there were now many more than there had been just a few days before.

"Man, look at this place," Lewis said. "It totally looks like *Ghost Recon II.*"

"Ghost what?" Garth asked.

"Ghost Recon. It's a computer game about special forces. But hey, now I'm living it."

"Whatever," Chris said. "I was going to say it looked like Bosnia."

The three teams advanced silently the rest of the way to their corners. Jason watched a cat trot down the street—perhaps the only creature able to see them in the utter darkness.

"Powerstrip and Scanner in position," Garth said.

"Copy," Jason said.

"Printer and Mouse in position," Chris said.

"Check. Sweep your field of fire and report."

"Hey, this is great," Lewis said, a curious squeaking sound audible with his voice. "You guys gotta see what we found."

"What is it, Lewis?" Rachel asked.

"Shh!" Jason said. "Keep the chatter down. And stick to code, Scanner."

"Sorry," Rachel said.

"Hey, Scanner," Lewis said. "We found us a full dining room set right here in this vacant corner. Table with tablecloth, nice chairs. And I found me a nice easy chair. Right on top of the mud and fallen down timbers. What a riot."

"Quiet," Chris said.

"Miss my chemical heatbag, though. Brrr. Gonna have to figure out a way to work those into our unif—"

"Hey," Chris said, *"be quiet!"*

"Monitor, this is Powerstrip," Garth said. "The field is clear on this side."

"Check."

"Looking good over here, too," Chris said.

"Check. Monitor and Keyboard moving in."

Rubble covered the ground as if a giant toddler had come in and knocked everything over. Bricks, upended furniture, burned rafters, discarded weapons, and plain old trash littered the ground exactly as they had in other war torn cities. While some buildings still stood, most were on the brink of collapse. Some were missing corners, some were blackened by smoke, and some were gone completely. Jason could see stars through the wall of one of the dingy white apartment buildings that lined the street.

Still not a human in sight.

Jason and Trieu reached the front of the orphanage. It had burned almost to the ground. A brick husk remained to mark the general layout of the building. The walls had five feet of solid concrete at the bottom. The first ten rows of pink bricks remained in places.

Jason signaled for Trieu to take cover and watch behind him while he went inside the ruins. She crouched against the wall. Jason stepped through the entryway.

It didn't look like anyone could've survived this fire if they'd been here when it happened. Everything that had been on the upper story was represented in the pile of dark rubble before him. The infrared imagers in his goggles gave him a green monochrome view of the destruction. He saw furniture amid the heap of ash and plaster: overturned desks, chunks of couch stuffing, a blackened refrigerator, and dozens of metal bed frames.

Jason's stomach constricted. In his mind's eye, he saw dozens of orphan girls having pillow fights on these beds. The frames were so tiny. Suddenly this wasn't a cut-and-dried FedEx op anymore: Now it was a rescue mission. If any children had survived this inferno, they were somewhere close, and they needed help *right now.*

"There's nobody here," he said, half to himself.

"Copy, Monitor," Chris said.

"Let's try the market square," Rachel said. "That's where I think they'd go."

Jason kicked around in the wreckage, half-dreading to find a little human ribcage. As he searched, his mind tried to reconcile this newfound desire to save the children with the demands of his own private plan. Probably there was no conflict. Probably he could still make sure the children got out safely. All along that had been part of the deal, anyway. His own little plot could proceed unchanged, he decided. It was just that before, the kids were just packages to be delivered. Now they were little girls who slept in little steel beds. It made a difference somehow.

"Monitor, Monitor," Garth said with intensity. "This is Powerstrip. Have one contact approaching your position. Repeat: One contact approaching your position."

Jason snapped into battle mode. He crouched and gripped his MP-5 with both hands. "Copy, Powerstrip. Is my partner exposed?"

A pause.

"Affirmative, affirmative. Keyboard, get inside."

"Monitor," Rachel said. "It's a child. I think it's a girl."

"Understood," Jason said. "Keyboard, come on in, nice and slow."

He watched Trieu duckwalk toward the threshold, her CAR-15 held down but ready.

"Twenty meters," Garth said. "Looks like she's carrying a two-liter bottle of something.

"Should we tranq her and take her someplace for questioning?" Lewis asked.

"Don't you dare!" Rachel said. "If anybody touches this little girl, they'll have me to answer to."

Trieu was almost across the threshold. Only her trailing leg remained outside. When she lifted it, a square of broken tile shifted against a brick.

"She's stopped," Garth whispered. "Contact has stopped."

Jason held his breath. He slid his goggles aside and dropped his eye panel down. He keyed his mouse to cycle through the images. He paused at the map overlay and saw where the red dot was in proximity to his and Trieu's green dots.

Finally he switched to the video through Garth's gun scope. The image here was straight black and white infrared. He could make out a dim figure crouched behind a mound of bricks. It did look like a girl. She had collar-length hair, but beyond that he couldn't see much. She was very still. And patient. If it weren't for the slight movements of the camera, Jason could have believed he was looking at a photograph.

In the distance, he heard another cluster bomb explode.

Damira flinched at the booming. She had to get back. The little ones would be scared of these new sounds that made the ground shake.

But she'd heard something from the orphanage. Probably a dog or maybe a jerboa. Damira thought of herself as a jerboa now: tiny, smart, quiet, and only out at night. If only she could jump as high as one of those little rodents, maybe she could find more food for the girls.

Still, everybody was counting on her. Best to not take a chance.

She eased away from the bricks and began backing toward the corner of the orphanage, her precious mineral water in both hands. She would take the long way, just to be sure.

"Little girl!" a voice called in Russian.

Damira froze. It sounded like a woman's voice.

"Little girl, don't be afraid."

It could be a trick. Damira rounded the corner but turned back to watch.

"I only want to talk with you. Will you let me come close to you?"

A part of Damira desperately wanted to go to the voice. Either this was a trap and she would be taken to some terrible place, like they did to Yulia—or killed, like they did to the others. Or this really could be a woman who only wanted to help her. Either way, her jerboa days would be over and she could get out from under her crushing burden. She took a step forward.

"I'm looking for the orphan girls who used to live at this orphanage," the voice said. "Do you know where they might be?"

A trap! Damira ran.

"Wait! Please don't run!"

She darted between the orphanage and the apartments next door. Where should she go? Not to where the others were hiding. The water sloshed in her arms and grew heavier with every footfall. She turned right at the next street, even though that was toward the place where the soldiers were. She heard the woman calling behind her and the sounds of someone trying to run across the shifting rubble.

A giant stepped out in front of her. He had a gun and wore a soldier's uniform, and was almost twice as tall as any man she'd ever seen. Even in the dim starlight she could see that something was wrong with his eyes. They were all black, with one eyeball right in the middle. He reached out a log of an arm to catch her.

She yelped in spite of herself. He clawed at her cloak, but she fell and backed away. Her cloak fell open and a rush of cold air penetrated all the way to her skin. People were coming, running up behind her. She rolled to her knees and stood, but the water bottle slipped out of her hand and rolled toward the giant.

"Please!" the woman's voice said. She was one of the ones running up.

Damira stood poised behind a twisted bicycle on the ground. Her eyes darted from the giant to the newcomers to the water bottle.

"Little girl," the woman said from the darkness, "we won't hurt you. We've come from far away to help the orphans who lived here. Please, can you tell us where they are?"

There were more than three, Damira could tell. The woman, the giant, and at least two others coming up behind. She should run. But what if it were true? She'd been given one miracle—she still wasn't sure how she got out of the orphanage alive. Who was to say another miracle couldn't have happened to bring strangers from another place to rescue her again?

"I'm going to step forward," the woman said. "I'm going to let you see my face so that you can see that I'm telling the truth."

Damira heard the woman whispering to her companions in another language. She caught some words she knew, but for a while she couldn't place the language. Then she knew.

"You speaking English," she said in that language.

The strangers weren't expecting that. They stopped talking and looked at her. One of them turned on a dim flashlight and pointed it at the ground. In the half light, Damira could see that they were all wearing the same soldier uniforms and that they all carried guns. She got nervous again.

"Now," the woman said, switching back to Russian, "I'm going to take off my hat so you can see my face."

The woman took her helmet off and let it hang over her shoulder on some kind of cable. She knelt amid the rubble and shone the light on her own face. She wasn't as old as Miss Ashirova. She looked about Yulia's age. It was a nice face.

"Do you see me?" the woman asked. "Will you answer my question?"

Damira didn't speak. No matter how nice this woman was, there was no getting around the fact that they were more than her, bigger than her, faster than her—and all had guns. She really wanted to run. If only she could grab her water bottle.

The woman must've seen her look at it, because she picked up the plastic bottle and offered it to Damira. "Here you are."

Damira held it to her chest.

"You're a pretty little girl," the woman said. "I can see you in my light. Can you please just tell me if you know anything about the girls who lived in that orphanage? Were they killed in the fire?"

That sounded like a fairly safe question. Damira shook her head.

The strangers mumbled. She could see six of them, including another woman. She looked Asian, like the Koreans in Baikonur City. Maybe there was a whole army of nice soldiers in the streets.

"Little girl," the woman said, talking faster than before, "do you know something about these girls? Can you take us to them?" She took her large backpack off and unzipped it. Out of it she pulled a blanket, a pair of thick pink socks, and some candy bars. "You see? We've brought things for the girls. We want to take them away from here, away from the danger, to another orphanage where they can be safe—and maybe find families to adopt them."

How could Damira decide to trust them or not without talking to Roza and the other girls? But how could she get to the girls without these soldiers following her and finding them? The hunger and the fear and the fatigue fell in on her like the walls of the orphanage.

She started to cry.

Rachel bridged the final three feet and took the little girl into her arms. That only made her cry harder.

Jason hadn't followed a bit of what Rachel had told her, but he could read this picture just fine. He turned to the others. "You guys stay sharp. We're in a dark alley in a town that won't appreciate our presence."

Rachel asked the girl something in Russian. They went back and forth for a while. Finally, Rachel kissed the girl's forehead and stood up.

"Blindfold me," she said.

Jason shifted his weapon. "What?"

"She's going to lead me somewhere. To the orphans, I hope, but maybe not. When she figures out she can trust me, I will call for you guys."

Garth produced a red bandana from his pack. "You're a brave woman, Rachel," he said softly.

The little girl said something and pointed at Garth.

Rachel looked at him. "She wants to know if you're an angel."

Chris coughed.

"She says someone with strong arms saved her from a burning

building. She thinks it was an angel, but one of the girls who saw it said it was just a very tall man. She thinks it might've been you."

Garth knelt down to her level. "You tell her that it wasn't me, but that if she ever finds herself in another burning building when I'm around, I'll come and get her for sure."

Rachel interpreted. The girl smiled shyly and tried to vanish into Rachel's shoulder.

Garth put the blindfold on, and the girl led Rachel away.

"Call us on the radio, Rachel," Jason whispered after her. "We're going to move back out to the front of the orphanage. Better fields of fire."

They stood in a line and watched the two green globs depart.

"Did we just send her off alone with someone who could lead her straight to bad guys with guns?" Chris asked.

"Um, Chris," Lewis said, "I think she just heard you on the radio."

Garth knocked on Chris's helmet. "Nice going, bird boy."

"Her helmet was off! Wasn't it?"

"Come on," Jason said, "let's go get settled again. We can watch her on the green dot screen."

CHAPTER 26

Uncle Monte's Used Camel Sales

"Looks like the game's over and the fans are leaving the stadium."

"Yeah," Lewis said to Jason, "except these fans are leaving at eighty-five miles an hour."

Jason nodded, one eye under his helmet panel. "And pretty much ignoring the roads. Yes, they're definitely in a hurry to get away from there. Can you blame them? How many cluster bombs would it take to make you want to leave?"

"None."

The view through Jason's eyepiece was black and white infrared again, but it was completely adequate for this shot. The banshee's camera showed a fleet of headlights—from cars, trucks, motorcycles, and three- and four-wheelers, their engines white in the infrared image—fleeing from the direction of the Baikonur Cosmodrome. Overturned hulks could be seen burning in the distance. Overhead, the MiGs made strafing runs. And after every one, fewer headlights were left approaching the city. But there were still enough coming to make life more complicated in the city.

"Printer," Jason said into the radio, "this is Monitor. How copy?"

"Monitor, Printer," Chris said. "Copy Lima Charlie. Over."

"Copy, Printer. Be advised that this ghost town is about to receive an influx of immigrants from the north. How copy?"

"Monitor, this is Printer. Understood." Chris said. "Can we head to the green dot yet?"

Jason looked over at Trieu. "What do you say, Keyboard? Is she still in that location?"

"Yes. And I can hear her talking with several young voices. I have even heard laughter."

"Excellent," Jason said. "But we'd still best wait for her call."

"Jason," Lewis said, his hand covering his microphone, "I'd better bring the banshee back home."

"Fine, do it."

The camera view swiveled away from the headlights and turned toward the south.

"Monitor, this is Printer," Chris said. "How copy? Over."

"Printer, this is Monitor. Copy Lima Charlie. Over."

"We found reliable transportation, Monitor."

Jason clenched his fists in victory. "Excellent, Printer. Well done."

"You're not going to believe what we found, Monitor." It was Garth's voice.

"What is it, PowerStrip, a blimp?"

"No, sir," Garth said. "We got us a special deal at Uncle Monte's Used Camel Sales. She's a real beaut. I think it's gonna be love at first sight."

Jason exchanged glances with Trieu and Lewis. "A camel, huh? Well, I guess that's fine. I was thinking more along the lines of a truck. But bring it on out here and we'll take a look."

"Monitor, this is Scanner," Rachel's voice said. "How copy? Over."

"Copy fine, Scanner," Jason said. "What's your status? Over."

"We've found the girls! Come on over. Some of them are sick and they're all cold and hungry. But they're safe and sound and ready to get out of here."

"Scanner, this is Monitor. Understood. Well done. We're on our way with provisions and a new set of wheels—er, humps. See you soon."

Lewis brought the banshee down and folded it into his pack. He and Jason and Trieu headed off toward Rachel's position.

This was going better than Jason could've hoped.

If Jason hadn't been using his green dot map, he never would've known that Rachel was behind the ruined Volkswagen Jetta. It was parked askew on a rubble-strewn dirt square that used to be the parking lot for a two-story office building. Even the thermal imaging didn't pick up any sign of her body heat.

"We're here, Scanner," he said.

She rose from a crouch. She had her helmet on again and the NV goggles over her eyes.

"Excellent concealment," Jason said. "Who was your teacher?"

"Um, some ex-special forces jock who thought he was all that." She took her helmet off. "Can we talk without mics for a minute?"

Jason took his helmet off, too. "Sure."

Rachel led Jason and Trieu and Lewis down beside the Jetta and an overturned Opel Vectra.

"They're very scared," she said. "They've seen things no child should ever have to see. We can't just all rush in there, not if we don't want to send them running."

"What do you suggest?" Jason said.

"Let me take Trieu in. They'll take to her because she's a woman and because they're used to Asian faces."

Trieu nodded. "I'll need you to interpret for me."

"Right," Rachel said, "but at least they'll let you close. Then I'll talk to them about you, Jason. You can come in next."

"What about me?" Lewis said.

"You can come in right after Jason." She looked around. "Where are the guys?"

"Bringing our transportation," Jason said.

"They said they got a camel," Lewis said.

Rachel stood. "Well, whatever gets us out of here. Trieu, you ready?"

Trieu shouldered her CAR-15 and slung her helmet over her shoulder. "I hope I don't frighten them."

Rachel took her hand. "Come on."

Jason and Lewis watched opposite directions on the street. Down Lewis's way, the dirt street was fairly clear. Where it intersected with another road, a building had completely collapsed. A fire truck lay partially buried in the avalanche. The view down Jason's way was more grim. It looked like photos of London during the Blitz. Airy skeletons of buildings lined the streets. Blocks of stone and concrete lined their perimeters like cookie crumbs. There was a smell of smoke and ash on the wind.

The building Rachel had led Trieu into was squat and square. If this had been America, it would've been a school district administration building. The right corner of it had caved in. Girders and electrical wires spilled out onto the lot. The rest of the upper story looked intact. Jason even saw air conditioner units in two of the windows, though the windows had no glass.

"Powerstrip, Printer, this is Monitor," Jason said. "How you doing with our. . .wheels? Over."

When Garth spoke, he seemed to be out of breath. "Monitor, this is Powerstrip. Having some trouble convincing our furry friends to go the direction we want. Neither one of us speaks camel. Headed to your current position soon. Over."

"Copy, Powerstrip."

Rachel's voice came through his helmet speakers. "Monitor, we're ready for you two. Over."

"Copy, Scanner, coming in."

Rachel met them in the entrance. "They're in the basement," she said.

At some point, this had been a decent place to have an office job. The walls had been white. There had been potted plants and maps on the walls. As the hallway opened into a reception area, there was even a hardwood floor. But now it was just another victim, first of the fall of the Soviet Union and then of the recent violence. The whole place reeked of broken sewage pipes. Rachel led them over piles of collapsed ceiling and dented metal filing cabinets.

She came to a metal door and pulled it open. A dark stairwell led down. At the end of it was another door. Faint light escaped underneath it.

"Take off your helmets," she said. "There are candles inside." She knocked three times and pushed.

The door swung open to reveal a squalid basement packed wall to wall with little girls.

Warm air greeted them, and Jason noticed the telltale orange light of an electric space heater in the center of the room. The plaster was largely gone from the walls, leaving a mostly brick look that restaurants back home paid big money to achieve. Dozens of girls sat on the floor or leaned against the wall or laid under blankets. Trieu knelt beside one, listening through a stethoscope. Thick white candles stood around the room on cinder blocks.

There were girls with wide Slavic faces and girls with round Asian faces and girls with pale European faces. Several of them were trying on new thick socks or spreading out new blankets. But when they noticed Jason, they all leaned away.

"It breaks my heart," Rachel said quietly to Jason, "all these girls here with no one to protect them. More than ever, I'm glad I said yes to Miss Eloise."

She spoke to the girls and pointed at Jason. He heard her say his name.

In a chorus, they said, "Dobrie vecher, Jason."

Rachel beamed. "They said, 'Good evening.' "

"Oh," Jason said. "Hello, girls."

She said something to them in Russian and they all giggled. Then she brought Lewis in.

"Dobrie vecher, Lewis." Actually, *Lewis* sounded more like *Loo-ees.*

Lewis waved and shook his head playfully. "Rachel, do you think I could show them the banshee?"

"You mean fly it? In here?"

"Just for a minute. I'll be careful."

She and Trieu exchanged a look. "Okay, Lewis," Rachel said, but let me explain it first.

While Rachel spoke to the children, Lewis unfolded the four-legged enigma. The girls' eyes widened and they scooted closer.

Lewis swiveled his head to Rachel. "Did you tell them it was going to be loud?"

She nodded.

"Okay," he said, "here goes."

Lewis keyed his vest mouse to power up the rotors. The whine increased until it seemed tremendously loud in the enclosed space. Several girls covered their ears, and more than one began to cry. But Lewis went on. The banshee rose from his hand and floated over their heads. The girls gasped and backed away, but their eyes never left it.

He flew it across the room and back. Then he brought it down to his hand, like a hunting falcon, and killed the engines.

You would've thought Lewis had just raised the dead the way the girls reacted to him. They surged around him, reaching to touch the banshee, petting his arm shyly. They asked him a hundred questions. He just smiled and made faces for them. They giggled and pressed forward all the more. "Loo-ees."

Jason stepped to Rachel. "Who knew that Lewis was Ronald McDonald in disguise?"

She smiled. There was something maternal about her now. Her

face glowed from more than the candlelight as she watched the girls having fun. "I wonder how long it's been since someone played with them like this."

He put his arm around her. "You've done awesome, Rachel. Getting that girl to listen to you, then arranging all this. I don't know how we could've ever gotten this far without you."

She looked up at him, not separating from his embrace. Instead of answering, she laid her head against his chest. "How do you do that?"

"Do what?"

"Make me feel like I can do anything."

He smiled. "Rachel, honey, I think God did that. I've never known anybody as capable as you of reaching any goal she wants. I'm just telling it like it is."

Trieu approached them. Rachel pulled away from Jason and he dropped his arm.

"Well, doc," Jason said, "are they fit to travel?"

She nodded. "Yes. It's a miracle. I didn't want to mention it before, but I was truly expecting to find a group of dead children here. This many days in this weather without heat would've left the youngest ones dead and the older ones with advanced frostbite. This five dollar space heater has saved all their lives."

Jason shook his head. "I guess the real miracle is that the power stayed on the whole time."

"Oh, it didn't," Rachel said. "They've had outages. Once they even started a fire in here, but the room filled with smoke and they had to do without. But always the power would come back on."

"How did they find this place?" he asked.

"Damira says she found it when she was out scavenging for food," Rachel said.

"Which one's Damira?" Jason said.

"Oh, sorry. She's the one we met outside. She's right there by Lewis. Anyway, the night their building burned down they tried to get to the

Russian Orthodox church. But it was burning, too. Somehow they found this place. Damira's been bringing mineral water from a stash she found in the basement of another house that got burned down."

"Amazing," Jason said.

"Thank You, Father," Rachel said.

"I am worried about one of the girls, Jason," Trieu said. She nodded toward an unconscious girl lying under blankets near the space heater. An IV bag hung from a cinder block beside her. "Liliya. The girls helped me understand that she's a diabetic. But since her insulin was lost in the fire, she's been without. Now she's in a diabetic coma. I've got her on saline and have given her a shot of insulin, but there's still a real chance that we could lose her." She looked at Jason. "When can we get moving?"

"As soon as the bus gets here."

"What about the hospital in the city?" Rachel asked. "Couldn't we go by there and get whatever Trieu needs, or even just leave Liliya in their care?"

"We might," Trieu said.

"You guys really want to leave one of these girls here?" Jason said. "Think about it: When they release her, what happens? Trieu, do you think she can make it to the plane?"

Trieu looked over at Liliya. "I just don't know. She is so small. I should be monitoring her blood sugar levels, but I need a blood sugar level tester to do that, so I'm only guessing at doses of insulin. And my supply of insulin is not large. I would like to take her to the hospital here, but I agree that is not the best solution. If we can hurry to another facility and if my dosage calculations are correct, she may be all right."

Rachel was looking at Damira. "Liliya is the one who said she saw the tall man carrying Damira out of the burning orphanage. Do you guys think it could've been an angel that saved her?"

"Nah," Jason said. "Probably she just walked out on her own and doesn't remember it. Like Lewis on the Versed."

"Perhaps," Trieu said. "But I would not be so hasty to discount the girl's story. I have seen many unexplainable things in my country."

The little girls whined. Jason looked up to see Lewis putting the banshee away. But he opened his pack and started handing out trick-or-treat sized Three Musketeers bars. Jason shook his head. "Who knew?"

He felt a tug on his sleeve. It was Damira, standing with another girl about the same age.

"Jason," Damira said, her English heavily flavored with Cyrillic pronunciations. "My name is Damira."

"Yes, I know, Damira. I'm Jason."

Damira turned to her companion. "This person name Roza."

Roza curtsied quickly. "Ochen priyatna."

"Roza speaking you a thing," Damira said.

"I'm sorry?" Jason said.

Roza launched into a Russian monologue that Jason had no hope of understanding. Whatever it was, she was deadly serious about it. It interested the other girls, too, because they all fell silent while she spoke. Rachel asked questions occasionally as Roza spoke.

As he listened, Jason's gaze was drawn to Damira, who was now tearing into a Three Musketeers bar. She was not the prettiest girl in the group, but the focus of her eyes and the tilt of her head bespoke intelligence. She had short, dark brown hair and black eyes. Her skin was darker than Jason's, but she didn't look Slavic or Asian. Jason felt foolish to think it, but to him she looked *American.*

Whatever it was that had begun in him back in the ruins of the orphanage picked up again at full speed. Here was a child who had been dealt a lousy hand, and yet she had taken responsibility for scores of girls and was out risking her life to keep them alive. She could even manage a smile now and then. She was a survivor and a protector. A little like him.

But she was tiny and vulnerable. So many things in this world—in this city—transpired to flick this little girl's life away. An unexpected fury arose in Jason. He had to get this girl and these others away from here—personally, himself, not by proxy.

Which presented a certain dilemma for him, since his private little plan didn't exactly allow for the personal touch on such things.

Finally Roza stopped, and Rachel turned to Jason.

"You should hire these girls as your information network."

"What did she say?"

"She knows where they're keeping Yulia, the young woman who worked at the orphanage," Rachel said. "She says that Yulia is alive, or was two days ago, and that some people she's calling Egyptians are holding her."

"Where?"

"In one of the older hotels in the city center. The Kometa. She could probably show you on a map." Rachel lowered her voice. "They are all very worried about Yulia. They've asked us—actually, they've asked you—to save her."

Though Jason knew zero Russian, the word *nyet* was suddenly on his tongue. "Rachel, this is not what we came here to do. That woman is in the heart of the city's worst conflict zone, probably surrounded by dozens of armed Middle Eastern zealots who are getting very nervous right now because the noose is tightening around the city. We'd have to spend a week gathering intel and planning the mission. No, Rachel. Let's just get these girls on the truck and get out of here."

"Um, Jason?" Lewis said, for the moment released from his adoring fans.

"What is it, Lewis?"

"I don't know, but I'm pretty sure that Miss Eloise would want us to at least try to rescue this girl. If you want, I can get Doug on the phone for you."

It occurred to Jason belatedly that what they were arguing about might actually be the break he'd been looking for to enact his plan. It was almost too good, as if God were handing it to him with a bow on top. Surely God couldn't be in favor of what he had in mind, though, right? But no matter why it was staring him in the face, Jason wasn't going to miss the opportunity it presented.

"Tell you what," he said, trying to sound like he were giving in reluctantly. "Find out from Roza where the hotel is. When Chris and Garth get here with the transportation, I'll go take a look. If it looks doable, I'll meet up with you guys and we can try to put something together." Was he making too much of a sudden change? That would arouse suspicion. Better amend the statement. "Something conservative, though. I really don't think it will work at all. But I'll at least go eyeball it."

Lewis nodded and went back to the kids. Trieu left them and wove her way to check on Liliya. Rachel got with Roza about the location of the hotel.

"Monitor, this is Powerstrip," Garth said over the squad radio. "Your limo is here. Over."

"Powerstrip, this is Monitor," Jason said. "Copy. Hang tight. I'll be right up."

Suddenly, the moment he'd been waiting for since that day in the ABL observation room was hanging in the air in front of him. Jason's mind volunteered a hundred reasons why his plan was wrong. But all he had to do to overrule the objections was conjure up his oft-replayed montage of Doug Bigelow.

In his mind's eye, he saw the man he was supposed to assassinate, with crosshairs over his face. He saw the little girl laughing in her father's arms. He saw the look in Lieutenant Semper's eyes when he found out Jason hadn't taken the shot. He saw Doug flying through the air and landing in the mud. He saw him tied down to the bed on the carrier. *I'll never forgive you!* And he saw Doug wheeling into his life again.

Bigelow's wheelchair was hanging on Jason now as surely as it had at the climbing tower. It was finally time to give in to gravity.

He walked solemnly to Trieu. She was taking Liliya's pulse. He waited and then stood her up to face him. "Trieu, I'm putting you in charge of getting these children onto whatever transport the guys have brought us, all right? I'm trusting you to see that they arrive at the airport in as good a condition as possible."

She cocked her head. "You are rejoining us, aren't you? And don't we still have to think about Yulia?"

"Right, right. I'm just saying that I might be concerned with other things and I wanted you to, you know, know what I expected of you." For the first time since they'd boarded the C-130, he was sweating.

"Of course, Jason," Trieu said.

"Okay, good."

He walked to Rachel, who was singing to a three-year-old girl on her lap. She looked radiant. He put a hand on her shoulder and luxuriated at the feel of her.

She finished singing and put the girl down. "I found out where the Kometa is." She pointed out its location on a map of the city Jason produced from a pocket.

"Um, Rachel. I. . ." He cleared his throat. "I've enjoyed getting to know you, Rachel. And," he added quickly, "I look forward to lots more time with you when we get back."

Her forehead wrinkled. "Are you okay, Jason?"

"Sure. Oh, yeah. Fine. So, I guess I'll be going now."

"Hang on." She escorted Jason to a dim corner. "Be careful, okay?"

"Oh, yeah. Always."

Her eyes narrowed. "Are you sure you're all right?"

"I'm fine, Rachel. Just. . .looking forward to getting on with things."

"Okay, well, I guess I'll let you go." She looked as if she were about to say more, but instead she brought her lips to his cheek. "Be careful, Jason. I think we have lots to talk about."

Despite the sudden spike in ambient room temperature, Jason managed to disengage from Rachel. He stepped over to Lewis and shook the boy's hand. Then, with a last look at Damira, he slipped out of the basement.

Jason had never seen a camel wagon before. If asked before this moment, he would've denied that such a thing were possible. Yet parked on the street was a two-camel team hitched to a flatbed trailer long enough for all the girls to ride on.

A camel is a strange looking animal anyway, Jason thought, but glowing in night-vision green these two double-humped beings looked positively extraterrestrial. Garth stood beside one of the beasts, holding tight to the bridle. Chris was offloading the last of the plastic PVC pipes that the wagon had been carrying.

"So this is what you got at Uncle Monte's?" Jason said.

Garth stroked one of the camels on the neck. "Ain't they beautiful?"

"We're not going to set any land speed records," Jason said, "but I suppose it will do. Good job, guys. Hey, Garth, do you think you can you rig something to keep the girls out of sight and out of the wind?"

Garth stroked his goatee. "I'll give it some brain juice, boss."

"The city's filling up," Chris said. "We've been seeing and hearing vehicle traffic behind us. And don't think I'm crazy, but just in the last ten minutes I think I've been hearing rotor thump."

Jason scanned the sky. "Slow movers, huh?"

"Possibly," Chris said. "I'm thinking the MiGs were just the opening act and maybe they've got some Night Havoc gunships coming in to really lay on the TNT. Meanwhile the troops are probably offloading at the airport."

"Hmm," Jason said. "Could get ugly. These camels come with a turbo setting?"

"You'd be surprised," Garth said. "Are the girls in there?"

"Yeah. They're doing really well, considering. Got one who's pretty sick, though. At least see about keeping her out of the wind, okay?"

Jason fastened his chinstrap.

"Where you going?" Chris asked.

"Oh, one of the girls thinks she knows where that other orphanage worker is being held. Lewis threatened to tell on me if I didn't at least go have a look at the situation. They want us to pull a hostage rescue, but there's no way we're ready for that."

Jason let the words sit there on the rubble between them. Surely he could count on these two to vote the way he wanted.

"Yeah," Chris said, "it's messy. And getting messier by the minute. Don't you guys hear that? Chum-chum-chum."

"No," Garth said, "and neither do you. I don't know, boss," he said to Jason. "Big Mama sounded pretty keen on us taking care of this woman, too. I figure she would tell us to go for it."

"Forget it," Jason said. "I'm not risking forty birds in the hand to go for one in the bush."

"Jesus left the ninety-nine to go after the one," Garth said.

"Yeah," Chris said before Jason could answer, "but the ninety-nine were already safe."

"Besides," Jason said, "it's also my job to bring all of you back home safe and sound. So forget it. I promised I would go check it out, so I will. You get the girls loaded on and get down to the river. Go straight upstream until you're a mile or so out of town and then get to the road. I'll catch up with you. But don't wait for me, understand?"

"Hang on," Chris said, taking his MP-5 off his shoulder. "I'll go with you."

"No," Jason said, perhaps too quickly. "No, I need everybody here working on the primary mission. I'll probably be back before you're even ready to leave. No, Chris, I'm fine. Thanks, though."

Jason shook hands with both of them. "You guys. . .take care of everybody, okay? Until I get back, I mean. I'm counting on you to pull this thing off. And I know I can count on both of you to watch out for Rachel and Trieu."

"Hey," Chris said with a shrug, "I watch out for everybody."

"Yeah, right," Garth said.

"Okay, I'm gone," Jason said. "You guys have fun on your hayride."

CHAPTER 27

A Simple Plan

JASON watched five green dots intersect with the river and start moving east. He sighed deeply. His responsibility was over. The girls were away, and the team was safely on its way out of the city. Now for one last thing.

He had been hearing increasing air traffic overhead and around the airport west of town. Trucks full of fighters armed with rocket propelled grenades sped by where he was hiding. These didn't look like farmers and fishermen. In fact, they looked exactly like Middle Eastern men in a holy war.

Where had the outraged Aral Sea people gone? Probably home. If they'd gotten here on the momentum of their dissatisfaction, that momentum would've suddenly deserted them the moment the first cluster bomb fell. But as he watched another pickup full of what looked like Muslim fighters roll by, Jason began to wonder if maybe these were the guys behind the insurgency in the first place. Everybody else had seen the light and gone back to their homes.

Jason stood outside the Kometa Hotel, a four-story cube that had probably looked futuristic back in the fifties when it was new. The

Kometa sign atop the building was accented with a rushing comet and its tail.

As he watched from the shadows across the street, a 4x4 king cab pickup—not unlike his own—roared up the street toward the hotel. Two men with shoulder-fired Stinger missile launchers rode low in the bed, scanning the skies. The driver skipped the curb, plowed over the few pathetic shrubs, and slid to a halt in front of the lobby doors.

All four cab doors opened, and five men who looked as if they could've once worked for the Taliban jumped out and ran for the lobby, their assault rifles banging on their backs. One of the five called to the men in the back of the truck. He pointed toward the top of the Kometa building. The two jumped down and followed him into the lobby.

This was good news and bad news to Jason. Assuming these men were part of the group holding Yulia, they were either about to skip town or dig in for a fight. If they were about to leave to escape the Russian onslaught, they would probably take care of Yulia—as in kill her—before they did. On the other hand, if they were preparing for a last stand, then they probably weren't going to appreciate Jason trying to check in at the front desk.

And, if he had understood that exchange with the guys and their missile launchers, some Russian aircraft were about to have an encounter with a couple of comets from the Kometa. Any way he sliced it, this old hotel just got a lot less hospitable.

Through his scope he could see men running around the garish silver lobby. One turbaned man, carrying two TVs, pushed through the doors and loaded his loot into the truck. He paused on the way back inside, hearing at the same moment as Jason did the unmistakable chop and hum of a helicopter. The man entered the lobby and shouted to his comrades.

Jason had no idea whether Yulia was in this hotel or not, or whether she was alive or dead. He didn't know what she looked like.

He couldn't communicate with her if he found her. He didn't know how many more bad guys there were in the hotel. For all he knew, he would have to search every room in the place before he found her—if she were there at all. In short, to walk in through the front door, alone, and start shooting would be suicide.

But that was kind of the idea.

Lord, I guess this is it. Now I might as well tell You the bottom line: You're not just. I'm sorry, but You're not. If You were, I would be paralyzed or dead instead of Doug. If You were just, Doug would still be a SEAL. But You're not, are You?

You called me to Yourself, but for what? To ruin a man's life and make myself unfit for the only thing I ever wanted to do? I thought I was hearing Your voice by not shooting that man. But if this is how You repay obedience, forget it.

I hope You've enjoyed Your fun with me, because it's about to end. If You love me at all, let me find this woman and get her out of danger before I die. Sorry it worked out this way, God. I mean, I loved who I was when I was with You. But this is for the best. Now I can do what You've left undone. See You soon.

Jason shook his head. What a pitiful speech. Chimp would laugh at him. But they were the words that had been poisoning his well for months. It felt good to finally draw them out.

He switched his toy pellet gun off safety, unplugged his radio and all his fancy computer gear, cradled a flashbang grenade in his fist, and trotted across the street.

When he got to the double doors, he locked his night vision goggles off his eyes and stepped through to do exactly what every moment of military training he'd ever had had taught him not to do: be a Rambo.

The high ceiling of the lobby was a striped sheet of reflective chrome. A statuette of a Soyuz spacecraft stood in the middle of the white tile floor on a round carpet. It felt like a set for a Buck Rogers movie. The men in their dirty robes ruined the effect, though. Three of them stood by a couch filling an anvil case with weapons and ammunition. A fourth sat on the floor nearby loading a clip for his Kalashinikov assault rifle.

Jason was five steps in before any of them looked up.

Finally, a young Mujahedeen in a tan skullcap noticed him. He rocked his head back and squinted, as if thinking, "Hey, that kinda looks like an American soldier." Then he pointed at Jason and shouted, his voice rising in pitch with every syllable.

By the time the others turned in surprise, the flashbang was already on the tile. Jason shut his eyes, plugged his ears, and shouted to drown out the sound. Even so, the high frequency component of the explosion made Jason flinch. When he opened his eyes and unplugged his ears, the men were only beginning to fall to the ground, and the low-pitched part of the sound was still echoing around the lobby. As they fell, he shot each one with pepperballs to the chest or back.

Without Trieu to come behind him with tranquilizer darts, they weren't going to be incapacitated for long, but for now he had the advantage. He collected their weapons and dumped them behind the check-in counter. He shut the anvil case and slid it behind the couch. Then he crossed to where five steps and a wall of glass bricks marked the entrance to the hallway to the rooms. He crouched behind a potted plant and watched the hall.

Behind him, the men were coughing and groaning. In ten seconds, they might be able to shoot at him. He was trying to get himself killed, but not yet and not like this.

He watched the empty hallway. *Come on. You heard something. Come out and investigate.*

Identical Persian rugs stretched down the straight passageway. Closed doors and dome lights demarcated the hall at even intervals. It looked like a perspective drawing for a high school art class.

In the lobby, the coughing transitioned into strained speaking.

Jason heard them struggling to their feet. He thought he was going to have to give them the cayenne treatment again.

Halfway down the hall, a room door flew open and a man burst out. He wore all black: black turban, black vest, black robe. His beard was very dark and contrasted sharply with his face. He readied his AK-47 and came forward, shouting a question to the men in the lobby.

When "Blacky" was one Persian rug length from where Jason was going to shoot at him, the door beside the man opened. Blacky spun and almost fired. But then he laughed and spoke to the newcomer with authority. Not one but three men came from that room and preceded Blacky toward the lobby.

Jason was fresh out of flashbangs. He could hit the front two with pepper and hope they dropped to reveal the back two, but it was iffy, and Blacky could probably get off a few rounds first. Behind him, Jason heard someone slide the anvil case out.

This was it. He gripped his MP-5 and coiled to stand.

And then, as almost always occurs on any mission, something unexpected happened. Halfway down the hall, the door Blacky had come out of bounced back against the wall and a young woman ran out of the room, retreating down the hallway without looking back.

Blacky spun and shouted at her. The three others stopped and became uncertain. Blacky raised his rifle and fired down the hallway. The sound was tremendously loud in the narrow space.

That was Jason's cue. He shot the closest two with double-taps of pepper. They brought their hands up to their chest in confusion, and then breathed the dust and folded onto the carpet. The third man watched them fall, a hand stretched out to them weakly. Jason double-tapped him, too.

Blacky fired again at the woman, but his aim was thrown off when his comrade collapsed on his leg. He stepped out of the way and went to fire again but then seemed to realize what he was seeing. He stared at his men writhing on the floor.

Jason fired a hipshot at him but had to spin around to face the threat in the lobby. The men there were on their feet now and pointing rifles at him. He sprayed a burst of pepperballs at them and at their feet, but knew he couldn't get them all in time.

He leapt onto the steps and charged up the hallway. Blacky's eyes tripled in size. Jason swept the rifle aside and drove his fist through the man's nasal cavity in a single flowing motion. Blacky hit the ground hard and his turban rolled down the hall.

Jason found himself in possession of the AK-47. Suddenly, he was in a moment of quantum stillness. A new way to handle the whole situation unfolded before him with the sound of an angel chorus.

Use the gun.

Surely these guys deserved to die. They'd taken hostages, incited rebellion, and murdered innocents. And if Jason and God were no longer on speaking terms, he wasn't bound by His rules anymore. It was almost as if he were back to his pre-Christian life as a SEAL: Why not mow 'em down and let the Russians sort out the bodies?

He fired the rifle into the lobby, intentionally missing. The shooters dove for cover. The gun's counterpunch felt sublime. The sound and the muzzle flash and the effect it had on the bad guys worked in his brain like a narcotic. He aimed at a man's head behind the couch and squeezed on the trigger.

But something wouldn't let him shoot to kill. Maybe it was that the tactical situation didn't require it. Maybe it was that he didn't want to get into a firefight when he really needed to be getting after the woman who had run away—if that was really Yulia and not some other kept woman. But he had a nagging suspicion that his real reason for not firing had more to do with his personal feelings about killing than he wanted to admit. Maybe God really had turned him into a conscientious objector, after all.

And just like that, the quantum moment was over. The men in the lobby were standing to fire, and Blacky and the others in the hall were rolling to their knees. Jason kept the assault rifle just to keep from being shot in the back with it, and sprinted up the hallway.

Someone in the lobby fired at him as he ran, but Blacky or one of his guards must've taken the bullet. A man grunted and then began shrieking in pain. The men shouted at each other and the firing stopped, but Jason knew they weren't giving up on him.

He risked a look inside Blacky's room. Were there other hostages in there? Was the woman who ran a hostage at all or just a disgruntled girlfriend? The room smelled of cigarette smoke and needed new carpet. But there was no one else inside. He tossed the rifle onto the unmade bed.

Jason wished now that he hadn't turned off all of Lewis's tech stuff. It would've been nice to poke the gun camera around the corner to see what was coming. But his imagination was happy to supply the images all by itself. He fired blindly up the hallway until he heard coughing, then he ran.

He didn't have much of a plan at the moment. "Run backwards firing pepperballs," was about the size of it. Hope to find someone who needed saving. Ride this wave as far as it would carry him. And then take one in the cranium. Well, all things considered, it was actually a pretty good plan.

At the end of the hallway, there was a door to the stairwell. About the time he lunged for it, his pursuers got their act together and opened fire. Jason was showered by plaster and asbestos, but spared any injury.

He took the first seven stairs, then turned around. Normally, this would be a good place to stand and fight: His enemies would have to come through the door one at a time and he would have the drop on them. But that wasn't going to work today. No matter how many times you pepper a guy, he can still get up and come after you. Jason climbed to the landing and kept going.

Then he had to make a choice. Would Yulia have stepped onto the second floor or kept going up? If he were the one running, he would go up one flight, cross over on the second floor, and hope to go down on the other side and get away. But maybe she had gone all the way up, hoping to climb down the fire escape. Or maybe she would try to hide in a room and wait it out. Maybe she wasn't Yulia at all.

When the door below him opened and many footsteps pounded up the stairs, his contemplation time dropped to nil. He rocked the door to the second floor against its hinges and ran onto the carpet.

The woman was at the other end of the hall. She cried out when she heard him and ran for the other stairwell.

"Wait!" he shouted. "Yulia, wait!"

She stopped and looked at him. "Kto tee?"

"Yulia, I'm here to help you." He jogged toward her, but she spooked and stepped into the stairwell. "Wait! I know Damira and Roza! And Liliya is very sick."

Whether this worked or not, this hallway was about to become a good place not to be. He ran down the hallway after her. The door swung closed.

Her head popped back through the door so quickly that Jason almost tripped in surprise. She was young and pretty, but her long chestnut hair was unruly, and her right cheek was deeply bruised.

"Tee znayesh Liliya?" she said.

"Yes, yes: Liliya."

He was halfway to her and coming at full speed, but it wasn't fast enough. The stairwell door behind him flew open and men shouted.

"Go on!" he called to the woman, motioning with his hand.

A bullet sliced the carpet beside him and another broke the window in front of him at the end of the hall. The crack of the gunfire arrived after the bullets did. The woman vanished from the doorway. Jason swerved from side to side erratically to at least make his pursuers aim.

The bullets came nonstop. Debris showered him like in the lobby scene in *Matrix.* Only he couldn't dodge bullets.

He finally felt what he'd been waiting for: a sharp sting. A hot ice pick high in his left arm. A thin red mist puffed out in fron him and sprinkled onto his face. His body spun around and caro off the wall. He dropped to the carpet like a sack of oranges. He a lt warm and numb.

And so it begins.

Down the hall, the men shouted and came at a run.

Jason stood and lurched to the door to the stairwell. Throug window he could see the woman waiting at the landing below hi The gunmen pounded to a stop halfway down the hall and open fire again.

As Jason stepped through the door, the hallway being blown to pixie dust behind him, something struck him on the helmet. His head slammed into the doorframe and he fell forward.

The woman was only now running up the stairs, so he must've been out for only a few seconds. She knelt over him and began to speak frantically.

"Uh," he said eloquently, rising to his elbow. His head was ringing like Quasimodo's bell. But he wasn't dead. Yet. If he lived, he was going to have to thank Lewis for this one. "Are you Yulia?"

"Da," she said, wiping her nose, "menya zavoot Yulia."

"Great," he said, pulling himself up on the railing. "Nice to meet you. Let's get out of here."

She said something and reached for his left arm as they descended.

"It's okay," he said, rounding the first landing and heading down. "Let's just—"

Someone entered the stairwell two floors above them. Jason tried to look up between the railings, but a sharp pain behind his eyes kept him from focusing. Through the blur, he could make out the form of one of the Stinger missile guys looking down at him. The man shouted and reached for another weapon. At least four feet began beating the steps above them. Jason grabbed Yulia's hand and lurched down the stairs.

bottom, he leaned heavily against the wall, painting it red entry and exit wounds in his arm. His head was pulsing. It o take all his concentration just to grasp the doorknob. He ng from the headshot, but the adrenaline was keeping him is. He couldn't pass out until he'd gotten Yulia to safety.

floor up, the stairwell door opened and his pursuers joined n coming down from the fourth floor. Somebody leaned over ing and fired down at them, the gunshots sounding like explo- n the concrete stairwell.

on's waning strength was just enough to pull the door open. gh his rippling vision, he was looking out into the hotel's restau- . Institution-straight rows of square tables and wooden chairs. obody in sight. Across the dining room he saw over a door a sign glowing in the universal red of emergency exits everywhere. He took Yulia's hand again and stumbled out into the restaurant.

Just as Blacky and his gang arrived from the lobby.

Not good.

Bad guys on his left, raising their rifles to shoot. Bad guys rushing up behind. Eighty feet of open space between him and the exit.

Nothing to do but go for it.

"Yulia, stay down!"

He sprayed Blacky's group with pepperballs—the last pepperballs in his clip, in fact—and pulled Yulia between rows of tables.

The attackers took cover. Two of them went down coughing. But the rest lifted their rifles to shoot. The stairwell door burst open and more angry men poured out.

But nobody shot. Blacky shouted orders and they held their fire. Jason wasn't going to waste the energy to think about why they were letting him go.

Twenty feet from the door the solution to the riddle manifested itself. The tallest, buffest Arab Jason had ever seen stepped through the exit and lowered the muzzle of a Degtyarev DP heavy machinegun at him.

Definitely not good. Well, God, so long, and thanks for all the fish.

Staring down the bipod-mounted gun with its flat disk drum on top, Jason held Yulia down and kept his body between hers and the Degtyarev. There was still a chance he could overcome the brute and spring Yulia, if he didn't pass out first or get his head removed at the neck by the 7.62mm barrel in front of him. At the very least, he was going to bleed on the guy's slippers.

Blacky was shouting. Somebody was coughing. Behind him, feet were shuffling for a clear line of sight. Yulia was crawling and whimpering. His shoulder was hurting. His head was suddenly too big for his helmet. The edges of his vision were going black. He was thirsty like the desert.

And he must've been hallucinating, too, because the big Arab suddenly disappeared. One second he was there, grinning over his iron sights. The next, a look of surprise crossed his face, and he fell away into the night.

Behind him, he heard disbelief. Footsteps in the lobby. And lots of clicking, like rulers slapping together, followed by more surprise, more clicking, and much coughing. There was also a very loud explosion and a light that would've normally seemed way too bright.

It seemed to Jason that the world had become an overwhelming place for a guy with a headache. What was really needed was a nice little nap. He decided to lie down and catch a few winks.

Well, God, it was worth a try.

CHAPTER 28

Hero Worship

THREE beautiful women stared down at him, worried looks on their sweet faces. Their hair was bathed in a soft glow and their eyes shone. When they saw him wake up, they sighed with delight.

Jason blinked. "Is this heaven?"

"No," one of them said, laughing gently, "but if you scare us like that again I'm going to send you there."

Jason looked at the upholstered seat beside him and the dome light on the low roof over him. "Are we back home?"

"Not exactly."

"Isn't this my truck?"

The angels looked worried. "Trieu," one of them said, "what's wrong with him?"

He remembered Trieu now, and Rachel. They were nice. He wasn't sure about the third one—*Oh, right, the girl.* What was her name?

"He'll be all right," Trieu said to Rachel. "Just a little disorientation from the concussion."

"Concussion?" he said, starting to sit up, "What concuss— Ow!"

Trieu laid him back down. "You've been shot in the arm. You'll be fine—if you rest."

"What concussion?"

"According to Yulia, you were hit in the helmet with a bullet and then hit your head on a wall. One or both of these impacts resulted in a concussion, which explains why you lost consciousness."

Yulia, that's right.

Rachel leaned over his face. Her hair tickled his neck. "You have been very, very brave, young man—and very, very stupid. Don't ever scare me like that again, Commander Kromer." She kissed his forehead. "I have to go see to the girls."

They were in the back seat of a king cab that looked a lot like his. Rachel reached for the door latch, but Yulia caught her arm and spoke to her in Russian.

Rachel turned to Jason. "She wants me to thank you for coming to her rescue. She's still a little confused about why we would come across the world to help her and the girls. That's given me a chance to plant some seeds about Jesus Christ. Anyway, she wants you to know that she's extremely grateful."

Jason's head seemed unable to decide which size it wanted to be: larger or smaller, larger or smaller. He looked at Yulia's face and noticed cute dimples. She beamed at him. "Um, tell her not to mention it."

"Considering what she's been through," Rachel said, "I think she needs more than that." She said something to Yulia in Russian. Judging from the enthusiasm she put into it and the reaction on Yulia's face, it wasn't *Don't mention it.* It was probably more like, "He says he would've climbed a thousand mountains and fought a thousand armies to reach your side." Wonderful.

Yulia leaned forward hesitantly and kissed him on the cheek.

Jason grinned. "Um. . .Rachel, those bruises on her face and neck: Did she tell you what happened to her?"

Rachel's posture seemed to stiffen. "She told me, Jason. I can't talk about it right now or I might break a window. Let me just say that the religion those men serve is supposed to punish them for what they did. They'd just better be glad I'm not God, or I'd have 'em screaming in a lake of fire right now."

"Oh," Jason said.

Rachel blew out a breath like a bull about to charge. "Anyway, she did find out that they are Muslim extremists. Apparently for a while she also had some contact with a couple of men from the Aral Sea area. They told her that guys like these have been appearing on and off over the years, always talking about how great it would be if Kazakhstan was run like a real Muslim country. But when the fighter jets came, her Aral Sea contacts decided they'd had enough."

Rachel opened the door. A rush of frigid wind swept the cab. She and Yulia hopped out of the truck.

"Trieu," Rachel said before slamming the door, "if he acts like he's about to go do something else stupid, cut off his legs."

The door shut with the tight Chevy thump. It was messing with his poor head to have familiarity inside and foreignness outside.

Trieu regarded him soberly. "How do you feel?"

"Okay, I guess. Except somebody put a timpani drum in my head. And my arm hurts." He felt the bandage on his left arm, only then realizing he didn't have a shirt on. He had one of the team's emergency reflective blankets over him. He peeked under the blanket to be sure he was decent everywhere else. He was.

Trieu checked his eyes with a tiny flashlight. "You are very lucky, Jason: The bullet did not hit any bones. That explains the small entry and exit wounds. You will heal completely. As for the head wound. . ." she had him follow the light with his eyes, "you are also very lucky. Or should I say *blessed?*"

More like 'cursed.'

He found her scrutinizing him. There was something behind her eyes besides medical concern. Did she know his secret?

Jason pulled up with his right arm and looked out the back window.

The hayride trailer was lined up behind the pickup. Some of the girls huddled under blankets in the bed of the truck. The rest shivered on the trailer. Rachel was climbing aboard it. Yulia was already there, hugging the girls and laughing with them. It was still dark, presumably on the same night that he'd made his assault on the Kometa. He could see Garth's dome bobbing up and down at the rear of the pickup. There was no sign of the camels.

"What's Garth trying to do, pull the trailer with the truck?"

"Yes," Trieu said, squeezing into the front seat.

Jason finally noticed a little girl—Liliya—asleep in the passenger seat. An IV bag dangled from the handle over the door.

"How is she?" he asked.

Trieu was taking the girl's pulse. "Her heart rate and breathing have slowed. She is stabilized for now. But I have only enough insulin for another six to eight hours. Somehow we must get her more, either at the hospital here or perhaps you could have some waiting for us in Kyzylorda with the airplane?"

Jason nodded, his thoughts arranging themselves better with every passing minute. "Where's Lewis? I'll have him call Doug. Have you guys updated him yet?"

"Yes. Lewis is with Chris. Chris wanted him to ride along to scout ahead while Garth tries to get the trailer connected."

"They rode? On the camels?"

"Yes."

Jason tried to picture it. "Camel jockeys, huh?"

"Mm-hmm."

"You say Chris *wanted* Lewis to go with him? What's up with that? Is Chris planning some kind of practical joke on the kid?"

She smiled enigmatically. "You may find that some things have changed since you left us, Jason."

He pressed his left deltoid gingerly. "What was that supposed to mean?"

The truck began to sway. Jason looked back and saw Garth

kicking at something out of sight behind the tailgate, probably the trailer hitch.

"I should be out there," Jason said. "Let the girls rotate in and out of the cab to warm up. Where's my shirt and my polyprope undershirt?"

"On the floorboard," Trieu said, "but I don't think you should—"

"Thanks, doc," he said, pulling on his shirts. "But I'm going out. If I blow a gasket I'll come back inside."

It was colder outside than he remembered. Was it a blessing or a curse to have someplace relatively warm to get to if you still had to go back outside?

The truck and trailer were in the depression by the river, due south of the city. All anyone would have to do to spot them was just walk over and look. But so far it seemed they'd escaped notice.

Most of the girls in the truck and on the trailer were either asleep or trying to be. But the few that were awake noticed him with a jolt. They whispered to their neighbors and awakened others. They looked at him and waved. What was he, a rock star? He saw Damira sitting against the upright at the front of the flatbed trailer, her blanket spread over the tiniest girls of the group.

Garth stood up at the back of the pickup. "What is it, girls? You see something?" He grabbed his MP-5 and scanned the horizon. Then he noticed Jason.

An unidentifiable expression appeared and vanished on Garth's face like a blue whale surfacing for air. Was it shock? Amazement? Relief?

"Well, well, Sleeping Beauty," Garth said. "I offered to come in and give you a smooch to wake you up, but Trieu wouldn't let me. Besides, I think I'd have to wait in line. You've got lips puckered up for miles around, seems to me."

Jason noticed the way the little girls—not to mention Yulia and Rachel—were watching him. They *did* seem awfully fond of him at the moment.

"What'd I do?"

"Yeah, right."

Garth laid his gun on the ground and stooped back down to the makeshift trailer hitch: two square poles and lots of leather straps loosely attached to a hitch ball on the back of the truck. He put his foot on one of the poles and shoved tentatively at the whole assembly with his leg. It began to come loose. Pieces of it slid off the ball and fell to the ground.

"Ah!" Garth said. "I haven't been able to keep the poles tight for distance and still have enough leather to secure it. Won't take much of a bump to break the link. I'm going to have to sit back here and ride it. Top speed no more than thirty, I'm thinking."

"Here," Jason said, pulling at the nearest pole, "let's try it this way. Take it all off and let me show you what I mean."

They worked quietly for a while. The girls began ducking back under the blankets. Jason heard shreds of noise over the wind, but it was indistinguishable. It could be engines, airplanes, gunfire, or killer bees, and he'd never know which.

He pulled the tailgate down and started tying a leather strap to a tiedown. "I take it you guys pulled me out of the hotel?"

"Nah," Garth said, working with a metal buckle. "There was this Girl Scout troop that happened by."

"No, really: What happened? I told you guys to go on without me. I even saw that you'd made it to the river. How were you suddenly in that hotel restaurant. And why?"

Garth dropped one of the poles to the ground. "Well, ya see. . . we got the girls onto the wagon and got the thing rolling and the camels pointed in the right direction. Some of us were watching your little dot on our helmet GameBoys. Then one person got to comparing notes with another person about how you'd basically said *goodbye* to us all before you left, like maybe you weren't expecting to catch up with the wagon train, after all.

"Rachel remembered how much you were against going after Yulia. Lewis and I remembered putting pressure on you to do it. And

Chris remembered what you'd said about it being your job to make sure we all got home safe and sound.

"About that time, your little green dot weren't on ye olde screen anymore. Chris said he thought he heard machinegun fire, but I think he's got feathers in his brain. Anyway, it just sort of clicked. Rachel said, 'He's going to try to rescue Yulia on his own.' You oughtta watch that girl," he said conspiratorially—definitely loud enough for Rachel to hear him, "I think she's takin' a shine to you."

"I'll keep an eye on her."

"Uh-huh."

Jason took one of the leather straps in his right hand. "We put these all along the end of the bed, here. See? Then we shut the tailgate and tie it over the top. What do you think?"

Garth handed him a tangle of harnesses. "Hold this." He began attaching straps to eyeholes on the pickup. "Anyway, we left Rachel and Trieu driving the Conestoga and the rest of us came to take a look. That Rachel was like a crazed she-dog to come after you, Jason. I had to break out the duct tape. It reminded me of a Proverb."

"It did?" Jason said. "Like maybe 'Let sleeping she-dogs lie'?"

"No. Like 'Better to meet a bear robbed of her cubs than a fool in his folly.' "

"So who was the fool in his folly: Rachel or me?"

"Ho ho. Anyway, imagine our surprise when we saw a mess o' gentlemen of Middle Eastern descent running around the hotel cursing your name and shooting the kuneezers out of anything that moved. Obviously you weren't dead yet, so we thought we might just pop our heads inside and offer to help them shoot you.

"Chris and I went to the front door. Lewis was supposed to come with us, but. . .Well, I should let him tell it. We found out later that he'd seen this stout fellow with a big stick headed in a side door, and decided to check it out."

Garth hummed and fiddled about with the harness. "Let's see. How's that going to hold? Hmm."

"Garth!" Jason said. "What happened next?"

"You were there, weren't you?"

"Not really. I passed out, remember? The last thing I saw was that big guy disappearing into thin air. At least I think that's what I saw."

"Oh, you saw it." Garth stood and faced Jason directly. "Jason, Lewis was a total hero. He pulled a major league takedown on that guy. Jumped up behind him and snapped him into 'the sleeper.' "

"No way. No. . .*way.*"

"Yes way, Ted. Then he shot him with enough tranquilizer darts to put a brontosaurus into a coma."

Jason looked at the river. "Lewis? Our Lewis?"

"Yessir, took on that bad boy like it was Saturday night. I think he believed what you told him about these guys not shooting back at him. Nobody's had the heart to tell him that it was the *fishermen* who wouldn't shoot back. These guys would!"

"I can't believe it," Jason said. "He's the last one I'd ever expect to save me in combat. Wow. I guess it just goes to show you that you can never tell who's got it where it counts, when it counts. Plus, it was because of Lewis that I wore that helmet that took a bullet for me. He saved me twice in one ten-minute span. I think I owe that kid a can of pop or something."

"Yeah," Garth said, "or something. Anyway, Chris and I brought pepper and fireworks to the party. We collected your sorry hide and the delectable Yulia—and a nice set of wheels—and went cruising for chicks downtown. And somehow we ended up here."

He fastened the last tether and stood up. "Let's give it the Nike test." He shoved at the new hitch configuration with his foot. It held tight.

"All right!" Jason said. "Still probably shouldn't go above thirty, though, or we're going to have orphans sliding onto the street."

"Yeah, that would pretty much defeat the whole purpose of us coming here, wouldn't it?"

"Can you get us moving?" Jason asked. "I'm getting real nervous about just sitting here."

"Sure."

As Garth walked toward the cab, two camel riders dropped over the river's bank ahead of them and came forward at a trot. "The odd couple's back."

Lewis vaulted off his creature and did a nosedive into the dirt. But he scrambled up and ran to Jason. "You're all right! Oh, man. This is great! Thank You, Jesus. Wow, dude, how do you feel?"

"Lewis, calm down, buddy. I'm fine."

"Dude, what you did. . .I mean, I can't begin to tell you how amazed I am at you," Lewis said. "I kiss your feet, baby. I grovel in your presence."

"Okay," Jason said, chuckling, "I get it. But it's me who should be licking your boots. I understand you took out Mr. Goliath back at the hotel."

"Aw, that. I guess I got a little excited. I saw you and Yulia over his shoulder, and I think I just flipped out. I thought, 'Man, if Jason can take on a whole boatload of those guys to keep us safe, I can try to take one of 'em out to keep him safe.' I don't even know why I did it. I was just there all of a sudden and my arm kind of went up around his neck. Before I knew what I was doing, he was on the dirt sucking air. But I shot him with the darts just in case. Do you think I hurt him?"

Jason put his hand on Lewis's shoulder. "Lewis, my friend, you did real good."

"You mean it?"

"I mean it. And you did even better than you know. Did you hear that that helmet you made me wear deflected a bullet? You saved my life, Lewis. Twice! I'm standing here talking to you because of you."

They embraced roughly.

"Thank you," Jason said.

"I hate to break up the love-in," Chris said, sliding off his camel, "but I've got some bad news."

Jason shook Chris's hand. "Good to see you too, Chris."

"Yeah. Hey. . .what you did. . .I just. . .I mean. . .*whoa.*"

"Don't mention it," Jason said. *Really, please don't.* "What's your bad news?"

Chris walked to the hood of the truck and spread out his map. He took out his small flashlight and pointed. "We're here, south of town. The railroad goes through town east-west, right here. And the road goes through here. We'd planned to head up the river for a mile or two and then join up with the road, right? Well, that ain't gonna work."

"Why not?"

"The Russian troops that have been deplaning at the airport for the last five hours have finally gotten their business squared away." He tapped the map east of their position, close to the river. "They've set up a fortified checkpoint right here."

"And guess what?" Lewis said. "They've got a big machinegun."

Jason looked at Chris. "They do?"

"Yeah. A sandbag nest."

"Hmm."

"You know what the worst part of it is?" Lewis asked.

"What?"

"They really will shoot us. Right, Jason? I mean, you told me before that only trained, professional soldiers would actually shoot to kill. Well, isn't that what these guys are? We're totally dead, aren't we?"

"Fugedaboudit," Jason said. "These are probably just conscripts, too, right off their farms in mother Russia. They're probably so ignorant and superstitious that they're more likely turn and run at the sight of you than try to get a shot in."

Oh, Lord, if only it might be true!

Jason looked at the map and tried to sound confident. "Can we just sneak by in the river gorge? Maybe put the truck in neutral and push it by?"

"No chance," Chris said. "The river gets wide and flat right there. There's no way we could slip by without them seeing."

Trieu got out of the cab and joined them. Rachel trotted up, too. "What is it?"

"Trouble," Garth said.

"Real soldiers," Lewis said. "Oh, man, if only I lived in Civil War times!"

"There's more," Chris said. "They're sealing the city. I saw them running razor wire. It won't be long until they spot us here."

"Oh, man," Lewis said.

Jason scratched his scalp. "Okay. Everybody stay cool. We'll figure this out."

"Why don't we just head out across the desert that way?" Rachel asked, pointing across the river. "Then turn northeast when we're out of sight."

"The trailer would never make the crossing," Garth said. "I guess we could go on foot."

"It's fifty miles to the closest town!" Chris said. "And it's east, not south."

They stood in a half circle, shoulder to shoulder. The wind gusted relentlessly. Above them, the Big Dipper sparkled like ice crystals.

"How many would you say at the checkpoint, Chris?"

"Ten to twelve."

"Infantry alone?"

"There's a small command tent, too. I'm guessing that's why there are so many at a little checkpoint. The way is blocked."

"Oh, no," Rachel said. "Lord, help us. We're so close! And we've done so well. I won't believe it's going to end here. There has to be a way out."

"There's one more thing," Chris said.

"What?"

"They have a bus."

Jason squeezed his injured arm. "A bus?"

"Um-hmm. A nice cozy bus that would be perfect for transporting forty girls and their chaperones across a dark country highway."

"What are they doing with a bus?" Jason asked.

"Who knows? Who cares? Maybe they decided it would be better to drive here from the airport than to walk. It looks like a tour bus or a hotel shuttle. They've got it parked across the road for their roadblock."

"Oh," Rachel said, "if only we could get that bus for the girls!"

Lewis put his fists on his hips, like Superman. "Let's take 'em!"

"What?" Chris said. "No, no, no."

"Lewis," Garth said, "nobody's doubting your courage, brother. Not after tonight. But charging the teeth of a fortified checkpoint is a good way to get yourself killed dead."

"I just think we can do it," Lewis said. "I mean, they can't be that much worse than the guys at the hotel, right? And look what we did with them. I don't know what it is, but it's like I'm deciding right now that I don't want to be afraid anymore. Yeah, they might point their guns at us and shoot, but that's only if we give them the chance, right? And they're not expecting us."

No one spoke. Lewis looked around for support. "Right, Jason?"

All eyes turned to Jason. Even if he hadn't had a concussion—or been shot, or just tried to kill himself—this would've been a tough nut. But now it was too much. "Let me think about it. Lewis, let's get in the cab and make a phone call. Maybe Chimp has some wisdom for us. Then Chris, you and me will go have us a look."

He was about to turn to go, but he felt something restraining him. He looked each of his team members in the eye. They had risked their lives to save his, while he was just trying to take the coward's way out of his life. They deserved better.

"I. . .I think Rachel's right, though," he said. "God's brought us this far, hasn't He? I mean, who's to say that He hasn't provided this bus just for us? Maybe it's ours to go and possess. Let's keep our eyes on Him and trust Him to bring us the rest of the way, okay?"

Hypocrite.

His words seemed to be fitting, though. They bucked each other up and went back to other tasks.

Jason and Lewis climbed into the cab. Liliya was still unconscious. Lewis initiated the link and handed Jason the phone.

"CPU, this is Monitor. How copy? Over."

Nothing. Jason checked his watch. Zero three-twenty local time. Which meant seventeen-twenty Akron time. Maybe Bigelow was at dinner? He repeated the code phrase. On the third try, Bigelow finally answered.

"Monitor, this is CPU. Copy Lima Charlie. Good to hear your voice, Monitor. Over."

Jason knew what his friend was saying. "CPU, Monitor. Good to hear yours, too, Chimp. Thanks. Over."

The short delay.

"I've got someone here who has a special message for you, Monitor. Motherboard says she's glad you're all right and that if you ever pull a stunt like that again, she will have you over her knee. Over."

Jason smiled. He could picture Eloise standing over Bigelow in the observation room. "Understood. CPU, be advised we need a supply of insulin at our extraction point. I don't care how they get it, but we need it and no buts about it. How copy? Over."

The pause seemed exceptionally long this time.

"Um. . .we'll, uh, get to work on it, Monitor. But I don't see how we can—"

In the background Jason could hear Eloise's voice. It was rising in pitch as she went on.

"Monitor," Bigelow said, "I have been informed that we *will* find a way to get you what you need. Over."

Jason smiled. "Excellent, CPU. And give my regards to Motherboard. Item next: It looks like your prediction was right: Our escape is being cut off as we speak. We've got a. . .virus blocking the free flow of information. Please advise. Over."

"Monitor, CPU. Afraid we're not going to be much help on that.

Can verify virus activity in your location, though. Military radio traffic heavy in your sector. Over."

"Understood, CPU. Over."

"Monitor, this is CPU. Big news, brother. Remember I told you I had a friend checking on our ill-fated Indonesian guide? And that if things checked out he'd have something to tell me? Over."

"I remember, CPU. Over."

"Well, buckle your seatbelt, Monitor, because my friend called me today. Are you sitting down, Monitor? Over."

"Check. What is it, CPU? Over."

"We were set up."

The words floated before him like motes of dust. The radio was silent. Lewis's forehead furrowed.

"Monitor, this is CPU," Bigelow said. "How copy? Over."

"No, I heard you. I just. . ."

"Understood, Monitor. We were plumb set up. Ibnu was part of the plan. The same group that caused so much trouble in East Timor was trying to take out one of their enemies—by using us as their weapon. They took out poor Ibnu to throw us off. It almost worked, too. We were supposed to assassinate their enemy and then walk into the ambush. Except you didn't want to shoot, did you? You waited and waited. Finally, when we didn't come, they left their ambush location and tried to catch us. If you'd taken the shot, we would've walked into their trap and we'd probably all be dead."

Jason's head was whirling. Bigelow was telling him something almost too huge for him to grasp. He was saying that the reality Jason had believed for the better part of a year—the reality that had led him to try to get himself killed—wasn't reality at all.

He needed to step back and think about it, but he couldn't get back far enough. He'd been the goat so long it was hard to wrap his brain around the idea that he'd actually been the hero the whole time.

"There's more, buddy," Bigelow said. "The man we were assigned to shoot was not the man intel wanted dead. He was not the butcher of East Timor. In fact, he was a Christian. One of the main tribal opponents of the real black hats. Causing so much trouble in the backcountry with his—get this—'evangelical Christian reforms' that they wanted him gone in the worst way. Are you hearing me, brother? You were right not to take the shot."

No words came to Jason. Only images. It all played again in his mind, except now he was cast as the hero instead of the villain. It was too much.

"Monitor, this is CPU. Are you there? Over."

On Jason's third attempt, words actually came from his mouth. "I hear you."

"I'm sorry for blaming you, my friend," Bigelow said. "You were right about all of it. Your instincts were right. You must be in tight with the Big Guy, bro, because you heard Him good that day. Not only did you not shoot the wrong man—a brother—you also busted up our welcoming committee and saved all our lives in the process.

"Jace, I said some terrible things to you after that day. But now I take them all back more than ever. Because if I'm choosing between my legs and the lives of four Navy SEALs, I'm choosing my legs every time. That's a no-brainer." Bigelow paused. "You there, buddy? Over."

"I'm here." Even as he spoke, the titanium padlock he'd locked long ago began to rattle against its cage. "But wait a minute. Didn't you shoot that man? You took my rifle. You said he was down. Over."

"He went down, yeah. But I never had a clean shot after the firefight began. My friend says the guy took a bullet but recovered. Talk about saving me some heavy-duty guilt. Over."

Jason laughed. He laughed so violently that Lewis jumped and people outside the cab turned to look. He laughed so hard that tears washed his cheeks and Liliya stirred in her coma. Deep in his soul something came unstuck. It floated up and got purged from his system through his involuntary laughter.

"CPU," he said when he finally could, "thank you for this news.

Whatever happens next, thank you for this news. Over."

"You got it, bro. You okay? Over."

"Yeah, buddy, I'm okay. More okay than I've been in my life, I think. CPU, I gotta go. There's something important I've got to do. Give my love to Motherboard. Over and out."

Lewis took the headset from Jason. "What in the world was that all about?"

Jason grabbed him by both shoulders. "Lewis, you're a genius. A boy genius!"

"I am?"

"Let's do what you said."

"What'd I say?"

"You said, 'Let's take 'em.' "

"Oh, that's right."

"Come on, then, Lewis: Let's take 'em. And I know just how we're going to do it."

CHAPTER 29

OPERATION: FIREBRAND

CUE the camel.

Jason sent the text message to his team over their computer displays. Somewhere in the distance to his right, a two-humped freak started walking toward the Russian checkpoint with its even stranger companions.

With that, the operation began.

Jason flipped his eye panel away and put his night vision goggles back on. In two hours, the sky would be brightening and their advantage would be gone. From the direction of the city he could hear the occasional muffled explosion. He checked over his left and right shoulders—Damira and Roza were there, crouching behind him, ready to do their part.

He looked across the forty yards of steppe to where the soldiers manning the checkpoint slept or stood guard or warmed themselves by the small fire, but he couldn't see Chris. Jason had to hand it to the guy: His claim about sneaking past Iraqi guards was no empty boast. He was inside their perimeter, somewhere dangerously close. Jason glanced upward, but he could see no sign of the banshee.

Jason and the girls were beyond the checkpoint. They'd come through the coiled razor fencing with Chris. From here they could've turned and walked free without being seen. If all they had to do was get the girls beyond the checkpoint, they could do it easily. But there was the little matter of the hundred and twenty-five miles to Kyzylorda airport. Jason was going to get them that bus if it was the last thing he did.

A green glob loped into view on his right. A camel. One rider, slumped over in the saddle. One runner leading the camel. Looking scared to death.

> *Oh, Lord. You and I have a lot to talk about. But for now can You just make sure this team You've made me part of makes it through this mission? Please help us pull this thing off and get these kids to safety. And then we've got a lot of catching up to do, don't we? I'm looking forward to it like crazy, Lord. Amen.*

"All right," he said to himself, feeling the small Bible in his pocket, "here goes nothing."

Rachel led the camel up the road toward the checkpoint, stumbling and whimpering. Garth, wearing robes found in the rubble of a home, moaned and swayed in the saddle.

"Stop," a soldier said in Russian. He shined a flashlight in her face and brought his assault rifle off his shoulder.

He is a cute boy, Rachel thought. Even younger than Lewis. He looked like a freshman in his green camouflage uniform and domed World War Two-era helmet. He was cleanshaven and had a spunky look to him. She noted that his flashlight beam strayed down her body, his eyes following it. For her purposes, his libido was a good thing. She rolled her shoulders back and waited until the full effect of her presence had registered on the boy's face.

"Oh, I'm so glad to see you!" she said in Russian, panting and clinging to the camel. "Please help me. Hide me!"

She saw heads popping out from pup tents and from around the back of the bus. A soldier who had been walking the fence line to the river quickened his pace toward them. A man with a crooked nose watched her curiously from the machinegun nest. The officer's tent danced in the steady wind.

"Hold on, young woman," Spunky said. "What is it that has you so frightened?"

"Oh, my brave Russian brother, please don't be so cruel. Let me come close to you so that you may keep me safe. Don't leave me outside where it can see me! I don't want to be alone!"

Spunky had a group behind him now. "What about him?" he said, jutting his chin at Garth.

Rachel turned the camel to the side. "This is my brother, Ivan."

At the sound of his "name," Garth moaned and let an arm fall loose.

"He is beyond hope," Rachel said. "He has been harassed too severely by the demon."

Spunky stepped back. "Demon?" Then he seemed to regain his fortitude. "Superstitious woman," he said to the other soldiers. They laughed.

Just then the wind seemed to shriek.

Rachel yelped. "It's coming! It's found me. Please, let us through the gate!"

"What?" Spunky said. "It's nothing." Nevertheless, he scanned the night sky.

"Look there!" another young soldier said, pointing up. "Did you see that?"

"Where?"

"I saw something fly in front of the stars."

The soldiers gripped their weapons and shifted from foot to foot. Two more pulled on boots and parkas and joined them. The man behind the machinegun rotated it around threateningly, looking ready to shoot at anything.

"Calm down, Sergei," a block-faced Slav said. "It is only an owl or a cloud. What is this foolishness? Woman, leave here at once."

Some of the soldiers made a show of dispersing. But when the block-faced man walked away, they reconvened at the fence.

Rachel moved right up to the closed gap in the fence, as close as possible to the soldiers. "It always begins like this. First you hear it. Then you think you see it. If you have seen it, it can only mean that it has decided to possess someone here."

Spunky's eyes shone white in the darkness. "It will not possess anyone. There is no such thing as demons."

His friend bumped into him from the side. "No, then why are you afraid?"

"I'm not afraid of anything."

Rachel spoke in a stage whisper. "If it has decided to possess one or more of you, you will feel a sharp sting somewhere on your body. This is the demon's teeth, probing you for an entry into your soul."

Demon's teeth was the codeword.

At that instant several things happened. Lewis swooped the banshee in lower for maximum psychological effect. Trieu fired her CAR-15 sniper rifle. Chris fired Rachel's MP-5. And Jason fired Lewis's MP-5. They each fired only once.

"Ah!" Sergei shouted. "The demon bit me on the leg!"

Spunky cried out. "My back, my back! It's coming for me!"

"There it is in the sky again!"

"It bit my belly!" another soldier shouted, dropping his rifle and clawing at his midsection.

The flap of the officer's tent flew aside and a man stepped out.

He was tall and lean and had a long narrow nose and very pale skin. He pulled his jacket on as he came, and flipped on a flashlight. "What is this commotion?"

At the sound of his voice, the soldiers recovered some of their self-control. They stood up straighter and held their ground.

"Sir, there's a. . ." Spunky started. "Sergei saw something in the air."

The officer looked up. "He saw what? Sergei, what did you see? One of our comrades in his fighter jet?"

Sergei stared at the ground. "I thought. . .I mean, I couldn't say, sir."

"I got bit by a demon, sir," Spunky said. "Right on my back."

"It got me in the leg," Sergei said, "and Alexi in the belly. Sir, we've got to get out of here before it possesses one of us."

"Possesses? What are you babbling about?" The officer pointed his light at each one of them. "A demon? What's got into you, men?" He looked at Rachel. "Who is this?"

Spunky stepped toward her. "She's the one who told us about the. . .we don't know exactly, sir. I was interrogating her when—"

"Well," the officer said, his flashlight on Rachel's face, "what do you want?"

"Please, good sir, have pity," she said. "I perceive that you are a man without equal. I and my brother here, we are not as strong as you. We fell too easily to the spirit's power. My poor brother, look at him. Poor, poor Ivan."

Garth moaned.

The officer shined his flashlight, went to Garth in his saddle, then back to Rachel, lingering a bit here and there before returning to her face. "What irrational talk is this? What spirit?"

The wind howled again. There was almost a supernatural edge to it. It sent a chill rushing up Rachel's spine—and she knew what it was. The soldiers bent their knees and walked backward, running into one another. One of them began to pray with urgency. Now none of the soldiers were sleeping anymore.

"I know you are much too intelligent to believe in superstition," Rachel said to the officer. "This is excellent. You can explain to me why the wind seems to wail and why we think we see a dark body blot out the stars. You can use scientific reasoning to explain why my brother sometimes speaks in strange languages. Please," she said, clutching his arm over the fence, "please explain it to me so that I will not be so afraid. And if you will not explain it to me, at least hold me in your arms where I will be safe."

"Now, now," he said, opening the gap and letting her through. "There is nothing to fear. Come, I will protect you."

She buried herself in his shoulder, taking care to lead the camel through the gap.

"Alexi!" one of the men shouted. "Alexi has died! The demon has killed Alexi!"

"No," Rachel said to the officer. "He has not died. The demon does not kill. It does not yet have that power, nor does it seek it. It only desires to torment, like my poor Ivan."

Garth suddenly rose in the saddle, his eyes locked open and staring straight ahead. "Four score and seven years ago," he shouted in English, "our fathers brought forth on this continent a new nation, conceived in liberty and dedicated to the proposition that all men are created equal."

"What is the matter with him?" the officer asked.

"You see what I mean about the strange tongues? It is the devil's work. Please, good sir, explain to me what is happening to him."

Beside them, Sergei fell to the dirt.

"Get up, Corporal."

"The next thing you may explain to me," Rachel said, clinging to his arm, "is how it seems that the spirit can possess structures and even vehicles. I have seen it do this in our village. Please explain it, good sir."

Structures and vehicles. Another code phrase.

Chris took up his position behind the officer's tent and gripped the poles. Trieu chose her next target. Lewis brought the banshee down to thirty feet, well behind the checkpoint, and sent it zooming at the troops.

Jason ushered Damira and Roza to the back of the bus. He opened the rear door and helped them inside. When they were hidden, he started the next phase of the mission: He gripped the door with his good arm and slammed it shut.

"Did you hear that?" Spunky said, his words slurring. "It's the deeee. . ."

The officer caught Spunky as he fell. "Stop this. I order you to wake up, Private." He kept ordering him to wake up—all the way to the ground.

"Now we are engaged in a great civil war," Garth shouted, "testing whether that nation or any nation so conceived and so dedicated can long endure."

The officer dropped Spunky. "What is happening?"

"Ow!" a soldier said, his hand shooting to the back of his leg. "Demon's teeth! It has entered my soul!"

"It is coming!" another said, holding his ears under his helmet. "The voice! Make the voice stop!"

Another soldier grabbed the back of his neck and cursed.

"We are met on a great battlefield of that war," Garth said, his voice waxing ominously. "We have come to dedicate a portion of that field as a final resting place for those who here gave their lives that that nation might live."

A soldier pointed at the officer's command tent. "Look! It's possessed the tent!"

The white tent seemed alive. It bucked and shivered violently, almost as if something were trapped inside it.

The wind screeched. Another man cried out and swatted at his shoulder. Flashlights strobed the area like broken-off moonbeams. The tent danced. Garth recited. Men fell to their knees.

The block-faced soldier ran to the officer. "The men are in some kind of hysteria, sir. There is nothing happening! Make them—Aagh! Something bit me."

Then the bus began to bounce.

It started small, but soon there was no mistaking it. It was moving up and down on its shock absorbers like a gorilla was jumping on it.

A soldier cried out hysterically and ran screaming toward the river.

Then something swift and fierce buzzed right through the checkpoint. Men dove for cover.

"What was that?" the officer said. "It–It shrieked like a. . ."

Flaming torches shot over the top of the bus and fell sizzling to the ground. The bus's lights flashed on and off. Something hard hit its roof. The passenger doors opened and closed, opened and closed.

Two more men fell to the ground.

"What is happening!" the officer shouted. "Help. I'll call for help. But the radio is in my tent. My tent. . ." He turned to Rachel. "You must help me."

"I will, I will. I can drive the bus away. If I take it, the demon will follow me, and your men will recover."

He didn't seem to be focusing. "You drive the bus. Drive it away? Yes, take it away? But, no! It would be too terrible for you."

"I must," she said, taking on her best B-movie voice. "It's the only way. Quick, where are the keys?"

A torch landed at his feet. "Ah! What–What did you ask me?"

"The keys! Where are the bus keys?"

He patted his pockets, looking around him. "This isn't right." When he brought the keys out, he dropped them on the dirt. "Something's not right about this. They shouldn't be—Ow! Something hit me. Ow! It hit me again!" His eyes were wild. "It's the demon! It wants me!"

Rachel pocketed the keys. "Not if I protect you."

Garth slid off the camel and walked like Frankenstein toward the bus, mumbling. "It is for us the living rather to be dedicated here to the unfinished work which they who fought here have thus far so nobly advanced."

"He is possessed!" the officer shouted, stretching toward his back. "And I am next!" He grabbed Rachel by the shoulders. "Save me! Take the bus away! Take it, take it, take it!"

"I will," she said, stepping away from him. "In just a minute, I will."

She watched as the last three soldiers staggered around on the hard ground. The bus continued to bounce and flash its lights, and the banshee zoomed by again, but the show was mostly over.

Or so she thought.

"No!" the officer shouted, seeming to throw off his fear. "You cannot have me, you spirit of the dead! You cannot have Yuri Tatarinova so easily!" He ran for the machinegun and chambered a round.

"Wait!" Rachel shouted.

He opened fire. Full auto. Tracers streaked into the inky night. He pointed upward and fired continuously, swiveling around the weapon's full firing arc. Shouting curses to the sky.

Then he stopped. His eyes snapped onto Rachel's. "You. You brought this upon us." He lowered the smoking barrel at her. "If you are gone, it will leave."

She walked backward, her hand held up in front of her. "No! I came to help—"

"Dos vidanya, pretty woman."

Rachel stumbled and fell backward.

The officer scoffed. "Now I will send you to where all demons come from."

"No!"

Something long and horizontal struck the officer in the shoulders. The machinegun fired. Hard dirt flew up beside Rachel in a staccato line away from her.

The officer landed on the ground. Jason was on top of him.

He rolled up to punch the Russian's lights out, but he was already losing consciousness, the tranquilizers finally taking effect.

Rachel collapsed backward. "Oh, dear Jesus, thank You!"

Jason held his arm gingerly. He and Rachel helped each other up. The Russians were all asleep.

"How many were there, Trieu?" he said into his radio.

"Twelve, counting the officer. How many do you confirm?"

Damira and Roza jumped out of the bus giggling and shouting. Rachel hugged them both.

Jason met up with Chris and Garth by the gap. He looked at Garth. "Four score and seven years ago?"

"Yeah. I didn't know if I still remembered it. I'm going to have to look up my fifth grade teacher, Mrs. Cooper, and thank her."

Jason clapped him on the back. "Okay, everybody, how many soldiers do you count?"

"Eleven here," Chris said. "And one out by the river."

"Okay," Jason said. "Chris, please plug each one of them again, just to be sure. We want them all sleeping. But do it in the legs and not at point-blank, okay?"

"Yes, sir."

"Garth," Jason said, "please go retrieve the guy who decided to go for a dip. Plug him with a tranq while you're at it."

"You got it, boss."

"Trieu," Jason said. "They're all accounted for. You and Lewis get the girls over here and into the bus, all right?"

"Coming," she said. "How's your arm?"

"I think I'll let you dress it again when we get going. Over."

Jason looked around at the carnage they'd caused. "Look at us," he said. "We're knee-deep in sleeping Russian infantry, but we haven't permanently harmed a one of them. We used our skills, and we used our brains, and we pulled it off."

"We're not out of it yet," Chris said. "It won't be long before they have a radio check or something and find out that these guys are sleeping on the job."

"I know," Jason said "but I don't want to miss this moment. Look around, you guys. WE DID GOOD!"

They laughed and high-fived each other.

Jason scooped Damira and Roza into his arms and hugged them till they squealed with laughter. "You girls did great! Rachel, tell them I think they did awesome."

She favored him with her knockout smile. "Oh, I think they know what you're saying."

Lewis and Trieu and Yulia arrived with the girls all in a line. They were sleepy but did not complain. Rachel and Yulia helped them board the bus.

Jason took the banshee from Lewis and gave the four-armed rotorcraft a sloppy kiss on the dome. "Great work, Lewis. You had my knees knocking."

"Thanks, Jason."

"And you," Jason said to Trieu, "great shooting, my friend." He gave her a hug.

She held the embrace. "Jason," she whispered, "I want you to know that I know what you were trying to do at the hotel."

Jason's blood turned to watered-down lemonade. "You. . .do?"

"Remember," she said, "a sniper is trained to detect things others don't see. That's how we are successful at attaining our objectives."

"Trieu, I'm not sure I know—"

"Yes, you do. You don't fool me, Jason Kromer." She brought her mouth very close to his ear. "But I understand. I think. And I promise not to tell."

He opened his mouth to speak, but she disengaged and trotted after the last girl in line. He was left staring at the camel, which wasn't much interested in anything that was going on.

"Hey, boss," Garth said, depositing his Russian next to the others.

"We still need to get the little one from the truck."

"I know," Jason said, already moving that direction. "I'll get her. You guys pick up all the darts off the ground."

Liliya was sleeping peacefully in the cab of the pickup. Jason moved a lock of stringy hair from her forehead. He stared at her in wonder. A little girl in trouble. No one to help her. He felt the raging, protective love surging within him.

Oh, dear Jesus, this is what it's all about, isn't it?

He'd never carried anything more gently than he now carried Liliya. He wrapped her in her blanket and held her IV in his teeth. His arm ached, but it seemed now to be a wound of love, suffered for little Liliya and the other girls. As he carried her nearly weightless body, he felt weightless himself. Jason Kromer, protector of the helpless. He could get used to that.

The bus was already started, and everyone was aboard. Jason climbed the steps and placed Liliya in the aisle on the pallet Trieu had made for her. The door shut with the familiar hydraulic *chhutt,* and Garth drove away.

EPILOGUE

"THE place is looking pretty full."

Jason withdrew his head from the doorway. "Who knew Doug had so many friends?"

In his tuxedo, Chris looked like a blond James Bond. Garth looked like he was ready to receive his award at the NFL Player of the Year banquet.

Chris took a peek through the door. "Nah, these are Jamie's friends. The ushers are only seating the groom's side to even things out."

"It figures that all his old SEAL buddies would be deployed when the guy finally gets hitched," Garth said.

Bigelow ran his wheels into Garth's shoes. "Shouldn't we have started already? Where's the preacher? Do you think Jamie's left? She's left, hasn't she? I knew we should've had a daytime wedding so I could track her easier."

"Relax, Doug," Garth said, "or I'm going to pin your boutonnière to your belly button."

"Well, shouldn't there be music or something?" Bigelow said. "The natives are getting restless."

"The natives?" Chris said. "What about you?"

"The band's coming now," Jason said.

The four members of the band from the Akron City Club stood from the third pew of The Lord Is on His Throne Scripture Church and walked to their instruments at the front of the church. But they didn't play. A slender woman in a long lavender dress joined them. She lifted a cello off its stand and held it beside her cheek.

"Funny," Jason said, "that looks just like. . .hey, did you guys know Trieu played an instrument?"

"Duh," Chris said. "Didn't you hear her practicing like every night back at the compound?"

"No! Where does she play?"

"Over on the girls' side," Chris said. "But I guess you don't get over that way too much, do you? You being not so good with the ladies, and all."

"Hoo hoo hoo," Garth said.

Trieu drew her bow across the strings, and a sublimely melancholic triad filled the sanctuary. She played with strength and artistry, her eyes closing at times. When the melody sank into the lower registers, Jason could feel it resonating in his feet.

The wedding guests became an audience at a concerto. They sat perfectly still, perhaps as mesmerized by the rich tones as Jason was. He saw Eloise in the second pew, sitting in as the mother of the groom, a broad smile on her face.

Trieu's eyes met Jason's. She continued to play, but now it seemed to be a concert for him alone. She was enchanting, this keeper of his secret. He basked in the warm sounds, marveling at her skill. When she lowered her eyes, he found that he was unexpectedly moved.

When her solo was over, no one spoke or applauded. Jason didn't know how to react, either. Trieu set her cello in its stand and walked up the aisle to the rear of the church. The quartet picked up their instruments and began to play Steven Curtis Chapman's song, "I Will Be Here."

Jason shut the door. "Okay, after this song, the organ will play and we go in." He looked at Bigelow. Behind the charcoal tux and pink boutonnière, he looked stressed. "You okay, Chimp?"

"Oh, man, Jace, what's wrong with me? I've jumped out of airplanes and been shot at and almost drowned behind enemy lines, but nothing holds a candle to this."

Jason would've laughed if Bigelow's eyes hadn't been so wild. He put his hand on his friend's shoulder. "It's a big deal, Doug. This is a big commitment. You're thinking maybe you can't hold up your end of the bargain?"

Bigelow grinned sickly. "How'd you know? Jace, I'm a skirt chaser. Always have been. I don't even know how to talk to women except to flirt. Up till now, it hasn't been, you know, *official* with me and Jamie. I haven't been too concerned if I took a look at another woman. But now! Jace, Jamie deserves better, man." He slapped the brick wall beside him. "What is she doing marrying me?"

Jason looked at Garth and Chris. "What do you think, guys: Is he right? Should Jamie marry somebody else?"

Chris stepped forward. "Absolutely. Doug, I volunteer to take this problem off your hands. Here, switch flowers with me."

"Now hang on," Garth said. "Doug, Jamie's a beautiful woman. And she's got character like nobody's business. I was thinking I might, you know, have a go with her. What do you say?"

"Hey," Jason said, "I wasn't meaning for you two. I was meaning for me. It was my idea."

"You guys are real funny," Bigelow said. "Well, you can forget it. Jamie's mine. And I'm gonna seal it right now. Jace, is that organ playing yet?"

"No."

"Too bad, we're going."

"Wait for the preacher, dude!"

"He can catch up."

Bigelow rolled through the door and down the side aisle. Jason and Chris and Garth fell in behind.

As Jason felt the weight of the guests' gaze fall on them, something came out of hiding in his mind. It was the old self-loathing. It lifted its horned head and spat out the old accusation: "The man in front of you is in a wheelchair because of you." But as soon as the poison was out, an ax came around and cut off the viper's diamond-shaped head. A verse came to him from out of nowhere: "Therefore, there is now no condemnation for those who are in Christ Jesus."

Take that, ya punk. Now leave me alone.

To his surprise, the accusations did leave him alone. And in the void left by its fleeing, a dam burst of emotion flooded in. Clean, cold water of the Holy Spirit.

Something told Jason this was going to be an emotional night for him.

The song ended and the organ began. Pastor Johnson, looking like an African monarch in his rich black robe, walked down the aisle and joined the groom and groomsmen at the front of the sanctuary. The organist went straight into the processional.

First down the center aisle was the flower girl, Jamie's seven-year-old niece. She carried a small basket and sprinkled rose petals as she came. Jason couldn't help being reminded of Damira. He could see her again on the street corner, bringing home water for the others. Oh, no: Was he actually going to cry at a wedding?

Next came the flower girl's mother, Jamie's older sister, an attractive soccer mom from Arizona. She step-pause-stepped down the aisle to the music and took her place on the bride's side at the front.

Then came Trieu. She looked to Jason like an Asian supermodel in the violet bridesmaid dress. Who was he kidding? This was a "beautiful people" wedding: They all looked like models. Except Lewis, maybe, who was standing in the corner on the right, the official videographer for the wedding. He just looked like Lewis.

Trieu stepped slowly to the front of the church. Only once did she look at Jason, but when she did it was like a sniper shot—potent and on the money. He was going to have to do some thinking about her.

But not right now. Next was Rachel. Everything she ever wore seemed to be made only for her, and this dress was no exception. Her hair was up like a princess's. She smiled openly, beaming her light on Jason and the others, walking in her own private super slo-mo. All of a sudden, he was sure the church's air conditioner had failed.

The organist played the familiar dum du-du-du-dum dum dum, and Jamie's mother stood up, followed by the rest of the congregation.

As the strains of the wedding march boomed through the church, a vision in white appeared at the top of the aisle. Jamie's dress was a sleeveless affair with lace up to her neck and down to the floor. Her hair was high on her head and she positively glowed. But she only had eyes for Doug Bigelow. Her father escorted her down the aisle. Jason could hear the chorus of "Isn't she lovely?" and "What a beautiful bride" from the guests.

Jamie's father took her hand and placed it in Bigelow's and gave his daughter away. The wedding party turned toward Pastor Johnson, and he began the ceremony.

Lewis got it all on tape.

"Admit it, Doug: You're in that chair so you can always be at garter level, aren't you?"

Bigelow gave Garth a solid thumbs-up.

"Okay," the photographer said, "take it off now."

With the guests crowding around the wedding couple in the church's fellowship hall, the photographer flashing away, and Lewis zooming in with the video camera, Jamie lifted her wedding dress and Bigelow slid the garter off her leg.

Eloise clamped Jason around the arm. "Would you look at him?" she said. "I believe he is actually blushing."

"All eligible males, over here," the photographer said. He was a thin man with a spot of gray hair centered in his otherwise brown hair.

"Go on," Eloise said to Jason. "But I want to talk to you after."

There were probably thirty single men at the reception, counting Jason, Garth, Chris, and Lewis. Bigelow wheeled in front of them and turned away. The photographer lined up the shot.

"Wait!" Rachel said. She plucked the video camera from Lewis's hands.

"Hey, I need that."

"Not for this you don't. I'll do it for now. You get over there."

Lewis walked to the front of the pack and crouched, as if ready for the tip off.

"Hold on!" Eloise said, hurrying across the tile. "There's one more." She went to where Pastor Johnson was talking to Jamie's father. "Unless you done made a change since the last time I checked, Pastor," she said, grabbing his arm, "you're a single man. Get out there and catch that garter, boy."

He protested meekly but stood with the other bachelors. He pointed at Eloise in mock warning, then smiled.

"Garth, man," Bigelow said over his shoulder, "are you standing on a chair?"

"No way, baby." Garth double-thumped his chest. "This is all me: Grade-A beef grown the American way."

"I always knew you were a heifer, Garth," Chris said.

"We better hurry," Bigelow said to the photographer. "It's getting ugly."

The photographer lifted his camera. "Whenever you're ready."

"Okay, you guys," Bigelow called, "here it comes. Three, two, one!"

The garter went farther then Jason expected. It acted as if it were going to fly over the whole pack, but at its apex it petered out and dropped. The men surged for it like a hail Mary pass. Jason reached for it, too, but a twinge in his arm kept him from going all out for it. When the whistle blew, the garter was found in the hands of. . .Lewis.

He stumbled to Bigelow with the prize in his hand. "Does this mean I get to kiss the bride or something?"

"No way!" Bigelow said, a bit too severely. He pulled Lewis down and grabbed him around the neck. "It means you get your picture taken. Smile."

"Huh?"

Flash.

"All right," the photographer said. "Let's move to the cake."

"What about the bouquet?" Lewis asked, placing the garter around his sleeve.

"Not until just before they leave," the photographer said.

Lewis went to retrieve his camera from Rachel.

"So," she said, "you caught the garter, did you? And you didn't get a kiss?"

"Aw, that's okay. I was—"

She kissed him on the lips. "There."

In years to come, whenever anyone watched the Bigelows' wedding video, they always commented that the camera was noticeably shaky for a few minutes after the garter throw.

Jason found Eloise talking to two members of the widows' prayer group. She was wearing a sequined red and white dress. She handed him a glass of punch and led him to some folding chairs a bit removed from the crowd.

"Do you want to talk business," she said, "or should I stick to comments about the bride's dress?"

"We can talk business," he said.

"All right. Well, I've heard from the orphanage in Paris," she said. "Madame Mazarin was able to house all the girls together, after all."

"That's great," Jason said. "What about Yulia? Is she going to stay?"

"She still hasn't decided. She's thinking she'll wait until her ninety-day tourist period is up and then decide. She'd like to stay with the girls, and they want her. And now that she's seen Paris, I'm afraid she may want to stay."

Jason took a sip of punch. It was a biting citrus blend, but so far it hadn't been spiked. "Liliya's still doing all right?"

"She's doing fine. Playing hopscotch like there's no tomorrow."

"And Damira?"

Eloise smiled. "Why, Jason Kromer, I'm surprised at you, checking up on these babies like you're starting to care about them or something. My, my, there may be hope for you yet. Damira's fine." She nudged his shoulder. "Why don't you fly out and see them in the next week or two? They'd love to see you."

Jason felt a warmth traveling from his chest down his arms. "I might, Eloise. You know, I might just do that."

"Sure, why not? And you'll be happy to know that Katie, that Peace Corps volunteer who started us down this path, has joined the girls in Paris, too. I've got some counselors I know meeting with them all, helping them work through some of what's happened."

"What about the red tape with customs?" he asked. "Still a problem?"

"Oh, I don't worry about things like that. If the Lord worked so hard getting these girls out of that place, He's not going to forget about visas and passports."

The photographer's flash went off. Laughter marked the moment when Jamie stuffed cake down her Bigelow's mouth. Jason could just see the action over the crowd if he stood. As he was sitting down again, Garth and Chris and Lewis rushed up, looking mischievous. They held plastic grocery bags under their jackets.

"Come on, Jason," Chris said. "We're going to 'decorate' the limo."

"Whoa," Lewis said, "wait'll you see what Garth's going to do."

Garth muffled his maniacal laugh.

"You guys go on," Jason said. "I'll catch up in a minute."

"Hey, wait a sec," Garth said, putting an arm around Eloise. "You're not trying to make a move on my woman are you?"

Jason lifted his hands. "Promise."

"All right," Chris said, "but hurry up. And don't let Doug see you leave."

They scurried out the door, looking like secret service agents hustling the president out of a state dinner gone bad.

"Those boys," Eloise said, chuckling. "I declare."

Jason drained his cup. "Say, with all your don't-ask connections, have you heard how things played out in Baikonur City? CNN didn't exactly tell us much when it was happening, and now they've moved on to other things. I mean, what happened to that whole Aral Sea revolution and the Muslim hardliners and everything?"

"Jason Kromer, you know I would never endanger a confidential source."

He shrugged. "I was just curious."

"Well," she said softly, "I can tell you that all those uprisings are over. Everybody from the Caspian Sea, the Aral Sea, the northeast where the nuclear testing ground was—everybody—they all went home. Once those troops started showing up everywhere, they decided maybe they weren't that mad, after all. They're still upset, but they're letting it ride for now.

"As for where you were, well, it's going to take a while to rebuild. The Russians are going load it out with more soldiers to protect their space business. But the city survived, and more money keeps flowing in. Nowadays everybody's got to be in space. These companies want to get their satellites up there to start making bank. They're not going to let a little revolution get in their way. Money flowing in can only be a good thing for the city.

"As for the Arabs you ran into, they're laying low. Wouldn't you? But they won't give up trying to use whatever they can to make Kazakhstan an Islamic state. It's still a wonder to me that they were able to drum up enough racial tension between the folks there." She tsked. "They must be awful good at stirring up hate."

"Right," Jason said, "it's hard to imagine a country where there's racial tension, isn't it?"

She poked him in the ribs. "Come on, let's get cake."

He stopped her from standing. "Wait. There's. . .I think I. . ." He sighed. "You should know that. . ." *Oh, boy. Here it comes.*

"Spit it out, son. I want one of them chocolate covered strawberries."

He licked his lips. "Eloise, I want you to know. . .that I am. . . *grateful* to you. I'm grateful to you for picking me for this team. You picked me up when I was at my lowest and gave me a chance at something I don't think I deserve. I. . .just wanted you to know. . ."

"You're very welcome, son. I kn—"

"No," he said. "That isn't what I meant to say. I am grateful. That's true. But it isn't what I need to tell you." He was at the brink again. Was he going over it this time?

He watched Bigelow wheel across the floor with his bride, and the old guilt was right back, threatening to crush him again. But again it was met by the new forgiveness and understanding.

And suddenly he was weeping. It broke out from somewhere and refused to be stuffed back down.

Eloise took his head to her shoulder. "There, there, baby. It's all right. Now, now. . .it's all right." She rocked him.

His throat seized, and his eyes and nose ran. What a dope. But it was beyond controlling for now. The fear and relief and old guilt squeezed out his soul and onto Eloise's shoulder.

With a stack of engraved napkins before him, he sat down and told her everything. When he was done, she held his chin in her hand.

"You're a good boy, Jason. I knew it the moment we met right here in this church. You have a great love, a great capacity to love. You've loved your Lord Jesus. You've loved your good friend, Doug."

As she spoke, the tears flowed again.

"You thought your love had died when he was hurt. But it can't die, baby, it can't. It just went on growing and giving even though you was trying to say it wasn't so. Your love spread out onto me, onto Lewis and Chris and Garth and Trieu and Rachel. Maybe especially on Rachel."

He gave a wet chuckle and blew his nose.

"And we're going to have to talk about me maybe making some

kind of policy that says nobody on this team gets to date nobody else on this team. But that's for another day. The kind of love I'm talking about now is agape. You got it, baby. Your agape love flowed out and wrapped around those sweet babies in that basement with their space heater. You are their hero, Jason, and for good reason.

"And I'm going to tell you something else. You trying to end your life at that hotel—even that was love. You loved your boy Doug so much you couldn't bear seeing him suffer. I don't care what you tell me, walking into that hotel alone was an act of love. Don't try to tell me otherwise. You were willing to lay down your life to save that girl and keep your friends out of danger. I don't know what Bible you're reading, but mine says, 'Greater love has no man than he who lays down his life for his friends.' "

Jason blubbered like a baby. She was right. Somehow, on some level, she was right about him. She had looked into his soul, much to Jason's surprise, found something worthwhile there. Deep within him, that cage with the titanium padlock, where he'd pinned his grief for so long, blasted wide open, and he basked in the forgiveness she was channeling to him from God. All the shame and self-loathing he'd foundered in for months leaked out through his eyes.

Eloise brought him to her shoulder again and rocked. "You're a good boy, Jason. The Lord and I had a long talk about you. And do you know what He told me?"

He wadded up his stack of wet napkins. "No."

"Nuthin'. He didn't tell me nuthin'. I'm not hearing no voices, are you?"

He laughed and shuddered and laughed some more.

"No," she said, "I didn't hear His voice. But sure as I know anything, I knew you were the right man for this job. What I didn't know is how much work He needed to do on you along the way." She kissed his forehead. "Come on, son, let's go bag us some calories before they're all gone."

After the cake was the bouquet toss. Though there was much

jostling and unladylike snatching between Rachel and Eloise and the widows' prayer group, the bouquet came to rest in the hands of the flower girl.

Finally it was time for the bride and groom to run the gauntlet toward the getaway car. The wedding guests waited outside, armed with handfuls of birdseed. The limo had what appeared to be a Wyle E. Coyote jet engine attached to its roof. Jason waited beside the car with the whole Firebrand team.

By some silent command, they linked arms and formed a circle.

"You guys," Jason said so that only they could hear. "I know this isn't the time or place for it, but I just want you to know that I'm super proud of you all. What we did together I honestly did not think would work. I would be lying if I told you that I expected all of us to be back in the States, safe and sound, with a successful mission under our belts. Thank you, guys. Thank you for coming after me. Thank you for befriending me and letting me into your family. Here's hoping we'll have time to train right before have to do anything like that again!"

They cheered.

"Yeah, right," Lewis said. "You mean before we take another *alleged* jump out of another *alleged* airplane."

Rachel flicked his head with her finger.

"Ow!" he said.

"Would you give it up, Lewis? You jumped, all right. Next time we'll take a photo."

Jason broke out of the circle, but Chris brought him back in.

"Hang on," Chris said. "Now we want to say something to you. Rachel?"

Rachel stepped forward and produced a plastic grocery sack. "On behalf of the five of us, we would like to bestow upon you our highest award." She drew out an old, black jogging shoe and presented it to Jason.

"Wow," he said, turning it over in his hand. "One whole shoe.

Previously owned, no less. Thanks. I don't know what to say."

"It's to remind you," Garth said, one large paw squeezing Jason's shoulder, "that you are no longer allowed to play Rambo, bonehead. It is to remind you that you are part of a team now, and that without us all working together, you're about as helpful as one black shoe. Got it?"

Jason was almost kneeling under the squeeze. "Got it!"

"Hey," Lewis said, "here they come. I gotta get this on video."

Bigelow and Jamie sped down the sidewalk under a barrage of parakeet feed. Chris got Bigelow into the limo and Garth tossed the chair into the trunk. The best man and maid of honor—Jason and Rachel—ducked into the car, and Jason pulled away. Ten feet from the curb the rocket on top flamed to life, showering fireworks sparks onto the street behind them.

Bigelow and Jamie weren't much for conversation on the ride to the hotel. Even Rachel seemed embarrassed and wouldn't look at Jason.

"Hey, guys," Jason said. "Get a room."

"You're driving us to our room!" Bigelow shouted. "Hurry it up, would ya?"

After they saw the happy couple off at the hotel, Jason and Rachel had to drive back to the church together.

Rachel was silent. Jason's attempts at conversation crashed and burned. He thought maybe he'd offended her, so he just drove.

Finally she turned in the seat and looked at him. "Jason, I need to tell you something."

Passing headlights illuminated her angular face and magnificent eyes. "Okay."

"You really scared me back in Kazakhstan."

He nodded. "I know. I'm s—"

"No, you don't know. Do you remember when we first met, that first day?"

"Do I ever."

"Do you remember what I said about how my father died?"

He scanned his memory. Then it hit him. "Oh, no! Rachel, I'm so sorry."

"That's right," she said. "My father was killed by Muslim terrorists inside his own hotel lobby."

"Oh, Rachel, I—"

"So when they told me you were actually fighting them instead of just going to check it out—like you told me you were going to do—I pretty much lost it. It felt like my father was out there being shot all over again. And once again I couldn't stop it! I knew I had to stay with the girls in case something happened to the rest of the team, but I hated it. Garth actually tied me to the wagon to keep me from following."

"He told me."

"The worst part," she said, and Jason saw tears on her cheeks, "was that. . .I've never. . .in all the. . ." She blew through her lips. "Jason, it's like this: You remind me of my father in some ways. No, in lots of ways. When I'm with you, you make me feel like I felt when I was with my father. He made me feel strong and capable and pretty. And safe. I've never thought about it, but I guess ever since I lost him I've been looking for someone to make me feel that way again. And you. . ."

She sighed deeply.

"Do you remember that first night, when we danced?"

He looked at her incredulously. "Rachel, how could I forget that? I've been trying to recapture that moment ever since."

"Do you remember I told you something in Hebrew? I said that one day I would explain it to you. Maybe."

Jason held his breath.

"Would you like to know what it was I said?"

He nodded rapidly, trying to devote at least some attention to traffic.

Rachel reached up and took her hair down. It tumbled over her shoulders. She repeated the Hebrew sentences she'd said before. Then she translated:

"All my life I have loved one man," she said. "My father. No one has ever come close to being the man he was. But my father is gone. From that day to this, I have prayed to God that one day I might find another man to give all my love to. I don't know, but perhaps you are the one. Time will tell."

He wasn't sure his heart was beating, he was so still. "Rachel, that's. . ."

"Shh. Are you that man? Still I don't know. But when I thought I would lose you, I felt something terrible was going to happen to me. To *me.* Isn't that selfish?"

Black mascara streaked her cheeks, and Jason thought she'd never looked more lovely.

"I know we have only just met, really," she said. "And I know that there are. . .others. . .who could love you and that you could love. I'm not trying to shut out the competition. I only wanted you to know that you are. . .someone that maybe I could love. Like that."

"Rachel, you have to know that Eloise wants to—"

"No, I don't want to talk about it anymore. I'm embarrassed. Just drive."

Jason drove.

Wending his way into the night, Jason felt like a new man. He had a renewed relationship with God. A new vocation. A new direction for his life. Expunged guilt. A beautiful woman—no, two—expressing romantic interest in him. And lots of hurting children out there needing his help. Correction: his team's help. It wasn't what he'd expected all those mornings ago when he'd walked out to kill a man in cold blood.

It was a lot better.

Would you like to offer feedback on this novel?

Interested in starting a book discussion group?

Check out www.promisepress.com for
a *Reader Survey* and *Book Club Questions.*

JEFFERSON SCOTT has written several thriller novels, including *Fatal Defect* and *Terminal Logic.* A graduate of both seminary and film school, he currently makes his home in the Pacific Northwest, where he writes full-time.

Coming Soon from

Promise Press

An Imprint of Barbour Publishing

Summon the Shadows by Eva Marie Everson and G. W. Francis Chadwick
ISBN 1-58660-490-2

When expensive gifts arrive at her office, Katie Webster, president and CEO of New York City's five-star hotel The Hamilton Place, believes her missing-and-presumed-dead husband has finally returned. Or perhaps her checkered past is catching up to her. . . .

Time Lottery by Nancy Moser
ISBN 1-58660-587-9

After twenty-two years of scientific research, three lucky individuals will receive the opportunity of a lifetime with The Time Lottery—to relive one decisive moment that could change the course of their lives.

Interview with the Devil by Clay Jacobsen
ISBN 1-58660-588-7

Investigative journalist Mark Taylor has landed the story of his career—an interview with Ahmad Hani Sa'id, the cold-hearted leader of a new terrorist network stalking the United States of America.

Vancouver Mystery by Rosey Dow and Andrew Snaden
ISBN 1-58660-589-5

Just days after Beth Martin's long-awaited facelift operation, Beth Martin is found dead—and her cosmetic surgeon, Dr. Dan Foster, finds himself playing amateur detective after being framed for the killing.

Available wherever books are sold.